Book One of the Reilan Trilogy

The King
of Nothing

Gordon Ian Barrick

Published by Gortfordshire Books
Copyright Gordon Ian Barrick 2013

ISBN: 978-0-9926490-4-3

The King of Nothing

CONTENTS

PROLOGUE:
Feirlan

The Birthday Party

The white stone battlements of Torr Sarvie blazed with torches and the castle glowed brightly in the dark Feirlan night. Below the hill on which the castle sat, the town of Obaln was settling in for the evening, yet, in Torr Sarvie, music and laughter carried through the night air. Celebrations were underway. King Fidiann's eldest son and heir, Ciro, was now eleven summers old and dignitaries and ministers from the whole of Feirlan had gathered to take part in the revelry. For the young prince it was a time of games, of treats and presents yet Ciro had no idea of the surprise which lay in store for him that night. Or the change it would make to his entire life.

It had begun innocently enough. The eleven year old prince had been leading the proceedings in the first game of hide and seek and had set out to hide from his party guests. While his younger brother and sister, Bdann and Penyatt, joined the other children in closing their eyes and counting to one hundred, Prince Ciro had raced from the crowded ballroom and quickly climbed the main stairway in search of a hiding place. He had heard his father, King Fidiann, wagering with the Chief Minister as he exited the ballroom door and, not wishing to disappoint his father's faith in his abilities, Ciro had decided to hide himself well.

Up the grand main staircase the prince had run, past the state rooms, the royal apartments and the nursery which until that day he had shared with his brother. The young prince sped on into the castle, not stopping until he had entered his new chambers and carefully closed the door. Ciro looked around his new room for the ideal hiding place and, after dismissing the bed, closets and curtains, had squeezed himself beside the empty grate of his fireplace; shuffling behind one of the large stone pillars which supported it. Here he had waited, his back pressed firmly against the wall, legs jammed against the pillar, while his pulse raced with the anticipation of the hunt.

Ciro waited. And with every passing breath his heartbeat slowed to normal. He listened intently for a sound beyond his door, yet none had come. No rapid footsteps, no shrill cries of pursuit. Nothing but the light sigh of his breath and the occasional scrape of his shoes against the stonework. He had realised then that his hiding place, though undoubtedly good, was nevertheless exceedingly uncomfortable. With this in mind, and the fact that his pursuers were obviously searching elsewhere, Ciro decided to stretch his legs. He would return to his hiding place only when the other children could be heard outside.

The young prince untangled his legs from their confines and moved to push himself from the wall; but as he did so his hand had grasped something soft behind him. Curious, Ciro craned his neck to look down to his hands but could see nothing in the darkness of the fireplace. Yet when he attempted to remove what felt like a piece of cloth, it strained but seemed stuck fast in the stonework. Intrigued the prince extracted himself from the fireplace, returned with the oil lamp from his bedside table and squeezed back behind the grate.

There it lay, a black silken scarf with white embroidered 'T's, jutting from the stonework behind the fireplace. Ciro moved the lamp closer, intrigued at how such an object could be set into the wall and, as he did so, the light revealed a flattened brass ring set into the wall by the pillar. Without thinking, the prince's hand had grasped the ring and, feeling it give, he had pulled with all his might. There came a low rumble from behind the stonework, and Ciro gasped as the rear of the fireplace slid back.

Shocked by the sudden appearance of the passageway, the prince paused to catch his breath. It was then that he heard the muffled sound of footsteps in the corridor.

With his heart racing again, Ciro pulled once more on the chain and to his relief the stonework slid quietly back into place. The prince snatched the scarf from the opening as it closed, shuffled backwards into his bedchamber and, returning the lamp to its original spot, slid underneath his bed. It was there, some minutes later, that his younger brother, Prince Bdann, had found him and the room had filled with the excited squeals of his party guests.

II

The day after Ciro's eleventh birthday had passed interminably, so occupied was his mind with what might lay beyond the hidden entrance in his bedchamber. His first impulse on rising that morning had been to share his discovery with his mother and father at breakfast, but his desire to explore the darkness behind the fireplace and the anticipated thrill of this unexpected adventure kept him silent. The young prince considered two possibilities would arise from his disclosure: one, that he would be forbidden from exploring further, or two; that they would solve the mystery in a single sentence and dash his hopes of finding hidden treasure. If the entrance was to lead to a mere coal cellar, then at least Ciro wanted the partial thrill of investigating the darkness.

All through his lessons that day, the prince attempted to focus on the work his tutors set him, yet time and again his eyes would drift to the sun shafts coming through the library windows and his thoughts would rove to the gentle grind of the stonework and the gloomy passage which sat behind his fireplace. Repeatedly, Ciro found himself fingering the silk scarf which now sat in his pocket.

As if to add substance to the endless scenarios flitting through his mind, another thought occurred to him then. Who had the scarf belonged to; and how had it become stuck in the wall?

It was not until that evening in the great hall with his family that such thoughts lessened their hold on his attention, and his mind became focused on beating Merion, the Chief of the Guard, at Soldiers. Ciro always found the Chief fascinating company, and though he never hoped to beat the old man at the board game, the tales of his campaigns in the Nelan desert and terrifying descriptions of Sand Devils always compensated admirably for the inevitable defeat.

'Do you know young sire,' Merion would often say, leaning back in his chair and cradling a large goblet of wine. 'That the move you have just made reminds me of a similar tactic from an old campaigner I used to know...' And so the story would begin, the game of soldiers an aside as Merion whisked the young prince away to a world of wonderful adventures. Occasionally King Fidiann, Merion's dearest friend, would gently interject from his nearby armchair that perhaps the Chief should temper his vivid descriptions for such a young audience. With an understanding nod Merion would always comply and then, with a sly, conspiratorial wink to the prince, would wander off on another tangent. 'Did I ever tell you of your dear father's escapade with a snow rabbit on the peak of Rachmon... ?'

That evening had been little different and Ciro's musings were kept at bay until his mother, Queen Irsa, had touched him gently on the shoulder and asked him to bid everyone goodnight. As Ciro did so and made his way upstairs to his chamber, he wondered whether, on the following night, he would be able to reply to one of Merion's stories with an adventure tale of his own.

As soon as Ciro had secured the door to his chamber and moved towards the fireplace, he felt the thrill of anticipation sweep through his body. Already his heart was beginning to race at the prospect of exploration and so he wasted no time in grasping the handle of his bedside lamp and crouching before the empty fire grate. The young prince had to stretch and grope behind the left-hand pillar, but within moments he had relocated the flat brass ring. Again Ciro found himself holding his breath as, with closed eyes, he pulled the ring downwards.

The sound of grinding stone seemed louder now: sharp in contrast to the stony silence that a second before had held the room. Ciro's heart beat just a little faster with the noise, and he did not let out a breath until the slab had swung to a stop.

Ciro waited as silence refilled his chamber, his ears straining to catch the slightest footfall beyond the door. None came and so, with deft and careful steps, the prince, with oil lamp in hand, clambered over the fire grate and into the darkness.

Ciro stood from his crouch and dusted his hands against his jacket: contemplating the tunnel which ran behind his wall. It was plain, high and narrow and the light of Ciro's lamp revealed little more than a few yards of stonework before its yellow glow petered out. Beyond that the passageway faded into an imposing veil of black. The prince felt a shiver run up his spine at the sight, a sensation which travelled to the tips of his fingers and the very roots of his hair before subsiding. With the lamp held high, Ciro gritted his teeth and stepped cautiously into the gloom.

He had not meant to, but the young prince found himself counting quietly as he walked on. Partly as a guide for the distance he was travelling, but mainly as a reassurance when the lights from his chamber dimmed into the darkness. Soon Ciro could see nothing behind or in front save his immediate surroundings until, at step two hundred and sixty two, a flight of stairs brought him to a halt.

Again, little more could be discerned past a few steps leading down into blackness, yet Ciro found his nerve begin to fail at the sight. He had had no idea of what to expect in the tunnel, yet in all his imaginings during the hours of the day he had not contemplated this. Where did the passageway lead? What could be down there? All too quickly, Ciro felt the darkness press upon him; a cold claustrophobia that left his mind awash with thoughts of fear.

Now Merion's tales of Sand Devils took on a new aspect, and all the old fables which Ciro's nanny had recounted on his repeated demand came back to haunt him. Stories of the monstrous Unmen who lived in the shadows, and the demon, Beck, that walked abroad when the moon was gone. Now they were here, past the weak boundary glow of his lamp and Ciro tried to fight his sudden compulsion to turn and run. In the midst of all these fleeting horrors, a phrase slowly rose to the fore. Part of something his mother had said to him one evening after he had asked her about the Beck Night.

'Of all the things that we may fear,' Queen Irsa had told the young prince. 'Perhaps the most terrifying for a child is the night. For we are all, no matter how old, the children of the sun, of the day; and night is a stranger to us. But, sure as Milla will shine, darkness will fall; every day of our lives. That is the way of things. But when darkness does fall remember to keep the sun in your heart and not let the night in, for that is where the fear really lies. Stand up to the dark, never fear it, for day must surely come.'

Stand up to the dark. Don't let it in. Day must surely come, thought Ciro, over and over again, so quickly in fact that all other thoughts were pushed aside. And then he realised that he was in the very heart of Torr Sarvie, surrounded by his family and friends and that no harm could come to him. I wonder what's at the bottom of the stairs? Thought the young prince, and with a slight smile, he skipped lightly down the steps.

The stairway turned twice as it descended, finishing in what appeared to be an identical tunnel to the one Ciro had just left. The prince stood for a moment and attempted to work out where he might be heading. By his reckoning this new tunnel was on the ground floor and at a right angle to the one above, so that would put him...Where exactly? Not near the great hall. The castle library? Perhaps... Ciro raised his lamp vainly to see further down the passageway and then caught sight of the intricately carved stonework which ran in a strip just above his arm. Fascinated - all thoughts of dark terrors gone from his mind - Ciro followed the unfamiliar swirls and patterns deep into the tunnel and was taken by surprise when a strange slab of marble ended both the passageway and his journey.

The prince reached out a hand and, touching the surface of the stone, felt its cool smoothness beneath his fingers. There were many rich and decorative types of marble throughout the castle, yet Ciro had never encountered anything with quite this lustre. It was a delicate yellow with strands of dull red running through it, muted by a thin film of grime which dulled the marble's sheen, but as Ciro brushed at the dust and moved the lamp closer, the strands flared brightly, as if with fire: holding the glow long after the lamp had been withdrawn.

After watching the fire strands surge and fade with every

move of his lamp, Ciro eventually moved his attention to the walls on either side of the block, scanning them for a means of entry. He was sure this tunnel was not simply a dead end, so perhaps there was a way of getting the marble to move in a similar fashion to that of his fireplace. After swinging the oil lamp around the walls for a few minutes, the prince finally noticed a circular shadow sitting proud of the final carving on the left hand side. Moving closer to investigate, Ciro saw with satisfaction that a brass ring was set into the wall, identical to the one in his chamber. Without a second thought he pulled it.

A familiar rumble of stone sounded beside him and, as the marble block slid smoothly back into the right hand wall, a rectangle of darkness expanded in its place. At the foot of the doorframe a tiled pattern could be discerned in the space beyond and at the sight of it, Ciro panicked: suddenly realising that he might have stumbled into somebody's private quarters.

His sigh of relief that he had not and that all was still was short lived; quickly replaced by a puzzled awe as his eyes adjusted and the blackness beyond the doorway lightened. Wherever he now was, it was a cavernous space which stretched both left and right with grey light beaming down through glass panes set high in the far wall. But where exactly 'here' was, Ciro had no idea: only that he had neither been here before or even heard so much as a whisper about its existence.

Even with the confined view which he had from inside the tunnel, the space beyond seemed disconcertingly large; bigger by some way than any hall he had ever been in. Ciro took a tentative step out of the passageway and, with a slack jaw attempted to take it all in.

The entire hall seemed to have been built from the same strange fire-marble, in a delicate style which Ciro had never seen before. The far wall, its base gloomy and

14

undistinguishable in the moonlight, rose to frame many slender windows which receded into the distance both left and right. Above the windows, elegant arches spread gentle curves towards a high but shadow hidden roof. The effect reminded Ciro of slender tree branches and he almost staggered backwards as he craned his neck to follow the lines to their apex. He looked towards the far right end of the hall but, beyond the dim illumination of the far windows, it was lost in distant shadow.

'Where in Feirlan am I?' whispered Ciro to himself as he stepped into what appeared to be the central walkway of the hall. He could see once dark shapes now revealing themselves both left and right so he stopped, swung the lamp around and turned to view the nearer wall to the left of the passageway.

Bookcases lined the base of the wall, crammed with countless leather-bound volumes. Above were set many heraldic devices, their detail too dim to see in the pale light. Ciro resisted the temptation to study the books just yet and turned his attention to the shadows at the far left end of the hall.

As he moved along the central aisle, Ciro suddenly noticed a glint of metal beneath his feet. He crouched and placed the lamp beside the glinting brass strip set firmly into the floor tiles and moved his head both left and right to follow its perfect line into the darkness. Now he knew where he was, and now he knew why he had never been here before.

The thin line of brass was called the 'King's Line'. It started at the quayside in Obaln harbour and had been set into the cobblestones since before anyone could remember. From the water's edge at the harbour the brass strip made its way straight up Line Street then curved up the hill road until it reached the castle. Once inside the grounds of Torr Sarvie the line of brass continued on until disappearing beneath two large ornate doors. Beyond those doors lay the Ascension

Chamber: and nobody, apart from the King and senior ministers, were allowed to follow the 'King's Line' inside.

Ciro chewed on his lower lip as the realisation sunk in. Of all the places in the castle, this was the one which was completely off-limits, and no amount of questioning or argument would change that fact. He knew; he had tried both on his father.

'Not before it is your time!' King Fidiann had said, about a year before in response to his son's insistent curiosity.

'But if I am to be King, why can't I go inside now?'

'Tradition dictates that no prince enters the Ascension Chamber until it is his time,' Ciro's father had responded. 'And in your case that time will be roughly eleven years from now. When you reach the age of Ascension at twenty one. Then it will be your time to ascend to the throne and accept your responsibility as King in Waiting. Not before!'

'But...'

'Enough!' Fidiann had cried in frustration. 'You will go inside when you reach Ascension. As I did, as your grandfather did and his father before him. That is the way it has always been and that is an end to it.'

So this was it, thought Ciro. He picked up the lamp and slowly paced the King's Line as if walking a tightrope. This is where I will come when I reach Ascension. This is where my childhood will end.

The prince guessed that behind him, at the far distant end of the chamber, sat the doors which barred the way and faced the harbour. Which meant that in front of him, hidden in the shadow of its recessed arch, sat the throne of Feirlan. Off-limits or not, Ciro could not resist taking a look at it.

To either side the bookcases continued, and Ciro could not help but notice how, even in the dim light, everything seemed neglected. It's little wonder the place is so dusty, he considered, if almost no one is allowed to enter. And yet it did seem strange that such a seemingly special place was quite so uncared for. Perhaps there was no point until Ascension Day, mused Ciro. Then, he felt sure; it would be cleaned and made ready for the ceremony. Before that day, perhaps there was little point.

Now Ciro began to make out large ornamental lamps on either side of the alcove and details of objects within the deep recess. In particular he could see the jutting shape of a high backed chair and a large banner which occupied the rear wall. With one more step his lamp burned brightly enough for him to see vague details of the objects, causing him to stop. Ciro turned his head to look back along the King's Line: unsure suddenly of his direction. He held the lamp aloft and fixed his eyes upon the banner.

'Where am I?' said Ciro with a frown.

The young prince stared for almost a minute at the banner behind the Ascension throne before the jumble of thoughts which were whizzing around inside his head began to slow and settle into place. The banner, or flag as it now appeared to be after closer scrutiny, was not the flag of Feirlan. It was blue, not white and green, and in place of the wild white rose which occupied the centre of their national flag, a golden, circled sun gazed dully down at the young prince. Slowly, Ciro mounted the two steps which rose to the alcove dais and shifted his gaze from the flag to the throne.

Again, the same circled sun was embossed in gold upon dust darkened leather, and Ciro had to stop himself from automatically reaching out to brush the chair clean. He pulled his hand back as if scolded. You are not supposed to be here, Ciro reminded himself. Wherever here is?

The young prince made a brief inspection of the other objects and artefacts clustered around the throne: finding the same sun symbol on every shield, suit of armour and chest which had obviously sat for an untouched age inside the alcove. Ciro could still not fathom what all these objects signified, but one thing was clear. This was not the throne of Feirlan. And that thought led to another. Why did the King's Line lead here? Perhaps he had been mistaken and this was not the Ascension Chamber after all.

The young prince yawned, feeling tiredness tug at his senses, yet he felt even more determined not to leave until he knew where he was. Ciro stepped down from the dais and returned to the brass line in the floor. He resolved to walk to the other end of the hall before retiring to his bed, to see if the King's Line led to the high arched doors which marked the entrance to the Ascension Chamber.

He walked on, past the numerous book cases, the vague dark square of the passageway and, close by it, a large table strewn with papers. Ciro once again felt a sense of awe at the size and simple grandeur of the place and listened as his booted feet gently echoed with each step. The prince divided his attention between watching the line at his feet and admiring the elegance of his surroundings until he entered the un-windowed shadows that he had guessed marked the far end of the chamber. Instead of the Ascension Chamber doors, Ciro found that the King's Line suddenly branched into two.

Ciro stopped at the divide, turning on the spot to see that the tiles beneath him marked a wide circle around the now divided line. One branch continued straight on from the sun throne which Ciro had just left, while the second veered off at a right angle towards the left side of the chamber. Intrigued by this unexpected development, the prince followed the left hand fork a few paces until the light from his lamp picked out the polished brass bands on the Ascension Chamber doors.

'So this is the Ascension Chamber,' said Ciro quietly,

reassured that his initial guess had been the correct one. Now all he had to find out was where the other line of brass continued to.

Turning to his right, Ciro could see that his original idea about the size of the Ascension Chamber had been wrong and that it was in fact twice as big as he had guessed. After a brief halt in the dim centre of the chamber, the moonlit windows continued again and proceeded on into what Ciro imagined must be a second, identical wing. That must be where the Feirlan throne is, Ciro mused, and ignoring the tiredness creeping through his body, he walked on.

The other side of the chamber was indeed identical in structure, but the prince noted an immediate difference in its appearance. This side of the hall had been scrupulously maintained and even in such poor light Ciro could see the sheen of the polished floor beneath him. There were golden railings on either side of the central aisle, and in place of bookcases, portraits of previous kings and bright heraldic devices lined the walls.

Ciro yawned loudly: blinking and shaking his head as fatigue continued to press upon him. He passed several display cases containing ornate suits of armour but gave them no more than a glance when he noted their similarity to others elsewhere in the castle.

'Nearly there,' he said leadenly to himself by way of encouragement and smiled when a familiar flag loomed out from the night. Here it was: the throne of Feirlan, and Ciro crouched on the lowest step of the dais to rest as he took it in.

It was set in an identical alcove to the other throne, yet filled with objects that Ciro was vaguely familiar with - having seen many of them used before on occasions of state. There were fire-lances and old fashioned pikes arranged in polished frames beneath the Feirlan flag and clusters of golden rods from which hung the white rose pennant. To his left Ciro could make out a rack of ceremonial breast plates that his father sometimes wore, while to his right, the marvellous, gem encrusted sword of office - which Ciro had always admired - hung with its scabbard and belt inside a glass fronted cabinet. Most surprising to Ciro, as he stood and climbed the remaining steps into the alcove, was the crown of Feirlan, sitting as if discarded upon the leather upholstery of the throne.

Ciro put down his lamp and picked up the crown, feeling its weight as he turned it reverentially in his hands and its jewels glinted in the feeble light. He smiled and lifted it to his head, knowing it was far too large for him and then returned it to the throne. One day, he thought to himself as he turned from the alcove, it would fit him perfectly: and he vowed to take better care of it than his father appeared to. After all, Ciro thought, that was the crown, the symbol of his land. Surely it deserved some respect.

Stifling another yawn, the young prince hurried to return to his chamber; deciding to leave the mystery of the second throne for another night. He imagined that the many bookcases would contain some clue to its purpose and perhaps explain why the King's Line led there as well. Whatever its function was, Ciro felt too tired now to think clearly about the matter. He had achieved his objective: found out where the secret passage went, and seen the Ascension Chamber ten years before he was supposed to. That was enough for one night. Ciro was almost to the passageway and passing the untidy table he had noticed before. He paused for just a moment to glance at the scattered papers and spotted the object which would change his life.

It was a map, made of hide and edged with gold braid, but it was not a map of Feirlan. Ciro had studied the Feirlan map enough times to recognise it in an instant, but this was something very different. Somewhere very different.

Intrigued by the unfamiliar outline, Ciro set down his lamp and extracted the large map from beneath some overlaying papers. He sat down on the chair beside the table and frowned as he viewed the strange contours, taking in the alien landscape which sprawled between his hands. He had never before considered - certainly never been told - that there could be another place: another country. The sudden realisation that it might not be the case sent a chill up his spine. Feirlan was all there was, wasn't it? To the south was the impassable desert of Nelan, to the north a craggy wasteland and all was surrounded by the sea. Ciro held the strange map closer to his lamp and stared at the gold seal which was attached to its bottom right corner.

Beneath a sun symbol surrounded by a circle, three lines of text had been embossed: Prince Ciro read them aloud.

'Made for Elson Torrman, Sixth King of Rial. Map of Reilan, its lands and domains. New Calendar: 720.'

Ciro felt his pulse race and put down the map, his body tingling with excitement: his tiredness gone. He looked over to where he knew the sun throne lay hidden in shadow and tried to digest the astounding information which the few lines communicated. The New Calendar date was now 1210, the map was almost five hundred years old and of a place he had never heard of: yet Ciro's surname, like that of the long forgotten King Elson, was Torrman.

III

Night after night, the young prince would descend through the darkness of the passageway to pour over works and records which had lain undisturbed and unopened for hundreds of years. Beginning with the nearest shelf to the passageway, Ciro diligently worked his way along the rows of ancient tomes and scrolls, marvelling at the information which each new book revealed about the ancient continent of Reilan. After many months, Ciro gradually began to piece together the distant, forgotten history of his people and, as he did so, he began to understand why his ancestors had consigned all knowledge of their original homeland to the oblivion of the past.

King Elson's old map showed the continent of Reilan to be a vast place, much larger than Ciro's own home of Feirlan and made up of many lands. In the north west of the continent was a place named Piir, to the north east a land named Taisin. In the centre, edged by mountains, forests and the sea, had been the Kingdom of Rial. Here, Ciro discovered, the ancestors of all the people of Feirlan had once lived for countless generations, building towns and cities across the land. Despite the cruel intentions of a warlike, southern race called the Makech, the people of Rial had prospered and their kingdom flourished. Until, that was, the reign of King Elson.

During this time the records which Ciro uncovered spoke of a terrible calamity which befell the kingdom: a plague of such devastation that the King hurriedly assembled a vast fleet of ships to sail the survivors to safety. A Rialan explorer, who had sailed further than any of his countrymen, was tasked with finding the exiles a new home – a safe haven from the death which had swept their land. The explorer, whose name was Feira, knew of only one place, a remote stretch of land which was far enough across the ocean to be completely secure. Named after the explorer, Feirlan became the new home to the survivors of the Rial plague.

Though King Elson had stayed behind in Reilan he sent his family away and ordered his youngest brother, Prince Idirnon, to take charge of the fleet and organize the survivors when they reached Feirlan. Years had passed, but no further vessel ever followed the initial exodus. All who had stayed in Reilan, it seemed, had become victims of the plague. In letters Ciro found collected into a large leather volume, the young prince was able to read of Prince Idirnon's efforts to quell the panic which had gripped the survivors when they landed on the barren shores of Feirlan and the great strides he had made in establishing their first town, which Idirnon named after his mother: Obaln. After ten years, Prince Idirnon's efforts had secured his people's future but the scars of the catastrophe ran deep within all the exiles. The fear of the plague and the fact that no ships had followed the initial exodus was compounded when Prince Idirnon himself sailed back to Reilan with two hundred men. Though he promised to return, no matter what the situation, not one man came back. Desperate to forget their lost loved ones and the glory of their old kingdom, the new people of Feirlan found that they had no choice but to let go of the past and forge a new life. King Elson's eldest son, Sarvie, who had been but a boy when the exodus had occurred crowned himself the first King of Feirlan when he reached the age of twenty one. He had lived for longer in the new land than in the old kingdom, so for him the break with the past was not such a hardship. He built a new throne and a chamber to house it and, to commemorate his coronation, the people of Obaln laid a line of brass from the shore where they had first landed right up to the throne. Out of respect for his father's memory, King Sarvie had the Rialan throne placed with all King Elson's regalia at the opposite end of the Ascension Chamber. In case, one day, his father returned to claim his place. But that day never came. In time King Sarvie came to accept that the old Kingdom of Rial and the continent of Reilan were as dead as those that had dared to return to it.

Despite the awful nature of Rial's fall, those records were a mere fraction of the history which Ciro found upon the shelves. And, with every new wonder that the young prince discovered, every thrilling account of the wars against the Makech, description of Peimonac's towers or sketch of Torr Adenair that he came across, Ciro knew that he wanted to go there. To stand and look upon Romunesse, or walk the cloud bridge at Circia. It was over a year before Ciro accidentally uncovered the means to achieve such a goal, and in doing so he discovered the truth behind Ascension Day.

IV

As the years had gone on, Ciro ceased to wonder how the scarf he had found had become lodged in the brickwork of his fireplace, or who it might have belonged to. But, at the age of sixteen and returning from another night of reading in the Ascension Chamber, the prince had been startled by a knocking on his locked chamber door. Ciro had quickly pulled the chain to close the fireplace but, in his panic, had remained inside the secret passage. He waited, breathlessly listening for sounds beyond the stonework but none had come and, after several minutes, Ciro deduced that whoever had knocked at such an early hour had gone away.

It was the first time Ciro had ever closed the passage entrance while he had been beyond it and, as he searched hopefully for a chain which would allow him back into his bedchamber, his lamp picked out a section of wall which had previously been hidden by the stone door. In the yellow light he discovered an inscription, carved into the stonework over two hundred years before.

May it be known to you, my dear, inquisitive reader

That I go, whether it is folly or no, to rediscover Reilan.
If you have come this far, I salute you as a fellow explorer
and wish you every joy in your nocturnal investigations.
Take care of my scarf for, if the Beck night has fallen upon
me,
it may be all that is left of me.
But if that is the will of Our Lady, do not let my misfortune
deter you from discovering the truth.
I have left a little something for you beneath the Rialan throne
which may interest, amuse or perhaps, who knows,
even inspire you to follow.
Good luck, wanderer of the night
May Milla shine on your every endeavour
Prince Tenlern Torrman.

Ciro had re-examined the scarf as he made his way back down to the Ascension Chamber, noting for the first time that the white embroidered swirls appeared to be an endless repetition of stylised 'T's. It explained a lot that such a notable explorer as Prince Tenlern was the one to have discovered the secret passage and it made Ciro anxious to know just what information he had left under the Rial throne. Tenlern was well known to Feirlan history as a fearless explorer, but he had died from his wanderlust in his early twenties, during a mapping trip to the northern wastelands of Feirlan. What, Ciro wondered, had happened to his plan to re-discover Reilan? Perhaps, Ciro thought, the information he had gathered was what awaited him in the chamber.

It was not long before Ciro had his answers. Stuffed snugly under the wide base of the Rial throne, hidden from casual sight, was a bulging leather satchel, cracked with age. Ciro cradled it under one arm as he made his way back to his chamber, upturned it onto his bed and fought sleep to pour over the varied contents.

There were letters, papers, inventories, provision lists, personnel lists, ship construction plans and navigational charts. In fact, Ciro realised, everything a person would require to organise a large nautical expedition to Reilan. The young prince spent the next week intently studying the documents and in frank, private accounts written by Tenlern, discovered a piece of history which had not made it into the public records.

Tenlern had been the younger twin brother of King Erin and the account described how both had occupied the same chamber as Ciro now did right up until Erin's Ascension. The two boys had discovered the passageway behind the fireplace in a similar fashion to Ciro and explored the Ascension chamber in much the same way. Tenlern wrote that they had spent many nights planning how they would both return to Reilan but, on his Ascension Day, Erin - much to Tenlern's disgust - had changed his mind and accepted the Feirlan throne instead.

"I cannot believe he fears the Beck night!" was the only explanation Tenlern gave for his brother's sudden change of heart, but Tenlern was angry enough to begin secretly planning his own expedition to Reilan.

From his mid teens, and seemingly inspired by what he had found in the Ascension Chamber, Tenlern had been travelling and exploring further than any previous Feirlaner. He then applied his skills and experience to the considerable task of mounting an expedition to rediscover the Kingdom of Rial. Ciro marvelled at the detail of the work, especially the plans for the ship which was bigger than anything previously built: sturdy, fast and capable of carrying two hundred men and a full hold of provisions. From correspondence and bills from the shipwrights, Curdain and Sons, Ciro found enough evidence to show that four such ships had been constructed: though how Tenlern had kept the building of such monstrous vessels a secret Ciro had no idea.

The final item, sealed in an envelope by a circle of cracked wax, was a note in Tenlern's fine script to the finder of the satchel. He wrote that all preparations were complete. He was resolute, ready to sail and had told his brother the King to "Look to the eastern horizon for sign of triumphant sails." The letter was dated 931, the year recorded in Ciro's official history book that Tenlern had lost his life mapping Feirlan's northern shore.

The truth of Prince Tenlern's demise shocked Ciro. Tenlern was a heroic figure in Feirlan history who had single-handedly mapped much of the known country; from its rocky northern tip right down to the impassable Nelan Desert. Tenlern was also a firm favourite of Ciro's younger brother, Bdann. Would Ciro tell his brother of his hero's real (and to Ciro's mind) much more daring final adventure. It was many years before the young prince did let his brother in on the secret, but Tenlern's story had a more immediate affect on Ciro. He searched the shelves for anything to do with Tenlern's brother, King Erin. To find out, if he could, what had made him change his mind about accompanying his twin to Reilan.

In a single scroll, tucked at the very end of a bottom shelf, Ciro found a letter bearing the royal Feirlan seal and signed by King Erin, it was dated 932, one year after Tenlern had set sail for Reilan, and addressed to a minister named Mairkam. It read:

Mairkam,
I do not know what the existing regulations are regarding
information concerning Reilan and I don't care. I know both

myself and my brother were not told by our father of the Rialan throne but I want to make sure that no other member of my family, no sons, grandsons, great grandsons and so on, will have to suffer the loss of a loved one as I have to that accursed continent. I have read enough of the information contained beside the Rial throne to know that in over two hundred years no one has ever returned from Reilan and, after having consulted the wise Saviours of the Children of Milla on this matter, we are agreed that I make this edict in the sure hope that I will save lives.

There is to be no discussion of Reilan or the Kingdom of Rial outside of the Ascension Chamber, even amongst ministers. I also want it decreed that only on the day of coronation is any future King to be allowed into the Ascension Chamber or be made aware of the other throne and the choice of kingdoms they can make. It is my firm belief that, with no knowledge of our past, any future King will merely see the Rialan throne for what it is - a relic and a curiosity - nothing more. Though I will not belittle the memory of my brother's folly or our distant ancestors by removing the throne I want that wing of the chamber left untended, unloved and unvisited. Let the past gather dust, for that is all that remains of Reilan. Any prince foolish enough to consider the Rialan throne will then have no illusions that they crown themselves the King of Dust. The King of Fools. The King of Nothing. Hopefully, such an unwanted title will never have an heir.

Carry out my orders.
Erin

Ciro read and re-read King Erin's letter. Now he understood why his father, King Fidiann, would not speak of what lay inside the Ascension Chamber and why the Rialan throne sat covered in dust. Tenlern's failure to return from Reilan had kept the fear of that continent alive and well within the Torrman family. Prince Tenlern's disappearance had been over two hundred years after the original exodus but, Ciro wondered, could a plague be so savage to still be deadly after such a time? Perhaps something else might have happened to Tenlern. Was the ship design not as good as was thought to survive the ocean? Or perhaps he had simply not bothered to come back. A hundred, no, a thousand things might have prevented Tenlern's return. But one thing Ciro did know was that he felt undeterred by Tenlern's fate and King Erin's warnings. It was now almost two hundred and fifty years since that lone voyage and times had changed. There were steam powered vessels now that did not have to rely on simple sails. There were fire lances and hand lances that were far more efficient than the old bow and arrow and medicine was now a science. Surely that would be enough to combat whatever Reilan might have in store? There were many improvements which Ciro could make to Tenlern's old plans and the young prince vowed to spend his teenage years doing exactly that. He would research, he would plan and he would succeed. In over five hundred years, Ciro would be the first to crown himself the new King of Rial.

LAND!

MAY IT BE KNOWN TO ALL
BRAVE & ABLE MEN
THAT HIS MAJESTY
THE ASCENDED
KING CIRO
OFFERS THE SUM OF
3 COPPERS A WEEK
& 50 ACRES OF LAND
PER MAN
FOR AID IN A VOYAGE
OF DISCOVERY
& THAT EACH MAN,
WHATEVER HIS PROFESSION
WILL BE CLOTHED, FED,
HOUSED & TRAINED
TO PEFORM HIS DUTIES
IN THIS
GRAND ENDEVOUR

◆

CONTACT YOUR LOCAL WATCHMAN
STATION FOR FURTHER DETAILS.
LONG LIVE KING CIRO!
LONG LIVE KING FIDIANN!

The Grand Voyage

On the morning of Ciro's grand voyage his father, King Fidiann, ruler of Feirlan slept fitfully. So frightening and vivid was the nightmare that played through his sleeping mind that he woke in the darkness with a tremulous cry upon his lips.

Throwing back the sweat-soaked linen of his bed sheets, the king was striding through the gloom of his bed chamber before realising that the sun had yet to rise and, reaching the thin sliver of light which spilled through the gap beneath his door, he stepped out into the lamp light of the grand hallway beyond and bellowed for the Nightwatch. He was dressed (a rare thing for him to do himself) before the guards had reached his chamber and the Nightwatch greeted him with apprehension when they found their monarch awake and waiting.

Fidiann was a tall man and, now aged more than fifty summers, his former slender frame had long since filled out to create an even more imposing presence. Silver-brown hair framed his angular features and fell to meet a grey-flecked, square cut beard – a rarity in Feirlan's warm climate. It was something the King had sported since his own Ascension Day many years before when he had become the King in Waiting to Ciro's Grandfather and so famous had 'Fidiann's Beard' become that the unusual sight had entered into the common vernacular as a statement of surprise. It also accentuated his piercing blue eyes which seemed to bore through those he cast his gaze upon. And now, dressed simply in dark greens and black, the king cast that dreaded gaze upon the yawning Nightwatch.

Of the four men, only their captain, Tilmose seemed as alert as Fidiann felt and, while the others tucked in shirts, buttoned their uniforms and avoided the King's stare, Tilmose saluted.

'Good morning, your majesty,' he said. 'How may we be of service?'

The nightmare which had woken Fidiann with such dread had faded now, yet snatches – confused jumbles of images – still lingered strongly enough for the king to feel no desire to return to his bed.

'What is the time?' he asked.

'Nearly dawn, your majesty,' replied one of the guards.

Fidiann nodded. Though the man's uniform was now straight, his ceremonial sword still hung crookedly. The king would normally have rebuked any man daring to enter his presence without carefully adjusting his dress but, this morning, his mind was elsewhere.

'I wish to take a walk,' he said.

Captain Tilmose looked blank. 'A walk, your highness?'

'Precisely, captain. A walk. To the South Quay.'

'Yes, your majesty,' answered Tilmose, attempting to mask his bemusement. 'I shall ready some horses.'

Fidiann was already striding past his men, his dark cloak splaying out behind him. 'I can't very well walk in the saddle of a horse, now can I, captain?' he replied testily and the guards hurried to catch up with their king.

As Fidiann walked swiftly through the halls and corridors of Torr Sarvie the castle came hurriedly to life in his wake. Servants scuttled through the shadows to light the lamps which their king had already passed and confused whispers echoed behind him as the castle staff attempted to fathom what on earth was wrong with their monarch. He never woke this early.

The guards at the main gate were equally flustered to see their king stride purposely towards them across the courtyard and, at Tilmose's command they drew back the brass trimmed doors to allow Fidiann outside.

The king took a few steps into the darkness beyond Torr Sarvie's gates then paused for a moment to gaze out over the sleeping town of Obaln which lay beneath the castle. Dawn was at least an hour away yet the sky was lit by an almost full moon. Its glow palely illuminated the cluttered rooftops below which jostled their way down the hill to frame the black and glittering ocean beyond. Fidiann shifted his gaze to the sky and watched a scrap of cloud creep past the moon: noting with a smile how Celestion blazed the grey shape to silver as it crossed its face. He shook his head in wonder. When was the last time he had stared at the sky?

'Your majesty?'

The inquiring tone drew the king from his contemplation and he turned to his guards.

'Come on,' he said with a frown, and marched off down the winding roadway towards the town.

Obaln, like Torr Sarvie, still slept and Fidiann felt an unusual sense of freedom as he reached the bottom of the hill to find Line Street deserted. He smiled, and took in the scene of shuttered shop fronts and the empty colonnades which stretched on towards the distant South Quay.

'Marvellous,' said the king to himself. He crossed the street and walked for a while beneath the lamp lights of the northern colonnade: enjoying the comparative solitude and the fact that he was on foot and not in the royal carriage. It was, he realised with some surprise, over twenty years since he had ventured out like this to experience the world beyond the confines of the castle. Twenty years since his father had passed away and he had gone from Ascended King to Monarch. Fidiann remembered that distant time well: it seemed like yesterday. The king's attention turned to his surroundings and he paused several times to inspect the wares of various establishments: making a mental note each time to later dispatch one of his aids to purchase the items he saw.

Half way down Line Street, Fidiann suddenly turned left into a narrow side road and started up its steady gradient. Away from the grand frontage of the lamp lit colonnade, wood and plaster walls leaned in upon the cobblestones and the guards watched the king's receding shape with some confusion.

'Your majesty,' called Tilmose. 'The harbour is this way.'

'Top Hill is this way,' announced the king by way of explanation and, without turning, continued on up the side street.

With shrugs and shaking heads, the Nightwatch quickly closed the gap and followed their monarch up the twisting road. After a few minutes climb the lane opened out onto the flat expanse of the market square which occupied the top of the hill. Here the king stopped again and stood for several minutes watching the towering shadow of Top Hill Clock: the hands on its illuminated face creeping towards four.

The clock, like the timber beamed tower which housed it, had stood for almost five hundred years: counting out the lives of every Feirlaner in Obaln. Fidiann gave a rueful smile. And every King, he thought. From King Sarvie right through to him. Fidiann: the last King of Feirlan.

The thought drew a veil on his happy musings and brought instead the object of his nocturnal wander back to the fore. In little more than eight hours from now Ciro, his eldest son and the rightful heir to the Feirlan throne, would throw that duty away in pursuit of some juvenile folly – dragging his younger brother Bdann along with him.

The king turned away from the clock as the first clear chime of four rang out and with a furrowed brow strode briskly towards the eastern edge of the market square. If his memory was correct the grey buildings ahead were divided by another lane which led down from the market to the South Quay. As he neared its entrance however, the tuneless singing which echoed out of the darkness ahead caused Fidiann to stop and the Palace Guard drew closer to protect their monarch as a dishevelled figure wandered from the shadows.

He was dressed in a similar uniform to Fidiann's own men yet, instead of the deep Feirlan Green with silver buttons, the man wore a cheap, misshapen beige tunic fastened with buttons of tin. Emblazoned upon his breast was an emblem of Milla, the sun goddess, which marked him as a member of his son's newly formed Rialan Army. Because of the un-dyed drabness of the uniform (a question of financial necessity for his son) Ciro's soldiers were commonly referred to by the king's circle as 'The Duns'.

The man, still singing, staggered closer: oblivious to his audience as his attention was firmly focused on his meandering feet. Fidiann drew his cloak around him, not wanting to be recognised and, watching the man, wondered how many other wretches had decided to drown their wits rather than themselves when the ships set sail at noon.

'Mi-Milla shine on brave King, King Ciro!' stuttered the man drunkenly as he finally spotted Fidiann's group. He waved an arm in uncoordinated salute then staggered closer, the broad grin falling to a scowl as he recognised the uniforms of the Nightwatch.

'Ha!' the man cried. 'Blo-Bloosandin' Green Jackets. 'ave ya seen this mates!' He turned on the spot as if to address some companions then wavered unsteadily as he scanned the darkness of the lane he had appeared from.

Captain Tilmose stepped forward, blocking the path to the king. 'Why aren't you on your ship?!' he barked and when the drunkard turned to face the group again, he seemed surprised to find them there.

'Wha...? Why...?' replied the soldier uncertainly, then some focus appeared in his eyes and he prodded the captain's chest. 'Because our illust-illus-trus young King gave all of us leave to spend our last night on shhhhore: that's why!'

Typical of the boy, Fidiann thought. How did he expect four thousand men to follow him with discipline like that?

'What a fool,' sighed the king with a shake of his head. He supposed he should be offended by the proximity of such an individual, yet it had been so long since Fidiann had seen such behaviour in his presence that he found the whole situation vaguely amusing.

The drunkard had started rambling to himself.

'Looks after his men, Ciro does,' he muttered. 'Not like, not like old Grey Beard up there.' The man threw a hand in the direction of Torr Sarvie. 'He don't care 'bout his troops –'

Tilmose, his eyes narrowing to a line, drew his hand lance. 'Right, that's enough,' he growled. 'You're under arrest.' He pointed his weapon at the man who stared drunkenly down its barrel for a second before shooting his hands into the air.

King Fidiann stepped forward and placed a restraining hand on the captain's shoulder. 'It's all right, captain,' he said. 'Just high spirits. Let the man go.'

Without a word, Tilmose holstered his hand lance, stepped back and warily the drunkard lowered his arms.

'Tell me,' Fidiann asked the man, 'why do want to go to Reilan?'

The man frowned and for a moment the king wondered if his wits were too addled by alcohol to understand the question.

'Land,' he replied as if it were the most obvious thing in the world. 'Good, fertile land. Nobody ever offered me land before, good or otherwise.'

Fidiann nodded. Land: the eternal Feirlan problem. Too many people, not enough land. Long Lake's southern shore was now nothing more than a salt flat and the Nelan Desert continued to creep its barren path ever northwards. What was the latest figure? A mile a month Fidiann seemed to recall. He'd dismissed it as scare-mongering at the time but knew that his current canal project had again failed to irrigate the Northern Flat Lands. Kensun's Fall was now a ghost town and the steady stream of southern farmers heading north was causing unrest in towns as close as Rurset. No wonder Ciro had caused such a commotion with his offer. But were these poor unfortunates really aware of the danger his son planned to take them into? It was the reason their ancestors had left Reilan and the Kingdom of Rial in the first place.

'Aren't you worried about the plague?' Fidiann asked.

'Plague!' The man's face split with a broad grin then, seeing Fidiann's impassive countenance, the smile lessened and he continued. 'No, your honour. By the stars, that's the last thing the boys an' me are worried 'bout. Fallin' overboard, yes. Plague no. We trust Ciro. 'e wouldn't lead us wrong an' that's certain.'

Fidiann could not help but smile at the man's simple faith in his son, and was surprised by the tinge of pride he felt at how successfully Ciro had engendered a confident spirit in his newly-formed 'Dun Army'. He still felt the voyage was a ludicrous and above all dangerous waste of time, money and resources but the king had learnt, on Ciro's Ascension Day particularly, that no amount of argument would dissuade him. His son was determined to pursue his Reilan folly to the bitter end.

Fidiann wished the man well and left to take the lane down to the harbour. As they negotiated the dim and meandering space, his thoughts returned to the strange, unsettling dream which had woken him.

If he were a superstitious man – which he wasn't – then perhaps he would have attached some mystic importance to the images which still flitted through his mind. But, unlike the repellent Saviour Engis who used superstition where wiser men would use facts, Fidiann's fear had subsided to the point where he now found the visions merely fascinating: it was not like him to have so active an imagination.

Of all the strange and disconcerting scenes which had eventually woken him, the image of the Songsmith, Calian remained the most vivid in the king's mind. Fidiann could still clearly recall the ground shaking beneath his feet and his surprise as he watched Ciro's friend run past him. The Songsmith's defiant cry had bested the storm which raged around them and inhuman shapes – mere grey shadows in the gloom ahead – had scattered in his path. Then one such shape had emerged from the angled veil of rain and a creature – born only of a nightmare-gripped mind – was suddenly bearing down upon the king. It was then that Fidiann had been startled awake to see nothing but the darkness of his bed chamber.

The shadows of the lane receded as they reached the harbour: moonlight bathing the quay side and glinting on the placid sea. Looking out into the broad bay, Fidiann shook his head in disbelief at the vast, dark shapes moored there. It was the first time he had seen Ciro's fleet other than as distant objects from Torr Sarvie's towers.

'Impressive,' he said to himself, watching the vessels rocking gently on the tide.

'Yes, your majesty,' muttered Captain Tilmose beside him and the king lent on the harbour railing to peruse the sight in silence.

Fidiann cast his gaze over the closest vessel, taking in the towering masts and vague spider's web of rigging before running his eyes along its sleek hull. From the bulky central arch of the paddle wheel the ship swept fore and aft in a graceful curve. Behind the paddle wheel the central cabins rose to the wheelhouse and, amidst the dull glint of brass railings and port holes, a dark figure moved along the starboard walkway.

'What's the name of that ship, captain?' Fidiann asked over his shoulder and, as one, the Nightwatch scrutinised the dim lettering written on its prow.

'It's the King Elson, your highness,' replied one of the men.

'And the one beside it?'

A guard jogged quickly along the quay side to get a closer look at the name and returned momentarily to inform the king that it was the Prince Meanon.

Fidiann nodded but said nothing. King Elson, Prince Meanon. Out there in the darkness, he surmised, would be a ship named after the third brother, Prince Idirnon, while seven other such titles would adorn the remaining vessels. Nowhere in that fleet however, would there be a King Colis, a King Sarvie or even a King Fidiann. No, the new King of Rial had no time for those who had guided Feirlan down the years, just those who had wasted their lives in pursuit of dreams across the sea. People who had never returned to tell their sorry tales but instead passed away into mysterious oblivion. Reilan by any other name.

The figure on the King Elson had disappeared into the darkness until the dull glow from a storm lamp showed that he was now on the main deck, swinging the lamp over the side. In response, Fidiann caught the sound of frantic paddling and guessed that some unseen boat – no doubt crammed full of more drunken seamen – was attempting to reach the ship in the darkness. Fidiann shook his head. Raising the spirit of the men his son had enlisted was one thing, but letting them wallow in spirits was a concession Fidiann would certainly never have allowed.

After a short time the sound of paddling and the lamp itself died away and the king focused his thoughts on the main cabin of the nearby vessel. In there, he knew, his son Ciro slept: while his brother, Bdann occupied an identical cabin onboard the Prince Meanon. Did Ciro dream peacefully? Fidiann wondered. Or was his sleep also disturbed by terrifying visions? No, the king decided, his son dreamt of bright things, things and places which existed only in the ancient Rialan documents of the Ascension Chamber and in Ciro's imagination. Of a future of adventure; of glory and discovery, where the practicalities of a Kingdom took second place to a young mind who, it now seemed, had never once grasped the first and foremost consideration required to be a Monarch. For Ciro, duty to his country and people was something he had circumvented with dreams.

Fidiann sighed. Beyond the grand ships, beyond the harbour and far out on the eastern horizon the sky was beginning to lighten. The sun: bright and glorious Milla would soon be rising to smile on another day and chase the baleful form of Celestion from view. The king looked up at the moon then: pondering the age-old question of what terrible, cosmic tragedy could have left such a sorrowful expression on its face. Was it the pain of a father, he wondered, whose offspring treated their father's wishes with contempt? Probably not. Only a fool would suppose that the lives of the sun, of the moon, were occupied by such mundane matters. Though Fidiann was sure that, if he asked Saviour Engis's opinion on the subject, he would be informed that all such things were inextricably linked.

'Now there is a fool,' muttered the king to himself.

'Your majesty?'

The king stood back from the railings and looked at the men around him. 'Tell me,' he said, addressing Captain Tilmose. 'Were you not tempted to join my son's little sailing party?'

The captain gazed silently at the dark ships on the water for a moment then shook his head. 'No, your majesty,' he replied. 'Not really.'

'May your King ask why?'

Tilmose shrugged. 'It just doesn't seem right, your majesty. Or feel right, anyway. This old kingdom everyone's heard about since the Prince's Ascension…Well, nobody but Ciro seems to know anything about it.'

Fidiann nodded slowly. 'We all did once but… Five hundred years, captain,' explained the king, 'that amount of time wipes away a lot of memories.'

'But, if I may ask, your majesty. Why now? After so much time?'

Fidiann did not bother to mask his pained smile. Why indeed? That thought had perplexed him from the moment his son had made his startling announcement to choose the Rialan throne on his Ascension Day. How had Ciro known so much about something so secret? He sighed and leant against the railings, regarding the captain with a sympathetic eye. 'Tell me what you know about the Ascension ceremony, captain.' he asked.

Tilmose thought for a moment. 'Well…Your majesty… It's to change a prince's position from that of Prince to King in waiting… So he can learn the ways of kingship and get ready to take his place on the throne.' The captain watched his monarch's face to see if he had answered correctly. To his relief, Fidiann nodded.

'And what did my son have to do on the day?' asked the king.

Tilmose pointed along the quay side to where the eastern

entrance to Line Street could just be made out. 'He walked The King's Line,' replied the captain. 'Like every monarch before him. From the harbour's edge to the Ascension Chamber up in the castle.'

'Quite so,' agreed the king. 'Following the brass line which has been set in those cobbles since before anyone can remember. But do you know what that brass line represents?' The captain shook his head while the rest of the Nightwatch listened attentively. 'It traces,' explained Fidiann, 'the path an eleven year old prince named Sarvie took more than five hundred years ago when he and our ancestors set foot on Feirlan soil for the first time.' The king shrugged. 'Or so the story goes. And it was that same Prince Sarvie who, all those years ago, built the Ascension Chamber and had the brass line laid into the cobblestones of Line Street. But what no living person except myself and several high ranking Aldermen knew – until my son made it public knowledge – is what happens to the line once it enters the privacy of the Ascension Chamber itself.' Fidiann looked at the blank faces around him and sighed. His son had mentioned these facts during his staggering Ascension Day speech but Ciro's words had obviously not been fully comprehended. 'It splits into two,' explained Fidiann, drawing his hands apart. 'One line leads to the Feirlan throne, while the other…'

'…Leads to this other, Reilan throne,' said Tilmose.

Fidiann nodded. 'That is what Ascension Day is truly about: a choice of kingdoms, old and new. But not one prince, not one, in the entire course of Feirlan history has known that fact until entering the Ascension Chamber. And not one prince has chosen the Reilan – or rather the Rial throne – until my son did.'

There was bitterness and regret in the king's voice and he turned back to face the sea where his son's fleet bobbed at anchor. Fidiann looked at the grey vessels for a final time and heard the steam whistle of a fishing boat sound across the water. As if the sound were a personal signal, he turned from the quay side and silently started back towards the castle. The fishermen would be returning with their catch and soon the market would fill with traders from Obaln, Rurset and Tarsin. Top Hill Clock, like it had for centuries, would count out another day but, by its end, something would be missing. Both Fidiann's sons would be gone.

The king felt the sense of loss deepen within him as he returned to Torr Sarvie but attempted to concentrate on matters at hand. The midday farewell ceremony at the quay side would allow him an opportunity to give Ciro, and that young rogue Bdann, a final chance to change their minds – but if they did not? Well, thought Fidiann, then he supposed he would have to wish them good luck and a fair tide. The king shook his head. Or would he once more remind his son of his duty?

The dilemma vexed him all the way back to his chambers – all morning in fact – and later, as he rode in the royal coach through the packed morning streets to the harbour, his Queen, Irsa found him muttering under his breath as to what to say to their sons. But the problem proved academic. Ciro, it seemed, had not wanted to face his father's expected anger. The harbour was empty. The young fool and his fleet had already sailed for Reilan.

The King of Nothing

PART ONE

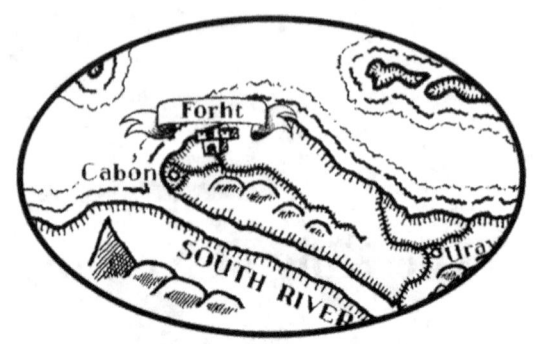

And so we reached our journey's end and stayed in the simple comfort of The Last Inn (and only Inn I hasten to add) in the rural town of Cabon: the most western outpost of our glorious Kingdom.

Here, far from the Heartwold - or even the firm bastions of Torr Betram - Cabon's only defence from Makech attack is an ancient ditch topped by a fence. An incongruously flimsy deterrent given that, situated as it is near the mouth of the South River which winds down towards deadly Kal Santra, such a threat can never be far from wary minds. In stark contrast to the token defence the people of Cabon seem as hard-eyed as hawks, rugged as the windswept landscape they eke a living from with a short sword hanging from every belt. Despite such menacing outlook and apparel however, they are a welcoming folk – even to 'towners' such as ourselves – and our arrival at the Inn was greeted with much cheer (and ale) by the tavern revellers. The same happy band later crowded the door of the small food hall as myself and my fellow travellers ate and Alderman Chaime (never one to enjoy digestion with an audience) was at last forced to divert attention from our famished selves by throwing two 'King's Promises' upon the tavern bar and calling for drinks all round.

In peaceful seclusion we ate our fill of mutton stew, sweet potatoes and apple dumplings and retired to our meagre rooms with the nocturnal vow that we would walk off our expanded girths the following morning. Alas, only myself and Alderman Fars ventured forth that morrow to see the bleak countryside give way to the sea. So only I and one other could claim truly that we had been to the very end of the realm.

Alderman Lacey. My Travels through the West Wold.

NC 659

Flotsam and Jetsam

I

It was bright as Igallianesh walked along the cliff top and the sea, mutely roaring on the rocks far below, rolled and glittered in the early morning sun. Gulls circled, calling overhead and she smiled as she carefully trod a barefoot path through the gorse. All was calm. A Gallia sea, she thought to herself and took off the shawl she had wrapped around her shoulders before leaving the farm. Far out, where the waves lost their shape to endless grey, tattered remnants of cloud hung faintly upon the horizon. Igallianesh wondered how the tempest of the previous night could give way so quickly to such beauty.

'Only other Gods and fools...' she said to herself and smiled at the recollection of the storm.

She had woken, as had the whole farm, when the first blast of wind had slammed against the stonework and quickly huddled beneath her blanket as the gale played its shrill tune on every nook and cranny it could find. There had been lulls, brief moments of peace as if the storm was attempting to catch its breath, before starting with renewed vigour as it did its best to wrench the shutters from her window. She had heard footsteps then – above the noise of the wind and first clattering of rain – running down the stairs. Then Menzir, her stepfather, had cursed faintly from the farmyard as he rushed to secure the flapping barn doors. She had pictured him standing in the mud as he berated Sakoom, Kolben Lord of the wind: drenched with rain while he shook a fist at the sky. Then the pitch dark of her room had flashed white for a second while a great peel of thunder bellowed overhead. As the house shook, Igallianesh had disappeared deeper beneath her blanket, now in turn cursing her stepfather for his stupidity.

'Only other Gods and fools know the ways of the world,' she had recited to herself beneath the bedclothes. 'But fools can't make the wind blow or the grass grow.' She had fallen asleep while the tempest raged on, reciting prayers to Fenya, and the other Kolben Ladies for the storm to stop.

Igallianesh was hopeful that the storm would have left its mark on her beach as well, washing up more shells and curiosities than she would usually find when she combed the shoreline and cliffs of her private haven. It was the same ritual she carried out once a week – twice if she could get away from the endless chores around the farm – and what she found she would polish or decorate and try to sell when she accompanied her stepfather and Tersic the farm hand to the monthly market in Cabon.

Menzir had never been happy with her beach combing and made no secret of the fact that he considered it a waste of time. Despite his reservations however, it never stopped him from taking what little money she could earn from selling her wares. It barely paid for her upkeep, he had once said, but that, Igallianesh knew, was just another excuse to bemoan the fact that she was not a thick-necked pack horse like Tersic and therefore, in his eyes, a constant burden. Her mother, Qisala, on the other hand, always encouraged her to collect her shells and flotsam because, as she always said, with a name like Igallianesh (Seashell), such pursuits could only bring good fortune. Igallianesh doubted her collecting would ever bring her any monetary gain, but the simple act of disappearing down to her private world and losing herself in the beauty of the ocean made her feel very fortunate indeed.

The cliff path veered away from the shore slightly and dipped behind the craggy headland which marked the eastern edge of her private cove. Igallianesh felt the same thrill of anticipation which she always experienced just before she got her first glimpse of the beach and she quickened her pace through the high banks of gorse to reach the rocky summit which overlooked the bay. As always the tide would be well past the middle rock which sat stranded in the centre of the bay and a crescent of pristine sand would stretch out before her eyes. On her way home she would always look back to see the footprints she had made meandering about the shoreline and know, like she knew now, that when she returned the beach would have been washed blank again. The centre rock peeked above the greenery as she strode the last few steps to the summit and with a glad heart she at last gazed down at her own little world – and found it disturbed.

The majority of the beach was untouched, but there, in the centre around the middle rock and cutting a messy swathe up towards the cliffs, was a jumble of dark, splintered objects which fanned out into the receding waves. Curious, because she had never seen such strange seaweed before, Igallianesh ran down the steep cutting in the rocks which gave the only access to the shore and sped across the sand to get a better look. It was only as she got closer that she could discern the angular shape of wooden boxes broken upon the sand and then a flash of gold made her gasp as she suddenly saw the figure of a man prostrate amongst the flotsam.

Igallianesh ran over, and then checked herself as she reached to turn the body onto its back. There was something very strange about the figure. The short blue jacket, trimmed around the shoulders and collar with some sort of gold, was like nothing she had ever seen before, certainly nothing like the black and iron armour of the vile Makech. She spat on the sand, displeased to even think about them here of all places. Beneath the jacket a thick black belt was studded by large silver stars and from it a tan pocket – like a stunted sword sheath – hung. If it contained a sword, it must have somehow broken, Nesh surmised, for a small handle poked out from the sheath at an acute angle. The leggings were a curious, beige coloured canvas and they sat above the most well made and sturdy looking leather boots Igallianesh had ever seen. Nesh frowned and looked down at her own dress, a shabby woollen shawl dyed green with nettles and a shapeless linen dress above bare legs and feet. These, she concluded, must be the clothes of a very rich man. But from where? And, more importantly, how did he come to be on her beach? Igallianesh gripped the sodden jacket at the shoulder and was about to turn the body over when there was a flurry of movement from the figure. Suddenly she was lying flat on her back and the shadow of the man loomed over her.

'C..Calian,' the figure stuttered: his words as weak as his shaking legs and he held out a hand towards her. Terrified, Igallianesh scuttled backwards – her heels leaving deep rents in the sand. Then she watched with her heart in her mouth as the man's legs buckled and he collapsed back onto the ground.

She jumped to her feet and breathed hard as she realised the figure was again prostrate and unmoving. Tentatively she took a step closer but, when she saw the large golden sun emblem pinned to his breast, she stopped dead and stared in disbelief. This was no Makech. Such symbols meant death to the wearer, yet no Rialan would ever feel suicidal enough to wear the sign of Milla so brazenly. They would carry it well hidden in their clothing, scrawl it on town walls or carve it into the bark of trees, but the only people she had ever seen wearing the sign in public were those accused of heresy and tied to the fire stakes in Cabon's main square. She furrowed her brow, cast her gaze around the mass of wooden splinters which lay all around her then picked out the shape of a broken box nearby. It too had the forbidden sign of the sun emblazoned on it.

51

Igallianesh bit her lip and looked down at the face of the unconscious figure. He was young, little older than herself she supposed, yet everything about him was outlandish. Odd. Even the straw blonde hair, matted and encrusted with salt as it was, looked trim.

The young man remained immobile as Igallianesh debated what to do. Despite the risks she felt determined to help him but, looking a good foot taller than her slender five feet, unless he awoke there was no way to get him back to the farm. She crouched down and shook the figure, hoping to rouse him, and saw the gash which sat above his left ear. The blood had matted the hair and Igallianesh pushed at it to get a better look at the wound. It looked deep and in response to her probing the man grimaced yet did not wake up.

The stranger's presence made Igallianesh feel nervous and she cast her eye along the cliff top, reassuring herself that she was not overlooked. She smiled, of all the places she could think of, she knew that this was the one place which nobody, not even her mother, knew about. She took one last look at the man to make sure that he was still breathing, and then ran as fast as she could to get help.

II

Kattis Capell stared despondently at the surf and then turned his attention to where the skeletal figure of Baramir Newman continued to stamp the wet sand and curse. Capell put his head in his hands and looked glumly at the receding tide. Despite what Baramir thought, he felt sure that the accident had not been his fault.

It had all happened so quickly. One moment they had been happily prizing open a food crate on the foredeck of the King Elson, the next the storm had hit and the King himself had been standing over them. Neither he nor **Baramir** had had much time to acknowledge the fact that they had been discovered before the whole ship had lurched and the entire stack of crates had collapsed and pushed them into the waves below. What little he remembered of that terrifying time, as the world turned to water and threatened to engulf him, he did not care to dwell on. And now they were here – wherever here was – with no hope of rescue and little chance of survival unless a miracle occurred.

Baramir stomped back to where the portly figure of Capell sat dejectedly on the beach. Around them, and spread about the shore was what remained of the crates that had been deposited with them on this unknown land. The dried meat that the boxes had held was now the subject of intense interest by the local gull population and every minute brought another wave of the screaming creatures to fight for scraps. Newman glowered down at his companion and, noting how the salt had stained and encrusted about Capell's uniform, realised that he too was similarly stricken. Baramir rubbed furiously at his 'duns', causing a shower of salt to rain down upon the miserable Capell and then looked vainly up the beach in the hope that some form of civilisation could be seen. A panorama of sand dunes interspersed with tussocks of grass was all that greeted his gaze, so he sank with a snort to the ground beside Kattis.

'Do you have any idea – at all – where we are!?' he snapped.

Capell turned to regard the same range of sand dunes. 'Reilan,' he answered glumly.

Baramir stood up again and flung his arms wide in exasperation. 'Where in Reilan!?'

'I don't even know where Reilan is, let alone where we are in it,' muttered Capell miserably.

To this Baramir sneered and prodded his companion on the shoulder with a bony finger. 'It's a pity your appetite is not matched by your intelligence. If that stomach of yours was less demanding, we would still be on the ship.'

Kattis said nothing. It was true that hunger had led him out of hiding and onto the foredeck of the King Elson to search the crates, but at the time Baramir had voiced no reservations about their course of action. After three weeks of cramped concealment onboard ship, Baramir had seen the distraction as a welcome one.

Capell watched the seagulls flock around the crates for a moment and wondered if all the food still inside had been spoiled by the water. He felt ravenous.

'I don't suppose,' said Baramir in a slightly softer tone, 'it matters much that we are here, rather than wherever the King and his men were going.' He gestured out to where the ocean passed the eastern edge of the bay. 'In fact, apart from our slightly undignified arrival, this could work out far better than I had thought.'

Kattis brightened. Now that Baramir had accepted the situation, he was putting his mind to work and that could only mean a rapid improvement to their circumstance.

'Perhaps we might be able to salvage some of the food?' Kattis said.

Baramir smiled: an action that always reminded Kattis of a dog snarling. 'Yes,' he replied. 'Well done Capell.' Kattis smiled back. 'Now,' continued Baramir, 'why don't you see off those gulls and see what you can rescue.'

The smile faded as Kattis watched the seething, fighting birds and then, with Baramir still grinning, tentatively stepped towards the battling flock.

Baramir Newman chuckled as he watched the bulbous frame of his companion begin vainly shooing the birds away and then returned his attention to the dunes. Somewhere, he thought, there must be some form of civilisation: and when they found it, they could start again. Here they would be unknown. Just travellers, not thieves or wanted criminals like back in Feirlan. Baramir searched inside his beige uniform and held his breath as he pulled out the gold pocket watch and held it up to his ear. It was still ticking. He smiled to himself, rewound it and then checked the compartment which held the metal tipped flights. The watch was a superb piece of cruel and cunning craftsmanship, allowing the user to eject one flight at a time from the base of the device by simply depressing the winder. At close range the effect was deadly. Baramir knew that well, he had killed twice with it before.

He returned the watch to his pocket and was just about to check on Capell when he cast his gaze back to catch the distant figure of a horseman appear above the dunes. He was swiftly followed by another, and then another until seven dark shapes lined the edge of the beach. Baramir caught his breath and then hissed at Kattis.

'Kattis! Kattis you fool! Come quickly!'

Looking up, Capell dropped his jaw as well as the armful of food he had collected. He walked woodenly to stand beside Baramir while the gulls dived screaming onto the pile of dried meat left behind him.

'Do you think it's the King?' he asked as the horsemen slowly descended the dunes.

'Don't be stupid!' growled Newman, betraying his nervousness. Even at this distance he could see enough to know that these were not King Ciro's men, and though there might have been horses stabled on one of the other ships, there had certainly been none aboard the King Elson. Whoever they were, they were native to Reilan, and Baramir prayed that they were friendly.

They would not have long to wait. The group had already reached the beach and were picking up speed as they cantered to meet the castaways.

'Whatever happens,' hissed Baramir, 'let me do the talking.'

Kattis's jowls wobbled as he nodded furiously.

The horsemen had now ridden close enough for the pair to pick out details, though what they saw did not improve their confidence. They seemed to be clad in black leather interspersed by strips of metal with high, white helmets perched upon their heads. Each rider carried a slender spear in one hand. The sound of clinking metal carried across the beach as the group approached and mixed with the bass thud of the horses' hooves which soon began to make the ground tremble. Kattis dropped his gaze and tried to stop his teeth from chattering as the men drew nearer and Baramir fought the urge to run back into the sea when the horsemen stopped before them.

He managed instead to regard them unblinkingly (more from shock than bravery) but any words he had thought to defend himself with died in his throat as he took in the sight of the grim-faced group which now stared back. They were clad in long leather coats, panelled with tiny iron plates and hung with a variety of trinkets and talismans. Most sported beards which draped down upon their chests and there the leather appeared stained the exact colour of blood. Each wore an iron helmet which curled down to cover their ears and chin which left a circular hollow from which they stared out. The armour appeared to be decorated with bones from the stars knew where but, upon the crown of each helmet, sat the unmistakable shape of a damaged human skull. The strangers exchanged some curious glances to one another before the closest horseman leaned forward in his saddle and frowned.

'Jo ui ekom lonar bi!?' he demanded.

Baramir blinked, unsure that he had heard the gibberish that the man had appeared to speak and, despite his nervousness, he managed to make his lips move.

'I'm sorry?' he said weakly.

The man's eyes widened, his brows shooting out of sight into the darkness of his helmet while the rest of the group seemed similarly amazed. The front man levelled his spear at Baramir.

'Lonar bi fetir? Nus yita itanta?!'

Baramir did not know what the man was saying but, coupled with the spear, there was enough expression in the gruff voice to convey displeasure. Baramir wracked his brains to think of something to say that would placate the man, but how could he do that if they did not understand him? After several long seconds of silence, the man muttered something to the group then handed his spear to another rider. He slipped from the saddle and drew a long curving sword, advancing on the pair.

'Ss...say s...something, Baramir, please!' stammered Kattis as the man stopped before them and pressed the tip of his sword against Baramir's chest.

'What do you expect me to say, you fat fool!?' Newman snapped in reply. 'They don't understand us!'

He looked into the eyes of the swordsman and saw hatred in his gaze. There was a pungent aroma of sweat and worse emanating from the man and Baramir wondered if this ugly, rank savage would be the last thing he ever saw. As if reading his thoughts, the swordsman split a gap-toothed smile and swung back his blade ¬with vigour before a blunt shout from another of the horsemen stopped him cold. Newman released a silent sigh as this intervening rider, similarly dressed yet younger and slimmer with a short, neatly-trimmed beard, dismounted and approached them. The younger rider exchanged a few curt words with the swordsman, shook his head and, in response, the swordsman stepped back. This man now regarded Capell and Newman's salt stained uniforms intently for a few moments. He then moved a step closer and prodded Baramir in the chest with nothing more dangerous than his finger.

'Jas' dara unar?' he asked. The words were indecipherable to the pair of castaways but the tone seemed conversational.

Baramir looked down to see him pointing at the sun symbol woven onto his jacket. "What is it?" Is that what he was asking?

'It's a badge,' Newman replied. The swordsman growled audibly at this answer, but the slim man simply glowered his companion into silence then returned his attention to Baramir.

'You know the penalty for speaking Rialan is death and yet you continue to do it,' he said, leaving Baramir and Kattis dumbstruck. 'So you are either stupid, as Yetzi: 12 thinks…' He indicated the man with the sword. 'Mad… Or probably both. And seeing that you also wear the symbol of Rial I am curious to know just how you where persuaded to come out in daylight.'

Before Baramir could reply, the man turned to Yetzi, said something in their strange tongue, and pointed to the broken crates scattered behind them. The swordsman returned his sword to its scabbard and hurried down the beach towards the flotsam.

'We mean no offence,' said Baramir. Kattis shook his head in frantic agreement.

'Every word you say offends me,' replied the slim man with a humourless smile.

'Please except our humblest apologies,' replied Baramir with earnest. 'If I knew your language I assure you I would not dream of speaking this one.'

To this the man grinned and shouted something over his shoulder to his companions. A roar of laughter erupted from the horsemen.

'The only people I know who stupidly speak your tongue are the scum Philiri,' the slim man said. 'But they live far from here and certainly wouldn't be dumb enough to wear that symbol openly. So who are you? And how did you get to be here?'

'We are not Philiri, I promise you,' said Baramir. 'Just travellers who were washed overboard from our ship last night. We are strangers here.'

To this the man snorted. 'Strangers?! Don't tell me: the Kingdom of Rial is alive and well. Back from the dead!'

'I think that's where we were going,' said Kattis helpfully before Baramir could stop him.

The smile dropped from the young man's face and he drew his own curved sword. 'You tell me who you are, now,' he said quietly, but with obvious menace. 'Or I will add your deaths to my total.'

Baramir put his hands up in sublimation and quickly gabbled: 'My name is Baramir Newman, his is Kattis Capell. We were washed overboard last night from a ship bound east – I think – for a place called Rial.'

The man pressed the tip of his sword beneath Baramir's chin and forced his head back. 'Bound east from where?' he hissed from between clenched teeth. 'There is nothing west of here except a wilderness. Or did Shernn spit you from the deep?'

'Feirlan! Feirlan! We've been sailing for weeks!' Kattis squeaked, panic breaking his voice.

Frowning, the man eased the pressure slightly on Newman's throat and turned his attention to Yetzi, who had returned holding a panel from one of the broken crates. Burnt into the wood was the Rial sun symbol and beneath it, in tiny letters it read: 'Dried beef. 50 pounds. Supplied by Tarmiir, Master Butcher, Obaln.'

The man removed his blade from Baramir's throat and levelled it an inch before his eyes. 'I want to know everything there is to know about this ship of yours and this place you say you come from,' he said sternly. 'And, if I don't like your answers, I shall turn your heads into hats.'

III

It was gloomy in the cramped forecastle storeroom of the King Elson and the single rocking lamp repeatedly threw Calian's profile into angular relief against the bulkhead as he secured the door against the night. Ciro had never known his friend to behave in quite such a conspiratorial manner, but he waited patiently for the Songsmith to explain why he needed to speak to him in secret and stifled a yawn as he leant against the cluster of steam pipes which pillared the centre of the room. The copper pipes were slightly warm to the touch and Ciro noted a strange gurgle sounding deep within its length. Above the noise, the familiar thud, thud, thud of the paddle engines could be heard, as the vessel pushed onwards through the gentle swell of the Inner Sea. The creak of the woodwork and squeak of the iron plating joined their straining harmonies to the voice of the ship but, after three weeks at sea, the young King hardly noticed it.

Turning to face Ciro, Calian's expression looked grim and his eyes were shadowed from the lamplight as he pulled a thick roll of parchment from his jacket and offered it to the King.

'I think that Saviour Engis has made other plans for some of the men in our party,' said the Songsmith and Ciro did not try to hide his confusion as he took the papers.

Engis was the leader of the Children of Milla, a dwindling religious order back in Feirlan. Although Ciro had never been interested in or involved with the church of 'The Eight', Saviour Engis had been a staunch supporter of the newly Ascended King. Particularly after Ciro's decision to renounce the Feirlan throne and return to Reilan became know. Engis had never been a popular figure in the royal court, yet even Ciro's father, King Fidiann – who openly disliked both the man and his superstitious ideals – had eventually seemed (however grudgingly) to accept his presence.

Yet Saviour Engis had stayed behind in Feirlan, waving them off when the fleet had sailed out of Obaln harbour, so how could he have devised anything that could affect this journey into the unknown? Ciro mirrored the Songsmith's frown and unrolled the papers, flicking his gaze at Calian before turning the top sheet towards the light and reading.

'Be it known to all you brave souls,' the letter began, *'that our prayers travel with you on this desperate journey into the night. The letters enclosed should give enough information as to where to begin your search and convince you, beyond all doubt, that you must not be swayed by the infantile dreams of the Fool King. The originals of these letters have been safely stored since the time of Prince Tenlern, the last fool to make this journey, and it is our firm belief that nobody in the royal court since the wise King Erin has ever seen them. If they had then I do not doubt that Ciro would never have decided on his present course of action, but then it is not our place to worry of the unbeliever's fate and we must give some thanks to his sacrifice for providing us with this 'golden' opportunity. Read these messages well, memorise every word so that you know you do Milla's work in retrieving her image*

from the darkness and, when you have it, return safely home. As for Ciro and his mindless followers, let their folly be the final one of our people. A pyre to light our way finally out of the darkness.'

The letter was unsigned, yet the religious overtones were unmistakably those of the Children of Milla.

Ciro shook the bundle of papers. 'Where did these come from? And why do you think Engis wrote this letter?'

Calian crossed his arms and looked a little sheepish. 'I take no pride in admitting this, but I took the letters from the cabin next to mine. The cabin of Captain Fars.' Calian met Ciro's incredulous gaze firmly. 'For some time now during the voyage,' continued the Songsmith. 'I've been hearing mutterings late at night from the Captain's cabin and, though they were never loud enough for me to hear distinctly, I found the cadence – the rhythm – always the same. It took me a little time to realise that I'd only ever heard the same meter in the Church of the Children of Milla and then I knew that it was Milla's Prayer being recited. Once a night, every night.' Calian sighed and gave a shrug. 'And, as you know, the captain's religious beliefs are well known.'

'Yes, Calian. Very,' Ciro replied with scorn. 'He has always derided the Children of Milla. I've personally overheard him make fun of Engis on many occasions.'

'As does your brother, Bdann,' agreed Calian. 'But never quite so vociferously. And for such a charming, polite man as Captain Fars is, doesn't it seem odd that he will always speak out on that one subject when on all others he remains so balanced? So stoic?'

'Are you saying that he tries to mask his true belief by deriding it?' Ciro chewed on his lower lip, considering the idea then shook his head. 'But that doesn't make sense. The

Children of Milla have never been persecuted. They may not be as popular in court circles or with the people as they once were. But why choose to mask a sentiment, a belief, that few people – least of all me – are going to be bothered by?'

Calian shrugged his broad shoulders. 'I don't know, perhaps they feel threatened. That first letter certainly hints at something of great importance to them. I have had no chance to read the others, but they must confirm it. Perhaps Fars is just being overly cautious.'

Ciro pulled a face and ran a hand through his straw blonde hair. He was not convinced that the letter had been written by Engis but, whoever had written the lines, its message seemed clear. Somebody had a hidden agenda that was tied to his own expedition. Despite the dubious acquisition of the documents, Ciro did not doubt Calian's integrity for a moment or a Songsmith's ability to recognise a half-heard tune. But he had to be sure of all available facts before acting.

'We'll return to my quarters,' said Ciro, 'and go through these papers thoroughly. We need to know as much as we possibly can about this issue before we confront Captain Fars.'

Calian nodded in reply before his expression changed suddenly. His face was now a deep frown and he sniffed the air. To Ciro's obvious bemusement, he turned and unlocked the storeroom door as quickly as he could.

'We've got to get back to the main cabins!' Calian said hurriedly. There was genuine alarm in his voice

'But...?'

'Please, sire, now!'

A strong breeze greeted them as Calian ushered Ciro out onto the moonless dark of the foredeck. With a quizzical glance at the Songsmith, Ciro pushed the rolled parchments into his jacket and was reaching for the hand rail as a towering wave of water rocked the ship.

Ciro stumbled as the whole vessel lurched beneath him and, missing his grip, was thrown towards the handrail on the starboard side of the ship. From nothing the wind had risen to a howling gale – the rigging screamed as if wounded – and the King clung tightly to the rail, gazing down at the now savage sea as rain began to pour in sheets upon the deck. He struggled to regain his footing as another wave battered the ship and looked down the length of the King Elson to dimly see the starboard paddle wheel rise clear of the water. The bright lamps of the wheelhouse glinted through the increasing rain and Ciro, with a glance back to see Calian gripping the rail by the storeroom door, began edging his way along the foredeck. He shouted to the Songsmith to work his way towards him and then inched ahead to reach the pile of food crates lashed to the centre of the foredeck.

The King Elson pitched and rose, ploughing across a vast curl of water and Ciro clung even tighter to the handrail as an arcing wave broke upon the deck and engulfed him. Spluttering, the king watched a flash of lightning split the night and two figures, several yards ahead, were suddenly revealed: working on the bindings which bound the food crates. Ciro strained to make out their identity as the lightning flash winked out to leave the ship in a deeper darkness and he edged his way forwards, hoping that the crewmen could secure whatever bindings had come loose. If the storm worsened, he thought, they might lose the entire stockpile. Then Ciro saw them wrench the side from one of the crates and realised that they had been untying the bindings.

'What in Fidiann's name are you doing!?' Ciro yelled yet, oblivious, the two men continued to frantically scrabble at the crate's contents, stuffing their pockets with whatever they pulled out.

The king moved along the handrail as quickly as he could, saw one of the men fall backwards as the ship rocked, then clawed himself close enough to be within earshot. Still unseen by the scavengers, Ciro paused for a moment and debated whether to draw his hand lance from its holster. It would have been a prudent measure in calmer waters, but the mountainous sea meant that both hands were needed simply to remain upright on the bucking deck. The two men seemed to have reached the same conclusion and ceased their frenzied clawing to hang on, like Ciro, to keep themselves standing.

The storm intensified and Ciro, glancing back to make sure Calian was still following, could dimly see that the Songsmith – still near the storeroom – was yelling and shaking a fist at the sky. Only Calian would think to blame one of his gods, thought Ciro, and turned back to shout at the two crewmen.

'Hey!' he yelled at the top of his voice. 'What do you think you're doing?!'

The two men saw him now and regarded their King wide-eyed as another lightning flash lit the ship. Ciro had never seen the two before and, even though there were over two hundred men on board ship, he felt sure they were not of his company. One was so obese that his frame was almost round and Ciro wondered briefly how such a man fitted the description of "all able men". The man stared back fearfully, hanging on to the flapping bindings, while the other – stick thin with a skeletal face – seemed to glower menacingly as Ciro shouted the question again.

He did not finish the sentence. Another spear of lightning flashed through the gloom, this time striking the foremast a shattering blow. The King Elson shuddered from the force of the impact and a sudden lurch of the deck knocked Ciro and the scavengers from their feet. Before the king could make sense of what was happening and hang on, an avalanche of crates tumbled him and the two men into the heaving sea.

Ciro sat bolt upright and gasped for air. The taste of salt water was strong in his mouth and it took his waking wits a moment to realise it came from the sweat which soaked his skin. He was out of the water.

How!? He had no idea but, as consciousness crept upon him, the more pressing question was: where? This was not his cabin. Bemused, Ciro stared around the unfamiliar room. He was in a strange bed in a gloomy room with a low, beamed ceiling and patchy, lime-washed walls. A single shuttered window occupied the wall beside him and shafts of bright sunlight shone in through the cracks and fell upon a small table clustered with unlit candles. His white shirt was clammy from the sweat and, as Ciro tugged at the buttons to remove it, he noticed it was all that remained of his uniform.

Are we back in Obaln? He thought, suddenly angry with Calian for his over-protective nature. Surely he hadn't been that badly injured? The thought drew his attention to the tightness around his temple and he felt at the bandage which was wrapped around his aching head. Where was he?

Ciro started as the door at the far side of the room squeaked open a crack but, instead of the familiar dark hair and sharp nose of Calian, a pale female face peeped timidly round the door to regard him with something approaching surprise.

'Bi'nar lindos?' she asked, coming no further into the room.

Ciro cocked his head to one side and frowned.

'What?' he replied, and to this the wide-eyed face disappeared and the door shut with a thump.

Soft, receding steps were quickly followed by a muffled explosion of voices somewhere beyond the door then the unmistakable clatter of many footsteps returning. Without thinking, Ciro was instantly out of bed, scattering first the bedclothes and then the candles as he lifted the small table above his head as the door reopened.

Four people crowded into the doorway. The slender, pale girl that Ciro had seen a moment before, a woman, similarly featured yet grey haired with a deeply lined face, a stocky, moon faced teenager whose neck matched his head for width and a wiry, black bearded man with striking green eyes. All looked shocked by Ciro's aggressive stance.

'Where's Calian? Where's my brother?' Ciro demanded, noting the surprise his action had caused.

The moon faced boy frowned back, muttered something harsh Ciro did not understand and advanced a step into the room. The grey haired woman put out a hand to restrain him and the bearded man slipped a hand inside his tunic. He withdrew the gold sun broach that had been on Ciro's jacket and held it towards him.

'Rial?' he asked with an uncertain smile.

Ciro nodded once in reply but did not put down the table. 'Where am I? Where are my clothes?' he demanded.

'We won't 'urt ya,' the grey haired woman said earnestly. 'We've been lookin' after ya. You were injured.' She gave a half smile and pointed at Ciro's bandage. Ciro flicked his gaze up and with that the moon faced youth charged across the room towards him.

Ciro barely had time to register the explosion of movement as the boy covered the short distance from the door but, before his attacker's lowered head could drive into his midriff, Ciro swung the small table down with enough force to send the youth sprawling onto the bed. The boy groaned but did not rise and Ciro again lifted the table menacingly and defiantly regarded the figures in the doorway.

The grey haired woman scowled, shook her head and moved to look at the unconscious youth. 'That weren't called for,' she said as she examined the boy for injury. 'Nesh,' she continued, turning to the girl in the doorway, 'fetch our guest's clothes please...'specially 'is leggin's.'

The girl sniggered, gave Ciro an amused look before disappearing through the door. Ciro looked down and realised that, standing as he was with his arms raised, his shirt was lifted clear of his naked lower half. Embarrassed, Ciro slowly put the table back in its place.

The bearded man, seeming nonplussed by Ciro's actions, introduced himself as Arper and held out the broach for him to take. 'Are ya 'ungry?' he asked. 'You've been asleep since Nesh found yer on the beach three days ago.'

Ciro nodded, took the broach and then the memory of the King Elson and the storm flooded back. His eyes widened and the realisation of where he was finally sunk in. He had made it to Reilan.

The king sat quietly in the kitchen of the farmhouse and attempted to digest the information his rescuers had given him. Reilan, and more precisely, the Kingdom of Rial, was not the dead land he had expected to find. After everything he had read about the plague – the savage blight which had decimated the country over five hundred years ago – he had never considered that some small pockets of people might have survived. Yet here was the living proof. All of the South West Wold of the old kingdom had seemingly been unaffected by the catastrophe which had driven away his forefathers to the safety of Feirlan. The reports and documents Ciro had pored over for years in the secret library of the Ascension Chamber had spoken of desperate times back then. Of the hurried decision to evacuate as many as possible before the blight reached the main port of Peimonac. In particular, the diary of his distant ancestor Prince Idirnon, brother of King

Elson, still conjured terrifying images in Ciro's mind: of bodies floating in wave after wave down the North Horn River to swirl around Idirnon's fleet as they departed Peimonac. The Prince's heartbroken description of the "bloated flotsam" still sent a shiver down Ciro's spine.

The kitchen was a large, lime washed room and appeared to be the centre of activity in the farm house. A single window looked out onto a rutted, muddy farmyard surrounded by a variety of barns and buildings and, from where he sat (if he had broken from his musing to look outside) Ciro would have seen Tersic, the farm hand; his head now bandaged like Ciro's, throw glowering glances in his direction whenever he crossed the space. The grey haired Qisala, along with her daughter Igallianesh – Nesh for short – were rummaging through the large larder at the back of the kitchen and from the wide, stone fireplace inset into the wall beside it the unmistakable sound, and smell, of bacon sizzling tantalised the young king's senses. Ciro did his best to ignore it as he listened to Qisala's brother Arper, who sat opposite him, but his three day old hunger made it difficult to concentrate on what was being said.

'Nope. Never 'eard about no plague – ever,' said Arper. He shook his head and for the third time in as many minutes twirled a finger in his beard while he ruminated. 'But,' he shrugged, 'like ya says – that were an age ago, an' way before the bastards came...' The curse seemed to leave a sour taste in Arper's mouth and he hitched a thumb towards the window. 'Makech bastards came later, but even that were before me... ' He sat back and counted off his fingers. 'Great... Great... Great Grandfather – I think.'

Ciro nodded and tried to keep the concern from his face. The presence of surviving Rialans was something he had never considered when organising the expedition, but the surprise at their existence was a pleasant one. The Makech, on the other hand, were an entirely different matter. He had read much about the battles his Rialan forefathers – King Betram in particular – had fought against them and, though King Elson had finally forced them back across the southern desert, the Makech threat had coloured much of ancient Rialan life. From what little Arper had told him of their expansion back across the desert from where their kingdom lay, it was clear that they posed just as large, if not a greater threat, than they had done more than five hundred years before. Ciro prayed that his brother, Bdann, and the rest of the fleet were safe and well but could not help feeling anxious about what might be there to meet them when they finally made landfall in the heart of Rial. Ciro tugged at the tatty silk scarf around his neck, wondering if that explained the disappearance of Prince Tenlern all those years ago.

The scarf was old, worn through in parts and heavily frayed at the edges. Black silk embroidered with small white 'T's which symbolised the name of Tenlern Torrman. Ciro had kept it as a good luck charm since the life-changing events on his eleventh birthday, and had worn it openly since his Ascension.

Despite Ciro's concerns about the Makech, and the fact that he blamed himself for not considering all the possibilities, he was determined that, if their presence in the old Kingdom of Rial had sealed Tenlern's fate, the same would not befall him or his people. Yet he could do nothing until he rejoined them.

'Where precisely did you say we were, Arper?' asked Ciro, hoping his mental image of the Reilan map was good enough for him to get his bearings.

'Few miles outside Cabon,' came the reply.

Cabon?… Ciro closed his eyes for a moment, picturing the old map which was now well on its way to Peimonac onboard

70

the storm battered King Elson. Ah, yes. Cabon, he thought. South Western edge of the kingdom, on the South River peninsular. Fifty miles or so west of Forht and roughly two hundred miles north of the city of Kal Santra. Or Torr Idirnon as it had been eventually called. The name was not marked on the map which Ciro owned yet he knew from chronicles that King Elson's youngest brother, Idirnon, had taken the city from the Makech to deprive them of their only foothold above the South Jaw Mountains. In honour of his brother's achievement, King Elson had given the city Idirnon's name. If what Arper said were true about the presence of the Makech – and Ciro had no reason whatsoever to doubt him – then it would undoubtedly be called Kal Santra again.

'I need to get to Rial,' Ciro said, thinking aloud.

Arper frowned. 'You're in Rial,' he replied. 'What's left of it.'

Ciro smiled. 'Further east,' he said, 'to...' He checked himself. He was alone in a strange and possibly hostile land. Should he tell them his final destination? The landing point for his entire expedition? Should he have even told them his name, when he could have stuck to the one they first called him when he had woken: Calian. He stopped the inner debate, feeling he was being overly cautious. How would anybody in this land know who he was? "King who?"

Ciro grinned. 'Torr Adenair,' he said finally. 'I need to get to Torr Adenair.'

'Good luck!' Arper replied. He threw his head back and guffawed at the ceiling.

Nesh and Qisala were also smiling at the apparent joke and both moved to join them at the table. Qisala carried a plate in one hand from which a mouth watering aroma rose and, the second it was placed before him, Ciro devoured the pile of bacon, tomatoes, mushrooms and bread as quickly as he could. Between rapid mouthfuls Ciro asked Arper to elaborate on why his destination seemed so risible.

'I ain't sayin' it ain't possible ta get there, but there's the black apples for one thing.' Arper shrugged, as if that explained everything. Then, seeing Ciro's blank look he continued. 'The 'ole land's covered with the things, see?' Arper swept his arm across the table. 'From The Channel to old Ebo's Mire. Field after field of 'em! An' every one a death sentence. I'd rather walk into a Makech Judgment Ring than walk through those damn things!'

Qisala shot her brother a stern glance. 'Ya shouldn't say such things, Arper. Not even in jest.' With her right hand she made a figure of eight motion around her head and heart: an action which instantly drew Ciro's interest.

'Do you have the Children of Milla here?' he asked (as best he could through a mouthful of food). The sign Qisala had made was the same one which Saviour Engis and his followers used back in Feirlan yet the farmer's wife looked blank.

'The sign you made,' Ciro explained, miming the action. 'It's what the Children of Milla always do in Feirlan.'

Qisala shrugged. 'It's for the Kolben.' Slowly, she repeated the action, this time reciting: 'Four fer our Ladies, full of grace. Four fer our Lords' to protect from their 'aste.'

'An' they can be most hasty,' added Arper. 'If Sakoom 'adn't thrown such a tantrum the other night, you wouldn't be 'ere.' He pointed a finger at Ciro. 'The old Wind Lord were most upset the other night.' He twirled a finger through his beard and shrugged. 'That's Gods for yer.'

Ciro was about to ask more about the strange, black apples Arper had spoken of, when Nesh suddenly stood up.

'Menzir's 'ere,' she said quietly.

With that the whole atmosphere changed. Arper, Qisala and

her daughter all rose and, craning his neck from where he sat, Ciro saw through the window a stout figure with a heavy stick and a trailing dog walk across the farmyard towards the house.

Arper edged nearer to Ciro. 'I'll talk ta someone I know 'bout yer...er, destination,' he whispered. 'But don't mention it ta Menzir.' He stole a quick, sideways glance at the window. 'Me sister's 'usband's a good enough man in 'is own way, but...' He shrugged, and then pointed to the gold sun broach Ciro had refastened to his jacket. 'I'd put that in a pocket fer now, not show it off,' he warned. 'Such things make some folk nervous – if yer follow me.'

Ciro didn't but was already removing it.

'I'll be back in two days...' Arper added. 'Three at most. 'til then – if you've any questions – ask me sister.' He hitched a thumb at Qisala who, along with Nesh was going through the larder again.

Ciro stood and was about to thank Qisala and her daughter for the food when the door opened and Menzir's dog sloped into the kitchen while the farmer himself paused on the threshold. He was a short, stocky man with a tanned face and florid cheeks and from under a thick brow he scanned the room quickly. A look of distaste creased his heavy features as his gaze met Arper's then his eyes finally settled on Ciro. He grunted and rubbed his nose with the back of his hand.

'Yer awake then,' he said flatly.

Ciro nodded. 'Thank you, yes.'

'An' eatin', by the looks of it.' Menzir pointed a finger almost, Ciro felt, in accusation at the empty plate before him.

Ciro nodded again. 'Thank you, yes, sir.'

The farmer gave the same, distasteful grunt and pointed to the yard were Tersic could be seen making his way from one of the barns. 'An' attackin' me farm 'and, so I'm told.'

'That were an accident, Menzir,' broke in Arper before Ciro could say a word. 'Ciro's already said sorry ta the boy.'

Menzir shrugged his broad shoulders. 'Not much of a way for guests ta be'ave, I'm sure,' he said, ignoring Ciro and addressing his comment to Arper.

'I really am very sorry for any inconvenience,' said Ciro. The farmer gave a half nod yet stared fixedly out of the window.

'Maybe you should come back with me,' Arper said to Ciro. The comment seemed to spur the farmer.

'No, no, no…' He shook his head in time with the words. 'I wouldn't take 'im back ta Cabon if I were you. Seems the Makech 'ave got wind o'somethin'. 'eard 'em askin' 'bout strangers when I was in town. He'll be safer 'ere – for now anyways.' Menzir waved a hand towards the farmyard. 'You go seek out them 'friends' o' yours, Arper, 'an we'll look after 'is lordship.' He looked at Ciro as if for the first time and nodded to himself. 'Can always use an extra pair o' hands around the place any road – pay for 'is keep.'

That seemed to settle the matter and Menzir lowered himself into a chair while his dog turned and settled at his feet. Arper smiled weakly at Ciro and moved towards the door. He passed Tersic as the boy skulked in then stopped on the threshold and turned back.

'Two days,' he said. Ciro nodded.

''e'll be fine, Arper,' muttered the farmer dismissively. 'On yer way now.' Menzir smiled over at Ciro but the sight brought him no comfort.

Tersic sat himself beside Menzir and Ciro as Igallianesh brought a precarious armful of clay jars to the table followed by two circular loaves. Both the farmer and his young hand busied themselves with removing the muslin jar tops and Nesh returned quickly with plates.

'Don't suppose ya'll be wantin' anymore to eat, will ya?' said Menzir with a wink at Ciro. The farmer returned his attention to his plate then frowned. 'Knife?!' he barked.

Qisala, without turning away from a bubbling pot, pulled two from where they hung on the wall and handed them to Nesh as she returned to the table with yet more jars. As Ciro looked on, the two men busied themselves heaping preserves and pickle onto their plates before sweeping hunks of bread through the various piles on the way to their mouths.

Menzir gave a sideways glance to Tersic; busily cramming his own mouth, and a thin smile spread as he regarded the bandage wrapped tightly around the youth's forehead. He gave a short snigger.

'Whacked ya good an' proper, didn't 'e?!' Menzir grinned and sat back in his chair, chomping loudly. Tersic shot a venomous glance in Ciro's direction but continued to eat in silence.

'Yer always been too 'asty, boy,' continued Menzir. He had a mouthful of food but it did not seem to prevent him talking loudly. ''ead down, pile in!' he continued, spitting dark flecks across the table. 'Won't get you nowhere!' The farmer grabbed another chunk of bread and wagged it at Tersic. 'You watch a bull,' he said. ''ead down, all a'rage and whoosh! Off it goes, 'eadlong inta trouble. Don't get it nowhere neither!' Menzir crammed the bread into his mouth, grinned and leant forward to slap Tersic on the shoulder. 'Don't ya feel bad 'bout it though, boy. If I'd wan'ed brains I'd 'ave got me women ta work the farm!'

Ciro did his best to ignore the farmer's jibes by focusing his attention on Qisala as she stood ladling out a dark stew from a blackened pot suspended above the fire. Menzir rubbed his hands with delight as the bowls were placed before both him and the farm hand. Unceremoniously sweeping the clay jars down the table to make a space, he grabbed the wooden spoon offered him by his stepdaughter and began shovelling the stew into his mouth. For a few moments the two sat noisily eating while Ciro and the two women looked on. At length Menzir paused enough to look up and jabbed his spoon in Ciro's direction.

'So where do people wear them sort o' clothes, eh?' the farmer asked.

Ciro glanced down at the blue jacket, cream shirt and trousers which he wore. 'Feirlan,' he replied. 'It's an island north west of Reilan, although not everybody dresses like this. Just the officers onboard my ship.' Feirlan was actually south west but Ciro had no intention of providing Menzir with accurate information. He felt a nagging guilt for being deceitful, but he also felt a strong mistrust towards the farmer.

'Your ship?' asked Qisala, her face a picture of surprise.

Ciro managed a smile. '…The ship I was on, I mean.'

Menzir was nodding over his plate as more food was shovelled in. 'Feirlan,' he repeated, through a mouth packed with stew. 'Can't say I've ever 'eard of it.'

Ciro shrugged. 'It's a long way across the sea and this is only the second time, to my knowledge, that anybody has come back.'

'From the look o' ya,' said Menzir. 'Why would anybody wanna leave such a place ta come 'ere? Ain't nothing here but 'ard workin' folk who wanna live in peace. Wha' business would outsiders 'ave with us?'

That we were once the same people? That I am the rightful King of this land? A whole range of thoughts flooded Ciro's mind but instead he shrugged once more. 'I wish I knew, sir,' he lied, 'but I was not privy to the thoughts of those who organised our journey.'

The answer seemed to satisfy the farmer, who grabbed at

what bread was still left on the table and began dabbing it into his bowl. He seemed lost in thought. 'You Fearers – Feraners...?' he said at length.

'Feirlaners,' corrected Ciro.

'Yeah, Ferrahners,' Menzir replied. 'Not the best sailors are yer?!' He grinned across the table, his teeth a visual record of the stew he had just consumed.

Ciro managed to smile back. 'Not really,' he replied. 'If we were, then I would not have had the pleasure of your family's company.'

To this Menzir revealed his stew again and waved a hand at Qisala. Without any further prompt, the farmer's wife brought out three mugs while Nesh pulled a large clay jug from the floor of the larder and struggled across to the table with it. Seeing the girl's difficulty, Ciro rose quickly and took the jug from her. Nesh smiled and, seeming embarrassed, turned away as Tersic and Menzir looked on. The farmer seemed to regard Ciro's action with considerable amusement while Tersic, apparently cursed with a single facial expression, glowered at Ciro as he put the jug onto the table. Ciro returned to his seat as Menzir pulled the stopper from the jug and poured a light liquid into the mugs. He pushed one up the table for Ciro, who sniffed cautiously at the brew.

'Cider,' explained the farmer.

Ciro nodded and took a sip. The taste was slightly sour but not as bad as he had expected.

''ere's to travellers,' Menzir said, raising his mug. 'An' all they bring.'

'Your very good health, sir,' Ciro responded. 'And I thank you for your hospitality.' He sipped at his cider while the two men drained their mugs in a few loud gulps.

Wiping his mouth with the back of his hand, Menzir pointed down the table at Ciro. 'That...That thing on yer sword belt?'

he asked. 'Wha' is that exactly? The boy an' me looked at it when yer was asleep but couldn't fathom for the life of us wha' it was for.'

Ciro pulled the device from its holster and held it sideways. It was slightly shorter than a foot long, made almost entirely of brass with a wooden handle and intricately engraved silver panels on its sides. A thin tube extended almost the whole length of the device while a rod of brass with a small wooden pommel at one end ran parallel with the barrel to disappear into a bulbous casing on the object's side.

'It's called a hand lance,' Ciro explained. 'It's powered by two clockwork springs in this side casing here and wound by this rod here beside the barrel.' Ciro had not had time to find out what damage the sea had done to it but, when he pressed a button beside the trigger to release any tension in the springs a crunching noise from within told him that salt had completely clogged up the works.

Both Menzir and Tersic seemed fascinated by the device and the farmer, after a pause, said: 'An' wha' does this... 'and lance thing do?'

Ciro released a catch on the stock of the weapon and drew out a long chamber from within the handle. Again Ciro heard the grind of salt as he removed the chamber and hid his bitter disappointment when he saw that the wood of the metal tipped flights contained within were swollen and encrusted with salt. He plucked one from the stockpile and passed it over to the farmer who turned it over in his fingers.

'It fires those,' explained Ciro. 'I suppose you could call it a miniature bow and arrow, but it seems the whole thing is little more than useless now, there's salt everywhere.'

Menzir passed the flight to Tersic who smiled. 'It's like some toy,' the farm hand said. He threw the flight on the table before Ciro rather than pass it back and both he and Menzir burst out laughing.

''ow many midgets 'ave you killed wi' that?!' The farmer managed to say before exploding with laughter again. Ciro smiled back and replaced the flight chamber: returning the hand lance to its holster.

'You'd be better off takin' that little table with yer,' continued Menzir, pointing at Tersic's bandaged head to emphasise the point. 'An' if you see a Boneman – ya'd do best ta run like the wind in the other direction!'

The pair continued to laugh at Ciro's expense for some time until eventually citing fatigue, Ciro asked if he might retire to bed. The farmer, noting the now dark courtyard and the candle lit kitchen agreed.

'Ya'd best get a good night's sleep,' he said. 'There's work ta be done tomorra.'

Ciro thanked the farmer once more for his hospitality before Qisala, with lamp in hand, led him up through the darkened farmhouse towards the loft.

It was a dirty, draughty space with bowing eves, straw strewn floors and an overpowering smell of rotten wood. Piled into one corner, amongst various junk that Ciro did not begin to recognise, was a tatty straw mattress, grubby sheet and a clump of half used candles.

'I'm sorry it's all we 'ave ta offer,' sighed Qisala. 'But the room ya woke up in is Nesh's. She's been sleepin' up 'ere the last few nights.'

Ciro smiled. 'You have all been very kind,' he said. 'Thank Nesh for letting me use her room.'

To this Qisala smiled back. She turned to leave but stopped and asked: 'Are all the men yer came with like you?'

The king balked at the question. 'I'm… Not sure what you mean?' he replied hesitantly.

'I mean… Are they good men, with trades an' such…' She

pointed at Ciro. '…That uniform?'

Ciro was puzzled by her interest. 'We have farmers, carpenters, master makers, bakers. Enough skills to establish ourselves. Only officers wear this uniform but –'

Qisala was nodding. '– Nesh needs a 'usband,' she interjected bluntly. 'A good man with a trade.'

'I see…' answered Ciro. 'Well, perhaps when I–'

Now the farmer's wife was shaking her head. '– There's nothin' 'ere for her. Nothing but fear an' 'ardship. Menzir'll 'ave 'er wed ta Tersic before the year's out: I know it. She needs a good man, not a brutal little farm boy. She's smart an' she's not afraid o' work.' The last statement sounded almost defiant and Qisala gazed levelly at her young guest.

'When I get back to my people,' replied Ciro, choosing his words carefully. 'I'll see what I can do.'

Qisala nodded. She seemed satisfied. 'Is there anythin' ya need before I leave yer?' she asked.

A thought occurred to Ciro and he pointed to the small oil lamp which Qisala carried.

'May I borrow that for the night?' he asked.

'O' course,' she replied and passed it to him. 'Sleep well,' she said and retreated into the gloom.

Ciro listened as Qisala's footsteps faded down the stairs then turned his attention to the candles and bedding. With the oil lamp, he lit the four stocky candles which sat beside the mattress then searched intently amongst the bric-a-brac around him. After a few minutes he returned to his bed with the small, flat nail he had found and, removing his jacket, reversed it and spread it out before him. He blew out the oil lamp, placed his hand lance on his jacket and with the end of the nail began taking the weapon apart. It was slow work – the nail a clumsy tool – but he patiently continued to strip, clean and oil his weapon back into use while his thoughts strayed to his friends, the fleet and his own isolation. He hoped they were safe and that the man, Arper, could somehow help him to be reunited with them.

It seemed that no sooner had Ciro's head touched the mattress than he was being shaken awake by Nesh and, bleary eyed and yawning, set to work sweeping the farmyard by Menzir. It seemed pointless work to him: the expanse of mud looking no different no matter how hard it was swept, but Ciro set about his given task without complaint and spent the time wondering how best to get east to Peimonac.

Between the barns and outbuildings which enclosed the farmyard he got his first, if slightly restricted, view of the countryside and marvelled at the lush plant life and rich greenery which poked above the roof tops and fences of the farm. It was all so different to the bleached scrub and salt flats of Feirlan and Ciro wondered what the farmers of Obaln and Rurset would give for something half as fertile. It was one of the main incentives of their expedition: to find good land. But such thoughts led Ciro to puzzle over something Arper had mentioned the previous day.

Nesh strolled out from the farmhouse a little later and found him still pondering the subject of black apples.

'Have you ever seen one of them?' he asked.

'No, but I've 'eard Uncle Arper tell Ma that they're like nuthin' 'e's ever seen. They grow 'bout this 'igh…' Nesh levelled an arm at her chest. 'An' they have this big black fruit all over 'em which bursts when yer touch 'em. 'e says 'e's seen animals run into 'em an… Well, they don't come back out. 'e says they're instant death.'

Ciro frowned and leant on his broom handle, staring off into space.

'Why d'ya wanna go there?' Nesh asked.

'To the east?' Ciro asked. Nesh nodded. 'My friends are there. The ship I was travelling on was heading there.'

Nesh was quiet for a moment. 'Ma and Uncle Arper think you're important…' she said hesitantly. 'I think Menzir does too… Are ya?'

Ciro smiled and resumed sweeping. 'No,' he replied, shaking his head. 'Not really. I was just one of the crew.' Which was perfectly true, Ciro reasoned, from a certain perspective. Even the king must be considered as one of the crew. 'But I do need to get back to them,' he continued. 'That's very important.' Because, he thought, my army need to know that not only are there Rialans here, but that so are the Makech.

'Would ya like somethin' ta eat?' Nesh asked with a smile but it dropped instantly as something over Ciro's shoulder caught her eye. Ciro turned to see Menzir appear from behind one of the barns.

Nesh turned away towards the farmhouse as her stepfather drew close and Menzir placed his hands on his hips as he inspected Ciro's work. The farmer scanned the courtyard then gave a derisive snort.

'It'll do, I suppose,' he said with a shake of his head and took the broom from Ciro. 'I need yer ta go an' 'elp Tersic now. In the wood past the lower field.' Menzir pointed in the direction he had come from. 'Go round the barn, through the gap in the 'edge an' then follow the field down. There's another 'edge at the bottom with a stream on the other side an' some trees: that's where Tersic is. Understand?'

Ciro nodded. 'Nesh was about to make me something to eat,' he said with a glance at the farmhouse. 'I'd best tell her to stop.'

'Don't bother, I'll tell 'er. You be off. Tersic's waiting.' The farmer pointed to the barn again.

With a shrug, Ciro walked towards the barn, wondering what other pointless chore Menzir had devised for him. Whatever it was it had to be better than sweeping dirt, but then again, Ciro was not so sure. He checked the thought. Here was a man who had taken him in, healed his wounds and given him shelter and up until now all he had done in return was to treat his actions with suspicion. Learn some humility, thought Ciro to himself: being a farm hand for a day or so was a small price to pay in return for such kindness.

Ciro turned the corner and followed a worn path which cut through the hedge and into the field beyond. There was a breeze blowing and the cool surge of air made him wish he had brought his jacket. He smiled to himself: getting used to a colder climate was something else he had not considered back in Feirlan. I shall add it to the growing list, he thought. With a smile on his face and the call of bird song all around him, Ciro strolled the gentle gradient down towards the bush line at the lower end of the field.

It took a few minutes to locate the gap that Menzir had mentioned and, as Ciro walked the hedge in search of it, he thought he caught the sound of Tersic's voice. He was about to call out to the farm hand but, having been warned that talking Rialan in the open was dangerous, he restrained himself. Instead he finally came across the gap in the hedge and pushed through to find the stream and the wood which lay beyond.

The stream at his feet was high banked but narrow and the leap a short distance: little more than a stride. But the surrounding earth was soft and, as soon as Ciro's foot struck the far bank, its edge collapsed beneath the pressure and he tumbled with a splash into the shallow water below.

Cursing, Ciro sat up: flicking silt from his hands as he grimaced at his now soaked and muddy clothing. His head was level with the ragged wild grass beside the stream and through it he caught sight of a figure who now stepped from behind a tree a little deeper into the wood. Wide-eyed, Ciro froze.

Clad in black leather overlaid with strips of metal, the man was pale-skinned, bearded and carrying a curved sword in his hand. He also wore what looked like a human skull perched on top of his helmet. Ciro held his breath, his heart pounding as he watched the figure scan the area of the stream. He knew this man, or rather his race – Rialan history was stained red with their presence. But in all his preparations, all the years of meticulous planning, Ciro had never once considered he would be unfortunate enough to confront these devils from the past. What were the Makech doing at the farm?!

The high bank and the grass must have obscured the Makech's view of Ciro for he made no move towards the stream and, after mouthing a few words to someone out of sight, disappeared back into the trees. With his thoughts racing like his pulse, Ciro silently cursed himself for leaving his hand lance in the farmhouse kitchen and, keeping his eyes on the wood, began backing slowly up the other side of the stream.

Ciro had cleared the bank and was edging warily towards the gap in the hedge when, from near where the swordsman had disappeared, Tersic suddenly jumped out from hiding.

'Unar ossa! UNAR OSSA!' the farm hand screamed. He pointed frantically in Ciro's direction and three armoured Makech rushed out from amongst the trees – their swords drawn.

There may have been more but Ciro did not wait to find out. He was already through the hedge and running as fast as he could back up the field towards the farm.

He heard splashes in the stream behind him as he ran and

someone shouting 'Qe ui oshana!' over and over again. Ciro however, was too occupied with putting as much distance between himself and his pursuers to glance back and it was not until he neared the hedge which backed onto the farm that he risked a quick look over his shoulder and found a single warrior in rapid pursuit.

The Makech shouted something unintelligible: waving his sword as he clinked and jingled his way up the field and Ciro sped on, turning into the farmyard to find Menzir standing by the kitchen door. He looked surprised to see the young King.

'Makech!' Ciro shouted as he ran, too panicked to realise that that was precisely why the farmer was surprised to see him return. To dispel any further illusion, Menzir bolted through the kitchen door in alarm and locked it, leaving Ciro cornered within the farmyard.

The king hit the door with his shoulder at full speed then hammered on the woodwork furiously with his fists. From within he could hear frantic shouts from both Qisala and Nesh but still the door remained firmly closed. Menzir had left the broom which Ciro had used earlier beside the door and now he picked it up to pound at the door latch. It was too dingy to see through the window beside the door but, listening between his strikes on the door handle, it seemed that the shouting within the kitchen was developing into a struggle. Then the jingle of armour drew his attention away and he turned to see that the warrior from the field had entered the courtyard.

The Makech, seeing that his quarry was cornered, now slowed his pace and Ciro – quickly considering his options – adjusted his grip on the broom handle and stepped away from the door.

Breathing heavily, the Makech approached and shook his head with apparent amusement at the muddy young man before him holding a broom like a sword.

'Vuimas unar esc, Rial,' he said slowly and pointed with his free hand to the broom.

Ciro only recognised one word, but guessed the rest and gripped the broom even tighter. 'No,' he replied. He had no intention of putting down the broom.

To this the warrior's eyes narrowed and, as Ciro fought the desperate urge to run, the man exploded into an attack: lunging the few feet between them sword first.

Ciro skipped sideways, turned and swung the broom as hard as he could onto the back of the Makech's helmet while his opponent's momentum drove his sword tip into the door. The blow buckled his legs: dented the plate on the back of his helmet but he did not fall and, with a pained grunt, the warrior wrenched his sword free of the woodwork and swung wildly to his left.

Ciro hopped back, swung again and this time struck the man's cheek guard. The Makech was startled by the blow but barely hurt, and Ciro could see that the only unprotected part of his opponent's helmet was a small exposed circle from his brow to his bearded chin. The man grinned, perhaps realising Ciro's frustration and swung wildly again, forcing Ciro back towards the farmhouse wall. The Makech chuckled, muttered something in the same incomprehensible tongue and moved purposely forwards, cutting off Ciro's space. He swung a few more times without success then lifted the sword above his head to charge: roaring at the top of his voice.

Ciro skipped back repeatedly to avoid the wild slashes then noted the shift of weight as the man committed himself to this two handed attack. As the sword flashed up and cleared the Makech's head, Ciro adjusted the grip once more on the broom, jumped forward to close the gap and thrust the wooden end of the handle as hard as he could into the man's face.

The wild roar stopped instantly while the impact threw the Makech onto his back and his sword into the dirt of the courtyard. No sooner had he hit the ground than Ciro was smashing the broom down once more for good measure: shattering the skull headdress in the process.

The man's face now looked a bloody state. His nose was twice its original width and Ciro breathed a massive sigh when the Makech did not get up.

'Thank the Stars for Calian,' he murmured, remembering the Songsmith's insistence that every member of the expedition – himself included – not rely solely on hand and fire lances but also master the archaic disciplines of sword and quarter staff. Calian's training had been an intense, and to some, irrelevant chore. But Ciro had insisted that everybody – even a less than enthusiastic Bdann – complete their training. The worth of Calian's wisdom and perseverance now lay at Ciro's feet. The Songsmith's training had just saved the young King's life.

The realisation drew Ciro's attention to his own nervousness and, while his heart seemed to struggle to free itself from the confines of his chest, he held his hand before his face and watched as it trembled uncontrollably. Then all his fear was forgotten as Nesh, her pale face tear soaked, opened the kitchen door. If Ciro had found the sight of his own hand disconcerting, it was nothing to the blood-soaked palms which the young girl mutely held before her and Ciro instantly left the prostrate warrior to find more bloodshed inside the farmhouse.

Nesh lent heavily on the door. Whooping for breath, her wide eyes followed the young King's approach and Ciro stopped on the threshold to survey with disbelief the result of the struggle he had heard beyond the locked door. The kitchen was in total disarray. The table was upturned, the chairs thrown to all corners of the room while pots and jars lay smashed: their contents strewn all over the flagstones. In the centre of it all, her blood still pooling around her, Nesh's mother lay dead.

'By the Stars…' whispered Ciro. He moved to kneel beside Qisala's body and numbly observed the knife handle still protruding from her chest.

'He…He…' gulped Nesh from the doorway, attempting to speak through her tears.

Ciro glanced round and found Nesh pointing to the far door which led through to the hallway of the farmhouse. Following her direction he noticed for the first time a trail of blood which ran from Qisala's body. Quickly, Ciro picked out the shape of his jacket from the carnage, retrieved his star belt, removed and wound his hand lance then went in search of Menzir.

He did not have to search very far. Throwing open the door to the hallway Ciro found that the farmer had barely made it from the kitchen before the knife thrust into his back had ended his flight. Menzir lay buckled upon the floor, one arm bent back as if he had attempted to remove the blade and, like his wife, a dark patch of red was still spreading from the wound. Further along the hallway the farmer's dog whimpered from the shadows for the loss of its master.

Ciro's thoughts were leaden as he looked down at yet another corpse and the clatter of approaching horses barely registered in his mind. It was only when Nesh screamed and slammed the kitchen door that the King managed to focus his attention on more pressing matters. He sped back into the kitchen to see Nesh crouch down then race on all fours across the kitchen to her mother's body. Tears streaming from her eyes, Nesh clasped her mother's limp hand and pointed to the door.

'Makech are here!!' She bawled.

Ciro ran to the small window to see two **Makech** warriors dismount from their horses and approach the farmhouse with swords drawn. They were cautious, the sight of their fallen colleague making them scan the farmyard suspiciously but, catching sight of Ciro gazing out from the window, they cried out as one and instantly began a violent assault upon the door.

With the sudden eruption of curses and thuds against the woodwork, Ciro's only thought was of escape. He turned to find Nesh still bowed over the body of Qisala and ran to grab her; but the thundering blows upon the door now splintered the woodwork and the two Makech burst through the ragged frame. Without a pause for thought, Ciro pointed his hand lance at the closest warrior and fired.

Whether it was the sharp mechanical SNAP! which accompanied the discharge, the force of the blow, or simply the carnage confronting the two men as they entered the kitchen that stopped them in their tracks Ciro did not know. What he did know was that, although his first shot had struck the warrior squarely in the chest with enough force to stagger him back into his partner, it had not been sufficient to completely pierce the metal strips of his armour. But, while the first Makech grimaced and gazed quizzically at the stubby flight which had half buried itself in his chest, the second gave a deafening roar, raced at Ciro with his sword held high and fell dead after the King loosed a second flight into his face.

Now the remaining warrior stood slack jawed in the doorway, his eyes wide as they moved from his fallen companion to Ciro, who rewound his weapon and advanced on the man.

'Get out,' the king snarled, but the **Makech** remained motionless: his shocked expression quickly creasing by degrees into rage.

Ciro felt a sickening chill run down his spine as he realised the inevitable outcome of the Makech's changing features. But, the second the warrior's sword arm twitched into life and the blade begin a slashing ascent, Ciro pulled the trigger of his hand lance. Its bloody impact threw the warrior flat onto his back: dead before he hit the floor.

Ciro blinked, yet time seemed to drag unnaturally as he looked up from the second man whose life he had just taken. Woodenly, Ciro stepped over the dead warrior at his feet and passed through the shattered doorway into the fresh air beyond. His wits still addled, Ciro found no peace awaiting him in the farmyard. The Makech he had previously rendered unconscious was now staggering across the sunlit farmyard towards the horses tied outside the barn. He held one hand to his injured face while the other gripped the sword he had recovered from the ground. Numbly, Ciro followed him.

As if walking through a dream – his hand lance held stiff-armed before him – Ciro trailed the warrior: catching his raged breath as the man stumbled on towards the horses. Whatever damage Ciro had inflicted on the Makech it was obvious he was experiencing difficulty merely walking and, on reaching the nearest horse, he buried his head in its flank and sagged, gasping for air.

'Why did you come here?' Ciro heard himself saying and with it the Makech turned his bloody face towards him and spat words the young King could not comprehend.

'Edun zeer fe!' cried the warrior.

'I'm…so…sorry,' mouthed Ciro numbly and ended the fight.

IV

'S. ARNUS ARMOURY, RURSET,' read the inscription on the silver panel. 'Presented with honour to his Majesty, King

Ciro Torrman, Ruler of the Kingdom of Rial.' Above the lettering, in place of the rearing stag which was the Arnus Armoury trademark, sat an engraving of the sun blazing down upon a rolling sea and on it, skilfully crafted, sailed a tiny representation of the King Elson.

Ciro was not sure how long he had gazed sightlessly at the panel set into the side of his hand lance, only that he had not taken his eyes from it since slumping to his knees by the horses and discarding the weapon before him some time ago. He felt drained, ashamed but above all overawed by the murderous events which had transpired at the farmhouse. As hard as he tried to accept the situation and get a grip on his emotions, his mind would not leave the engraving of the tiny ship on the weapon he had cast before him or the memory of happier, carefree times when Reilan was only just a dream. Not the nightmare reality he was now experiencing.

'Ciro?'

The word was like sunshine. As if a thousand thunder clouds had been parted by a single ray of light, banishing the darkest shadows to the far corners of his mind. Ciro looked up to see Nesh, her eyes still red from tears, her face creased with sorrow as she looked down at him.

Ciro managed to find his voice. 'I'm so sorry...' he muttered.

Nesh nodded, wiped her eyes and without a word curled herself onto his lap – holding him tightly until she drifted into sleep.

Ciro, listening to the soft sigh of Nesh's breathing, gazed fixedly at the lane which curved out of the farmyard and wondered how long it would be before more Makech appeared. He wanted to rouse himself into action – get away from the farm – but instead felt consumed by an overwhelming sense of fatigue and isolation. Where was

Cabon from here? Which way was Forht? He knew he was in the Western Wold and that Peimonac was east: but that was not enough. What would he find if he travelled the lane? How many more Makech – how much more death – would be encountered down that unknown trail?

Nesh would know, Ciro realised but, as wretched as he felt, he was loathed to wake her. So he sat in the dirt and watched her peaceful face as she slept and tried not to think about the bodies that were scattered all around them or where they would go when she finally awoke.

Ciro woke with a start to find the light was fading and an unfamiliar sound had joined the rustling of the wind through the trees. Then he recognised the creak of cartwheels turning slowly in the half light beyond the farmyard and was wide awake: fearful at the prospect of more conflict.

He roused Nesh urgently, placing a hand over her mouth so she would not cry out and, though she struggled wide-eyed for a second, the sound of the approaching cart quickly caught her attention. Ciro placed a finger to his lips and released Nesh from his grasp.

'Who is it?!' hissed Nesh.

Ciro shook his head, retrieved his hand lance from the floor and quickly led the girl to the gap in the hedge beside the barn. He checked the tension in the weapon, rewound for good measure then aimed at the opening to the lane.

Nesh peaked over his shoulder. 'Can ya see anythin'?' she whispered.

'Enough,' replied Ciro with a conviction he did not feel. Daylight was fading by the moment and their surroundings quickly merging into deeper shades of grey. He could still hear the cart approaching however and watched as a vague and bulky shape suddenly plodded into view.

'Beck!' said someone from the cart. ''orses!'

Nesh got to her feet so fast she knocked Ciro sideways and her pale shape raced across the farmyard towards the cart.

'Uncle!!' she cried at the top of her voice, throwing herself into Arper's arms the second he jumped down from the riding board. Surprised, Arper held her tightly as Nesh burst into tears.

Ciro followed as another, taller man climbed from the ox drawn cart to stand beside Arper. Catching sight of the young King's muddy, bloody state, Nesh's Uncle frowned.

'What 'appened?' he asked.

Ciro let out a deep sigh. 'Makech,' he answered tiredly.

To this both Arper and his companion exchanged a worried glance.

'M-Menzir…' stuttered Nesh through her tears. ''e killed Ma!' Her voice was lost to another bout of wracking sobs and Arper's face fell.

'Oh, by the Stars…' whispered Arper faintly and hugged his niece even tighter.

Ciro looked on, knowing that whatever pain he felt inside it was nothing to the grief of Nesh and Arper. The tall man moved a step closer and Ciro regarded him blankly. He was a good deal broader than the King, as well as taller than Ciro's own six feet. Dark, shoulder length hair framed a grim and weathered face.

'I'm Amec,' said the stranger, his voice a bass rumble. 'You're the Rialan?'

Ciro nodded.

'We came as quickly as we could when we heard,' continued Amec. 'Cabon is buzzin' with rumours.' He looked towards the grey facade of the farmhouse. 'Have the Bonemen gone?'

Ciro turned and pointed to the slumped corpse of the

warrior by the horses. 'They're all dead.' He indicated the farmhouse and hung his head. 'Qisala too... And Menzir.'

To this Arper looked up. 'You killed the bastard?!' he asked.

Ciro shook his head and fixed sad eyes on Nesh. Arper nodded and kissed his distraught niece on the top of her head.

'Do you have a change of clothes?' asked Amec, looking Ciro up and down.

The question caught the King off guard. 'Do I have a what?' he answered, incredulous.

'A...change...of...clothes,' repeated Amec slowly. 'Because if you travel wearing the strange garb you have on now we won't get very far.'

Ciro regarded his Rialan clothing and saw the sense in Amec's question. 'No,' he responded with a shrug, 'this is all I have.'

Amec gave a curt nod. 'We have to get ready and go, Arper,' he said firmly. 'Once the patrol is missed you know the Bonemen will send more.'

'I know,' Arper replied faintly. He gripped Nesh firmly by the shoulders and slowly she lifted her head to meet his own tearful gaze. 'C'mon Nesh,' he said gently. 'We have ta go.'

To keep Nesh occupied, Arper helped her lead the Makech horses to the barn, striping them of their saddles and baggage while Amec and Ciro made their way over to the farmhouse to move the bodies of Menzir and Qisala to more respectable resting places. Before they reached the shattered kitchen door, Ciro looked back towards Amec's cart.

'Wouldn't it be better to harness the horses to the cart?' he asked when he realised that was not the reason for removing their saddles.

Amec's expression was incredulous. 'You really are a stranger, aren't you?'

'What does that mean?'

The big man frowned and pointed to the cart. 'It means that if the Makech so much as catch a glimpse of us usin' horses, we'll be sent straight to the Judgment Ring. An' that, my naive young friend, means death.'

'So we can't ride horses?'

'Oxen is the finest stead a Rialan can ride these days. Horses are for our bloody masters alone.'

'I had no idea,' said Ciro.

'I'd guessed,' replied Amec dryly and entered the farmhouse.

With as much ceremony as was possible in the circumstance, Ciro and Amec moved the bodies of Menzir and Qisala upstairs: the farmer to the room usually occupied by the missing farm hand, Tersic, and his wife to the main bedroom. To Ciro's eyes, the tragic scenes within the farmhouse looked markedly bleaker by candlelight and, though Amec regarded the other dead Makech with something approaching disbelief, he remained silent as they carried the farmer and his wife up the narrow stairs. To take his mind from the task and break the deathly silence, Ciro recounted the events that had taken place that afternoon.

'Those Makech came from Cabon,' Amec informed Ciro once Qisala was laid upon her bed.

They had drawn a blanket up to her chin to make it appear she was merely sleeping but the effect was marred by the knife handle still jutting from her chest. Ciro winced when Amec unceremoniously wrenched the blade free and threw it to the corner of the room.

'It wasn't until they'd ridden out this afternoon,' continued Amec, unfazed by his actions, 'that word got to the Last Inn about where they were going. The Landlord's brother tends the stables at the Cabon garrison,' he explained, 'so secrets leak from it like a sieve.'

'The Last Inn,' repeated Ciro with a wan smile. 'I've read of it. Do they still serve apple dumplings?'

'No,' replied Amec bluntly and began to search the room.

Ciro found himself staring down at the lifeless face of Qisala, not really knowing what to do next. He reached out a hand and straightened her grey streaked hair as best he could while, behind him, Amec pulled open a door to reveal a deep cupboard containing the clothes of the farmer and his wife. He eyed the back of the mud-covered King then began pulling items from Menzir's rack.

'C'mon,' he said. 'There'll be time to grieve later.' Ciro turned to regard the clothes pile Amec was creating. 'Change into these,' insisted the big man. 'We can't do anything about your hair but at least we can make you dress like a local.'

Reluctantly Ciro dragged his attention away from Qisala and removed his shirt to try on the clean one Amec had thrown at him. It felt wrong to be ransacking the possessions of the recently departed yet, somewhere deep inside himself, Ciro felt a grudging admiration for this strange man's practicality. To divert his mind from the far stronger sensation of guilt however, he asked Amec what the problem was with his hair.

Amec frowned, as if the answer was obvious then elaborated when he realised Ciro's query was a genuine one. 'It's too short,' he said and indicated his own, wild shoulder length hair. 'Nobody has hair that short, not even us Philiri.'

'Philiri?!' echoed Ciro, incredulous. 'You mean you're from Philire?'

Amec shrugged. 'There about's,' he said and returned to piling clothes at the young King's feet.

Ciro continued to change in silence, pondering the importance of what Amec had said. The town of Philire was deep within the Kingdom of Rial, beyond the city of Peimonac where Ciro's fleet was heading and far beyond the peculiar barrier of black apples which Arper had described to him. How many more people had survived the blight? He wondered.

By the time the pair returned to the farmyard, Ciro was transformed. Gone were the blue jacket, white shirt and trousers, now he was dressed in nettle green with a calf skin jerkin and dark green cloak – his old clothes bundled in his hands. Arper greeted them by the ox cart and managed to smile at Ciro's new appearance.

'That were the jacket Menzir wore for Solstice,' he said with relish. 'It looks better on you.'

Ciro nodded and gazed past him to where Nesh sat, her legs dangling from the back of the cart which was now piled high with straw. She looked up and gave him a watery smile.

'We salvaged as much as we could from the Bonemen,' Arper told Amec and prodded the pile of bags at his feet with the toe of his boot.

The Philiri nodded and picked up an empty one to pass to Ciro. 'Put your things it this,' he said, and then addressed Arper. 'We need to get as much food as will keep and we can carry before we go.'

Arper kicked the bags again. 'Done,' he said.

'Then we need to get out of here. Right now.'

Ciro was about to ask Amec where they planned to head, but Nesh's voice cut faintly through the gloom

'I need my shells,' she said.

The Philiri, about to climb onto the riding board of the cart, paused. 'If they're light enough to carry,' he said with a sigh. 'You don't wanna weigh yourself down.'

Nesh nodded, climbed down from the cart then looked hesitantly at the dull glow of candlelight from the farmhouse.

She looked at Ciro. 'Will ya come with me?' she asked.

Ciro gave her a sympathetic smile. 'You don't have to go back inside, Nesh,' he said. 'Just tell me where your shells are and I'll get them for you.'

Nesh shook her head and squeezed Ciro's hand. 'I want ta say...Goodbye...Will ya come?'

The young King nodded and together they walked towards the farmhouse.

'Do you wanna join 'em, Arper?' Amec asked as the pair disappeared inside.

Arper took a deep breath and shook his head. 'Nah,' he replied, the emotion plain in his voice. 'But when they come out, I'm gonna make a pyre of the place.'

Amec looked wide-eyed at the suggestion. 'That's not wise, Arper. The flames'll be seen for miles.'

Arper shrugged, and when he spoke there was resolution in his tone. 'You know what the Bonemen'll do with the bodies when they get 'ere,' he said then fixed his gaze firmly on the Philiri. 'I lost me wife ta Ebo, Amec,' he continued. 'I'll not leave me sister ta the same fate.' Arper pointed to the dark sky. 'I'm sendin' 'er to the stars no matter what.'

The Philiri regarded the farmhouse for a moment then nodded reluctantly. 'I just hope we don't end up following her,' he said and climbed up onto the cart.

With a candle before him, Ciro guided Nesh through the farmhouse until they reached the top of the stairs. Here Nesh lit another candle and disappeared momentarily into her bedroom, returning with a small shell covered box clutched under her arm and a roll of tatty parchment in her free hand.

'These are yours,' she said, handing them to Ciro. He looked blank. 'They were stuffed inside yer jacket when we brought ya 'ere,' Nesh explained.

'Oh, yes. Thank you,' responded Ciro. He had forgotten all about the papers Calian had given him: it seemed a lifetime ago.

'I 'aven't read 'em,' said Nesh, mistaking his surprise for concern. 'They're all stuck together.'

Ciro smiled. 'I haven't read them either,' he replied and stuffed them into his bag.

Nesh moved to the threshold of her Mother's bedroom then stopped and asked Ciro to wait on the landing. She gave him her shell box, removed two brightly coloured shells from within then disappeared beyond the door, returning moments later to retrieve her box with a strange expression on her face.

'Are you all right?' Ciro asked, a little perturbed by the girl's stern countenance.

Nesh nodded. 'We should go,' she said with determination and made straight for the stairway.

Ciro followed, then paused half way down the stairs when he realised the landing above now appeared brighter. He turned to see flames curl around the door Nesh had just exited.

'Blood…and…sand,' Ciro mouthed, amazed by the speed at which the fire was spreading.

Within seconds the whole landing was filled with smoke and Ciro descended the remaining stairs in leaps to follow a rapid grey shape from the farmhouse as Menzir's dog also ran from the growing blaze.

'C'mon!' Amec shouted from the cart.

The Philiri had manoeuvred the cart to the entrance of the lane and Ciro raced across the farmyard to catch it and clambered up onto the straw where Nesh and Arper were already sitting.

'Get some rest,' said Amec from the front of the cart. 'We'll be at Forht tomorrow.'

The king nodded, and then noted with some bemusement

the smiles of both Arper and Nesh. They were gazing back at the farmhouse as the cart entered the high-banked lane and Ciro realised that an orange glow lit each face. He too glanced back to catch a last glimpse of Menzir's farm and saw that the roof now spouted flames.

'Goodbye, sis',' said Arper quietly and hung his head.

Nesh gave a deep sigh and, with a quivering smile, fixed her tear-filled eyes at the stars. 'Safe journey, Ma...' she whispered.

The King of Nothing

PART TWO

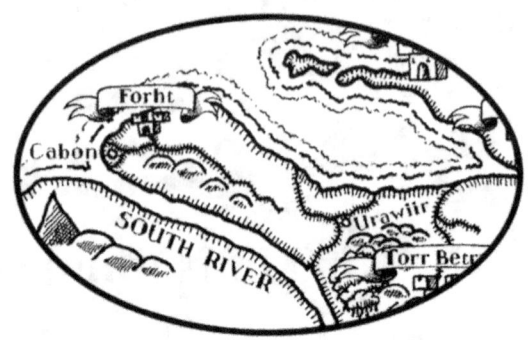

Despite the remonstrations of Alderman Chaime, I for one was glad to see the solid walls of Forht appear at the end of our long road. As I have already told, Urawiir brought my learned colleague little comfort and in truth his spirits have been rarely lifted since leaving the splendour of Torr Betram and venturing out on this final leg of our journey. For Chaime, Forht's battlements and general resemblance to Torr Betram in all but size only exacerbate his continuing sense of 'isolation' and, while we others debated jovially what would be found inside those high walls, Chaime merely shook his head.

'The capital of wilderness,' he said, then said little else for the rest of the day.

I had sent Begwood on ahead at first sight of Forht with papers announcing our arrival and so, when we finally reached the East Road Gate, a deputation from the castle of Lord Ross greeted us cordially. Even Chaime's dark mood seemed lifted by the invitation for us to stay as Lord Ross's guests but, while both he and Alderman Baulenus made instantly for the castle, myself, Captain Sharce and Begwood followed the main town road until we discovered Forht's hidden wonder.

Reaching another high wall, I was at first convinced that we were about to exit the town's western side, but the bright sunlight instead illuminated a graceful bridge which spanned the river gorge that bisects the east and west halves of the town. At the far end of the bridge, another high battlement hid the west of Forht but our collective attentions were lost on the sight of the bustling harbour which sat at the base of the gorge. It is not, I must say, quite as far a drop as the Cauldron Harbour of Torr Betram but, where the mist from the Grand Falls all but obscures that spectacle, here there was nothing to distract the eye from the bustle of the distant quay side and the sight of vessels gliding silently to and from the harbour. Our distance from this activity and the wonder of it to our eyes is best encapsulated by Captain Sharce, whom I found as we looked on, squinting with one eye while he pointed a finger towards the harbour.

'Are you quite alright, Captain?' I had inquired, concerned by this strange activity.

The captain had blushed and replied sheepishly: 'Your pardon, sire. I was attempting to push the boats into harbour with my finger.'

I laughed, instantly joining in the fun and for some time the three of us tried in vain to direct the harbour traffic with outstretched arms. How long we stood and gazed on that marvellous sight I cannot say only that we left when a deep shadow crept across the water and we realised it was almost evening and time to inspect our new lodgings.

Alderman Lacey. My travels to the South West Wold.
NC 659

Amec's Charge

I

Baramir Newman and Kattis Capell had never heard of Forht before and, they decided after less than a day that, if they never heard of it again they would be happy. After being herded, shoved and beaten by the Makech patrol for several days across a bleak and windswept landscape, they had been given the dubious pleasure – for the patrol said they were lucky to be alive – of sharing a cell in the rotten bowls of a castle which overlooked the eastern half of the town. Not that their accommodation offered anything in the way of a view, and even the decrepit sight of their surroundings was denied them once the torch light had receded with their guards.

'There ain't nothin' to see,' one of the guards had laughingly told them in broken Rialan and, after the fleeting glimpse of the damp, crumbling brickwork around them, both were inclined to agree.

'What do you think will happen to us, Baramir?' Kattis had asked more than once, but his companion would simply curse in response and return to his musings by the cell door.

It was, Baramir thought, a difficult enough position without Capell wittering on the whole time: and if the man didn't stop his damn stomach from rumbling every few minutes, what the Makech would do with him would be the last of his worries. Newman tried not to let his friend's whining distract him from his line of thought. He had never been in quite such a bind but, while he could still breath, while he could still think: then there was hope. His own stomach rumbled.

'Now see what you've done!' he shouted: the exclamation creating a strange echo in the confines of the cell.

'Sorry, Baramir,' Kattis replied meekly.

Newman sighed. 'If they wanted us dead,' he said, thinking

aloud, 'and let's face it, they've gone on about little else since the beach. Then why keep us alive? We don't know anything… '

'I've been wondering much the same thing mysel-'

'Shut up!' reprimanded Baramir. 'Heavens Capell!' he exclaimed into the blackness. 'Can't you see I'm trying to think!?'

Newman rubbed his chin and returned to pondering over their predicament. He closed his eyes to shut out the oppressive darkness and concentrated his attention on the matter of just how he might extricate himself from their perilous position. After a timeless period of quiet, Baramir felt he had successfully identified the one and only opportunity their difficult situation presented.

'Of course!' he shouted, standing up. 'That's it!' He cackled gleefully to himself and rubbed his hands together with joy. 'Kattis, I've got it!… Kattis? Well say something, man!?'

From the gloom, the sound of gentle snores reached him and Newman lashed out a boot into the unknown. There was a small explosion of breath and a cry from his friend as his swing connected and Kattis spluttered. 'What's happening!? What's happening!?'

'I've got it you lazy fool!' cried Baramir. 'I know why our guards want to keep us alive.'

'Do you think they'll feed us soon?' said Kattis feebly.

Baramir snorted. 'If we can play this right we can eat like Kings!… Well, Lords at least, listen… ' Newman sat down and began outlining his theory.

The Makech, he explained, were like any people: nervous of strangers. You only had to remember the consternation and worry that the arrival of the Songsmiths had caused in Feirlan – how everybody had believed the Nelan Desert in the south impassable until that odd group had walked out of it. And look what became of them! Now they were firm favourites of King Ciro.

The Makech probably felt the same way about their unexpected arrival. There had perhaps been trouble (how, Baramir was not sure) between this old Rial Kingdom which young Ciro was headed for and the Makech before and now they were naturally cautious about encountering them again: violent even. But the reason they had been kept alive was because the Makech wanted as much information as they could from Baramir and Kattis.

Kattis said nothing at this point, hoping his friend was building up to some greater revelation. He had deduced this much himself.

'Now,' continued Baramir, 'who, are we?' He winced in the darkness, half expecting Kattis to reply: "Capell and Newman?" but his companion remained thankfully silent. 'Why,' Baramir explained, 'we are whoever we tell these people we are. We are not fugitives, not criminals, and certainly not stowaways. We are whatever we say we are!'

'True... ' Kattis responded, 'But... '

'Yes... ' Newman did his best to sound indulgent.

'But how does not being a stowaway and being somebody else instead help us?'

'Ahah! That's the clever bit,' Baramir replied triumphantly.

'It is?'

'Yes. Now shut up and listen closely. If these people are after information, who would they most want to talk to? – No, let me rephrase that. Who would be in a better position to give these people information? Just a couple of stowaways? Or a couple of important personages who just happened to be washed overboard?'

'Well, the important ones. But... '

'Yes?'

'But wouldn't it be safer to say we know nothing, rather than say we know lots?'

'Ordinarily, yes. But what use would two stowaways who know nothing be to these people?'

'None.'

'And then what would they do with us?'

'Let us go?' The quaver in Capell's voice belied his confidence in that outcome.

'Go? Where? Feirlan?... What will you do, Capell, swim back?' sneered Baramir. 'Or find the King so he can imprison us for stowing away? Use that overly large head of yours and think, Kattis. There is nowhere for us to go.'

'But, then... '

'So we make ourselves useful to these people: they are quite obviously in charge here. But we do it as allies – helpers to their cause.'

'But how can we make peace between King Ciro and these people?' replied Capell doubtfully. 'We don't even know where he's gone.'

Baramir laughed. 'We aren't going to make peace! Damn the King! If he hadn't thrown us overboard we wouldn't be in this mess in the first place!'

'Washed overboard, Baramir,' corrected Kattis, 'Not thrown.'

'Washed, thrown: what difference does it make to our position?!' Newman stood up and kicked out at the wall beside Capell. A gentle patter sounded in the darkness as crumbled brick hit the floor. 'No,' he said, 'the King deserves all he gets... I mean, look at it from the Makech point of view. There they are, going along minding their own business, and up turns Ciro with a load of ships, dumps us on a beach to face their wrath and then buggers off! How would you feel?'

'But we still have to face their wrath,' said Capell. '... In a

107

way, you know, we're facing it now.'

'Oh, shuttup! Keep your half-witted philosophising to yourself. We aren't going to face any wrath! In fact, just the opposite. We are going to happily co-operate with these people in giving them just what they want, and we will do it because we were thrown overboard, Kattis, not washed. Thrown. Do you see?'

Capell was silent for a moment. He was about to admit he didn't see when caution and common sense made him instead say: 'You mean?!'

'Yes!' cried Baramir, happy that his friend finally understood. 'If we are enemies of Ciro's, then that can only make us allies of these people! And valuable ones too – to a people who don't know the first thing about us.' Baramir smiled at his own cleverness and puffed out his bony chest. 'Yes...' he said, thinking aloud. 'We could be leading dignitaries – perhaps generals – who were opposed to the King's hostility to the Makech –'

'– But we don't know King Ciro was hostile,' Kattis interjected.

'Heavens, Kattis!' bellowed Baramir in exasperation. 'Neither do they! But that was not a welcoming committee on the beach, was it?!'

'No.'

'No. So these people see a threat. And we are in a position – if you keep your mouth shut and let me do the talking – to capitalise on their suspicions. It's like any business transaction, Capell: supply and demand. And they have a demand for information which I can most definitely supply.'

Baramir was about to expand on exactly how they were to profit on this situation when the distant creak of rusted iron sounded through the darkness and the tunnel through the grill of their cell door began to brighten. Both stood, expectation and nervousness in their hearts as the footfall of an approaching guard came down the passageway.

'Remember,' said Baramir quietly. 'Let me do the talking.'

The guard, dressed in the now familiar black and metal armour came to a halt before the door and placed the torch he was carrying into the bracket on the wall. He drew his sword and turned to face the grill and for a moment the prisoners wondered fearfully at his intentions. The guard gave a grin of broken teeth, unlocked the door and swayed the curved blade several times before pointing it down the passage.

'Fulan,' the guard said, waggling the sword once more. Baramir and Kattis remained immobile.

'Fulan! Fulan!' The guard thundered at the prisoners and jabbed savagely at the damp cobblestones beside him. Tentatively the pair shuffled out to stand against the wall and watched the guard with wide and wary eyes. The Makech warrior pointed down the passageway.

'Fulan!' he repeated loudly and shoved Kattis in the direction he had pointed.

Followed closely by the guard, Capell and Newman left the cells and climbed the tight stone staircase which led to the ground floor of the castle. Waiting for them were several members of the patrol that had brought them here hours – a day ago? Neither man was sure anymore, but Baramir deduced it had to be night outside for torches were lit all around the sparsely furnished hall in which they now stood. The Makech they had seen before – Yetzi: 12 and the younger man with the trimmed beard who they had learnt was called Tanikalin: 26 – exchanged a few words with the guard then looked Baramir and Kattis up and down. For a moment Baramir was sure he saw humour in Tanikalin's expression but the illusion was quickly dispelled. Tanikalin frowned, stepped forward to each in turn and, with a single sharp wrench, ripped away the breast pockets of their uniforms which showed the Rial sun emblem.

'Thank you,' Baramir said, risking the Makech's wrath for speaking Rialan. 'That damn symbol has brought us nothing but trouble.'

Yetzi growled in response but Tanikalin reacted with the same humoured expression he had worn a moment earlier. 'More than you could possibly imagine.' He replied and ushered the prisoners towards a large wooden door at the end of the hall.

'Our Lord has ordered that you be shown the penalty for not co-operating with us,' Tanikalin said conversationally as they passed through the doors.

'I can assure you, sir,' Baramir replied, managing to keep his voice from fluttering like his stomach. 'That we wish to aid you in any way against our foul King. We feel his treatment of us and intentions towards you good people to be an outrage –'

'– Outrage –' echoed Kattis with frantic nods. He kept his eyes on the floor and tried not to think about their possible destination: or what this menacing individual meant by "the penalty".

Tanikalin smiled in response to Baramir's statement but was silent and they walked swiftly down a windowed passageway where smudges of light could be seen through the darkened glass. Two guards stood stationary beside doors at the far end and from beyond came the muffled roar of voices.

'Our laws here are very simple,' Tanikalin said as they approached the end of the passageway. 'If you do not co-operate, you will be brought here for judgment.' He waved a hand at the guards who immediately swung back the doors and the noise beyond rose on a wave of fresh air.

'This is our Judgment Ring,' he announced with obvious

pride.

Capell and Newman looked through the doors to see a wide, torch-lit arena surrounded by tiers of wooden benches sparsely filled with warriors. Beyond the seats a wooden wall blocked out any view of what lay outside the arena bar a star lit sky. A gentle breeze flapped the many strange banners which dotted the rim of the enclosure. The Makech patrol leader led the way down the central aisle which descended beyond the doors and a shove from Yetzi enticed Capell and Newman to swiftly follow.

The cheers appeared to be in response to two men who had been led out onto the sand covered pit which formed the focal point of the arena. They stood dejectedly, their hands bound, their faces bruised and bloody in the torchlight while the Makech who had led them out addressed the crowd.

Turning right, Tanikalin proceeded to a large, empty platform which commanded a grand view over the central pit and ushered both Baramir and Kattis to sit on the cushioned bench which was there. He himself remained standing and pointed to the battered men in the ring.

'These men are criminals,' he said, then crossed his arms. 'The sort of scum that your people seem to have an endless supply of.'

Baramir nodded, guessing by Tanikalin's emphasis on 'your' that he meant Rialan. *The sooner I can distance myself from that, the better,* he thought and looked on as the warrior in the ring continued to jabber unintelligibly and gesture at the prisoners. Whatever it was he was saying it seemed to spur the small crowd to further cheers.

Tanikalin pointed to the warrior. 'He is offering them a chance of justice.' He shook his head. 'Though Sakoom himself knows they don't deserve it.'

Baramir watched as the warrior in the pit drew his curved

sword and split the bonds which bound the two men's hands. He stole a glance at Kattis beside him and smiled as he noted his friend's gaze locked upon the wooden floor of the platform. Had he also seen the dark stains soaked into the sand? If so then Kattis realised, like Baramir himself did, that this was a place of stern and harsh justice – completely alien to the Alderman Courts back in Feirlan. But, unlike Capell, Newman was perfectly happy to watch some strangers be dealt their punishment. What did he care if there were blood stains in the sand? Capell's problem was thinking too much for no purpose. And all that achieved was worry. He should think more about our position here, thought Newman, and learn the rules.

Fascinated, Baramir watched as a small boy, dressed in a poor facsimile of the Makech warrior's armour, scurried out from the side of the ring and dropped two swords in the sand before the prisoners.

'What... What is their crime?' Capell asked nervously to no-one in particular.

Tanikalin turned from his vantage at the edge of the platform, his half-shadowed features beginning to form a frown in the torchlight.

Before he could say a word Baramir had slapped his partner on the arm and spat. 'They are obviously criminals, you fool! Does it matter!?'

This seemed to please Tanikalin who, though he glowered briefly at Capell's lowered head, nodded curtly to Baramir and returned to watch the 'trial' below.

The warrior in the pit was now directing the boy as he scooped handfuls of a dark substance from a pail and smeared it onto the rags which the prisoners wore. This done, seemingly to his satisfaction, the warrior shouted a few words to the audience and withdrew with the boy leaving the two prisoners alone with the weapons. Neither prisoner moved. A dull chime, like a broken bell, sounded through the brief quiet that had fallen upon the arena and drew Baramir's attention to the far side of the enclosure. Here, he saw two figures standing on a platform which was illuminated by a glowing brazier. Together, the men slowly turned what looked to be a large sand glass over and the small amount of sand within began rapidly pouring into its lower half. Baramir checked to see if the two prisoners had moved – they still stood immobile – then fascinated, returned to watch the sand glass. The men on the platform withdrew briefly to the darkness beyond the brazier, before returning with the unmistakable (though terribly old fashioned, Newman thought) shapes of bows in their hands.

'I wonder, sir,' Baramir said, his curiosity getting the better of him, 'What exactly are the archers for?'

Tanikalin did not turn, but Baramir saw plainly one corner of his mouth upturn into a smile.

'Justice,' said Tanikalin in reply and Baramir returned his attention to the small amount of sand still left in the upper glass.

The sand lasted about another minute and in that time the shouts and calls from the crowd became louder and more insistent. At last, with a few grains still left in the upper glass, one of the prisoners picked up the sword before him and raised it above his head. The crowd cheered his action, but the support turned sour as he pointed the sword to the crowd and shouted in a language which Baramir had no difficulty understanding.

'May Milla shine!' the man cried at the top of his voice and instantly ran at the stands directly before him.

Baramir smiled at the guts of the man, but wondered at such a suicidal action. Both prisoners appeared to have lost their defeated air and now the second man was picking up his sword and running in the opposite direction, towards the doors through which they had originally entered. He reached them and, after quickly ascertaining that they were firmly shut, began hacking at the woodwork in fury. While this went on and the scant few warriors in the overlooking stand jeered down at him, the other man, to a similar and strangely passive response, was attempting to climb the barrier at the opposite side of the arena.

Baramir noted that, though there was no physical response on the part of the crowd, all the men in the arena were drawing swords – even Tanikalin and Yetzi – though they were far from the disturbance. Then his attention was caught by a flash of fire blurring through the dark air and flames erupted close to the first prisoner. It was followed quickly by another streak of flame and Newman saw that the two archers were passing their arrows over the brazier before loosing them into the pit. Curious, he thought, and looked on eagerly.

The first prisoner was unable to scale the barrier. In frustration he began ramming the high wooden pillars with his shoulder and it was while pursuing this futile course that the first flaming arrow caught him. His scream carried through the tumult of voices to where Capell and Newman were seated and even Kattis seemed spellbound as the distant figure span round in agony and erupted into flame.

Baramir nudged Kattis with a bony elbow. 'They covered them with pitch!' He exclaimed with a grin. 'Can you believe it!?' Kattis shook his head, his jaw slack as Baramir chuckled and returned his attention to the pit.

The second prisoner had also failed to breach the solid barrier of the doors and his exertions left him panting and doubled. Newman thought he made the perfect target for an arrow but was disappointed to see the archers had discarded their bows and were again turning the sand glass.

Another dull bell chime sounded and with it the crowd surged forward towards the barrier. Baramir shook his head, completely perplexed by the strange antics as a swarm of bodies began dropping into the arena where the last prisoner stood.

The prisoner was also bemused by the sudden rush over the barrier and pointed his sword above his head as a warrior fell on top of him. Far across the sand, Baramir seemed to see the figure fall in slow motion to meet his fate, grimacing despite his total fascination as the upheld sword split through the man's thigh in a gush of blood before his full weight crushed the man underneath him. The injured warrior was screaming, thrashing helplessly upon the sand as he tried vainly to stop the gapping wound from streaming blood before the remaining mass of people converged and hid the scene. A brief thrashing of sword arms amidst the throng followed and finally a bloody head was held aloft to the hearty cheers of those Makech who had remained in the stands. Yetzi and Tanikalin joined in the revelry and then the patrol leader addressed his own prisoners.

'That is what will happen to you if you don't co-operate,' he said sternly. 'I hope the point is clearly made.'

Baramir smiled. 'We have never sought any other course than co-operation, sir, and want nothing more than to aid you in whatever way we can. You seem a fair and... ' Newman wracked his brain for the appropriate expression. '... Just people, and I know I speak for both of us (Kattis nodded dumbly) when I say that I look forward with pleasure to working with you.' He smiled more broadly while Tanikalin, his mouth half open, blinked back at him.

'You talk too much,' replied the Makech coldly, and motioned Yetzi to begin escorting them back to their cell.

On the way Baramir suddenly remembered something and, turning to the trailing Tanikalin said:

'Would it be possible for my friend and I to have something to eat?'

The question stopped the whole group dead and for a moment it looked as though the patrol leader had frozen to the spot. Baramir's heart quickened at the thought that he might have overstepped the mark but then Tanikalin's face split into a broad grin and he laughed.

'Of course!' he exclaimed, much to Baramir's relief and Kattis's delight, before muttering a few words to Yetzi. Yetzi spluttered a laugh, smiled a crooked smile in return, and then disappeared back to the arena while Tanikalin ushered them on.

'I really can't thank you enough, sir,' said Baramir as they were returned to their cell.

'Think nothing of it,' responded the Makech. 'After all, we would not want you dead before you have been questioned.'

The guard who had originally released them was standing by the wall holding another torch. On Tanikalin's instruction he placed it into the socket opposite the cell.

'Soon,' said Tanikalin, 'you will have the honour of meeting a very important gentleman. And have the opportunity to tell him everything that you know.'

'Splendid,' replied Baramir.

'Hm,' scowled Tanikalin in return, and then spoke a few words to the guard who unlocked the cell. 'Yetzi will be here with your food shortly... I hope you enjoy it.'

With that the patrol leader slammed closed the door and he and the guard withdrew. The torch however remained burning on the wall.

As the footsteps receded a faint laugh could be heard and Kattis collapsed onto the ground with a groan. 'I have never been so frightened in my life,' he muttered from the cell floor.

'Or so hungry, I'll bet,' said Baramir with a smile. Kattis shook his head before slowly rising. He looked haggard, his eyes heavily bagged and skin grey. Probably much as I look, thought Newman.

'I just thought that, the whole time we were there,' said Kattis tiredly, 'they would throw us in next.'

Baramir tutted. 'You should have more faith in me, my dear Capell,' he said. 'We have something that these people need, and I have every intention of exploiting that.' His eyes narrowed. 'We have a score to settle with our young King for getting us into this predicament. To that end these Makech should prove very useful.'

'But Baramir,' replied Kattis, 'how can you trust these people? They aren't friends, they're fiends. Merciless – you saw it yourself.'

'Merciless to whom? Criminals? What of it? How are we to judge in one day the ways of another people? Besides –' Baramir stifled a yawn and realised he had hardly slept for nearly, how long had it been? He pulled out his pocket watch and checked the dial in the torchlight. More than a day had passed since he had last looked at it. '… Besides,' he repeated, 'we do not know the crimes of the men they killed. They could have been murderers. Perhaps if we were better informed I – even you – would have been jumping into that pit to help slay them.'

Murderers…Like us, thought Kattis, and then his stomach growled ominously. 'Sorry Baramir,' he said.

Baramir waved the apology away. 'That thing of yours will be fed soon, and then perhaps I can get some peace,' he said and then, despite his desire to remain awake until the food came, Newman crouched by the door and fell fast asleep.

II

There had been few words spoken after the glow of the farmhouse had disappeared into the night and the darkness seemed all the blacker for the sombre silence which descended upon the group. At times Ciro could barely see his hands in front of his own face and he longed to break the silence which gripped the cart if only to ease his own sense of loneliness. He fought the urge however and was gratified to hear at length the gentle sound of Nesh as she slept.

By degrees the night lightened to a murky grey and the stars, hidden for a time by cloud, broke free once more to stud the sky. Rocking and rustling in the straw Ciro watched dark outlines of trees and hillsides cut across the sky and to the steady creak and bounce of the cart he gradually drifted into sleep.

He woke to find it light and, as the misty morning came into focus around him, so the dull, aching memories of the previous day returned. Ciro sat up and looked instantly around for Nesh but instead found Amec leaning on the back of the cart.

'Awake, then, are ya?' he asked.

Unsure whether the observation was a rebuke, a joke or a genuine question; Ciro nodded, collected his thoughts and climbed down from the cart. There was a slight chill to the air and the king put a hand to his jacket thinking it must be unbuttoned. He looked down to find that it was not. 'Where are the others?' he asked, brushing straw from his clothing.

Amec pointed beyond the cart to where the trace of fire could be seen through the mist. 'Over there, 'avin' breakfast.'

Ciro surveyed what little of the landscape could be discerned in the mist then followed Amec towards the fire. 'Where are we?' he asked, frowning at the gloom.

'Still between Cabon an' Forht,' came the Philiri's reply.

'An' a long way from the road. Best place to be if we don't wanna get spotted. We've been 'ere a while but Nesh thought you should rest.'

Ciro nodded and the pair walked on in silence.

Getting closer to the fire, Ciro could see that it was in fact a roaring blaze set in the centre of a leaf strew hollow. There was a patchy circle of bushes – grey in the mist – set around the depression and by the fire Ciro found Arper and Nesh. The farmer's daughter looked up and managed a smile while Arper pulled out a branch which he had been poking into the fire.

'Ere,' he said, pointing the glowing end of the branch towards Ciro as he moved closer to the pair. 'Ave some breakfast.'

Ciro saw that a sizzling piece of meat had been skewered onto the wood and gingerly plucked it from the branch. 'Thank you,' he said, tossing it from hand to hand then sat down beside Nesh.

Amec stood in silence for a few moments as Ciro ate then called on Arper to help him with the cart. As the pair faded into the gloom beyond the hollow, Ciro asked Nesh what they were planning to do.

'Amec wants to put some planks 'e took from the barn 'cross the back of the cart,' she replied. 'E says we can lie under 'em while 'e puts the straw back on top. That way the Bonemen at Forht won't know we're there.'

'Makes sense,' said Ciro. He wondered if the farmhouse blaze had drawn attention from Cabon – that was probably Amec's concern. If so, then whatever force was at the next town would be on the look out for them. He gnawed the last of what had turned out to be a chop and threw the bone into the fire.

'Would ya like some water?' Nesh asked. 'We've got some.'

Ciro picked up the jug which Nesh pointed to and took a few, grateful swigs.

'Amec wan'ed ta wake ya earlier,' Nesh said, watching Ciro drink. 'But I said: "Any man'as kills three Bonemen in a day deserves to sleep. Oo knows 'ow many 'e'll 'ave to kill today?"'

Ciro gave a thin smile: it was not a subject he wished to dwell on. 'Let's hope we don't meet any today,' he said, putting down the jug.

'Or no other day,' agreed Nesh. With those words, she fell silent, drew her legs up to her chest and lent her chin against her knees. Rocking gently she gazed into the fire and began to sing quietly:

'I was born a wanderer,'
'An' never 'ad no 'ome,
'From Romunesse to Circia,
'Torr Betram an' Tion.'

'I walk the roads,'
'an' stride the 'ills
'an' sleep beneath the stars,
'the forest is an 'ouse to me,'
'Milla is my 'earth fire.'

'I've met the Kings an' Princes,'
'aroun' Torr Adenair,'
'What 'ave ya seen? They ask of me,
'an' then I do declare.'

'I've travelled south,'
'An' climbed The Jaw,'
'An' spied the foreign lands,'

'An' then I came straight back again,'
'cause all I saw was sand.'

'You 'ave been far, dear wanderer,'
'the King 'e says to me,'
'Now 'ere's a gift ta take with 'e'
'when next you go afar.'

'An sayin' that, the King gave me,'
'A bright an' shinin' sword,'
'to show to all the desert folk,'
'when next I was abroad.'

'So now where 'ere I wander,'
'I march be'ind the King,'
'An' show me blade to anyone,'
'what dares to fight with 'im.'

'Oh, I was born a wanderer,'
'An' never ad' no 'ome,'
'But now I'm one of Betram's men,'
'An' don't wander alone.'

'That was beautiful,' said Ciro after Nesh lapsed back into silent contemplation of the fire. 'I've never heard that song before.'

'Uncle Arper says it's the song everyone asks for when 'e travels the road with Amec.' Nesh replied. She frowned slightly and looked over at Ciro. 'What's 'e like?' She asked.

'What's who like?'

'The King. What's the King like?'

Ciro shrugged and resisted the smile which threatened to split his face. 'He's… A good man, I think,' he replied.

Nesh nodded. 'Will 'e come 'ere if you ask 'im? Get rid of the Bonemen?'

Ciro's expression grew grave. 'Yes Nesh, he'll come. You can be sure of it.'

Nesh smiled, her eyes still locked on the fire. 'Before she went, Ma said I should marry one of 'is men. D'ya think I could? She said you'd ask for me.'

Ciro nodded. 'You'll be spoiled for choice, Nesh. Every single man in the army will be calling on you.'

'Ma would 'ave liked that,' said Nesh and fell silent again.

Ensconced beneath planks and straw, Ciro, Arper and Nesh travelled the rest of the journey to Forht in relative silence. It seemed an age before they regained the road they had left during the night and another before the plodding oxen rattled them into sight of Forht just before sunset.

Through a crack in the planking of the cart, Ciro watched the woodland which had bordered the road for so long begin to thin and fall away. In its place an expanse of course grass swept down towards the town and, on either side of the rutted track, Ciro noticed countless shallow mounds dotting the area. He would have identified them merely as tussocks but, from many of the mounds, large, arrow-shaped pieces of wood pointed out from them towards the sky. Ciro drew Arper's attention to the curious sight.

'Graves,' he replied and let out a deep sigh. 'The Bonemen don't let us build pyres for our folk to let their souls go to the stars: 'specially those that 'ave been 'judged'. So they bury 'em in the earth, in the dark, so that Beck and Ebo will take 'em. The arrows are there so that, if they can somehow escape, their souls'll know which way to go.' Arper paused for a moment. 'Me wife's buried there somewhere,' he added then lapsed into silence.

Nesh murmured words of comfort to her Uncle as they squeaked and rocked their way through the pitiful graveyard and, with a sad heart, Ciro stared out towards the approaching gates of Forht.

Back in Feirlan, hidden away in the depths of Torr Sarvie, Ciro had poured over so many maps and writings from, and about, Reilan that he had always considered he knew the Kingdom of Rial back to front. Yet Forht, the last strong point on the far western edge of the old kingdom, was virtually unknown to him. He had seen it mentioned in dispatches from King Elson's younger brother, Prince Idirnon, as the staging post for his naval assault on Kal Santra, and there was a brief mention of it in the travel journals of Alderman Lacey. But, apart from those scant descriptions, the town was a mystery.

Ciro wondered if Idirnon or Lacey would recognise the place now. He doubted it. The encircling wall looked on the brink of collapse – had done just that in some places – and swathes of dark ivy clung to the stonework as if trying to pull the rest of the decrepit structure back into the earth.

Amec was slowing the cart as they neared the arched entrance to the town and Ciro twisted his neck to better see through his vantage point as something in the stonework caught his eye: a panel of large, bright stone which sat directly above the entrance. Countless years of weathering seemed not to have affected its brilliance yet some brutal hand had deliberately marred what was once carved into the stone. Scratched almost to the point of oblivion were the remains of a Rialan sun and beneath that a single word in his own tongue which he could just make out. 'Welcome,' it read.

Ciro smiled, even though the symbol was almost gone, it was still enough for him to feel that he had at last achieved his ambition. Hidden in the back of a cart and covered with straw was not quite how he had envisaged what should have been a triumphant occasion but even so, this was a moment he had dreamed about for more than ten years.

There was a sentry waiting at the entrance and a trickle of people entering and exiting the gateway. The Makech, seemingly disinterested in guarding the gate, ignored the thin traffic, preferring instead to lean against the entrance arch and carve his initials into the stone. He looked up as Amec approached and hollered out a sentence in the Makech tongue.

'You're a bit late for market!' he said with a sneer.

Amec shrugged. 'Farmer Dernic wants this for his cattle.' He nodded to the straw piled high behind him. 'I've got to cart this stuff all the way to Urawiir.'

To this the sentry laughed. Urawiir was a good four days away by horse, let alone the single oxen which Amec had. Meanwhile, Amec coaxed the cart through the entrance way and the sentry, his grin fading, watched the procedure with blank disinterest. Suddenly, his expression changed and he launched himself from the wall and waved his sword.

'Hey! Peasant!' he cried.

Amec flinched at the sudden shout but the guard seemed oblivious.

''ave you seen any strangers on ya travels?' he asked.

Within the cart, Ciro's pulse raced when the sentry yelled and the cart lurched to a halt. He could not understand a word of what was being said so, like the others crammed beneath the straw, he listened hopefully and held his breath.

Amec gave the sentry a bemused look. 'Strangers?' he repeated as the Makech drew level. 'What d'ya mean by that?'

The sentry frowned. 'Just what I say I mean,' he growled. He looked back down the road then stared at Amec with narrowed eyes. 'I've been asked to ask people if they've seen anythin' odd... ' He brought his sword close to Amec's face.

'… So I'm askin'.'

Amec seemed to consider the question for a moment. 'I saw me boy get up early an' do his chores yesterday. That was beckin' odd.'

The sentry's frown turned into a grin. He stepped back from the cart and returned his sword to its scabbard. 'If ya see anythin', or anybody strange, you let us know, alright?'

Amec nodded. 'I'll do that,' he said.

'Oh, an watch the bridge,' the sentry added, pointing through the arch. 'Beckin' thing's nearly ready ta go.'

Amec nodded again and drove on.

The first thing that Ciro noticed about the town within the walls was the smell. If the crumbling battlements indicated a state of decay, then here was the conclusive proof that Forht was completely rotten. It stank. The farm had possessed a rich, earthy smell which was unusual but not too unpleasant to Ciro's unaccustomed senses, yet this was something far different. Sewage blocked the deep stone channels on either side of the main road and from it rose a stench which made him want to gag. He covered his nose and mouth with a handful of straw and tried to concentrate his attention on the new sights before him which, he had to admit, were as rank as the gutters.

He had expected to see some splendid, further evidence of the old Rial Kingdom but, to his disappointment, was reminded more of the Lantern Tavern in the north harbour of Obaln. Like the tavern, the buildings were a piecemeal patchwork of stone, wood and plaster, but here they combined to produce an effect that looked not only shabby, but downright dangerous. The Lantern looked like a beached hulk but was solid none the less and had stood on the harbour side for generations. Ciro had great difficulty believing the houses

– if they qualified for such a distinction – would survive a strong breeze.

There were people going about their business all around them and a few more Makech, but the whole atmosphere seemed subdued. There were distant noises: clatters, cries, but he heard no distinct conversation, no signature sound of a place full of life. Beside him, Arper had also covered his mouth with a handful of straw but he lowered it for a moment and pulled a face which seemed to sum up his own feelings towards the town. The cart travelled a few yards further when an explosive sneeze from Nesh made everybody's hearts skip a beat and Ciro stared through the gap in the plank to see if they had drawn any attention. No one appeared to notice that the noise had come from a mobile pile of straw. As disinterested as the sentry had been, Ciro thought to himself, with equal measure of curiosity and relief. Then he realised they were approaching another gateway, and with it the Forht Bridge.

From north to south, edged by another two high walls, a river split the town in two. Ciro could not recall the name of it, only that it had been wide enough and deep enough to accommodate Prince Idirnon's fleet as he prepared to storm Kal Santra. The cut through which the water flowed was deep, allowing even high masted vessels easy passage beneath the single span that joined the two sides of the town.

That, Ciro realised as they passed out from the shadow of the western gate and into the bright early evening light, had been during another age. Now, there were only the shattered ends of the stone bridge, clumsily spanned with plank and rope: as vocal as they were visual in their distress. The groans and movement as Amec spurred the oxen to brave the crossing reminded Ciro of the King Elson during that eventful storm and he found himself holding his breath as the ground

126

slipped away and the river, swaying slightly far below, glittered orange in the late sunlight.

There were piles of rubble poking intermittently from the water, both from the main part of the bridge and the battlement walls and Ciro retraced the probable descent of one green edged rock pile up the far wall to find a large gap on the eastern bank. He could see little from his narrow viewpoint of how high the gap climbed but it was enough to see through into the other part of town. Past another collection of makeshift hovels, a more sturdy structure showed what looked to be battlements.

'What's that?!' whispered Ciro, unable to contain his curiosity. Arper twisted to peer through the gap and snorted.

'What, the castle?' he whispered back. 'It's where the Bonemen live.' He narrowed his eyes. 'An' worse... ' he added.

The west of the town was as lifeless and putrid as the eastern half had been: with only one exception. As they passed through the open expanse of the market area, Ciro saw at its eastern edge a high, curving wooden structure which lay beneath the castle. Many strange flags and pennants fluttered at the summit of the wall and just as he was about to enquire about it to Arper, a distant roar of voices rose up from within.

'Bastards... Filthy bastards!' Arper muttered and shook his head. Ciro looked back out as Nesh muttered prayers to herself.

'Quiet in there,' hissed Amec under his breath.

The cart approached a crossroads, turning right into another hovel-edged street which led to the eastern gate. As the round structure slid from view, another, more disturbing feature came to Ciro's notice. A gibbet, twelve feet high and wide enough to swing ten people was doing just that. A line of limp bodies swayed gently in the evening breeze. As the first shock of this mass execution passed, Ciro realised that it was unlikely they had died from the hanging. All the bodies had been charred by fire – blackened in some cases to the bone – and badly disfigured by brutal sword strokes. Many were headless and suspended by their arms while others had heads but little left of their limbs. Someone had thrown flowers at the base of the gibbet and a single white arrow – pointing upwards – had been hastily painted on each chest. Unable to remove his gaze from this scene of torment, it was a moment before Ciro realised Arper was crying. While Nesh whispered comforting words to her Uncle, it slowly dawned on the King that the same, terrible fate had probably befallen Arper's wife.

Ciro was beginning to see that what historic records there were about the Makech did nothing to show the true nature of them as a people. They had always been reviled in the old texts but here was the root cause of that hatred in all its stark and gruesome reality. A reality that had continued for these unlucky people while the rest of the country had fled from the plague. Ciro wondered about the Makech garrison strengths. Could four thousand men reclaim this country? He made a mental note to quiz Amec and Arper on the subject as soon as possible.

At the final gate, two Makech sentries sat drinking from a single bottle while they played pitch and toss with coins against the edge the cobbled street. As Amec guided the cart through the final few feet before the open arch, the men yelled out for him to stop.

'What the Beck, du ya think ya doin'!?' bellowed the first sentry in the old tongue.

'Stop that damn cart!' shouted the second.

Amec brought the cart to a stop and the two men tried with some difficulty to get to their feet. They were clearly drunk, their eyes wide, their actions uncoordinated and both used the wall to balance and finally lever themselves upright. The first sentry waved wildly as he approached Amec and pointing to the road before them.

'Whadaya thin' ya doin'?!' he bellowed. 'We're trying to bet here! Any fool can see that!'

'I'm very sorry,' replied Amec, eying the man warily. 'I had no idea. I was just trying to pass through the gate.'

'Jus – jus trying ta pass through tha gate!?' spat the first sentry. He gripped the riding board of the cart with one hand and snatched the reigns from Amec with the other. 'Did ya hear tha?!' He said, turning to where his partner was picking up their coins from the road. 'I said, did ya hear tha?'

'Yeah, I 'eard,' replied the second sentry. He still had the bottle in his hand and swigged from it as he walked towards the cart. 'You ain't goin' nowhere, peasant,' he said, pointing the bottle at Amec.

'Please,' pleaded Amec. 'I don't want any trouble; I just want to be on my way.'

'Too late for that, boy,' replied the first sentry, who grinned and shook his head.

The second sentry tossed the bottle over his shoulder and drew his sword. 'Shoulda thought o' tha' before ya stopped our game, peasant,' he said and then, gripping the sword with both hands, flashed the blade down onto the neck of the oxen as hard as he could.

The oxen bellowed in agony and pitched sideways, almost toppling the cart as it hit the ground. The sentry gave a triumphant, drunken roar and struck again, nearly severing the head from the body. With that Amec leapt from the cart and bolted through the gate.

'Get im!' shouted the Makech with the sword and his partner dashed after the man, laughing as he went.

The sentry lent on the cart, his attention divided between

watching the pursuit beyond the gate and admiring his bloody sword work. Then the sound of rustling straw caused him to glance behind him. He was surprised to see a young man, dressed in green and covered in straw emerge from the rear of the cart, but what was more surprising than the man's appearance and his neatly cut hair was the strange brass object he held in his hand.

'Jo lonar bi?!' exclaimed the sentry, turning to face the man as he skirted the cart. Unnerved by the keen gaze which met his own he took a step back and readied his sword.

'Put that down or I'll shoot you,' said Ciro, aiming the hand lance at the man's head. He glanced past the sentry to make sure Amec had not been caught and saw that the Makech had stopped pursuit and was now running back to aid his friend. Ciro's immediate thought was to get everyone out of the cart but, before he could utter another word, the Makech before him roared and leapt forwards sword first. The 'SNAP!' from the hand lance echoed in the archway and the Makech collapsed.

'Get out, quickly!' shouted Ciro to the pair still in the cart, then looked back towards the market to see that his actions had not gone unnoticed. There were several locals in the street they had just travelled down and all were looking on intently. Now Arper and Nesh tumbled out of the cart with an explosion of straw and Ciro returned his gaze to the other sentry.

The first sentry had tired of chasing the cart driver and turned back to see his partner facing a stranger. He had instantly started back to help confront this new threat when he saw his friend raise his sword and, with a muffled thwak reaching his ears, saw his fellow sentry simply drop to the floor without a fight. Unnerved he slowed his pace, and then stopped dead when he saw two more strangers clamber out of the cart. The warning they had been given the previous day returned to him and with it all courage disappeared. This was the thing they'd been warned about! The strangers were here! In his sudden panic he didn't register the sound of running feet behind him and turned in time to meet Amec's fist square on the jaw.

Standing over the unconscious guard, Amec shook the pain from his knuckles and shouted back to the others. 'Come on! Run!'

Arper passed Ciro his bag and from it he fished his star belt. He strapped it on, re-holstered the hand lance then ran with the others towards Amec.

'Where to?' he asked as they drew level.

'It'll be dark soon,' Amec replied. 'But we have to try and make it to the hills.' The Philiri pointed to a dark range on the horizon. 'As soon as they realise what's happened they'll send out riders. If we can get to higher ground we should stand a better chance.'

Ciro took Nesh's pack and resumed running; fighting the urge to look back. He swore that the next time he saw Forht it would be at the head of his army.

Away from the road the land beyond Forht was a patchwork of high grass and bush lines interspersed with coppices. It provided enough cover for the group to move relatively unseen as they ran from the town but only with the cover of a larger wood and the fall of night did they begin to feel more secure in their movements. As they had crossed the open ground around Forht Ciro had noticed the faint bulge of a hillside which seemed closer than the main range. After hours of constant jogging and, though the fading light and their current path through the wood afforded little in the way of a panorama, the King felt sure that it was their ultimate destination. It had to be: they would not be able to run much longer.

Beside him, Nesh was beginning to breathe heavily: her head drooped upon her chest. Her exhausted state confirmed Ciro's fears and he voiced the question which had been on all their minds.

'How much further, Amec?'

'We have to reach the hills,' came Amec's reply, through several pants. 'So don't tell me you're tired. We all are. But we have to keep going until we're safe.'

'How long to the hills?' persisted Ciro.

'I don't know!' Amec growled. 'It's dark and I can't see. Alright?'

'It shouldn't be too far, Nesh,' said Ciro quietly and in response she lifted her head and managed a smile.

Now at barely a trot, they continued on into the night until their weary legs felt an incline and at last the ground began to rise. To everyone's relief, Amec called a sudden halt.

Ciro clutched his sides and breathed deeply while Nesh collapsed onto the ground. Arper was clutching the trunk of a tree for support while Amec, no less tired, attempted to get his bearings.

'There's a bolt hole, not far from here that we can use for the night. We'll be safe there.'

A half moon, shining through the canopy of leaves gave enough light for Ciro to discern the others. Nesh looked dazed – her chest heaving maniacally as she gasped for air while Arper had slid down the tree trunk onto his haunches. 'How far is the bolt hole?' Ciro asked.

'Not far,' Amec replied, but there was an edge to his words.

'Is it walking distance?' Ciro continued, shrugging off the irritation his companion showed to being questioned.

'It's… Not… Far.' Amec expelled each word like a flight from a hand lance. 'Or would you rather sit here and be killed?'

Ciro lent his back against a tree to momentarily ease his weary legs. He thought better of sitting down for fear he would not be able to get back up. 'I would rather we had enough strength left to continue running,' said Ciro wearily, 'but that isn't the case. So, if we are going to get to this place of yours, the only way will be to walk.'

Amec snorted something which Ciro took to be grudging acceptance of his words then went to rouse Arper. Ciro did the same with Nesh and, very slowly, they continued on up the rise.

The wood they had travelled through became patchy as they trudged their way up the steepening hillside until it gave way completely to the open sky. As the group walked on into open ground Ciro glanced back to find that they had risen above the tree line and, far back in the darkness, the distant lights of Forht were burning brightly. The King looked to see if there were any lights closer than the town but was relieved to see none. He turned back to resume walking and found that Amec had dropped back to join him.

Amec frowned at Ciro and placed a hand in front of him, stopping him from moving on. 'If you want to get back to your people,' he growled quietly. 'Don't question my authority again.'

Ciro sighed, his reply as weary as his legs felt. 'I'm not your enemy, Amec – my people are also your people – and the sooner I'm back with them, the better it will be for all of us.'

Amec snorted.

'As for questioning your authority,' Ciro continued, 'I don't. You know this land better than I ever will and I have every faith that you can get us to our destination. But I will question anyone's judgment if I feel it's detrimental to our survival.' Ciro shook his head. 'None of us are used to this type of exertion,' he explained with earnest, 'and I would imagine that the more exhausted we are at the end of this day, the less energy we will have for tomorrow. Don't you think?'

'I don't know what passes for an army in this land you come from,' replied Amec with obvious contempt, 'but if you want to survive to reach your destination you better do as I say and stop whining. I ain't noticed anyone else complainin'.' With that the Philiri increased his pace to move back to the front of the group leaving the King alone.

Ciro picked up his own pace to keep the others in sight and reflected on Amec's words. He felt some sympathy with the man's attitude but was concerned with his blunt rejection of any other opinion. It was a frame of mind Ciro hoped he seldom displayed, having surrounded himself with people whose council he trusted implicitly. But then that was back at Jirasinne, when the dream of Reilan had begun to take shape in a flurry of activity. There had been plenty of time to take the council of others there but what, Ciro wondered, would those wise friends of his do in this unseen situation?

Bdann would probably allow his temper get the better of him and simply confront Amec. Or was he being unfair about his brother's temperament? Alanti, that rock of logic, would never have been stupid enough to fall off his vessel in the first place and Calian…? Calian, Ciro suspected, would either be in complete charge of the situation by now or else have already set out on his own. The Songsmith, like all his fellow Songsmiths, had an enviable affinity with nature which would have suited their present circumstance perfectly.

'By the stars I wish you were here,' said Ciro to himself and began to hum one of the Songsmith's tunes as his aching muscles pushed him on. Despite his overwhelming tiredness, he smiled and felt his spirits lift.

The king caught up with the others as they reached the

summit of the hill but Amec simply pointed to the darkness beyond and, without a word, kept on walking. Stumbling after him, it took another hour of leaden plodding before they reached the hidden cave and, no sooner had Amec announced that they could rest than the group dropped as one to the dusty ground and groaned themselves to sleep.

Ciro woke to feel a cold wave pass over him: a shiver which ran the whole length of his body as he took in the view from the vantage of the tower window. Some five miles beyond – past flat plains, fog shrouded forests and streams – the pale morning abruptly ended in a wall of night. Tall as the sky itself, the darkness stretched in a straight line as far as he could see in each direction and, as he watched, seemed to creep its way a little closer.

Ciro pulled his gaze away from the mind numbing view and glanced down at the bulky metal armour he was clad in: the dark band of King Elson's star belt circling his waist. Instead of the familiar sight of his hand lance, the King was surprised to see a lavishly decorated long sword hanging from the belt.

This isn't right, thought Ciro. He had personally seen all Elson's regalia stored aboard ship before the voyage. How did he come to be wearing it?

A muffled sound resolved itself into a voice behind him and Ciro turned from the window to see for the first time the chamber he stood in. It was high-arched and half-shadowed, the grey stone walls hung with rich tapestries and filled with men clad in similar armour to his. It should have shocked him to be in such strange surroundings but the budding notion of unfamiliarity was quickly curtailed when one of the men broke away from the group to approach him. He carried a lavish helmet crested with white feathers under one arm and another, golden helmet emblazoned with the Rial sun symbol

135

in his other hand. He held the golden one out for Ciro to take. The man's face was grave as he spoke but the voice was still muffled – distant – and Ciro turned back to take one last look at the menacing horizon before putting on the helmet.

The landscape beyond the window appeared to have shifted: the black horizon closer now and, though he felt a strong sense of apprehension at the brooding vista, the fear was met with a grim determination somewhere within him. An unwavering resolution seemed to set itself in his mind. Then that firm certainty slipped completely and to his horror Ciro realised what the men behind him in the chamber where waiting for: where they were all going.

'No!' he heard himself cry at the black horizon and then the darkness was replaced by light.

The day hit Ciro brightly in the eyes and for a moment his blurred vision showed the whole world to be a rainbow. The trees through the entrance to the cave seemed to flare with an inner light while the patch of sky between the branches swirled with colours. The birds made a deafening cacophony and Ciro blinked: sat up and saw the dawn return to normal – the bird song lessen. There was a dull pain in his neck and Ciro twisted to see the lumpy pillow which had caused the ache. He knew he had been exhausted, but had no memory of laying his star belt on top of the bag before resting his head there. He massaged the indent which one of the bulbous silver stars on the belt had made to the back of his neck during his sleep and, with a grimace, looked around the dim interior of the cave. Nesh was curled beside him, snoring quietly while Arper, opposite, was beginning to stretch and stir. There was no sign of Amec.

With a loud yawn, Arper sat up and narrowed his eyes at the day. He scratched his head, looked over at Ciro and managed a crumpled grin.

'Damn this runnin' about,' he exclaimed quietly and, with a pained expression, began massaging his legs.

Apart from the stiffness which lying on his belt had caused, Ciro felt no ill effects from the exertions of the previous day. Just the opposite, in fact. He felt completely refreshed and rested: as if he had slept a lifetime rather than hours. He seemed to recall waking to find it dark, but the memory slipped away as he climbed to his feet and stretched.

'I'll see where Amec has got to,' he said as he squinted at the daylight outside then left the cave to find the Philiri.

The cave was well hidden within a brake of trees which led out into a rocky hollow. The sides were steep, overhung with blossoming bushes and somewhere close by was the sound of running water. With a blue sky above, the fresh scent of morning strong in the air and the cheerful sound of bird song all around, Ciro merrily clambered upon the large, moss gripped rocks beyond the cave to search for the source of the water. In the process he also found Amec.

The Philiri was sitting hunched over a fire by a sandy pool which was fed by a trickle of water. He made no acknowledgement of Ciro as he negotiated a path amongst the boulders to reach him, but tended four skinned rabbits suspended on sticks above the flames.

'Good morning, Amec,' Ciro said as he came closer. 'How long have you been awake?'

Amec turned to regard Ciro with a blank expression then flicked his gaze at the sky. 'Hour, maybe more,' he said then turned his back on him to tend the fire.

Ciro leaned against a rock and watched the man aimlessly poke the cinders. He cast his gaze around the hollow. 'This is a good spot,' he said brightly, attempting to draw Amec into some form of conversation: ease the tension which had been evident the night before. 'How long have you used it?'

'Couple o' years.'

Ciro nodded to the back of the man's head. Alright, he thought, skip the small talk, let's get some information. 'Philire's a long way from here, isn't it?' Ciro said. Amec shrugged in response but did not turn round. 'But with the land overrun with Makech,' continued Ciro, 'what do Philiri's like yourself hope to achieve by coming here?'

Amec turned and gave Ciro a half smile. 'Philire's a lot closer than the place you say ya came from. What did you 'ope to achieve by comin' here?' he asked.

The question caught Ciro off guard. 'Do you mean personally?' he replied, stalling. What do I say? He thought: that I'm King but not a very good sailor? Amec was gazing at him with a mixture of amusement and expectation written on his face. Oh, what does it matter? Ciro thought, they'd find out anyway when we get to Peimonac. Why bother hiding who you are? And anyway, it would wipe the smirk off Amec's face. He took a deep breath. 'I personally came here to reclaim my Kingdom, Amec.' It sounded a little more pompous than Ciro had intended.

Amec's half-smile broadened to a grin. 'Your kingdom?' he said, pointing a questioning finger at Ciro.

Ciro nodded. 'My name is Ciro Torrman, I –'

'–Torrman!?' echoed Amec with evident shock. He stood up, turned his back on Ciro and exclaimed to the sky: 'Oh! By Ebo's mire, I should have guessed! Another bloody Torrman! Just what this land needs.' Amec turned, his grin now humourless, and shook his head.

'What do you mean: "Another Torrman"?' Ciro asked, perplexed by the man's attitude.

'Are you descended from the same Elson Torrman that once ruled here?' Amec asked. Ciro nodded. 'Then how much do you know about your family? About what they did to this country of ours?'

Ciro was impressed that the lineage of the Torrman family was still remembered after so long, but less taken with Amec's obvious disdain.

'My family ruled this land fairly,' he replied, slightly more defensively than he meant to. 'From King Adenair to King Elson, they –'

Amec waved a dismissive hand. '– Adenair I know nothing of,' he said. 'But Elson, we know all about him.'

'Meaning what?'

"Meaning," mimicked Amec, 'that if it hadn't been for his power mad stupidity, this land would still be a paradise and not the Omerk infested, Makech overrun cemetery it now is!' Amec punched the air with his fist.

So, thought Ciro, the strange Omerk that he had read about in the old texts where also here. But what power mad stupidity was it that King Elson was guilty of? There was nothing in the texts but praise for the man, and sadness for his loss. Ciro's prompting drew another tirade from the Philiri.

'Our Elders still tell tales about the fall of Rial,' Amec sneered. 'How your forefather, Elson, didn't think King was good enough for 'im! Oh no. The people gave him praise – and he took it. They gave him tribute and power and he took it all. But that wasn't enough for Elson's lofty ambitions! 'e wanted the stars themselves in his back pocket. The sun herself at his feet!' Amec spat the words and pointed to the sky. 'But Milla: blessed, blazing Milla, was far too powerful for such a feeble schemer, and so to teach the upstart a lesson she sent Beck, the god of night to show him just what the world would be like without 'er. An' how do you best punish a King? You take away his Kingdom, that's 'ow, and so a wall of darkness swept the land: devouring anythin' an' anybody that couldn't escape. Elson, they say, hid while the world was ravaged by the blight, an' the poor subjects that had raised him up so high died in fear: in the dark. An' those that survived curse his name to this day.'

Ciro had never paid much heed to superstition, nor for that matter did most Feirlaners. There were certain groups, primarily 'The Eight': the Children of Milla, who believed in the sun and the moon as physical embodiments of the gods, but time had eroded their voice to a minority amongst the populace. The Songsmiths too, though they were not strictly speaking Feirlaners, were a very spiritual group: in some ways more so than The Eight. But Ciro had always found their reverence for nature and its supposed controlling deities a quite poignant expression of man's connection to the world around them. And, unlike the Children of Milla, they did not particularly care if they were chided for such 'primitive' beliefs. He was lucky, he supposed, to have been brought up in such an enlightened society, but here, for those descendants of the survivors of the catastrophe that had befallen the old Rial kingdom, life had been a continual struggle. Society seemed to have broken down.

Elements of Amec's tale were vaguely familiar, but Ciro had never heard the 'Beck Night' children's story applied in such a ridiculous way; certainly not in such an historically distorting one. He supposed that the fall of the kingdom, coupled with fear and ignorance could eventually make even a bedtime tale about the moon disappearing and the evil Beck walking the earth into the cause of their calamity. And, Ciro supposed, as King, his distant ancestor Elson would become the focus of the blame. But there was still a grain of truth within the superstitious whole, a glimmer of rational light in an otherwise preposterous hypothesis.

'This blight you speak of, Amec,' said Ciro. 'It wasn't some punishment of the gods, but a plague. That's what swept the country.'

'Ha!' Amec chided. 'Were you there?'

'No, no more than you were,' responded Ciro. 'But the one thing that did survive from Elson's time intact were the texts brought over with the exodus. I'm living proof that others survived the calamity and they took a library of written proof with them. I have read the old reports from the Aldermen of Peimonac from that dark time. They speak of panic, mass evacuations of the cities in the north and bodies floating in the water. That's why Elson ordered the fleet to leave Rial. Taking as many people as they possibly could.' This seemed to make Amec pause for thought and seeing it, Ciro attempted to drive home his argument. 'I don't know the exact details, but I do know that it was a calamity big enough and bad enough to virtually destroy the entire kingdom. And the memory of it made our – 'my' if you will – people turn their backs on the land they had once called home for generations.'

Amec nodded as if reviewing the new information. 'How do you explain the curse upon Rial? The Black Apples?' he asked, 'Or the demons in the mountains? Or the fact that not even the vile Makech will step one pace past the swamps of Ebo Pamessi?'

Ciro had no idea what or where Ebo Pamessi was but he shrugged. 'I can't, no more than I can explain what caused the plague. But I promise you, Amec, it was no act of King Elson's against the sun which wrecked the kingdom, but a very real and very deadly disease. When I began my plans to return here, I never, nobody ever, thought we would find a living soul still alive. That's how bad this blight appeared to us.'

'Well,' muttered Amec, 'you can believe what you want to believe. Maybe what you say is true, maybe what I know is true.'

'I have papers,' Ciro continued, trying to make Amec see sense. 'An entire library which is at this minute on its way to the heart of Rial. You can read the reports for yourself if you decide not to believe me. But I would ask you not to speak in such terms about Elson again. He refused to leave the kingdom until everyone he could find was safely aboard ship, and died as a result.'

Amec shrugged and poked at the fire again. 'So,' he said, changing the subject. 'Now glorious Elson's heir is back! And what would your title be exactly, Ciro Torrman?'

Ciro sighed. 'King,' he said.

Amec smirked. 'So, valiant King Ciro has returned from – ' he waved a hand in the air '– the Kolben know where, to reclaim his throne and clear the name of poor Elson: is that right?'

'King Elson has no need of my help in that respect,' replied Ciro. 'But otherwise, yes.'

Amec pulled a piece of flesh from the rabbit and chewed absently. 'Not a very good sailor, are you?' he said with a greasy grin, then stood as Arper and Nesh clambered into view.

'Somethin' smells good!' Arper said as he climbed down the rocks. Ciro gave Nesh a helping hand.

'Wha' was all the shoutin' about?' Nesh asked. In response Ciro gave a sideways glance at Amec, who said:

'Our Lord here was giving me a history lesson.'

Ciro frowned while the eyes of the others turned on him. 'I am nobody's Lord, Amec,' he said.

Amec gave a low bow. 'My apologies, sire. I meant no disrespect. I meant to say King.' He looked up grinning. An expression Ciro did not mirror.

'What ya talkin' about, Amec?' Arper asked.

'Ask his Majesty. He'll tell you,' Amec replied.

Ciro sighed and sat down on a flat boulder. 'My name is Ciro Torrman, I –'

'– Tell 'em your title,' interrupted Amec.

Ciro scowled. 'I'll explain this myself, if you don't mind, Amec,' he said.

Ciro ran both hands through his hair, felt the bandage that had been there for days come loose. He screwed it up and dropped it to the floor. 'Why don't you both sit down?' he said with a weary smile. 'And I'll try to explain exactly who I am and what I'm doing here.'

Intrigued, Arper and Nesh made themselves comfortable on the grass beside the boulder while Ciro collected his thoughts. Amec continued to play with the fire and the food.

'My name is Ciro Torrman,' began Ciro again. 'I am the son of Fidiann Torrman, the King of Feirlan.' Arper's eyes narrowed while Nesh regarded him with an open mouth. Ciro continued: 'Two years ago, as Prince of the realm and eldest child I ascended to the Feirlan throne,' Ciro anticipated the blank looks. 'That means,' he explained, 'that had I taken the Feirlan throne I would have become a sort of apprentice King and begun learning the practical ways of governing the kingdom and –' They were following him but, Ciro guessed, only just. Get to the point, he told himself. '– To cut a very long story short, there is provision within the Feirlan ascension ceremony to choose the Rial throne instead of the Feirlan one and, though in the five hundred years or so since we landed in Feirlan it had never been done before, that is what I chose to do. For the last two years I have been preparing for an expedition to return to my people's natural home and I was on route when a freak storm washed me overboard… The rest you know.'

Arper's frown deepened until it ridged his brow. He

scratched his head. 'A..Are you sayin' you're the King?' he asked. Ciro nodded. 'The King o' Rial?'

Ciro's face broke into a broad grin and he laughed. 'Arper,' he replied, 'look around you. I'm the King of Nothing: of nobody, and have been ever since I was washed into the sea. I had over four thousand men under my command, ten ships, but at the moment they will be under my brother's charge.' The smile left Ciro's face. Poor Bdann, he thought, he must think I'm dead. The fact hadn't really struck him before.

'I thought ya said you were just one o' the crew,' said Nesh.

'I was alone in a strange land,' Ciro replied. 'I'm sorry Nesh; I didn't mean to mislead you. I was just being cautious.' How many Makech might have turned up at the farmhouse if I had not been, Ciro thought to himself.

'So where're yer people now, Ciro?' Arper asked.

'Peimonac,' Ciro replied. 'They should have landed several days ago.'

'An' if we can get ya there, will ya people 'elp us?' inquired Arper. 'Y'know, against the Bonemen?'

Ciro nodded. 'I guarantee it. They are not just my people, but yours as well. As soon as I get back we can begin working out a plan of attack. But for that I'll need your help. Yours too Amec.'

Amec raised an eyebrow. 'Really. How?' he asked.

'Troop numbers, garrison strengths and locations,' Ciro ticked the words off on his fingers. 'When I come back with my men I want to know as much about the Makech as possible.'

The request seemed to evaporate Amec's former hostility. 'I do know a certain amount about that,' he admitted. 'But it may not be as simple as you think.'

'How so?'

'Well, first we have to get to Peimonac and I'm not sure

that's going to be easy. You've already stirred the Makech up.'
Ciro was about to speak but Amec indicated the food. 'We
should eat now and be on our way – we'll 'ave plenty of time
to talk later.'

Ciro nodded and moved closer to the fire with the others.
Nesh fished out a loaf of bread from her bag which she split
between the four of them while Amec passed around pieces
of scorched rabbit. The whole group ate in silence and Ciro's
mind wandered from thoughts of his friends in Peimonac to
vague recollections of the strange dream he had had in the
night. It puzzled him that he should dream of a wall of night
descending on the kingdom just like the one which Amec had
spoken of.

III

Baramir and Kattis were rudely awakened by a tumult of
noise on the cell door. For a moment it sounded as if the roof
were falling in and, with the sudden influx of guards – their
boots and fists striking out to wake and raise the pair – that
was exactly what it felt like. Wide-eyed and terrified at the
sudden brutality, within seconds they had both been lurched
to their feet and manhandled though the door.

'What's the meaning of this?!' cried Newman as they were
shoved along the corridor. He received a cuff around the back
of his head for his enquiry and turned to see the snarling
figure of Yetzi behind him.

'FULAN! HAISAN!' the Makech bellowed into Newman's
face and spurred his prisoners into a fast trot by drawing his
sword.

They were run rapidly out of the depths of the castle and
hurried up several staircases. Struck and berated in equal
measure, they arrived panting and petrified at a large set of

doors on the second floor. Neither had glimpsed this part of the castle before and, despite his situation, Baramir noted with abstract interest that the floor here was carpeted. Kattis was pushed beside him as the two waiting sentries drew back the doors and, with violent shoves, the pair were propelled into the large, sunlit room beyond.

One wall was dominated by four huge, stone-carved figures which seemed to represent thunder, fire, earth and water while the other walls were hung with large tapestries depicting the effects of the same elements on terrified people. There was lightning flashing from a dark sky to strike an army in one, a wall of water consuming a village in another, fire devouring more helpless individuals in the third while the final tapestry showed a large city falling into a crack in the earth. Apart from these vivid depictions the chamber was sparsely furnished. Before the windows a large stone table dominated the centre of the room and it was here that Capell and Newman saw Tanikalin standing with what looked at first glance to be a bear standing on its hind legs. The figure turned as Baramir and Kattis were pushed to their knees on the floor several yards before him and both saw that it was indeed a bear of a man: his long hair and bushy beard flowing over a large fur robe upon which sat a heavy gold chain. Despite their situation and the evident tension in the air, Newman found himself wondering how much such a fine piece of gold work would fetch in Obaln market.

Tanikalin, now pacing before them, gave a sour glance at the pair then curtly addressed the guards behind them. There was silence for a few moments as both Newman and Capell studiously studied the carpet and then a distant cry of fear grew louder as the guards returned with another prisoner.

A young man with a moon face was thrown onto the floor before them. Beaten and bloody – his clothes torn and stained

– he writhed upon the carpet as Yetzi and another guard kicked him repeatedly. Watching impassively for a moment, Tanikalin drew his sword, stepped forward and placed a foot upon the youth's chest. The boy ceased his movement but continued to whimper in Makech.

'Silence!' Tanikalin shouted in Rialan and levelled his sword at the prisoner's throat. He stole a glance at Baramir – holding his gaze – while he prodded the boy with his sword.

'Tell these… 'gentlemen',' (the word forced its way past his lips) 'who you are.' The prisoner remained silent so Tanikalin dug the tip of his sword into the prisoner's shoulder. 'Tell them!' he barked.

'Tersic! Me name's Tersic!' screamed the prostrate figure in pained reply.

Tanikalin nodded. 'He's a labourer from a farm not far from where we found you two.' He gestured with his sword towards Baramir and Kattis. 'Now,' he continued, regarding the boy beneath his boot. 'Tell them what you told us earlier. About the young man who stayed at your farm.'

The boy gulped. 'Nesh found 'im on a beach. 'e was injured an' slept for days.'

Tanikalin smiled menacingly at Baramir. 'Describe him.'

''e was strange. Short 'air, clean lookin'. 'e had a thing, a sun thing on 'is blue jacket an' this strange thing he showed us which he kept on a belt.'

Baramir's mouth dropped and he turned to see Kattis mirror his expression even before Tersic said that the stranger had called himself 'Ciro'. Their surprise did not go unnoticed.

'So,' said Tanikalin stepping away from Tersic. 'You know about this man, do you?' Kattis gave a nervous nod and Tanikalin, with a flick of his hand, got Yetzi to drag Tersic to his feet.

'I see,' replied the patrol leader, pacing. He stopped

momentarily before the bear-man and bowed his head curtly, speaking a few words of Makech. The giant in furs nodded back and Tanikalin resumed speaking in Rialan. 'What you probably don't know,' he said, 'is what happened when we sent a patrol from Cabon to find this man…' He pointed the sword at Tersic but kept his eyes locked firmly on Newman. '…What this boy ran all the way from the farm to tell us.'

Baramir looked blankly back in answer and shrugged his shoulders.

'Well… ' Tanikalin gave a humourless smile then, in a sudden blur of movement, span around and flashed his sword into Tersic's skull. There was a sickening crack as the blade connected and the farm hand toppled, lifeless to the floor: a pool of blood quickly spreading into the carpet.

Tanikalin eyed the remaining prisoners with malice. 'That's what we found!' he spat and kicked the corpse as hard as he could. 'Our entire patrol dead!'

Capell and Newman were transfixed by Tanikalin's sudden violence but, unlike the others in the room, it was in open-mouthed horror rather than fascination. The bear-man – whoever he was – placed a restraining arm on Tanikalin's shoulder and a large door set into the wall with the statues opened to admit a strange and terrifying figure.

Over six feet tall and dressed in highly polished scale-mail armour, it took both Kattis and Baramir a few moments to realise that there was a man beneath the hideous red mask which completely covered his head. Around his torso was a cross band of wide leather straps and at the centre of these sat a large square of brass showing a crescent moon. Beneath it was embossed a strange symbol which neither prisoner recognised. A decorative sword hilt showed above his left shoulder, but it was the mask which drew both Capell and Newman's chief attention.

It was a bulbous and unearthly visage. Blood red leather with white, snarling teeth where the mouth should have been and two curving horns made of bone which jutted from the top of its head. The only sign of life was the unblinking gaze which stared out from two eye holes and the chamber fell silent as the figure advanced through the doors. He gazed down at the bloody mess of Tersic, glanced at the now calm Tanikalin then addressed himself to the man in furs.

'His reverence grows impatient,' said the figure dispassionately, a tone at odds with the ferocity written on his face.

After a brief pause as Tanikalin also looked to the bear man for guidance, all eyes fell upon Capell and Newman. Kattis wrung his hands and tried to stop his lip from trembling.

'Oh, dear, Newman… ' he whispered as he stared firmly at the carpet. 'What will become of us?'

Newman shook his head a fraction in response but kept his eyes firmly on Tanikalin. If the Patrol Leader was about to fly into another unexpected rage, Baramir wanted to know about it. Instead they were ordered to stand and shoved by Tanikalin and Yetzi through the connecting door into a second, equally large chamber.

If the scene in the last room had been strange, the sight which now met them was completely outlandish. There were another three of the red gargoyles awaiting them and they stood rigidly to attention behind two figures whose appearance was something which stopped both Capell and Newman in their tracks.

The first was an old man: so thin that it was as if he had been squeezed through a carpenter's vice. His clothes were long and flowing; richer, Newman surmised, than anything he had seen so far in this strange land. Yet, despite their obvious splendour they seemed grubby and uncared for.

Around this old man's neck hung a linked metal scarf covered in unusual symbols and, circling a sore-pocked and flaking forehead, was a similarly adorned band of silver-like metal. Whatever this rare substance was, it was like nothing the prisoners had ever seen before and it glowed like a pale flame in the dimly lit chamber. The old man's angular arms, lost amidst the heavy folds of a cloak ended in skeletal hands which rested upon a slender silver staff. The overall effect made Newman think of death.

The other figure, which sat at the feet of the ancient, was harder to analogise. It was short and child-like in frame but with a head far too big for that to be the case. It had, like the old man, a band of the same glowing silver around its bare head but was otherwise naked apart from a scrap of cloth tied around its waist. It too was filthy: its pale, almost white skin, stained with mud and whatever else it had deigned to lie in. Its eyes, which remained closed as the prisoners were brought in, were huge and Newman wondered just what illness it was that this grotesque thing suffered from.

Capell and Newman were pushed forward, gently by normal Makech standards, until they stood before the two strange figures. The old man had kept his gaze on the head of the creature at his feet all this time: his eyes hidden by grey brows. Now he lifted his thin face to look upon the prisoners for the first time and smiled. In response, Kattis locked his view upon the floor and kept his gaze firmly down – he had already seen enough.

Newman on the other hand, though no less nervous, wanted to know exactly what was going on. The sudden killing of the boy had upset his plan to begin explaining themselves, but more than that the sudden discovery that their young king, Ciro was at large and causing problems made it imperative he sow the seeds for his tale of being thrown overboard before the King himself was captured.

The old man was still smiling and staring at Newman, his jet black eyes locked upon Baramir's own, which flitted and darted about the room in order to escape the continual inspection. Then the man muttered something and raised a palm: to first Capell and then Newman. The thing on the floor still appeared asleep and the old man glanced sideways to one of the red-masked guards. He made a sudden nod towards Kattis who was instantly dragged back by the arms leaving Baramir alone before the pair.

The sudden removal of his friend finally spurred Newman to talk. 'Wait a minute –' he began, but his words were cut short by Yetzi's sword butt on the back of his skull. Wincing, he collapsed to his knees and looked up to see the child-thing's face mere feet away from his own, its large eyes now wide and focused upon him.

The creature's eyes were huge white spheres, sitting proud upon its pale and grimy cheeks, the pupils mere dots of black which seemed to bore their way into Newman's very soul. Baramir tried to blink – look away – anything to get those searching orbs out of his sight but he found himself powerless to redirect his own gaze.

'Good… Good,' he heard a voice say and attempted to shout out to Kattis to help him. He felt his lips quiver: the muscles of his mouth spasm momentarily and then lock. Then he saw the thing's pupils widen: growing and expanding far beyond the confines of its face until he realised with numb horror that the dark spots were unchanged and that he was falling helplessly into the dark recess inside. He still could not find a way to voice his rising terror and so, in his frustration and fear, did the only thing he could do. He cried.

Kattis, still held fast by the two red-masked guards, had finally removed his attention from the floor to see Baramir kneeling before the infantile horror which sat at the old man's feet. He saw the thing open its bulbous eyes to stare fixedly at his companion and the shudder which ran down Newman's frame. The old man closed his eyes and held out a bony palm towards Baramir.

'Good... Good,' he whispered and then, with his eyes still shut, gripped the staff he carried with both hands and began hesitantly to speak. As he did so, every sound and every syllable he shaped was mirrored by the diminutive oddity whose gaze remained locked on Baramir's face.

'They are Rialan,' said the old man. 'Though these two have no real comprehension of what that means, or indeed, where they are... ' He paused and blindly turned his head: as if searching for something. 'Aahh... ' he continued after a few moments. 'I can see ships. One... Two, three ships... Possibly more, anchored in a wide harbour. O..Obaln, they call it. A hot place.' The old man suddenly smiled. 'These two are stowing away. Hiding themselves on one of the ships... '
Kattis, who had been flitting his attention from the rigid Newman to the unintelligible words of the old man, jumped when Baramir's voice suddenly poured from the old man's mouth. "Be quiet, you fat fool!" he hissed. "I've not come this far to have your bumbling antics ruin everything!" The old man laughed then, but what he continued to say was unintelligible to Capell. 'They are thieves, but this one – this Baramir Newman – is a sly one.'

To this, Tanikalin, who stood with Yetzi behind the Beck Iph guards, narrowed his eyes at Kattis. Once this is finished, he thought, we can put them in the Judgment Ring where they belong.

The old man had raised his face until it pointed towards the wood panelled ceiling and smiled again. 'Oh, very good! Very, very good,' he announced. 'Baramir treads our master's

path. Death after death…Merciless… Effortless. Beautiful…
But they are pursued, hunted by the Watchmen, and so they
run to find sanctuary on the ships… On the King's ship!' The
old man was nodding to himself. 'The little King… The Fool
King they say… They must hide from sight. Aaah! Baramir
knows the captain… Captain Tolwood. He daren't give them
away… Sly Baramir…The fat fool wants food again so they
raid the provisions on deck… Hello? Who's that? The young
king… Ciro, rocking along the deck towards them.' The old
man frowned, bobbing his head with concentration. 'Is there
someone else there… Yes! Who is that?'

The wide-eyed creature suddenly leapt to its feet as if
scolded and grabbed at the old man's cloak. At the same
instant the old man's eyes flicked open and he patted the
creature gently on its bald head, calming its sudden agitation.
Baramir, immobile for a second, slowly toppled sideways to
lay prostrate on the floor.

'Baramir!' Kattis cried out, suddenly struggling against his
restraint to reach his fallen friend. The two Beck Iph guards
however, held him firm, and a gloved hand was slapped
against his mouth to prevent any further outbursts. All other
eyes were on the old man who took a deep breath and then
addressed Tanikalin.

'Where is your lord?'

'In the next chamber, your reverence,' replied the Patrol
Leader with a slight bow.

'Fetch him. I have news.'

Tanikalin dipped his head again. 'What of the prisoners,
your reverence?'

The old man shrugged. 'The fat one, there –' he pointed at
Kattis '– is of no use whatsoever, so do with him as you see
fit.' He looked down at the immobile form of Baramir. 'This
one, however,' he said, prodding the body with his foot. 'Is

something very special. And I have you to thank for bringing him to me. You've done well, Patrol Leader.'

'Thank you, your reverence.'

'Now bring your lord to me.'

Tanikalin bowed lower and, as the guards, accompanied by a grinning Yetzi, dragged Kattis out of the chamber, he went to fetch Lord Chinek.

Lord Chinek, the bear man, was in the midst of watching two Makech sentries clean Tersic's blood from the carpet: the corpse having been removed to hang from the gibbet near the market. He looked up as Tanikalin and Yetzi returned and watched absently as the latter took over dragging Kattis from the chamber. Tanikalin strode forward and bowed.

'The Soulcatcher, Gidus, says he has news, Lord.'

Chinek nodded and returned his attention to the carpet. Tanikalin waited dutifully for a few moments before breaking the silence.

'He says it's important, Lord, and he wishes to speak with you.' Inwardly, the Patrol Leader wondered how much longer it would be before Chinek was replaced. A reputation forged striding the river of blood was one thing, but a Lord and master who could no longer think straight could be a liability in these strange times. He wondered if Dinevre, Chinek's second in command and presently on some unknown business in Kal Gians, had the guts to challenge for his superior's position. He doubted it; the venomous Dinevre was too cowardly and too shrewd to ever openly oppose Lord Chinek. He might poison him, Tanikalin mused: that would not only suit Dinevre's sly disposition but may well have explained Lord Chinek's current state of health. But, even if Dinevre had some hand in Chinek's mental demise, the toad would probably have gotten someone else to actually carry out the deed. Though Commander Dinevre had over fifty kills to his name, the Patrol Leader knew of no one who had ever seen him in combat. The joke amongst the Makech was that Dinevre possessed a very long sword and had swung it, just once, in a room full of Rialan children.

Tanikalin remembered his own first kill as a child. His parents had purchased a Rialan slave for his ninth birthday and strapped the man to a pole in the centre of a specially built blooding circle. Little Tanikalin had killed the man with his first thrust but had difficulty reaching up to lop the head off. He imagined Dinevre would have had the slave lowered onto his sword to save effort.

Such thoughts made the Patrol Leader frown. Dinevre was just a symptom of a far greater malaise in the Makech people. They had gone soft in these endless decades of supremacy: far from the invigorating life of war which was chronicled in the old stories. Perhaps it was a good thing that these new Rialans were here, considered Tanikalin. It provided an opportunity to fight a proper adversary for a change, instead of the humbled cattle which roamed the land and the stupid Omerk who massed in the mountains around Nish Huiss.

Tanikalin's thoughts were ended when Chinek suddenly broke from watching the carpet being cleaned and walked towards the connecting door. The Patrol Leader quickly fell into step behind his superior and returned through the doors to where the Soulcatcher, Gidus was addressing one of his personal guards.

'Go down to my chamber and return with the silver box that sits inside my travelling chest,' said the old man. The red-masked Beck Iph guard bowed in response and exited the room.

Lord Chinek and Tanikalin stood seemingly unnoticed as the Soulcatcher then ordered Baramir's limp body picked up from the floor and laid upon the absent Commander Dinevre's ornate desk. Tanikalin had been in this room many times, standing dutifully before his Commander's immaculately tidy desk, so could not resist a grin when the Beck Iph swept every object – every paper, every neatly stacked document and quill onto the floor. Dinevre would rage like Sakoom when he returned from Kal Gians and saw what had been done but, Tanikalin knew, that anger would quickly subside when the perpetrators were revealed. Nobody – not even high ranking officers with over fifty dubious kills to their name – would dare complain about the activities of the Dark Square.

The Wraith, Gidus's deformed Omerk, was waddling on bandy legs around the table: gibbering to its master as the Soulcatcher proceeded to arrange the supine prisoner to his satisfaction. Tanikalin watched with equal measure of fascination and unease as the little beast completed yet another circuit and tried to count its shadows in the shifting torchlight. Though it was morning outside, the windows to the chamber had been blocked to protect the monster from Milla's burning gaze and, as it stopped for a moment to babble at Gidus' side, Tanikalin managed to count at least eight grey shadows blossoming from its feet before it scampered around the table once again.

Gidus, his narrow frame bent over the immobile form of Baramir, nodded his satisfaction at the three Beck Iph guards and then paced the short distance to stand before Chinek.

'You seem distracted, Lord Chinek,' the Soulcatcher observed, his eyes mere cracks beneath grey brows as he squinted momentarily into the large man's face. Chinek stood impassively before him and Gidus shrugged. 'No matter, you can still listen.' He pointed to Tanikalin. 'Your officer has done the Empire a great service, Lord: brought us news of grave consequence.'

'What?' Chinek replied blankly as if realising for the first time the Soulcatcher was standing before him.

'These men you captured were washed overboard from a ship,' explained Gidus. 'One of several which were sailing towards Rial. They were very strange vessels; with something Baramir calls engines... And they carried the Rial sun emblem on their sails.'

Chinek looked at the old man impassively but made no sound.

'Sailing from where, your reverence?' asked Tanikalin, daring to interrupt. 'Everyone knows that Rial is a dead land.'

'Sailing "towards"! Not "from"!' snapped the Soulcatcher. He shot a venomous glance at the Patrol Leader which dropped the latter's gaze to the floor. 'Now, if you will listen, rather than interrupt,' Gidus continued, his tone softening, 'I will attempt to enlighten you.' The old man sighed and closed his eyes for a moment before directing his attention towards Tanikalin. 'Now... Where was I? Oh, yes, the ships... These ships – and there are at least five of them – were sailing "from" a place far to the west and had been travelling for more than four weeks before our Kolben Lords, Shernn and Sakoom had their fun. "Sailing from where?" you ask?' Gidus said, mimicking the Patrol Leader. 'Well, I will tell you. There is a place called Feirlan, exactly where in the west I do not know – and neither does he.' The Soulcatcher hitched his thumb at Baramir. 'But it is a place of deserts and heat and where these people have lived for as long as our two prisoners can remember. They, like most people in this land, have never heard of Reilan, let alone the Kingdom of Rial, and they have certainly never heard of us. They consider themselves... What was the word? Feirlaners, I think, and have, or rather had, no interest in Reilan whatsoever. Close your mouth Patrol Leader; I know what you're going to ask: "What changed their minds?" Yes?'

Tanikalin, who had just parted his lips to ask that very question, closed them again and nodded sheepishly. The old man smiled.

'It appears,' continued Gidus, 'that their King, Fidiann, has an adventurous son who found out – somehow – about their ancient connection with Reilan and decided, as hot-headed youths will, to reclaim the ancient Rial throne for himself. To that end he formed a thing called "an expedition": which is merely a polite word for "army", to come from Feirlan to Reilan. He even named his own ship after the last Rial King – who was?' The Soulcatcher flicked his gaze between the two men.

'Elson,' Tanikalin replied. He knew the name well; it was vilified in the ancient texts.

'Very good!' smiled Gidus. 'I like a man who knows his history… Now, this ship, the King Elson was the same ship that our two captives were on and, from what my guards have told me, you believe they were not the only ones to get washed overboard.'

Tanikalin nodded. 'We found out this morning that there is another man, named Ciro, at large. Reports say he has killed four men - the last one at the east gate last night.'

Gidus nodded in return. 'So I have heard,' he said. 'But isn't there something curious about the deaths? Hmmm?'

Tanikalin looked uncomfortable and glanced sideways at his superior: he should have known that such a secret could not be kept from the Dark Square. Beside him, Lord Chinek had a smile on his face and, seemingly oblivious to the conversation, was watching the Omerk continue to run round and round the table. Tanikalin considered gaining his Lord's attention for a second before thinking better of the idea and returning his gaze to the Soulcatcher. He fished a pointed object from his pocket and handed it over to Gidus.

'It was found buried in the sentry's skull at the east gate,' explained Tanikalin. 'We don't know what it is but he had no other injuries. It must be what killed him.'

The Soulcatcher thumbed the metal tip of the flight. 'I know what it is,' he said. 'And, what's more, I know who fired it.' He smiled slyly at the patrol leader.

'This man? This Ciro?'

'Oh... He's not any man, "This Ciro",' replied Gidus with a shake of his head. 'He's none other than the adventure seeking son of King Fidiann: the new King of Rial.' The Soulcatcher watched with amusement as the emotion played across Tanikalin's face and the information sank in. It did not take long before the emotion found voice.

'Do you mean to say that this Ciro, this Rialan scum at large, is their king?!' Tanikalin blurted. He jabbed an accusing finger at Baramir.

'I think that's exactly what I mean,' the Soulcatcher replied. He gave a humourless laugh. 'Baramir didn't know Ciro had also been washed overboard, even though he was there when it happened. But I saw it: saw it with his own eyes. A man named Ciro – their king – dressed in blue with a golden sun on his breast fell into the sea with them.'

Tanikalin made to turn away. 'I'll organise the whole garrison to begin searching –' he said but Gidus gripped his arm.

'All in good time, Patrol Leader, all in good time,' said the Soulcatcher. 'We have many things to consider first... Do you have any patrols out looking for him at the moment?'

'Yes, your reverence,' Tanikalin replied. 'One was dispatched to find him soon after the murder at the gate.'

'Then send a rider to find the patrol,' said Gidus sternly. 'They are not to kill him. Do you understand? Anyone stupid enough to do so will answer to me.'

Tanikalin nodded and, with a bow, left to find a horseman. He got as far as the chamber door when Gidus called after him.

'When you've found a rider, come straight back to me, we have more to talk about.'

The Patrol Leader bowed once more and, as he left the chamber, heard the Soulcatcher talking to Lord Chinek as if he were a child.

It did not take long to dispatch another rider and soon Tanikalin had returned to Dinevre's chamber. He entered to find that the fourth Beck Iph guard had brought back the silver box which the Soulcatcher had asked for and Tanikalin hung back as he watched Gidus bend over the still immobile Baramir.

'Come in, Tanikalin,' said the old man without turning. 'You might be interested in this.'

Hesitantly, the patrol leader approached the large desk and as he did so the smell of burning flesh reached his nostrils. He glanced around for the source and saw that Baramir's forehead now had the symbol of the Dark Square burnt into the centre of it as well as bloody words carved into the skin on either side. He had heard of such ceremonies but was at a loss to understand why it was being carried out on a Rialan. Wasn't this the initiation right for a Soulcatcher?

'You look perplexed,' said Gidus with a smile. 'So you should be. It isn't often that we gain such a prize.' The Soulcatcher fished around inside the silver box and pulled out a strip of glowing silver tied with a leather strap, and then a small phial made of the same metal.

'Are you going to...? To make him...?' Tanikalin stuttered the words: partly from a sense of awe that he was privileged to see such a ceremony but mostly from the fact that, if he had misinterpreted the situation, he did not want to appear stupid.

'Make him a Soulcatcher?' finished Gidus. The Patrol Leader nodded. 'Yes. That's exactly what I intend to do.' The old man turned to one of the Beck Iph guards. 'Hammer,' he said and without pause the guard went in search of one.

The Soulcatcher placed the glowing objects on Baramir's chest and peered into the prisoner's lifeless face before addressing Tanikalin. 'You see,' he said conversationally, 'this man is a very rare find. In fact I cannot think of anyone like him in living memory... It's quite fantastic...' The Soulcatcher seemed lost in thought for a moment.

'How so,' asked Tanikalin. '– If you'll excuse my ignorance,' he quickly added.

'Quite alright,' Gidus replied with a wave of his hand. 'Quite alright. I am indebted to you for bringing him here, as I said, and for preventing that fool – what's his name? – Yetzi, is it? From taking his head off on the beach. A wise and thoughtful decision.' To this Tanikalin bowed. 'Now,' continued the old man, pointing at Baramir. 'What we have here is a Rialan who already walks the Square – and how he walks it! A killer of almost perfect conscience, with such slyness and style that I'll warrant the victims were never even aware of the action until Ebo snatched at their bones.' Gidus chuckled. 'You should see it in there, my boy,' he said, tapping Baramir's head. 'A Rialan more Makech in spirit than most Makech.'

'But can he be trusted, your reverence?' queried Tanikalin. 'Is he worthy of such an honour?'

'He will make a fine Soulcatcher: a veritable master given time and, as far as your concerns go, yes, he can be trusted. He hates his own kind, especially the little king, Ciro. He has been attempting to communicate that sentiment since he realised we were not like his own kind and – Aahh, good,' said Gidus as the guard returned with a hammer. 'Now we can proceed. Would you be so good, Tanikalin, to hold one of Baramir's arms? Rebirth is always a painful experience.'

Nodding, the Patrol Leader did as instructed while a Beck Iph guard moved forward to hold the other arm and another gripped his ankles. Tanikalin watched, fascinated as Gidus then removed the top of the phial and gently shook out a tiny sliver of black crystal into his palm. Tanikalin gasped at the sight and to this the Soulcatcher nodded agreement.

'Indeed,' he said, moving his hand so Tanikalin could get a better look. 'A piece of God: chipped, so legend has it, from the throne of the mighty Unzekka himself.'

Tanikalin closed his eyes and dropped his head. 'I am not worthy of this honour, your reverence,' he said quietly.

'Hm, maybe not,' replied Gidus. 'Now where's that hammer?' The Soulcatcher took the small hammer from the guard and positioned the black sliver in the very centre of the design burnt into Baramir's forehead. The little Omerk began chanting.

'Now, hold him still,' advised Gidus and then, with a single, swift blow, drove the crystal into Baramir's skull.

The effect was instantaneous. Newman, with a flash of pain the like of which he never thought possible, was awake, screaming and attempting to rise. Gidus grabbed the glowing band he had previously placed on Baramir's chest and, with a speed Tanikalin found impressive for one of his age, rushed around the table to strap the object around Baramir's head. The Patrol Leader watched as the Celesdain band faded for a moment upon contact with Newman's skin before bursting into a fire more radiant than before.

'Alright,' said Gidus, flicking his gaze at his assistants. 'Let him go and stand back!'

They all complied and the second he was free, Baramir leapt from the table to stand clutching at the band which seemed stuck fast. Gidus, motioning everyone else to move away, approached the new Soulcatcher as Baramir collapsed to his knees.

'Listen to my voice, Baramir Newman,' whispered Gidus. He moved cautiously forward and placed his hand gently on Baramir's shoulder.

Like a cornered animal, Newman looked up suddenly. His eyes were wide – pain filled and frightened – and the moon iron band around his head glowed more fiercely. The old man winced as Baramir's gaze bored into his own but managed to keep his voice steady.

'Feel the pain subside, my friend,' Gidus said. 'Feel it fade away.'

Baramir blinked, shook his head a fraction and then searched the Soulcatcher's eyes again.

'What can you see, Baramir?'

The searing pain that seemed to have lit Newman's head from the inside was indeed subsiding. He blinked again and heard the old man's voice for the first time. What could he see? He could see… ? Baramir got to his feet and stepped back: looking the old man up and down. There was a dark band around the man's entire body: like a glow of inner light but, instead of light it was as if the fellow was radiating darkness. Amazing, thought Baramir, before his natural suspicion returned and he remembered looking into the eyes of the little monster. Keeping half an eye on the old man – who did nothing but smile at him – Newman took a pace to the left and scanned the room. There was Tanikalin and the four red-masked gargoyles and beside them the little creature with its eyes wide open. They, like every other eye in the room, where directed at him. What is going on?! Thought

Baramir. Something's changed… And where's Kattis got to?

Newman took a few steps towards the group. Why isn't anyone shouting at me? He wondered. He looked back at the old man who was still smiling, then moved a hand to touch the thing on his forehead. He felt a warm glow on his fingertips.

'It will take a little explaining, Baramir Newman,' the old man said, 'but everything you have ever wanted has just come true.'

'Where's Kattis?' asked Baramir. 'I want to see Kattis.'

The old man smiled. 'I'll take you to him. And on the way I'll explain about your good fortune.'

Baramir nodded and was about to speak when he realised the man was not speaking Rialan. 'Very well,' he said in return, but the words came out as: "Gil jamain."

If Baramir's fortunes had veered swiftly upwards, his companion's had taken an opposite, yet equally rapid direction. Unhindered now by any concerns about keeping him alive for questioning, Yetzi:12 had decided to have some fun and his only real dilemma was how close he could bring Kattis to death while still leaving him alive enough for the Judgment Ring. Rules where rules after all, he thought as he treated himself to one final kick in Capell's face.

Kattis had long since stopped desperately trying to cover that area of his body and, having been unconscious for some time now, had been mercifully spared the worst of the ordeal. Yetzi stepped away from Capell's battered form, took the torch from his Makech companion and brought it back into the cell. He crouched down and looked at his handiwork, noting with some small pride the blood, the shattered mess of Capell's nose and the broken tooth on the floor which his last kick had removed.

'Is he dead, Yetzi?' asked his fellow guard.

Yetzi shrugged. 'Who cares?' he replied and stood up as the sound of distant footsteps sounded in the corridor.

'Beck, Yetzi,' whispered the other guard, looking into the shadows. 'I think it's the boss!'

Frowning, Yetzi peered around the cell door and saw Tanikalin – now Tanikalin: 27 since the murder of the farm hand – pass through a pool of torchlight at the head of the four towering Beck Iph guards. They were coming their way and Yetzi shot a worried glance at his companion before handing him the torch. What did they want? He thought. Don't say they wanted to question the prisoner! Beck! The Soulcatcher had said he didn't need him! Yetzi looked quickly back into the cell but, even though Capell was all but hidden in shadow, he knew that the man would be in no fit state to do anything for a while – if ever.

Their Patrol Leader was closer now and the stern look on his face confirmed Yetzi's worst suspicions. He was in trouble.

The four Beck Iph guards, their massive frames filling the cramped corridor, stopped a few feet from the cell. Tanikalin stepped forward, the same grim expression on his face.

'Where's the other prisoner, Yetzi?' he asked and the dispassionate, almost leaden tone of his voice made the guards quail.

Yetzi said nothing in response but moved aside from the door and dropped his head. Tanikalin, his eyes still firmly locked on his colleague, stepped into the cell and took a brief look at the battered figure of Capell. He stepped back and Yetzi looked up to meet his eyes.

Slowly, Tanikalin shook his head. 'He's in here, your reverence.'

Yetzi had not been able to see past the bulk of the Beck Iph guards but now he watched nervously as the old Soulcatcher pushed his way through. Only it was not the old man, and the sight of Baramir Newman, celesdain band strapped upon his forehead made Yetzi's nerve fail. He dropped to his knees as the thin frame of the new Soulcatcher passed him and felt a numbness overwhelm his senses as the footsteps stopped in the cell. Yetzi searched Tanikalin's face for some sign of compassion but his Patrol Leader had locked his eyes on the brickwork of the corridor: his face an impassive mask.

There was a moment of silence, during which time Gidus silently led his little Wraith through the gap in the guards but all Yetzi was aware of was the rapid beating of his own heart.

'Hm,' said Baramir from the cell before stepping out into the light. 'I suppose I have to ask – although I already know the answer – but perhaps you could tell me, Tanikalin, who reduced my friend to a bloody mess?' He raised an eyebrow at the Patrol Leader who dropped his gaze towards Yetzi.

'I would hazard a guess that it was Yetzi: 12, your reverence,' Tanikalin replied. Baramir nodded and followed the Patrol Leader's gaze.

'Yes,' he agreed, smiling down at the top of Yetzi's head. 'I would hazard that guess as well.' He flicked a glance at Gidus and saw the old man chuckling.

'No finesse,' continued Newman with a shake of his head. 'No style whatsoever. Yetzi: 12, bludgeoning his way to thirteen.' Baramir crouched before the kneeling Makech. 'An unlucky number for some, they say,' he whispered and then a broad grin split his face as Yetzi raised his head to stare venomously back.

'I should have killed you on the beach!' spat Yetzi. To this the four Beck Iph guards raised their arms to the sword hilts on their shoulders and Tanikalin too touched the pommel of his own weapon. Baramir continued to smile.

'Yes,' agreed Newman, 'perhaps you should have. But then we can't be blessed with good looks and brains, can we? Or in your case, Yetzi, neither.' To this Gidus laughed out loud and Baramir stood up. He looked at the grim face of Tanikalin beside him. 'My Master, Gidus, informs me that you do not know what killed your guard at the gate?'

Tanikalin nodded. 'Yes, your reverence, it's true.'

Baramir fished inside his jacket and pulled out his pocket watch. 'It always puzzled me –' he said conversationally while winding the mechanism, '– both Capell and myself in fact, why you never took this from me.' He held the object before Tanikalin's face and the Patrol Leader shrugged. 'Just as well, I suppose,' Baramir continued. 'Can you tell the time, Yetzi?' he suddenly asked and crouched before the guard again. 'Hhmm?'

Baramir gripped the watch in his hand, his thumb on the winder. He looked across to see Gidus's face alive with interest, smiled at the old man then returned his attention to Yetzi.

'Time's up, Yetzi!' Newman said and pressed the winder.

There was a sharp snap, magnified in the confines of the corridor and a sudden explosion of blood on Yetzi's forehead as his head was thrown back. His body followed and Yetzi fell backwards: dead before he had hit the floor.

Baramir stood up, pleased by the look of unrestrained awe on everybody's face. Even the impassive masks of the Beck Iph guards seemed impressed.

'It's called a clockwork repeater,' explained Newman, handing the device to an open-mouthed Tanikalin. 'I had it specially made a few years ago by a master craftsman in–' Baramir stopped in mid-sentence, frowned and looked down at Yetzi's body sprawled upon the flagstone floor. It was still moving. He cast a glance at Gidus.

'Look closely Baramir,' the old Soulcatcher advised and Newman returned his attention to the strange motion of the body.

The grey glow which had previously surrounded Yetzi was moving now, like a morning mist slowly evaporating in the sunshine. Tendrils of grey, sparking here and there with patches of light swayed and swept around the body. Baramir moved closer, fascinated by the strange sight and felt a warmth began to spread itself through his mind as the strands of mist changed course towards him.

Newman could see some recognition of shape within the swirling forms now and found it difficult to suppress his surprise. It was Yetzi! Where are you going, Yetzi? Baramir thought to himself, before, in a sudden surge, the grey mist that was Yetzi's soul formed a vortex and sped its way into the new Soulcatcher's forehead.

Newman staggered backwards. Images, faces, landscapes of a world he had never seen before flooding into his mind.

'Hold him,' he heard Gidus say distantly and then a firm grip on his arm prevented him from falling.

Newman smiled: the chaotic flashes of memory receding to a part of his mind he had not experienced before, as if a whole new chamber of thought had opened its door to him. What was Yetzi's – all that Yetzi had seen and had been – were now stored beyond that door: a frightened form out of its proper place. Curious, Newman examined the thing – the Yetzi form – prodded it with his own intellect and felt its fear. He laughed. Was it out loud? Or just in his mind? No matter. The old man had been right: this was the greatest fortune imaginable.

'Thank you, Tanikalin,' Baramir said over his shoulder and the Patrol Leader withdrew the supporting arm. Newman retrieved his watch and turned to face Gidus.

'How do you feel?' the old man inquired.

Baramir nodded. 'Better than ever, Master.'

'And so you should; you are now twice the man that you were,' Gidus replied. He looked thoughtful for a moment then peeked into the cell. 'My men will carry your friend to your new chambers, Newman, where my Wraith will heal his wounds.' His eyes strayed to the lifeless form of Yetzi. 'And then,' he said, 'I think we should eat.'

IV

The day threatened rain which never materialised and the sky, first marbled then patched with white and grey finally cleared to a hazy blue by the afternoon. Amec marched them north at first, clear of the hill range, then east again as the sun reached its zenith. Ciro had never seen, certainly never read, anything about the strange landscape that existed here beyond Forht but became quickly bored by the maze-like qualities of the countryside. The entire region snaked with miniature rocky canyons choked with tree and plant life and from a distance it seemed as if some demented stone mason had practised his wall building skill across the whole area. Only when they drew close to the first line of 'walls' did it become apparent that no hand had made the rocks this way and, after leading them another mile to the north, Amec seemed to find the route he was looking for and prepared to take the group deeper into the maze.

The cave outside Forht had supplied the party with two rusting swords, left there a long time ago, Amec informed them, by other Philiri. Keeping one for himself, the big man had given the other to Arper and now the pair drew the yard-long blades to hack their way deeper into the plant choked confines of the stone maze.

Ciro had noticed the curious way in which Amec suggested they carry their swords, the scabbard strapped to their backs rather than at their side. He remembered the Songsmith, Calian's explanation of why his group always carried their quarter-staffs in the same position.

'A prince will rarely find himself without a swift horse,' Calian had explained. 'Yet, for an ordinary man, fast legs are his only carriage. A sword at the waist is for those who ride and a sword on your back for those who run.'

Ciro remembered doubting the logic of the arrangement at the time, but then, no one in Feirlan had used swords since the invention of the hand and fire lances many years before. It had only been later, when the young King found himself fettered with such a weapon, that he had realised how Calian's words made perfect sense.

It had been during his own Ascension Day Procession, when he had had to walk, and not ride, the 'King's Line' from the edge of Obaln Harbour to Torr Sarvie. Amongst the Royal regalia he had been duty bound to wear on that dry, hot day, was a ceremonial sword which had clanked, squeaked and banged itself against his leg with every step of the two mile journey. Ciro still believed that, had he not been irritated to distraction by its continually noisy presence, the ensuing confrontation with his father, King Fidiann in the Ascension Chamber might never have happened. Perhaps even the course he had set himself might have failed at that final obstacle if his emotions had been less strained. How many times had he spoken to his father since? Ciro mused. Three? Perhaps four times? Arper broke his train of thought.

'Why don't we just go round?' he said after taking several half-hearted swipes at the foliage.

'Because,' Amec replied with a frown, 'if it's not easy for us, just think how difficult it'll be on horseback. No Makech would bother trying to come this way, which means we'll be safe.'

'But,' Arper replied, shaking his head, 'this'll take us an age.'

'About a hundred yards in it'll thin out,' said the Philiri with certainty. 'And once we're on the wall it'll not take us long to reach Olbas Osanti.'

Arper nodded and was about to resume hacking when Ciro held up a hand. 'Wait a minute, Amec. Arper.' he said.

The Philiri cocked his head and raised a brow as Ciro stepped forward. 'Don't tell me,' Amec said wearily, 'you've thought of a better idea.'

Ciro smiled in response and shook his head. 'Before we cut a path clear through these bushes, I was just wondering what a Makech patrol might make of finding such a recently made clearing in this tangle.' He cast his gaze around the group to see if they were following his train of thought. There seemed to be some signs of recognition on the faces of the others yet Amec simply looked more exasperated.

'If we had walked along and found the path we are beginning to make,' Ciro continued, 'wouldn't we know that someone had recently cut it?'

'Are ya sayin' that we shouldn't cut a path?' asked Arper.

'There's no other way in,' growled Amec. 'Either we cut a path or we walk around some twenty miles. In the open.' He levelled his gaze at the young king. 'Is that what you want to do, your Royal Highness?'

Despite himself, Ciro found there was an edge to his voice as he replied: the same tone, he realised afterwards, that his father had so often used on him when patiently re-explaining matters of state or duty. 'We cut a path, but we don't start it here. We push through the bushes for ten, perhaps twenty feet – then we start the path. That way this foliage will look exactly the same as is does now: untouched. And the Makech will not have the benefit of following our trail. Understand?'

Arper and Nesh both lifted their heads back as one: their mouths silent 'O's as the explanation sank in. Amec's forehead became a mass of parallel ridges.

'This is a big country,' the Philiri replied, 'and the chances of the Makech discovering this clearing are slim.'

'I'd rather they was none,' said Nesh and Amec let out a heavy sigh.

'Right! Come on then,' he declared, pushing both arms then a leg into the greenery. 'Let's do what his Majesty orders!'

Ciro gazed on impassively as the large shape of Amec slowly disappeared into the tangle of bushes. Arper sucked his teeth and cast a sympathetic look in Ciro's direction before he too followed Amec's lead.

Nesh drew near and gripped Ciro's arm. 'I'd rather 'ave Amec un'appy than the Bonemen right be'ind us... An' besides,' she said, regarding the hole the two men had made, ''e seems to be un'appy so often.'

To this Ciro shrugged as the sound of frantic chopping came from beyond the bushes and, after a few moments they followed the two men into the maze. They kept their distance as the dull blades cut a slow path in the greenery ahead and, feeling surplus to requirements, Ciro wondered how long it would take them to pass through the thick tangle.

An hour later Ciro was beginning to think that Arper's original idea about circumnavigating the area had been the right one. Arper and Amec had spent over an hour creating explosions of wildlife in the foliage before them but the further they progressed the thicker the intertwined branches seemed to become. He had asked several times if he could help but, though Arper seemed exhausted, Amec had snapped at him both times to stay back. Reluctantly, Ciro watched the slow progress of the pair and quizzed Nesh about Olbas Osanti.

'If I remember right,' Nesh said, 'it's an old village in the centre of this warren. Old folk say it was the last refuge of the rebels before the Bonemen took the 'ole country.'

'Does anyone still live there?' Ciro inquired, Nesh shook her head before making the sign of the Eight.

'The story goes that the Makech decided to make an example of the villagers. Those that weren't carted across the desert an' inta slavery were taken to all the surrounding towns an' strung up in the main squares.' To this Ciro looked grim. Nesh continued: 'Nowadays, I think Olbas Osanti's where the Philiri go to swap old stories from round the country.' She smiled, the first Ciro could recall since the farmhouse, but it was tinged with sadness. 'They say it was beautiful once – but I don't suppose it is now.'

'Where many Rial taken into slavery?' asked Ciro.

Nesh shrugged. ''bout 'alf of every city, town an' village were 'erded south ta begin with – less as the years wen'on. You don't 'ear of it 'appenin' much nowadays, but that's because there're so few of us left. They're probably waitin' 'til our numbers go up again – I wouldn't put it past the bastards. They see us as nothin' more'n cattle as it is.' With that Nesh lapsed into silence and tugged at a bright wildflower which drooped from the high rock wall beside them. She sniffed at the bloom, span it momentarily between her fingers then pushed it behind her ear. She seemed self conscious that Ciro had witnessed the act then gave him a wan smile.

'Ma always liked fresh flowers,' she said and a wave of emotion suddenly crumpled her face. She blinked back tears and clung onto Ciro as he put a consoling arm around her shoulder. He felt her sobs shiver down her thin body, and looked ahead to where Arper and Amec hacked mechanically at the bushes.

'I'll get Arper,' said Ciro quietly. It was the only thing he could think to say.

Nesh sniffed and pulled away from him, wiped her eyes and attempted a grin. 'S'alright,' she replied, her face red. 'I'm fine. Don't bother Arper, 'e'll only worry.'

Ciro nodded and gave Nesh another hug. 'I think I'll get him anyway,' he said, pointing to her uncle. 'It looks like he could do with a rest.' Before she could protest, the king strode forward to fetch Arper and take his place

Nesh's uncle needed no persuading, and this time Amec made no complaints. Arper stretched life back into his aching arm, handed Ciro the sword and stepped away from the wall of ivy which stood before him. Ciro winked at the sweating Amec and started vigorously chopping at the plant life.

An hour later the swords were unneeded: the vines and bushes scant enough to allow unobstructed passage and Amec led a circuitous route between the snaking maze of rock until the ground rose to a wide plateau, level with the top of the walls. Here the Philiri called a halt and, as the others rested, Ciro and Nesh surveyed the maze of rock lines which could now be seen snaking out in all directions.

'I didn't appreciate it from down below,' remarked Ciro, 'but from up here it looks incredible.' He turned to take in the complex swirls of stone that faded into the distance. 'I can't believe it's natural.'

'It ain't,' responded Amec from behind them. The tall Philiri had taken the scabbard from his back to stretch out with his head on his backpack but he now sat up to point past Ciro. 'Legend says that Ebo came here once – fell asleep – an' his snores shook the earth so much that this was formed.'

Though Calian and the other Songsmiths had often spoken to Ciro of the Kolben – the mythical Lords of the Elements –

the young king still had difficulty remembering what each one represented. 'Ebo is the Lord of the earth, isn't he?' He said. Amec nodded.

'I've 'eard the same tale, but with Lady Fenya sleepin', not Ebo,' added Arper.

'Well,' shrugged Amec, leaning back, 'whoever it was, they certainly could snore.'

Ciro returned to viewing the maze and sat down beside Nesh as she dangled her legs from the edge of the wall.

'Ma named me after one of the Kolben,' she said, nodding to herself.

'Which one?' Ciro asked.

'Gallia,' Nesh replied. 'I-gallia-nesh – means seashell.' To this Ciro nodded silently. Nesh shrugged and frowned at the landscape. 'It's not really, I mean, not properly 'er name, but… Well, 'er name is in there.'

Ciro smiled. 'It's a lovely name, Igallianesh. It suits you.'

Nesh's face lit up as if an inspiration had suddenly occurred to her and she scampered over to where her bag lay beside her uncle.

'That's why I've always collected seashells,' she said: returning to show Ciro the small box she had rescued from the farmhouse. It was packed with black and white striped shells. 'Ma always said they'd bring me luck an'… Well…' Nesh's face clouded for a second. 'I used to sell 'em in Cabon market,' she continued, 'to the Bonemen sometimes – but never the good 'uns.' She shook her head. 'Menzir didn't like me makin' money but –'

Her face clouded again, a deep frown ridging her brow and Ciro saw tears begin to well in her eyes. She fought them back, closed the box of shells and let out a huge sigh.

'D'ya think the Makech'll find us here?' she asked distantly, looking out across the maze.

It was a question Ciro had been considering himself since their rapid exit from Forht: just how would the Makech go about finding them? Would patrols be sent out, or an army? How big a threat did their actions pose? How long would it take for the news to travel? For the garrisons to be mobilised? He voiced his concerns to the others and for once Amec chose not to find his questions an affront.

'There's maybe a hundred Makech garrisoned back in Forht,' replied the Philiri, 'and... What would you say Arper? About thirty, forty, in Cabon?' Arper nodded. 'But,' continued Amec, 'I doubt they'll send 'em all – they don't have that many horses. An' they'll not search for us on foot.'

'So,' replied Ciro, thinking aloud. 'We're safe in this warren... But what about when we leave it?'

Amec shrugged. 'I never claimed the journey would be easy, but let's not worry about things too far ahead, yer majesty.' With that the Philiri stood, lifted his pack onto his shoulder and pointed east to where a group of distant trees could be seen poking above the rock lines. 'Once we've arrived at Olbas, we can plan our next move. I've a friend there from Philire an' another who visits from Urawiir. They'll be able to help us.'

'This place we're heading for,' said Ciro, following Amec's outstretched arm. 'What's to stop the Makech getting there? Is this route the only way in?'

A shadow of disdain flashed quickly across Amec's face, but it passed as suddenly as it appeared. He shook his head. 'Olbas Osanti sits in the middle of this maze and the only clear route in is a small river. The road has been disused for so long you'd need good eyes to spot it. The Makech never go there.'

'There's nobody left to kill,' said Arper with a bitter smile and with that the party began to make ready to move on.

Amec walked onto the foot-wide top of one of the rock walls and stood for a moment with his hands on his hips, scanning the path before him.

'Watch my lead, and watch your feet,' he said, turning to the group. 'Some of this rock ain't safe and a lot of it's overgrown. If I stop, you stop. If you fall – 'He kicked a stone over the twenty foot drop and Ciro noted a rabbit suddenly bolt from a bush. 'If the fall don't kill ya, you'd be useless for travelling, so… ' He shrugged. 'Don't fall.'

One by one they fell into step behind Amec, Nesh first, then Arper and finally Ciro. The young king cast his gaze south towards the vague hill range they had travelled from that morning and wondered just how secure the area really was from the Makech. If Amec saw this place to be the safest around, wouldn't their pursuers think the same?

As he negotiated the narrow path before him, Arper flicked his gaze back and grinned at Ciro. 'Tell us more 'bout this other country of yours,' he said. 'This Feirlan.'

'What would you like to know?' answered Ciro.

'Oh… I dunno,' Arper replied with a shrug. ''ow big is it? Is it as big as Reilan?'

'No,' said Ciro, 'it's much smaller: though twice as big as we once believed.'

Arper laughed. 'What's that mean? Is it a riddle?'

'No,' replied Ciro, his attention momentarily at his feet to negotiate a crumbling depression in the rock. 'What I mean is that Feirlan's a very hot country, with a vast wasteland called the Nelan Desert in the centre. Some brave souls had travelled into it in the past, but no one had ever crossed it. We just assumed it went on for ever… We were wrong. It transpires that part of the original exodus from Rial sailed further south and those that survived the ocean reefs settled in a place they call New Kindor. We didn't know they existed until a wandering band of these people walked out of the desert about three years ago.'

'If yer desert's anythin' like the one past Kal Santra then they must've bin tough ta survive it.' Arper stretched out his arms for balance as the wall thinned and walked slowly forwards. 'I saw it… ' His voice trailed off, lost for a second in concentration. 'Yeah, I saw it once,' he continued once the wall had widened. 'Beckin' awful place! Sand, heat… Makech everywhere.'

Ciro crossed the same space, watching his every step and the bush-filled drop on either side.

'The people who came out of the desert call themselves Songsmiths,' Ciro said, 'and they have a peculiar affinity with nature.' The king grasped Arper's outstretched hand and cleared the narrow part of the wall. He nodded thanks and they moved on.

'So they didn't find the desert 'ard ta cross?' queried Arper.

Ciro laughed. "It's all a question of trust," so the Songsmiths informed me. But what amazed us most was not that they had managed a feat we thought impossible, but that they were there at all. We had lived for nearly five hundred years without looking beyond the boundaries of Feirlan so you can imagine how the sight of outlanders seemed.'

Arper chuckled. 'I'd wager money it's a bit like findin' a king washed up on the beach.'

Ciro smiled back. 'Almost identical, I should think,' he replied. 'But the Songsmiths are a very special group – a sort of religious order back in their home of New Kindor – and their music has to be heard to be believed. When we get to Peimonac I'll introduce you to Calian and the others.'

'I'm not such a bad musician me'self,' said Arper. 'I've played inns from Cabon ta Kal Santra.' He sighed. 'I brought me flute with me but 'aven't 'ad the guts ta play it… Ya never know oo's listin'.'

Ciro nodded. 'The Songsmiths carry their instruments wherever they go too. They wear these jointed, wooden belts around their waists which they lay flat and they play on them with these slender, 'L' shaped hammers... Quorum hammers they call them. It's an amazing sound, like nothing we'd ever heard before in Feirlan. Have you ever come across anything like that on your travels?' Ciro asked.

Arper shook his head. 'Amec's ya man fer anythin' strange,' he said. ''e's wandered all over.'

'Hm,' replied Ciro. 'It's fascinated me since the Songsmiths travelled into Feirlan how five hundred years can change the same people.'

'I don't folla,' said Arper with a frown.

'Well, Feirlan has advanced in a different way to New Kindor, or so the Songsmith's say.'

'You've not bin down ta this New Kindor then?'

'Nooo,' Ciro shook his head. 'Even after – or rather – especially after Calian and the others described the journey they had made, I had no desire to make a return trip through the Nelan Desert. Feirlan's hot enough as it is without having to endure... What was it they called it?' Ciro wracked his brain to think of the expression Calian had used. "Milla's stare!" That was it,' he said finally.

Arper laughed. "Milla irasii", that's what that is in the Makech tongue. If you ever wanna insult a Boneman, say: "Milla irasii emo bi!" It means the sun's starin' at ya: an' they don't like bein' reminded that Milla's on our side.'

'There's little record of the Makech religion,' said Ciro, always fascinated by such archaic detail. 'Don't they worship the Kolben?'

'Oh, they worship the Kolben alright!' Arper said, before the attention of both men was drawn by Amec, now quite

179

some way along the curve of the wall.

'Come on!' yelled the Philiri, waving back. 'What're you doin' back there?!'

Ciro and Arper exchanged a quick glance. Neither had particularly noticed how far they had fallen behind. The young king shrugged, and they continued on their way.

'So,' said Ciro, after a minute of wall walking had passed silently. 'The Makech also worship the Kolben.'

'The Bonemen only follow the Kolben Lords: Shernn, Ebo, Sakoom and Sosh. They've got no time for the Ladies.' Arper shook his head. 'Stupid bastards don't think they're strong enough.'

'And you?' Ciro asked. 'Who do you follow?'

'All of 'em!' Arper said. He turned and grinned, then pointed at the sun. 'But above 'em all is Milla. Without 'er there wouldn't be no Kolben.'

'And what about Beck?' Ciro inquired.

'Beck?' Arper shrugged. 'Some Makech follow 'im only an' they're the worst.' He took a few more steps before stopping and when he turned to face Ciro there was a grim expression on his face. 'An' even worse than that – if ya c'n believe it – are the ones't call 'emselves the Beck Iph: the Dark Square. I ain't seen 'em meself – Amec says 'e 'as – but one day I will.'

'Why?' asked Ciro. 'Why would you want to see them?'

To this Arper sighed. 'Word is, they're the scum that killed me wife.' His lips compressed to a hard line and he stared blankly out across the maze. 'Soulcatcher 'e was, plucked 'er right off the street in Forht. Dunno why, dunno what for. Bonemen never need no real reason. All I know is next day she's 'angin' from the gibbet by the market.'

'I'm so sorry, Arper,' said Ciro.

Arper shrugged. 'It was a while back, but I ain't forgotten.

An' now, with all this 'appenin', 'oo knows? I might get ta find 'im. An' when I do – sure as the sun shines now – I'll catch 'is Beckin' soul an' stamp on it.'

With a look of firm resolution, Arper turned away and strode the rest of the wall's summit as if daring it to harm him. Ciro, more cautious in his footing, attempted vainly to keep up with Arper's reckless pace until slowly, through twist and turn, they had reached their destination and the remains of Olbas Osanti sat before them beneath the trees.

Derelict for more than a generation, nature had done its best to reclaim the village. Beneath the branches of the oaks which grew in profusion beside the rock wall they had just negotiated a single, raged wall could be glimpsed below. Ivy covered, with a large hole which must have once been a window; it seemed to be all that remained of the village. Ciro wanted to ask Amec if that was the case but the Philiri had wandered further down the wall and was intently studying the trees.

Ciro paused for a moment and gazed down into the shade beneath the oaks, listening to the twitter of birds and the rustle of a gentle breeze through the leaves. Nesh and Arper had followed Amec along the wall but Ciro hung back for a few seconds more, enjoying the unexpected sensation of tranquillity. The place seemed like a hidden pocket of calm, he thought, wrapped within the barrier of the maze. Ciro glanced back to where the green line of the southern hill range could still just be made out.

'It's more like the eye of a hurricane,' he corrected himself. 'With the Bonemen waiting for us when we go back outside'. The sentiment broke Ciro's mood and with a sigh he checked that his hand lance was fully wound then walked on after the others.

He caught up with them beside a tree whose branch blocked

181

their path. Amec was leaning on it, while Arper and Nesh stared over at the vertical drop.

'So this is 'ow we get down?' Nesh asked. She did not sound happy at the prospect.

Amec nodded and pointed along the branch. Where it met the trunk a line of wooden pegs had been driven into the bark which faced the wall. Amec shrugged his pack from his shoulders and dropped it down to the base of the tree.

'Watch me,' he said then gripped the branch with both hands and swung out from the wall.

With slow sways the Philiri moved hand over hand towards the trunk before steadying his foot on a peg and descending to the ground.

'C'mon,' he shouted up. 'It's easy!'

One by one, they threw their packs down near Amec's and clambered out from the wall. Nesh went first: cautiously and with much encouragement from the others, then Arper and finally Ciro.

The young king retrieved his pack from the base of the tree then joined the others by the ruined wall as they surveyed the landscape beyond. Dusk was descending and the oaks threw long, cool shadows over the group as they helped one another re-shoulder their packs. Ciro sniffed the air.

There was a strong smell of earth beneath the trees but it mixed with a pungent fragrance which Ciro did not recognise. Arper, noticing the king's nose wrinkle, pointed to where the tree line stopped. Beyond was open ground which climbed gently to a tree lined rise and the space in between was filled with countless wild flowers.

'That's what 'appens when ya leave yer crops untended,' said Arper and gradually Ciro could make out a rough symmetry in the space past the wall: the remains of more walls marking overgrown field boundaries.

Nesh pointed at the ivy covered ruin beside them. 'Is this it?' she asked, voicing Ciro's earlier unspoken question.

Amec shook his head. 'This is one of the old farms,' he said, then pointed up the hill to the trees. 'The main village is over that rise, less than half a mile.' The tall Philiri glanced at the deepening sky. 'Plenty o' light left,' he said to no one in particular before wading into the waist high wild flowers.

The others followed in his wake and quickly found that the smell from the wildflowers became overpowering. From a distance the fragrance was pleasant but here, in the midst of them, the aroma strengthened to a cloying stench. They also discovered that the flowers grew from tangled stems which caught at the feet and it was not long before they all adopted Amec's strange but practical step which brought their knees up to their chest with every stride. Walking beside Ciro, Nesh giggled and stopped.

'What is it?' the king asked.

Nesh covered her mouth and looked apologetic. 'It's them two,' she said, pointing forward to Arper and Amec. 'They look like string puppets from the show in Cabon market.'

Ciro had no idea what show Nesh was referring to but if it was anything like the Children's Theatre in Obaln he knew exactly what she meant. He watched the pair for a moment as they high-stepped clumsily and gave a half-smile. 'I bet we look worse,' he said and they continued on until the farm land ended with a stone wall and the flowers gave way to patchy grass.

'Who do you expect to find in the village, Amec?' Ciro asked as he vaulted the perimeter wall which sat at the bottom of the rise. He turned to give Nesh a hand as she scrambled over the ragged stonework and the pair brushed vainly at the orange pollen which had stained their clothes.

Amec, a few paces in front plucked a tall grass stem from

the ground and stuck it in the corner of his mouth. 'Tenc'll be there,' he said, chewing on the stem. 'Mara maybe… We'll have to see. But Tenc'll be there,' Amec stated with a nod. 'He lives here.'

''ope e's got some food on,' muttered Arper. 'Me stomach thinks me throat's been cut.'

'We've still got cheese, Uncle,' Nesh said. 'An' bread,' she added. 'An' pickles.'

'Ooh,' Arper groaned and patted his shirt. 'Don't go on so – me stomach'll 'ere ya.' His face was distorted in agony for a second, then he winked and gave Nesh a smile.

'Tenc should have plenty of food,' grinned Amec looking on. 'He's been cultivatin' the far farm for years now.' He patted Arper on the shoulder. 'We'll all eat well tonight, an' then we can plan for tomorrow.'

The group strolled up the rise and into the woods at its summit. Ciro found the same peaceful air present beneath the trees and listened contentedly to the gentle sounds of nature all around them. The others didn't even seem to notice. The undergrowth rustled with every step they took deeper into the wood and each tree that they passed seemed filled with a dozen different sounds. The ground began sloping down almost as soon as they made the summit and a moss banked pond steered them south before they could descend towards the village.

'There's fish in there,' Amec said casually as they passed its southern bank and he turned to see that Ciro had stopped. 'What's the matter with you?' he asked, almost breaking into a grin at the comical look of concentration on Ciro's face. Arper and Nesh also stopped to regard the king.

'Does Tenc keep horses?' Ciro asked, his head still cocked to one side.

Amec snorted. ''e doesn't even have oxen! An' you know

the Bonemen don't allow –' Amec stopped in mid sentence as the sound which Ciro had heard a moment before came again, loud enough for them all to hear. There was a horse in the village – and that meant only one thing.

'Stay here!' hissed Amec to Ciro and the others and he drew his sword. Ciro shook his head and pulled his hand lance from its holster.

'I'm coming with you,' he said firmly. 'Arper, you stay with Nesh until we come back.'

Arper nodded and slowly drew his own sword. He looked pale, nervous and eyed the wooded slope warily. Ciro drew close and gripped his shoulder lightly.

'Listen out for us,' Ciro said, addressing Nesh as well. 'If you hear either of us shout 'Milla irasii!' Run back to the maze.' They both nodded and Ciro grinned at the worried look on Arper's face. 'We'll scout the village and see what's down there, then come straight back. We'll be no more than a few minutes.' He patted Arper's shoulder and the man managed a grimace.

'C'mon,' hissed Amec and, with a last smile back at the others, Ciro followed the Philiri cautiously down the slope.

The remains of Olbas Osanti were more recognisable than the farmhouse by the maze wall had been and, as the trees thinned, Ciro could glimpse complete shells of cottages jumbled amongst the ever-present vegetation. He followed Amec's lead: keeping low and only moving from bush to bush when the Philiri gestured him forwards, until they reached the spot which Amec had been creeping towards.

To the north of the village the wooded slope rose dramatically and a chalk-faced cliff split the grass where before there had been a gentle slope. From a gap between two trees which clung to the top of the cliff, the pair surveyed the village: Ciro listening as Amec described the various buildings.

'Tenc always uses the mill,' the Philiri said and drew his companion's attention to a large weathered structure in the distance partially obscured by a willow tree.

Ciro, with an almost unrestricted view of Olbas Osanti and the river which meandered through its heart, moved his gaze from the bridge just visible at the other end of the village and left along the curving street of roofless cottages which swept towards them on both sides of the river. On the opposite bank the curve ended with the mill beside the water.

'Is that where you want to head for?' Ciro asked.

Amec gave a single short nod in response but his attention seemed elsewhere: his eyes flicking continuously around the village for signs of life. He let out a small snort of air, his jaw set.

'D'ya think we might 'ave been mistaken with the noise?' he asked.

Ciro too scanned the peaceful scene of Olbas Osanti then shook his head. 'No,' he answered quietly, 'that was definitely a horse we heard. We may not be able to see them but I'll bet you a 'King's Promise' they are down there.'

Amec snorted again: a reluctant agreement. 'We'll have ta make for the bridge at the far end, then move back down towards the mill.' He weighed his sword in his hand then pointed to Ciro's hand lance. 'How far does that thing of yours fire?' he asked.

'Well... ' shrugged Ciro. 'It can fell a running deer at two hundred yards –'

'– We aren't hunting deer,' Amec observed tersely. 'We're hunting Makech.'

'Yes,' Ciro replied with a smile, 'and they don't run as fast.' Amec's brow furrowed. 'Don't worry,' Ciro continued. 'It can fire far enough to keep the Makech at arm's length if necessary.' He pointed to the row of cottages that ran along their side of the river. 'Shall we explore?' he said and, with Amec leading the way, the pair doubled back through the woods.

The undergrowth had not appeared imposing from their vantage point on the ridge but now, shoulder high amongst ferns and bracken, Ciro questioned the wisdom of travelling along what had once been the main street. Like the tangled maze before, the enclosed space was choked with plant life which made progress not only slow but noisy. Ciro felt another looping line of bracken grip around his leg and pulled it free with a loud rip. He looked over to where Amec was attempting to keep his large frame below the fern line and heard the same sound of tearing bracken emanate from his companion.

'Amec!' he hissed, keeping his gaze on the road before them in case of company. 'This is no good. We should go back into the forest and circle around.' Amec pushed forward a few more paces and then stopped.

'Keep closer to the walls!' the Philiri growled back. 'The ferns are thinner there.'

Ciro shook his head but complied, moving slowly to the cottage shells which backed on to the river. The plant life was indeed thinner, but not by any great degree and here the hidden ground was littered with broken stonework. Ciro stumbled and tripped his way along for several more minutes before, in a narrow gap between two cottages, a worn path of trampled ferns and nettles appeared which provided an unrestricted route down to the riverside.

'Amec!' Ciro hissed again and the Philiri shot a venomous glance in his direction, expecting, Ciro had no doubt, some further complaint to be voiced. Ciro pointed between the cottages. 'Pathway!' he explained and moved into the space, waiting for Amec to join him.

While he waited, Ciro walked down the path to see what lay at the other end and pondered the question of why the foot-worn ground suddenly ceased at the fern clogged road. The answer, it seemed, lay at his feet in the form of rotting apples and above the walls on both sides of the path, apple trees rose up into the early evening sky. Someone, it seemed, collected apples often enough to keep the path well trodden. Beyond the passage a strip of short grass ran along the rear of the cottages with a ragged line of bushes and willows hiding the murmuring river from sight. Ciro shivered, the shadows beneath the apple trees cold as the warmth of the day faded with the light and he returned to the road to find what was keeping Amec.

The Philiri was nowhere to be seen and Ciro felt a deeper chill run through him as he searched the road for signs of Amec's whereabouts. It was replaced with exasperation when he saw his companion's head bob above a stone wall much further along the street and Ciro almost gave voice to his frustration. Why had Amec ignored him and gone on alone?

Ciro chewed his lower lip. He really did not understand this man at all. Not only did his actions not make rational sense to Ciro, they didn't make tactical sense either. And, if he remembered the view from the hillside accurately, Amec was now almost at the point where the vegetation in the street ended and the bridge began. There was no way he could wade through the ferns fast enough to catch this hot-headed wanderer before he reached the bridge so Ciro retraced his steps down the passageway until he reached the riverbank.

The ragged peaks of the cottages on the far bank could just be seen through the foliage which enclosed the river, and the same barrier provided almost perfect cover for Ciro as he made his way swiftly along the path in the direction of the bridge.

A small brake of trees nestled beside the steep arch of the bridge and, as he reached to grab a branch and scramble onto the stonework, Ciro froze when the sound of laughter came from close by on the opposite bank. The bridge wall was more than head high at this point and, as quietly as he could, the young king tentatively pulled himself up onto the branch then peeked through the leaves to get his first view of the far side.

The other bank was so free of the undergrowth which held sway on the west side that the cobbles of the street could clearly be discerned and the bordering ferns and wild flowers hugged the cottage walls in neatly trimmed lines. There was a wide, circular mound of grass planted with wild flowers immediately after the bridge and it was from here that the sound of laughter had come.

A Makech patrol, four strong, stood laughing upon the green while a fifth walked to the wood line on the far side of the village where their horses were tethered. The four Makech where drinking from an earthenware bottle and, amongst much humour and back slapping, seemed to be toasting a wooden pole set into the centre of the green. It was only when one of the men stepped to one side for a moment that Ciro saw the real cause for their joviality. The upturned figure of a man, his head and shoulders buried beneath freshly turned soil was strapped to the pole.

Ciro's jaw dropped as one of the Makech stuck a hand into his britches and began to urinate on the base of pole and before he could recover from that shock, a bellow of anger from his side of the bridge announced the arrival of Amec.

There was little Ciro could do to prevent the Philiri's charge across the bridge: he was as unaware of Amec's presence as the Makech on the far bank until that bloody roar split the evening sky. By then Amec was already charging, his sword held high before him, his massive frame thudding the stonework of the bridge as he ran screaming to meet the enemy.

There was a frozen moment where all – including Ciro – stood transfixed by the Philiri's charge. The Makech who, an instant before, had been merrily relieving himself on their captive now stood open-mouthed and wet legged as Amec raced forward. Ciro, his eyes glued to the stunned figures on the green was reminded of the two Makech who had burst through Menzir's door. They wore the same shocked expressions that had greeted his presence.

The thought spurred Ciro into action. He knew that, like before, the incredulity would pass swiftly as fear transformed into anger and already the group were beginning to flick their gaze from the oncoming Philiri to each other. The spell was broken.

Ciro was already clambering over the bridge wall as the first two Makech drew their swords to meet the oncoming threat. The young king ran to the brow of the bridge and crouched to aim as Amec clashed swords with the first Makech: the big man's strength and momentum sending the first swordsman reeling to the floor. The second Makech had rushed in on Amec's left and, as he prepared to swing, Ciro loosed a flight and caught the man on his right arm. The injury was not fatal in itself, but he dropped his sword in shock from the impact to grab at the wound and died as a wild slash from Amec all but severed his neck from his torso.

The first swordsman was using the pause to scrabble from the ground as the other two Makech leapt to the fore. Ciro's arrival had given the enemy two targets to worry about and, while one attempted to thrust his blade into Amec, the second ran on to meet Ciro.

The king ran the few paces needed to cross the bridge then

raised the hand lance to the oncoming Makech. He lined the barrel up with the man's un-helmeted head to fire and the appearance of the strange object was enough to bring his adversary to a wary halt. Ciro shot but missed: the sharp snap dying away and, seeing the disconcerted expression on the young king's face, the Makech warrior grinned in triumph and rushed on.

There was no time to rewind the mechanism as the armoured man bore down upon him, so Ciro took the only attacking course he could think of. He threw the hand lance as hard as he could into the face of his enemy – hoping that the distraction would give him time to manoeuvre. Beyond his foe, Ciro saw that Amec's impetus was lost as he struggled valiantly to fend off the two remaining Makech – while the fifth man, originally far away by the horses – was now making his own charge towards the outnumbered Philiri.

The hand lance span through the air, striking the swordsman square on the nose and bringing an instant grimace from the attacking Makech. He flinched with pain, brought his hand to his face reflexively and before he could utter the curse which began to snarl upon his lips, Ciro had locked his left hand onto the man's sword arm and landed several frantic blows to the Makech's face. The swordsman collapsed under the violent barrage and Ciro wrenched the sword from his weakened grasp and ran to help Amec.

The fifth swordsman was almost upon the Philiri – still battling and retreating before the combined attack of the two Makech – and Ciro saw the Boneman lift his sword to swing as he reached striking distance behind Amec.

'Milla irassii!' Ciro screamed, running even as he shouted to meet the warrior. The insult, combined with Ciro's rapid approach was enough to distract the Makech's attention away from Amec and he barely had time to protect himself before the young king was upon him.

Amec was still just managing to keep his opponents at bay but Ciro, now close by, could hear the Philiri's breath labour as he engaged his own Makech.

Watching his adversary's body for some sign of potential attack, Ciro thrust his sword tip towards the man's stomach and tested the response. The Makech skipped backwards, awkwardly parrying the blade with a downward stroke but Ciro, reading the move, jumped forwards to thrust again: this time at the man's throat. The blade struck, and a strained whine mixed with the Makech's cry of pain as he clutched his hand to the fatal wound. He collapsed slowly to the floor, but Ciro was already turning to face the men who battled with Amec.

Both warriors eyed Ciro warily as he leapt to Amec's side and one instantly transferred his attack to the newcomer. With short, rapid chops, the Makech attempted to hack through Ciro's defence but the young king simply used his own blade to redirect the force of each blow. The two pairs of fighters moved apart and Amec continued to retreat, attempting to catch a second's breath. Ciro was now oblivious to the Philiri's increasing fatigue, focused intently as he was on the man before him.

Letting his attacker tire of his assault, Ciro suddenly fainted to the man's midriff as he had done with the last warrior. He watched the reaction as his opponent tried to counter the blow before swiftly flicking the blade towards the Makech's face. Both forays were resisted but, as Ciro pulled back from the second strike, the Makech attempted his own counter.

Stepping in quickly as Ciro withdrew, the warrior stabbed his sword in low towards the king's groin. Seeing the sudden lunge, Ciro skipped right but, too close to use his blade, instead clubbed the man across the side of his head with the pommel of his sword. The warrior staggered, dazed by the swift blow and Ciro brought his blade round to strike before a scream from behind distracted him.

Amec, the Makech's blade buried deep in his stomach was slowly sinking to the floor: a look of shock upon his face as he clamped onto his opponent's sword arm and tried to counter with his own. Ciro saw the Makech mirror Amec's move to leave the pair locked when he glanced back to see his own adversary's sword blurring to connect with his face. Then Ciro did what Calian had always warned him against doing in a sword fight. He lost his temper.

With a snarl, Ciro ducked the slashing blow, gripped his sword with both hands and flashed the blade up at the point where the Makech's swinging arm met his armour. The warrior screamed as his arm was almost severed but the sound was cut short as Ciro span on the spot, drove his sword under the brow of the Makech's helmet and buried it into his temple. Amec, either dead or unconscious, was now sprawled upon the floor but his adversary, attempting to reach Ciro while his attention was elsewhere, had freed his sword to charge at the king.

As Ciro landed the fatal blow to his opponent, the other Makech had got close enough to attack and Ciro cursed loudly as the sword sliced through his cape and jacket. He attempted to knock the sword away with his own but it had become tangled in the leather and cloth. The Makech, realising he had less than a second to retrieve a weapon now stuck fast in his enemy's clothing, instead dropped his shoulder and rammed into Ciro's chest as hard as he could. Caught off-balance by the desperate attack, Ciro stumbled backwards and both men tumbled over the legs of the body behind them to land in a flailing heap.

Ciro struggled to turn the Makech who was now on top of

him while his opponent finally wrenched free his own entangled sword. Ciro grabbed the man's wrist as he tried to stab his blade into the young king's side and used the impetus of the movement to roll sideways so that he was now on top of his adversary. Still holding the Makech's sword arm, Ciro swept his own blade down to strike but the warrior shot out his free hand to prevent the blow. He missed Ciro's hand by an inch and with a wail of pain gripped the blade just above the hilt. He screamed as Ciro jerked the sword free and stabbed down frantically into his enemy's neck.

Ciro stood up. His clothes were bloody from the battle and a numb sensation emanated from where the Makech's sword had ripped through his clothing. He looked at the bodies littered around him, then limped over to crouch by Amec.

There was a pained expression set on the Philiri's face and it grew more intense when Ciro touched his hand. Amec flinched, struggling to sit up while Ciro moved to support his head but, though his lips moved, nothing but blood and pain emanated from his mouth. Amec's hand clasped and unclasped rapidly at his side and his gaze flickered like his expression until finally settling onto Ciro's face. With a determined heave, the Philiri managed to raise his head and, in a strained and pain-ridden voice said:

'You're wrong Ciro Torrman… You're wrong. Go–' Amec winced. '… Go to Philire… See the Eldermen… '

'You must rest,' Ciro said, concern in his voice. 'I'll get help.'

To this Amec shook his head and gripped his bloody stomach as another wave of pain washed over him. 'No… ' he finally whispered. 'I go to… To shine amongst the stars… … '

'You shouldn't speak, Amec,' Ciro said softly. But the Philiri had already spoken his final words.

Amec's body, rigid a moment before with pain now became limp and, though he still gazed at Ciro's face, there was no longer any life within his eyes. Ciro felt tears well up as he held the man he had barely begun to know and looked up at the darkening sky where the brightest stars where now beginning to glimmer.

'Shine brightly, Amec,' he whispered, and closed his eyes. Vainly trying to hold back the despair which quickly overwhelmed him, Ciro clutched the Philiri's lifeless body and wept as night fell on Olbas Osanti.

Nesh found him in the darkness a little later, still cradling Amec's body. Arper had done as Ciro had asked and taken Nesh back to the wall when they had heard the sound of cries and clashing swords but, when the night fell, Nesh had insisted they go back to find out what had happened.

Ciro looked up as Nesh touched his shoulder then slowly released the body of the Philiri. He hung his head.

'I couldn't stop them,' he said through tears. 'I tried, but...' Ciro's voice trailed off and he surveyed the shapes of the Makech warriors in the gloom.

Arper had hung back, cautiously inspecting the dead Makech. 'Five. Ebo's Mire!' he murmured then regarded the body of Amec with sadness. '... Is he?... ' he asked, already knowing the answer, then walked to crouch down beside Nesh. 'What 'appened?' he asked but Ciro gave no response.

Nesh frowned at her uncle and indicated the bodies around them. 'Ain't it obvious, uncle!' she hissed, then softened her tone. 'Go get our bags from the bridge.'

Arper looked crestfallen for a moment but acquiesced and returned to the place where they had dropped their baggage. At the foot of the bridge, the bloody-faced body of a Makech lay sprawled and beside him Arper spotted the bulky shape of Ciro's hand lance. He picked it up and lent on the low wall of the bridge, turning the weapon over in his hands: admiring the craftsmanship.

''Mazin',' he said to himself.

Arper considered taking the device straight to Ciro but decided he was probably best left alone with Nesh for the time being. She seemed to cope well with death, he thought.

'Huh,' he snorted. 'Better 'an me.'

Arper had been terrified by the sounds of the sword fight – the ringing clash of metal which had broken the tranquillity of the wood – and wasted no time in dragging his niece back towards the maze wall. Nesh had resisted the move, wanting to go back at once, but it was not until night came on that Arper managed to pluck up the courage to return. After all, he had told himself, he was a musician, not a fighter like Amec.

Arper put the hand lance on his lap and gazed up at the stars, thinking about Amec's death. He shook his head. He had travelled quite a few times with Amec: through the taverns of Forht, Urawiir and Kal Gians. He'd play his flute and sing for food and lodgings while the Philiri preached resistance and rebellion to the revellers. Both the music and the sentiment were always received well but, apart from a few Rialan slogans daubed hastily onto walls, the rebellion never reached beyond the tavern door.

'One day, Arper. One day,' Amec would always say, his face a mask of firm intent: his fist clenched. 'We'll strike 'em with somethin' sharper than words.'

And now, thought Arper, Amec's wish had come true. He had faced the Bonemen in battle and died fighting. Arper furrowed his brow and stared off into the gloom. The thought had only just occurred to him but, with Amec dead, what were they going to do now? Getting as far as Kal Gians would have been difficult even with the Philiri to aid them but getting through the barrier of black apples and the marshes of Ebo Pamessi would be impossible without someone who knew a safe route.

A sudden movement from the ground near Arper's feet froze both his mind and his body and the Makech which he had assumed to be dead shook his head and slowly began to rise.

Nervously, Arper inched further along the wall as the warrior sat up with his back to him. The Boneman put a hand to his face – muttered a stream of expletives when the pain from his broken nose resurfaced – and focused his attention on the barely visible bodies of his comrades. Arper too looked into the darkness, vainly hoping that Ciro would suddenly appear: but the night had deepened, and all that he could see was a faint outline of black treetops against a star-dotted sky.

Arper continued to shuffle along the wall, holding his breath in case the mere expulsion of air should alert the Boneman to his presence. Then he remembered the weapon in his lap.

He had seen Ciro use the hand lance in Forht and, though he had no real idea as to how it worked, he slowly raised the device until its barrel pointed at the Makech.

Arper cursed the fact that he had put down his sword somewhere but knew in his heart that he was more of a danger to himself than anyone else with it. Hacking plant life was easy, hacking people – even vile Makech – was an entirely different matter. One which he had neither the experience nor the stomach for.

His fingers had been searching all the while for a way to make the hand lance fire and then, more by luck than judgment, a ring of metal set before the handle suddenly gave way beneath his grasp. The sharp click which sounded from the mechanism made him jump but failed to make the device fire. It did however alert the Boneman to his presence and, with a roar of anger, the Makech jumped to his feet and charged at Arper, quickly knocking the weapon from his grasp.

Under a sudden barrage of blows, Arper struggled desperately against the Makech, but his frame and strength was no match for his opponent's fury. With one hand clamped tightly around his throat, the warrior clubbed and struck through Arper's flailing defence and, by degrees, the musician was pushed backwards over the river.

'Huirness! Inshek! Tik! Rial!' the Makech grunted: each word punctuated with a brutal blow.

Arper's head rang with the impacts and he attempted to claw at the warrior's hand locked around his windpipe. Yet his efforts only increased the ferocity of the attack and he felt his wits begin to cloud.

Somewhere – it seemed very distance – Arper thought he could hear Nesh screaming. His head was ringing, his vision blurred and, though he tried to catch his breath, the hand locked around his windpipe made it almost impossible. Arper looked up into the leering face of his assailant to realise he was going to die.

There was a jolt which loosened the Boneman's grip and Arper gasped with relief for air. At the same instant he felt a strange sensation in the pit of his stomach, followed instantly by a smack as his falling body hit the stream. On the bridge, Ciro stood wide-eyed and trembling over the body of the last Makech: as if daring it to rise again. In his hand he carried Amec's bloody sword.

Nesh ran to aid the spluttering Arper. The water was deep enough to have cushioned her uncle's short fall, but his addled senses left him floundering wildly until Nesh's hand found his. With all the strength she could muster, Nesh pulled Arper to the bank where he lay gasping and coughing as he attempted to gulp in air.

'W..Wha' 'appened?!' he finally managed to splutter.

Nesh looked up to where Ciro still stood immobile on the bridge and briefly explained how the sound of the struggle had made Ciro race into the darkness like a demon to strike the Boneman down.

Arper nodded, grinned then fainted dead away.

Nesh patted her uncle on the hand, and then went to join Ciro on the bridge.

The king had lent Amec's sword against the bridge wall and was checking his hand lance when Nesh approached him. She stopped a few feet away as, oblivious to her presence, Ciro held the mechanism up to his ear, pulled the trigger, and then swung the winding arm round twice before returning the weapon to its holster.

'Is –?' Nesh began then recoiled in shock as Ciro span round and levelled the hand lance at her face. '– It broke?' she finished, her voice now a whisper.

Ciro dropped the weapon to his side, gave a deep sigh and let his shoulders sag. He rubbed a hand across his face and the ferocity which had flared in his eyes vanished.

'It's fine,' he replied then nodded towards the riverbank. 'How's Arper?' he asked.

'Bruised, bedraggled... But 'e'll live.'

'Good... Good... ' Ciro replied, but his mind seemed to be elsewhere: his eyes continually scanning the darkness behind Nesh while they spoke.

'We've a sayin',' Nesh said. 'Often used for those that survive the Makech Judgment Ring. We say they're "Bearin' the Bonemen" 'cause almost everyone who survives it wears a haunted look for ages after. I don't think I've ever seen no one bear the Bonemen quite like you.'

Ciro managed a strained smile. 'We should prepare a pyre for Amec,' he said. 'And for these savages too.' He prodded the body at his feet with the toe of his boot. 'If they found this place, so will others and I don't want them to know that we were here.'

Nesh shook her head. 'We need ta rest – you most of all,' she said softly. 'Amec can wait.' Ciro frowned but Nesh crossed her arms defiantly. 'We can set pyres at first light. But for now, even if you can't see it, we all need ta rest.'

Ciro took a deep breath and nodded. His instincts screamed for him to cover his tracks and move on but perhaps he wasn't thinking straight. Amec's death was not only hard to bear but his last words still stung the young king. There had been the same bitterness in the Philiri's dying words as there had been in most of his conversations with Ciro: as if, the young king thought, he blamed him for the incident. All that kept running through his mind – apart from the continual threat from the Makech – was that, without his presence here, Amec would still be alive. How did that fit into the Reilan dreams of his youth?

A groan from beneath the bridge made Ciro peer into the darkness and there, pale and round in the dim starlight, he could vaguely make out Arper's wide eyes staring back at him. With their Philiri guide now dead, would Nesh and her uncle be looking to him for guidance? Ciro's mind quailed at the prospect but he tried his best to counter his fear with the stark facts. No matter how insecure he felt about his own abilities, if he could not remain in control, there was a high probability they would all end up like Amec.

Ciro sighed. Nesh was right, he was tired: not thinking straight and had almost made a fatal error. If they had lit pyres, from how far away would the flames have been visible? That could have cost them dearly. Ciro shook his head, marvelling at his own stupidity and gave Nesh a weary smile.

'We should tend to the horses before we do anything,' Ciro said, sounding more like his normal self. 'Then we'll move back over the bridge and into the forest to sleep.'

'Why bother with the 'orses?' asked Nesh. 'You know we ain't allowed ta ride 'em. Why risk drawin' attention?'

'The Makech are searching for us,' Ciro replied, 'so it's imperative we move fast tomorrow. If riding a horse will get me to Peimonac twice as fast then I will ride a horse.'

Ciro holstered his hand lance, picked up Amec's sword and the pair left the bridge to check on Arper.

'Besides,' Ciro continued, 'the Makech will undoubtedly kill us on sight either way – so why worry about horse riding?' There was a hint of a smile on Ciro's face as he delivered the remark but it compressed in a moment to a thin line as a grey shape flitted in the shadows past Nesh's shoulder.

'Get down.' he hissed.

Nesh was shocked by Ciro's sudden change in temperament but the young king was already drawing his hand lance and pointing it into the darkness.

'Stand still or die!' Ciro shouted, advancing towards where the grey shape stood by the trussed body on the pole. Now the shape suddenly dropped to the ground, attempting to hide behind the pole but there was enough starlight for Ciro to retain sight of the figure.

'If you can understand Rialan, I want you to know that the weapon I have in my hand can kill you from here,' Ciro announced. 'One more move like that and I'll use it. Now, stand up slowly and walk towards me.'

The figure did not move and again Ciro felt nervous tension rising within him. He didn't want to have to kill again, but what option did he have? To protect himself – and the others

– no-one must know they had been here.

How Ciro longed to be back aboard the King Elson. Just to spend an hour where such hostile thoughts had no place in his mind. He aimed the hand lance at the very centre of the grey shape and watched with relief as it slowly rose. Cautiously, the shape stepped towards him and resolved from the night into the figure of a stout, grey bearded man wrapped in a dirty linen cloak. He came forward hesitantly, his eyes flicking past Ciro to where (Ciro surmised) the shapes of Nesh and Arper were just visible, then stopped as he reached the fallen figure of Amec. Ignoring Ciro, the man dropped to his knees beside the Philiri then looked up to meet Ciro's gaze with silent hostility.

'Who are you?!' the man demanded. 'What happened here?!' He stabbed an accusing finger at Amec's body.

Ciro holstered his weapon and moved closer to the man, crouching a few feet away. The stranger did not shift his gaze.

'Are you Philiri?' Ciro asked, his former harsh tone softening. 'Like Amec?'

To this the man's eyes narrowed, but he said nothing.

'My name is Ciro; the others are Arper and Nesh. Amec travelled with us from Cabon and was trying to guide us to Peimonac until… ' Ciro's voice faltered, the memory of what had happened to the Philiri was still too painful, and he patted Amec's hand as he drew a deep breath. 'We came across this patrol at dusk,' he said quietly, withdrawing the hand to point out the other shapes spread around them. 'Amec fought like a veteran, but the odds were just too great.'

The stranger nodded but still looked keenly at Ciro's face. 'I heard it,' he said, a frown creasing his brow. 'But why would Amec be taking anyone to Peimonac? There's nothing but trouble there. In fact, why would Amec be guiding anyone?'

'Because 'e's our King,' said Nesh. Both she and her uncle had moved over from the bridge to stand behind Ciro. Nesh's statement made the man grin.

'Our King?!' the stranger repeated. Ciro nodded but said nothing. 'By whose authority?' the man inquired.

Ciro sighed. If this man was Philiri, then he would almost certainly know the same version of history as Amec. 'It might take a little explaining,' said Ciro, 'but, here goes... '

With expressions of surprise, incredulity and disbelief, the man listened in silence as Ciro explained briefly who he was, where he had come from and how he came to be in Reilan. At length, Ciro produced his crumpled blue jacket with its Rial sun emblem and showed him his hand lance, but it was not until he described the Feirlan fleet bound for deep within Rial that the grey-bearded man saw fit to comment.

'How many ships?' he suddenly interjected.

'Enough,' Ciro replied, unwilling to divulge too much information.

The man smiled. 'It would, I suppose, be unwise to trust all your secrets to a stranger, so allow me to introduce myself. My name is Tenc, and I am, as you surmised, a Philiri. I don't know how much of your remarkable story is true, but I've heard enough to know that you at least seem sincere.'

'Weren't Tenc the one Amec said lived 'ere?' observed Arper.

'Yes,' Ciro replied, 'and there was someone else, someone from Urawiir who was supposed to be here...'

'Mara should have come today,' Tenc replied with a nod. 'But the Makech patrol probably scared him away.'

Ciro chewed his lip and wondered if that was the identity of the figure strapped to the pole. Reluctantly he put the question to Tenc before he, Tenc and Arper uprooted the Makech's victim.

'By the stars!' Tenc exclaimed, his voice choked with emotion.

He turned away as Ciro and Arper gently laid the body upon the grass and untied the ropes which bound it.

'Mara?' Ciro asked.

He looked at Tenc, who nodded but did not turn around then, aided by Nesh, the pair of them moved Amec's corpse to lie beside Mara's.

'We shall send them both to the stars at first light,' Ciro said.

'But first we all need to rest,' said Nesh firmly. No one argued.

Feeling weary to the point of exhaustion, Ciro still insisted that the Makech horses were unbridled, unsaddled and fed before they themselves rested. Once done he forced his leaden limbs on as Tenc led them down the main street of the deserted village towards the mill house which was his home. There was little any of them could discern of the structure beyond its ragged outline framed against the stars but an overwhelming warmth mixed with the smell of decaying vegetation assaulted them as they ducked through a low beamed door set into the side of the building.

'Not much, but it's home,' said Tenc through the darkness and the others listened to the Philiri's clumsy passage as he went in search of candles.

'Smells like our barn,' Nesh muttered with a grimace as the noise of a squeaking hinge sounded somewhere ahead of them.

'Ssh, girl!' Arper responded. 'We're guests 'ere.'

A few moments later Ciro was stifling a yawn when a pale glow framed the door that Tenc had disappeared through. The room they stood in brightened as their host returned with two large candles.

'I have some food if you're hungry,' said Tenc.

With the light from the candles the group could now see the clutter which filled the high beamed room. Wicker baskets, grubby sacks and a jumble of broken furniture occupied most of the space and, as Tenc negotiated the chaotic piles he indicated a sack brimming with apples.

While Arper helped himself to the fruit, Ciro and Nesh followed Tenc to a wide table in the corner of the room. Obscured like everything else with various detritus, Tenc placed both candles at one end of the table and made short work of clearing it. Two long, split logs mounted on short wooden legs acted as benches and Ciro sat down gratefully as Arper joined them. What had been a dull pain at his waist suddenly flared into savage life as Ciro sat down and the young king felt at his hip where the Makech's blade had torn his cloak and jacket.

'Wassup?' said Arper, munching noisily.

Ciro grimaced. 'I think one of the Makech had better aim than I thought,' he replied and pulled back the clothing to reveal a dark slash across his hip.

'Lie on the bench,' Nesh ordered, moving round from the other side of the table. Arper and Tenc left their seats to gather around him.

'It's really nothing serious,' protested Ciro but Nesh's stern expression made the king do as ordered. Reluctantly he stretched out upon the log as Nesh peered at the wound.

Tenc brought a candle closer to reveal Ciro's blood-stained side and after a few moments deliberation Nesh asked Tenc if he had any moss.

The Philiri shook his head. 'I don't, but there's plenty outside.'

Nesh nodded. 'Uncle, can ya go outside and gather some moss? Tenc, could ya boil some water?' To this the man nodded. 'An' could ya find some cloth?' she continued. 'Anythin'll do so long as it's long enough ta wrap round Ciro's waist.'

'Is this really necessary?' complained Ciro as the others went off to complete their tasks. He felt not just uncomfortable – balanced as he was upon the narrow bench – but undignified as well. 'I'm sure I'll be fine in a day or two.' Ciro raised his head to see Nesh scowling at him.

'Menzir got slashed on the same spot by our bull a few years back,' she replied brusquely. ' 'e left the wound 'till it festered an' 'ad to walk with a stick ever after.' Nesh furrowed her brow. 'Pity that's all the bull did to 'im,' she added with feeling.

Ciro guessed the memories of the farmhouse were beginning to cloud Nesh's thoughts again but in that instant he could think of no words to comfort the girl. Instead he gripped her hand. Nesh nodded to herself and managed a thin smile.

'It's funny,' she said, staring off into the darkness beyond the candlelight, 'but the only reason Ma stayed with 'im was because she thought it was safer there than in town. She never said it, but I'm pretty sure she wan'ed ta make sure the Bonemen never got me.'

'Got you?' echoed Ciro.

Nesh grimaced. 'Slavery,' she explained.

'I thought the Makech had stopped taking slaves?' Ciro replied.

Nesh shook her head. 'It still 'appens, there's still markets about. There's one in Kal Gians apparently, where they sell girls ta the 'ighest bidder an' send 'em south across the desert.' Nesh sighed. 'But, though the Makech still want slaves, they want food more, an' I think Ma thought I'd be safe on the farm.'

'I'm sorry,' Ciro said, 'for all that's happened.'

Nesh shook her head. 'Not your fault,' she replied firmly. 'It's the beckin' Bonemen. None o' this would've 'appened if Menzir 'adn't told 'em about ya.' Nesh took a deep breath. 'It still 'urts ta think about Ma, but I know she would've agreed with what I'm doin'. Ta get away from the threat o' the Bonemen is all any Rialan wants.'

Ciro smiled, patted Nesh's hand and a cool breeze swept the room heralding Arper's returned from outside.

'Ol' Sakoom's about,' he said as he pushed the door to. Arper walked to the table and held out a pair of muddy hands full of moss. 'Did ya really want this, Nesh?' he asked dubiously.

Nesh nodded. 'I'll take it to Tenc,' she replied and relieved Arper of his burden.

Left alone, Arper gazed down at Ciro's wound and grimaced. 'Nasty,' he said.

Ciro frowned. 'It's not so bad,' he answered, trying to ignore Arper's pessimism. 'Once it's dressed and bound I'm sure it will be fine.'

Arper nodded and swept his gaze around the room. He looked up to the rafters where flowers – long since dried – had been hung to mask the smell of the place but now provided nothing more than a playground for spiders.

'Wonder 'ow long 'e's been 'ere?' Arper mused, hitching a thumb at the door Nesh had disappeared through.

Ciro shook his head, sat up and winced. Wearily he stood up so as not to pull on the wound again and considered Arper's question.

'I just hope he's not too attached to the place,' said Ciro, half to himself.

Nesh and Tenc returned a few minutes later carrying a steaming pot of water between them. Inside was the boiled

207

moss and strips of rag which Tenc had torn from an old sack and with these Nesh dressed and bound Ciro's wound. Bleary-eyed, the grateful travellers were led by the Philiri in search of a place to sleep.

A small hayloft provided an ideal mattress for the entire group but Ciro fought his overwhelming exhaustion to address the others. He stifled a yawn with the back of his hand and said:

'We should keep a watch just in case more Bonemen come: I'll keep the first one.'

'You ain't doin' no such thing!' admonished Nesh. 'You c'n barely keep yer eyes open!'

'We should be safe for this evening,' said Tenc. 'I don't know where those Makech came from but there won't be another patrol along soon. The way into Olbas Osanti is hard enough during the daylight, but I'd say it would be impossible during the night. We shouldn't expect anybody for a day or so.'

'Yep,' said Arper, 'an' we'll be long gone be'then.'

Nesh gripped Ciro's arm and gazed up into his half-lidded eyes. 'I ain't no expert,' she said, 'but 'ow long do ya think yer gonna last tomorra if ya don't rest now?'

The king's eyes narrowed but the hint of a smile played upon his lips. Wasn't that the same argument he'd used with Amec during their escape from Forht? Had Nesh overheard, Ciro wondered. Not that it mattered, she was right: he felt dead on his feet. Ciro managed a grin.

'I defer to your wise council, Nesh,' he said and stretched himself out on the straw.

'I think that means 'e agrees with ya,' observed Arper.

Nesh smiled and gazed down at the young king. He was already asleep.

Ciro sat on the edge of his cot and stared at the two leather bags on the floor before him. There was no doubt that they were there – no matter how hard he stared at them – yet the king did not want to accept the brutal truth. The tent in which he sat was grass floored, spread with furs and richly woven rugs and from beyond its pale wall of canvas came the unmistakable sound of horses. The noise broke the wretched spell cast by the bags and Ciro wrenched his gaze away to concentrate on the chest which sat at the foot of his cot. On top of its deep, polished surface sat a crown of exquisite beauty inset with several large precious stones: but Ciro had no eyes for it. Instead he focused his attention on the strange, glowing words which lay along side it. They were a line of large, unfamiliar letters and, though the king could not comprehend the meaning of the sentence, he somehow felt an understanding of their importance. Whatever that sentence meant, it was powerful.

Ciro's gaze shifted back to the two leather bags and the blood stains which had discoloured the lower part of each. The bags had been tied tightly at their tops and the stretched leather made it easy to discern the shapes of the severed heads which had been placed inside. One was Oltrek's – the other Bamile's – and, with a grief greater than he could contain, Ciro had to accept the bitter truth. Mala had carried out his threat. He had killed Ciro's son and his son's bride. Not wanting to think any more, Ciro picked up the words at the end of the bed and strode from the tent.

The day was grey, the rolling plain patched with fog as Ciro's horse thundered on towards the vague sunrise. Hunched into the saddle, Ciro's gaze stayed locked on the horizon before him and the single hill which began to rise up from the continuous undulation of the Long Lands. It was a cold morning and though the chill air beat upon his cheeks as he rode, the king felt nothing. He was already far colder inside and the pounding of his mount's hooves accompanied the single word which repeated over and over in his mind. Revenge... Revenge... Revenge.

Near the top of the hill Ciro jumped from the saddle and shoed away his faithful horse: he would ride no more today. Icashem was reluctant to leave her master but such was the king's rage that the stead was soon scared off. Ciro left it to the mercy of the fog and ran to the summit.

At its top he paused and gazed down at the plain beyond, easily picking out the black tents and massed rabble of men through the drifting banks of mist. The glint of spears and armour were easy to discern but there was little structure to their ranks: they still thought the day too young for battle. Ciro filled his lungs and cried down the hill like thunder.

'MALA!!... INDEC!!' he bellowed, instantly noting a ripple of movement pass through the army as they turned to regard him on the hill. 'I have come to avenge my son!' He thundered from the hilltop. 'Come face me if you dare for, as sure as Milla shines, I will have blood!'

A great cry went up from the men below, followed by a surge of motion as they ran towards the foot of the hill. Ciro gazed back: impassive at the sight of the eager warriors as they jostled to be the first to mount the summit and face him. Calmly he scanned the black tents to see if Mala and Indec would take up his challenge. He felt no fear at the prospect of facing the onrushing enemy. Ciro no longer felt anything. He simply stood his ground and waited.

As the first of the warriors breasted the hill, Ciro saw recognition in their eyes as to who it was that awaited them. Some he had known well – they had feasted at his table many times – and now their footsteps faltered; their eagerness was diminished. Black though their hearts had become they were not brave and before them was a foe they knew too well. Ciro smiled and beckoned them forwards.

An arc of armed and armoured men began to surround him at a safe distance, their expressions stern yet unsure. Words of caution were thrown amongst them as the rear ranks attempted to push forward to better see their prey but still Ciro stood immobile. Waiting for the two men who he had trusted with the life of his son.

Then the glint of celesdain armour shone through the ranks and both Indec and Mala forced a path through their nervous men to meet their challenger. Now Ciro found that the words he had taken from his tent were suddenly in his hands and at their appearance the faces of the men before him drained of colour. With a scream on his lips he rushed straight at Mala and began the carnage.

Again and again the words swept before Ciro's eyes as he wielded them sword-like against his foe. By the dozen they fell before his irresistible rage and soon the ground around him was red with blood and piled with broken bodies. Still they came on, unsighted by the brow of the hill to meet their deaths and wave after wave of charging warriors were scythed by the dreadful words which Ciro brandished before him. Milla climbed high into the sky and still the battle raged on: the king thrashing his tired arms at anyone foolish enough to face him. At length the enemy began to thin until, exhausted and finally alone, Ciro clambered through the bodies to view the enemy camp. It was difficult to see in the twilight but the place looked deserted and looking west Ciro saw that the sun was now dipping below the horizon. He looked back down towards the rolling plain and saw the pale glint of armour. What was left of his enemy was running away.

Tired beyond belief the king fought for breath and sank to his knees. Hazily, he regarded the hilltop and realised he could no longer see it, just bodies strewn in every direction. He sighed and toppled forwards amongst the slain, not caring that his was the last life to be claimed upon the hill. That, he thought as he closed his eyes, was a reasonable price to pay for revenge.

'Ciro!'

Ciro felt a kick against his feet and sat up quickly, instantly putting a hand to his neck as pain stabbed through it. He blinked and gazed around groggily. The dark wooden walls of the hayloft were now cracked with daylight and a single bird was singing outside.

'What?' he muttered, focusing on Nesh as she stood over him.

'Are ya alright?' she asked with a frown. 'You were shoutin'.'

Ciro rubbed at his neck, frowned back at Nesh then regarded his pack behind him. He made a mental note to stop resting his head on it.

'Shouting?' he replied with a yawn. 'I was dreaming…' Ciro's mind wandered to the diminishing images of his dream. He seemed to recall standing on a strange hilltop. Hadn't he been holding a sword? A word? –

'You was shoutin' 'bout revenge,' said Arper from the opposite side of the hayloft. Nesh's uncle plucked straw from his beard as he sat up and grinned at Ciro. 'Said ya was gonna avenge yer sons or som'in like that. Dunno exac'ly, but it woke me up alright.'

Ciro nodded, his weak smile fading as the memory of Amec's death returned to him. 'I'm sorry,' he said, 'It must have been from…' he let the sentence tail off, his thoughts returning to the sword fight by the bridge. Were his nights now going to be like his days – constantly invaded by scenes of bloodshed? He grimaced at the fear which welled up in him at the thought; he had to be strong.

Ciro got up and stretched while Nesh and Arper collected their packs and cleaned themselves of straw.

'We should find Tenc,' said Ciro, looking towards the door. 'Then make arrangements for Amec.'

'What about the Bonemen?' asked Arper, 'Should we burn them an' all?'

'No,' replied Ciro with a humourless smile. 'I have plans for them.'

They trooped out from the hayloft and followed the smell of frying bacon in search of Tenc and breakfast. It had not occurred to either Nesh or Arper to inform him of the fact but, when Ciro had cried out in his sleep, he had been talking in the Makech tongue.

The King of Nothing

PART THREE

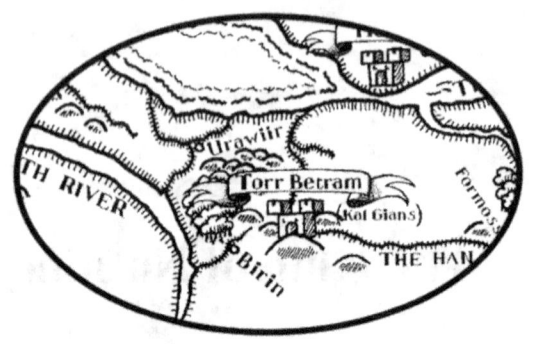

After the grandeur of Torr Betram we had stolen ourselves for the bleak prospect of the final leg of our trip into the windswept west. Deciding to avoid the Port town of Birin (and the risky venture of sailing the South River) we instead procured a large, four horse carriage with which to ride along King Antius's Grand Avenue. To escort us, the ever-helpful Captain Sharce decided to join our little party and, as we took in the marvel of King Antius's statue at the entrance to the avenue, he informed me that the entire roadway had been hewn through the forest by captured Makech soldiers.

Such talk, though jovially put, did little to ease the apprehensions of my fellow Aldermen. Beyond Torr Betram's stout defences the threat of Kal Santra seems far closer to those more used to life in the Heart Wold and it was Alderman Baulenus who wondered aloud about the village named Urawiir which was our next – though distant – destination.

'Was it,' he inquired, 'because of these Makech prisoners settling there that the place had a foreign name?'

To this Captain Sharce answered: 'No Sire, the prisoners were marched south after they had completed their task but, even so, you will find many things strange in this part of the Kingdom. The locals refer to the Grand Avenue merely as 'The Cut' and, though some will call their village Three

216

Rivers the place has changed hands so many times over the years that the name Urawiir seems to have stuck. That,' the captain went on to explain, 'was why the Grand Avenue was built in the first place – to protect the farthest part of our Kingdom.'

'Well, let us hope,' grumbled Alderman Chaime, 'that it does not change hands again while we are there. I had intended to see the far end of our land – not leave it.'

Alderman Lacey. My travels to the South West Wold.
NC 659

Birin Bridge

Upon the narrow bridge which spanned the river west of Urawiir, Pronyes:7 and Siort, Makech guards from the Urawiir garrison debated the implications of their brand new shields: a device no Makech soldier in Rial had carried for generations. A new recruit of eighteen, Siort had only been in Rial a month and the deep tan from a life in the desert climate of Makech still marked him easily from his paler companion. Siort adjusted the chin strap which cut through the wispy beard he had been attempting to grow since arrival and hefted the wooden shield which he, Pronyes and the rest of the garrison had finished making just that morning.

Pronyes had lent his own shield against the hand rail to peer over at the water below and, after a brief pause to aim, spat at a family of ducks which swam beneath him. He missed, cursed, then wiped his beard with the back of his hand and squinted at his young companion. It was not the boy's fault, Pronyes supposed, to be so eager for battle because the helmet which he wore had nothing but a point on the top of it: no first-kill skull to mark him as a true soldier. A group of them had planned – as they always did with new recruits – to take Siort to the garrison's blooding circle at the turn of the moon so that he could get his first kill but, with the events of the past evening, it was only natural that the boy should want to claim his kill in open battle. Switching his gaze past Siort, Pronyes could see from the thick smoke which greyed the sky that the village of Urawiir was still burning.

The Beck Iph had come with the dusk. Unannounced, the first the garrison had known about the Soulcatchers' presence were the screams from the village square and the flames from thatch burning in the darkness. Both Pronyes and Siort had been mustered with the twenty others of their garrison to investigate the sudden disturbance but their march had been halted by the gargoyle sight of a Beck Iph soldier standing sentinel-like at the edge of the village square. Beyond that terrifying shape, framed against the blaze which gripped the surrounding houses two gaunt, black figures stood immobile while the populous ran – seemingly blind – around them.

Pronyes, glancing to his side to catch Siort's gapping–jawed profile against the flames of a nearby building, had realised that he too was as awe struck by the sight as the new recruit. The presence of a Soulcatcher was a rarity, even back home in Makech, but to see two – side by side – was something Pronyes had never even heard of, let alone seen. And whatever magic was being used beyond the red-masked guard was, even at this distance, making the hairs stand up on the back of his neck. Pronyes had circled his heart for protection against the spirits and, by degrees, the seasoned soldier that he was reasserted itself. More to show the lad what experience could make of such a spectacle than for any lack of incredulity he pointed to the two stick figures in the square.

'Ever seen so many Soulcatchers?!' Pronyes had to holler the words above the roaring, cracking blaze of thatch and, much to his disappointment, Siort nodded.

'I saw five leave Gatch on their way to Nish Huiss,' the youngster shouted back. He held up a hand with all fingers splayed to emphasise the number. 'It was what made me want to join the Legion…' Siort gave a slight shake of his head. 'Thought I'd end up following them: never thought I'd get posted here.'

Pronyes had shrugged. Every soldier in the Legion wanted to help reclaim Nish Huiss from the Omerk, but every veteran knew that there was more to being a soldier than a four number kill count and striding the river of blood. Pronyes had scratched at the lice in his beard and, looking on at the proceedings, saw a tiny Omerk run into the firelight. He went to point out the strange creature when there was a shove from behind him and their commander pushed his way through.

Tzimek was a dull man, Pronyes thought. Slow witted and dull. A man more at home wielding a quill than a sword in battle and so it was a complete mystery to the entire garrison how he had got his 23 kills. Ink poisoning was the current theory amongst the garrison troops. Deeply shadowed by the constant flicker from the fire as he took in the events before him, Tzimek's face quickly assumed a frown of irritation. Pronyes knew from experience that this was their commander's favourite expression.

'You, Pronyes,' Tzimek barked. He had prodded the old soldier in the chest and pointed to the red-masked Beck Iph guard. 'What's going on here?'

After two years in the Urawiir garrison, Pronyes was used to Tzimek's inability to grasp the obvious. He had regarded the statue figure of the Beck Iph guard for a moment, caught several wide-eyed glances and sniggers from the men behind him and, after dismissing the first caustic response which sprang to mind, had answered: 'Looks like the Dark Square are here, sir.'

'I can see that!' the commander had snapped irritably. 'What is it they want?'

Pronyes had looked again at the red-masked man. He knew where this line of questioning would lead: Commander Tzimek was attempting to have Pronyes inquire of that frightening figure just what the Beck Iph were doing here. The answer was something Pronyes already knew. The Dark Square were a law unto themselves and could and did do anything they wanted, without hindrance. Only the terminally brave or the exceptionally stupid would dare question their intent. As Pronyes mulled over the daunting possibility that Tzimek would order him to approach the guard, the Beck Iph soldier suddenly spoke.

'Commander,' the Beck Iph said in a voice both stern and clear above the noise of fire. 'My master would wish that you should withdraw at this time. We do not require your assistance.'

Tzimek had looked dumbly at the figure for a moment before mutely nodding his head then turned as quickly as he could and barged back into the men behind Pronyes and Siort.

'Come on men!' The pair heard him declare. 'Let's get back before this blaze gets out of hand!'

Few had moved to follow, so engrossed were they all in the bizarre spectacle before them and, though he could not be positive in the flickering light, Pronyes was sure there was the hint of a smile on the Beck Iph guard's lips. Beyond, as the villagers ran and screamed above the noise of the flames, the tiny Omerk continued its own frantic circuits.

Bandy-legged with a black cloth wrapped tightly over its huge eyes, the strange creature ran in and out of the screaming villagers as it circled the two Soulcatchers still immobile in the centre of the square. Pronyes had heard many strange tales of the Beck Iph but he could not fathom why the villagers seemed unable to escape from the square. Round and round they went, circle after circle, but never once did they attempt to burst past the Beck Iph guards stationed at the four exiting streets. More and more frequently as the silent soldiers of the garrison looked on, villagers began to loose their footing and fall or simply slow from exhaustion. Time and again those running beside their friends or family members would encourage, cajole or simply wrench the weary back to their feet and Pronyes pointed out to Siort how the villagers always seemed to be looking back over their shoulders – into the flames – as if there was something tangible that was in pursuit.

'Look there!' said Siort and Pronyes saw first one Soulcatcher then the other lift their hands to cover their eyes and a glow brighter than the blazing village shone from their foreheads. A wild cry went up from the tiny Omerk who now stopped his running and wrenched off the cloth which had obscured its face to reveal two beacons of light burning fiercely in its eye sockets. Now it seemed as if a whirlwind had descended upon the square and one by one the screaming, running villagers were hurled from the ground and thrown like extra kindling into the surrounding blaze. In unison, Pronyes and Siort made the sign of the square but they, like the rest of the garrison, could not wrench their eyes from the grim spectacle until the screams of the locals had become consumed by the ever-crackling flames.

It had been a little later when Siort had pointed out a strange discussion between Tzimek and an unfamiliar officer of the Legion and the pair, supposedly on patrol, had crept into the deep shadows of a nearby derelict barn to look on. The stranger, wiry with angular features and a sharply trimmed beard was holding a square bronze plate an inch from their commander's face and, though they could not catch the words, the stranger obviously spoke in a manner menacing enough to drop Tzimek to his knees. Pronyes guessed that the brass plate was a Beck Iph insignia, which meant that, though the fellow wore the uniform of the Legion, he did in fact 'Walk the square'. Which meant that he, whoever he was, answered to no one but the Soulcatchers. Certainly not Tzimek, who had seemingly made the same mistake they had by thinking he was one of them.

'Do you think we should intervene?' Siort had said, but his tone left Pronyes in no doubt he had not mean it.

Pronyes had grinned. 'Serves the slug-witted bastard right,' he replied and watched as a red-masked guard joined the group and Tzimek began prostrating himself on the floor.

They left, disappointed, after Tzimek got timidly up and left with the two men and they returned to the garrison at the end of their watch to find the place a hive of activity.

'Commander says we're to make shields, lots of 'em,' announced a guard when Pronyes asked what the commotion was about. Pronyes had laughed at the idea.

'Shields were for the ancients,' he had replied. 'We don't need 'em.'

'Maybe so,' said the guard, 'but you don't wanna be the one to tell Tzimek that.' The man shook his head. 'Never seen 'im so angry. 'Says everyone gotta 'ave a shield by morning or they'll be for it.'

Pronyes had grinned and nudged Siort. 'I bet this's got somethin' to do with that little conversation we saw our illustrious commander have earlier.'

Siort returned the grin. 'So, what do we do?' he asked.

'Simple,' Pronyes had replied. 'We go and make some shields.'

Pronyes had returned his attention to the circling ducks beneath him.

'But it has to be the Philiri!' exclaimed Siort for the third time. He too had removed his shield and now lent his back against the handrail of the bridge and fiddled with the strap of his helmet.

'Why do you keep insistin' it's the Philiri when I've already told you it can't be!?' Pronyes replied. He spat at the ducks again and was rewarded by a sudden chorus of quacks and splashing as his spittle struck home.

'Because there isn't anyone else!'

Pronyes raised an eyebrow and stood up. 'Isn't there?' he asked.

Siort laughed in exasperation and flung his arms wide. 'Alright, Pronyes,' he exclaimed, still laughing. 'Who is it that makes the Beck Iph kill half the cattle in Urawiir and gets us so defensive we have to have shields for the first time since anyone can remember?!'

'Not the Philiri, that's for sure,' Pronyes said. He lent beside Siort and watched as the smoke rising from Urawiir suddenly plumed black. His partner went to speak but the older man held up a hand. 'Even in the old days – long before our grandfathers where warriors – the Philiri were not enough of a threat to make us carry shields. Which miracle do you think took place to make them anything more than the vermin pest they are?'

'Who knows what goes on beyond the black apples these days,' Siort replied with a shrug. 'And why are we to watch out for "Anything unusual"? Perhaps the Philiri are in league with the Omerk now.'

To this Pronyes snorted. 'The Philiri would rather side with us than the Omerkfel. Just how much do you know about these rebel Rialans?'

'I know they're scum!' Siort replied defensively. 'Who knows how low their kind might sink.' He paused for a moment then wagged a finger at Pronyes. 'And what about Nish Huiss? Why are we suddenly fighting the Omerk? It doesn't make sense unless the Philiri are behind it.'

'Well, you're right that it don't make sense, I'll grant you that,' Pronyes replied. 'But then I never understood a thing about the Omerk anyway. I mean, you saw that thing last night –.' The memory of the Wraith from the market square made Pronyes shudder but he mimicked its waddling gate and let out a strangled howl.

Siort grinned. 'I remember my father telling me the tale of Souza and the South Jaw,' he said.

Pronyes nodded. 'My father told me the same story.'

'Yes, I'm sure,' Siort replied. 'But my grandfather was there. Right beside Souza when he found Ebo's Lake, and he killed ten massive Omerk when they had to retreat back to Huiss.'

Pronyes fixed a smile on his face and looked away. How many fires had he sat around and heard the same type of boastful tale? "My father single-handedly took Torr Idirnon!" "My grandfather killed the man who killed Commander Marlenz!" 'I suppose he killed a Fireheart too?' Pronyes said, looking back with a grin.

Siort frowned. 'Don't mock me, Pronyes. It's true!' The young soldier kicked his own shield to emphasise his irritation. 'My grandfather named my father Souza in honour of the man himself and there's a statue of my grandfather in a square in Gatch… It's not a very big statue,' Siort continued with a shrug, 'but it's there.'

Pronyes arched a brow. 'Well, perhaps they'll build a statue to you one day. Bigger than your grandfather's. Just as soon as we spot "Anything unusual".'

'If only,' Siort replied. He picked up his shield then pointed to the far end of the bridge. 'Patrol,' he announced, and turning, Pronyes saw that four Makech horsemen were about to cross the bridge. He too picked up his shield and moved to stand opposite his partner, standing to attention as the group clattered their way slowly towards them. The riders looked tired, heads down, shoulders slumped forwards and as they came closer Pronyes could see the mud caked against them and their horses. They had either ridden hard from Forht, he decided, or been off track for days. Searching for something unusual perhaps?

While Pronyes considered the point, the lead rider lifted his head to stare hard at him and, for several long seconds, Pronyes found he was unable to do anything but stare back. There was something about the man which seemed unusual, but he was at a loss to identify just what it was that intrigued him. All the while the riders moved closer and the man did not shift his stern gaze an inch from Pronyes's.

Pronyes looked down as the patrol came level, a thought striking him on why the man had continued to stare at him so hard. We must look like fools with these shields, he thought. What soldier in his right mind would carry a shield for Sakoom's sake!? He sighed and lifted his head again as the last rider passed then flicked a glance over to Siort who stared back at him wide-eyed.

'Did you see that?!' Siort hissed, his eyes darting to make sure the patrol did not overhear. Pronyes checked to see that the riders were far enough away to be out of earshot then crossed to his companion.

'See what?' he asked quietly.

Siort looked again at the receding riders, now clear of the bridge. 'One of them had no boots on!' His voice almost squeaked with the incredulity of the fact.

'No boots...' Pronyes repeated dully. He frowned: his own thoughts racing back to his own curiosity with the lead rider. He had carried no spear, had a beard as sparse as Siort's and – a shudder ran down his spine. The staring rider had blue eyes... Ebo's Mire! Blue eyes! Only the scum Rial had blue eyes!

'HEY!!'

His heart racing, Pronyes found himself shouting at the departing patrol before he'd had a chance to think about the tactical disadvantage he and Siort were in. Two men in a confined space against four on horseback. He put his hand on the hilt of his sword, caught his companion's look of surprise at his sudden animation then took a deep breath as the patrol slowly stopped. The lead rider wheeled his horse around to face him.

Pronyes thought better of his actions and waved his sword hand in greeting. 'Any news from Forht?!' he shouted and managed a smile.

The lead rider stared unflinchingly for a few seconds then slowly shook his head. He continued staring but the old soldier just hung on to his smile and nodded acknowledgement before turning away and looking out onto the river. The patrol moved off again.

'Are you alright?' Siort asked. He laughed and patted Pronyes's arm. 'I thought you were going to ask why one of them had no boots on!'

Pronyes nodded but gazed sightlessly at the ducks beneath him, thinking of the implications of what he had just seen. "Anything unusual" Commander Tzimek had said, but he had not expected something quite so out of the ordinary. That had been a Rialan on that horse – he was positive of it. Which meant they had all been Rialan. Brazenly riding past... RIDING!! On stolen horses wearing the uniforms of Makech soldiers. Pronyes shook his head, disbelief giving way to nervousness at what he had just seen and, more importantly, what he should do about it. He took a deep breath and looked past Siort at the patrol which had picked up its pace slightly.

'I think I know what's going on, Siort,' he said with a mournful sigh.

Siort frowned. 'What do you mean, Pronyes?' he replied.

'The Soulcatchers, the shields,' Pronyes said. 'I think I know why.'

Siort laughed. 'Go on then, let me in on the secret.'

Pronyes tugged at his beard abstractly and watched the

horsemen, now small against the rising ground as they skirted the southern edge of Urawiir: unsure what he should do. He had to warn the garrison so they could capture the Rial scum before they got too far away, but to do that he would have to admit that he had not challenged them – had let them get away without even a harsh word. Siort was right; it had to be the Philiri that had, somehow, gotten bolder than they had ever been before.

'C'mon!' Siort's jovial exclamation broke Pronyes's train of thought and he frowned at his young, unblooded colleague. 'What is it you know about what's going on?' Siort demanded.

Pronyes shrugged. 'Nothin',' he replied, 'but I think we should report back about those boots.'

Siort burst out laughing. 'Boots!?' he cried gleefully. 'No, Pronyes, we can't! Tzimek would rage like Sakoom! You aren't serious?'

Pronyes's stern expression quelled his partner's joviality. He nodded and, making certain that the horsemen were now out of sight, placed his shield against the handrail and made to go back to the garrison.

'You stay here,' he said to Siort.

'Tzimek will go mad,' Siort replied.

'Perhaps,' said Pronyes quietly and walked away.

II

Kattis Capell felt as if he existed in some waking nightmare. Bar the terrifying memory of pain he remembered little of the injuries inflicted on him by the brutal Yetzi, but he had woken several days later to find the strange world he was stranded in had become even stranger. Whatever damage had been done to him in the cell had – apart from several missing teeth

– miraculously healed and Baramir now sported a silver-like band around his temple and claimed to possess the spirit of the now dead Yetzi. Added to that, they both seemed (well, Baramir seemed) to be an honoured guest of these savages and their dank cell had been exchanged for sumptuous quarters better than any Kattis had ever seen before. Capell had done little after regaining consciousness than rest and eat but Baramir had spent most of his time in consultation with Tanikalin and Gidus, the wizened old man who was known as a Soulcatcher.

Baramir had returned from one such meeting dressed in fine robes like those of the old man and presented Kattis with similar items of clothing.

'They are a mark of distinction,' Newman announced. 'No one but the Beck Iph wears such things and,' he grinned, 'wearing it means you are untouchable.'

'Wish I'd had them in the cell,' Capell replied as he sifted through the garments and felt the various textures and weaves. 'Perhaps Yetzi would have left me alone.'

'Don't whine, Kattis,' Baramir responded. He strolled around the room and settled himself into an ornate-backed chair beside a circular table. Adjusting his elegant robes he placed his elbows on the arms of the chair and rested his chin on his hands.

'You're alive aren't you?' Newman said. 'Thanks to me, while Yetzi is…' He waved an arm and flashed his rictus smile. 'Would you like to meet him?' he asked. The question seemed to hang like a dark cloud in the air.

Kattis shook his head but the action simply made Baramir's grin broader. 'Too late,' he said. 'Watch the chair.'

On the other side of the table an identical chair to that which Baramir sat on began to vibrate slightly. Kattis frowned and was wondering whether the movement was simply his imagination when a large copper pot which had occupied the centre of the table suddenly launched itself into the air and flew with tremendous speed straight for Kattis. Capell gave a terrified yelp, threw himself sideways and there was a snarling Makech curse from Newman as the heavy object smashed into the wall just inches from Capell's head.

Kattis's desperate dive had tumbled him out of bed and he took a few moments to untangle himself from the bedding that had been dragged in his wake. He stared wide-eyed at the large hole in the plaster behind him and the squashed remains of the metal pot which now lay on the bed.

In the centre of the room Baramir was still yelling in guttural Makech and Kattis noticed how the metal band around his temple glowed with a ferocious light. At length the light faded and Newman sank back down into his chair: seemingly exhausted by his bizarre activity. Capell rose from behind the bed, poured out a mug of water and crossed to his friend.

'Are you alright, Newman?' he asked, offering the water to Baramir.

Baramir chuckled and rubbed at the flaking skin around the celesdain band. 'I think Yetzi still bears you a grudge,' he said and smiled weakly as he took the water.

The next day Patrol Leader Tanikalin had accompanied Baramir to Kattis's room: the patrol leader sitting himself in the same seat Newman had occupied the previous day. Capell was still unsure of the Makech in general, and the patrol leader in particular, so he glanced nervously in his direction as Newman ordered him to get out of bed and dress. Tanikalin, seemingly without a care in the world grinned back before picking up the squashed pot Newman had insisted be returned to the centre of the table. Baramir followed Capell's gaze and smiled at Tanikalin.

'Do you see that, Kattis?' he said, pointing to the patrol leader. 'That is the happiness of a man who has not only joined an elite group but who has just jumped two levels in rank. Is that not right, Commander Tanikalin?' Tanikalin remained silent but the reinforced smile spoke volumes.

'That lovingly polished brass plaque on his chest,' continued Newman, 'proclaims that he is now a novice officer in the Beck Iph Guard. A very rare and envied position.'

'Con-congratulations, Tanikalin,' stammered Kattis with a wan smile. Tanikalin scowled.

'Commander Tanikalin,' he replied icily and pointed to the shining brass plate which hung from his neck.

'Co-Commander Tanikalin… Sorry,' Capell muttered and, as the proud new member of the Beck Iph reset his smile; he hurried into his new robes while Baramir paced impatiently.

They left less than an hour later with Gidus's group in a cart that had been 'procured' for Baramir from a local tradesman. It was a simple affair: its bleached and buckled wood stained from a thousand journeys and drawn by oxen, not horses. Even so, Baramir held the reigns as if he were the proudest man alive. Beside him on the bench Kattis wrinkled his nose as the rancid smell from the streets of Forht assaulted his senses and shifted in his seat to look back as Newman negotiated the cart through the shadow of the town gates. Mere yards behind them Commander Tanikalin led ten horsemen from the garrison and, though his eyes were shadowed by his skull-topped helmet, Capell was sure that the man's icy gaze followed his slightest movement. Quickly he turned back and found Newman grinning.

'Soon, my dear Kattis,' Baramir said cheerfully, 'we shall ride around this land in a fine carriage like that one.' He pointed to Gidus's coach up ahead. Drawn by four black horses, its pristine black paint work and velvet curtains were a far cry from their own ramshackle transport. Behind it was tethered two spare horses, one for Gidus and one for the Beck Iph guard who held the reigns of the carriage. The remaining three guards rode ahead of the entire procession.

'Why does Gidus travel with those curtains drawn?' Capell asked.

'That's to protect the Wraith,' Baramir replied. Kattis looked blank and drew a frown from his friend. 'The Omerk,' explained Baramir testily, then in exasperation when Capell still failed to comprehend. 'The bloo'sandin' big-eyed midget! Remember?!'

'Ohh…' Kattis said, remembering the strange, wide eyed monstrosity. They sat in silence for a few moments before Capell voiced the question which kept buzzing around in his head. 'Why?' he asked and Newman's cheerful demeanour fell away.

'Why…what?!' Baramir drawled menacingly. He frowned at the horizon.

'Why, if you don't mind me asking,' continued Kattis despite the edge in Newman's voice, 'do the velvet curtains protect it?'

Newman sighed and flicked the reigns several times in irritation. 'It's to protect it from the sun. Milla's glare.'

Capell looked at the overcast sky but refrained from asking anything further on the matter. Instead he changed the subject. 'Where are we going, Baramir?'

The question returned the smile to Newman's lips. 'We are going to find the Fool King my dear Kattis,' he replied.

'King Ciro?'

'The very same,' nodded Baramir. 'Gidus believes that our illustrious, wandering monarch has found a group sympathetic to his cause called the Philiri. And, thanks to Yetzi, I know quite a lot about them myself.'

'How did Yetzi tell you?' Kattis asked.

Newman's smile grew broader and he gave a low and hollow chuckle. 'You still don't understand, do you?' he said. 'About what's happened to me? The gift I've been given?'

To this Capell looked nervous and shook his head; half expecting Yetzi's – whatever it was – to suddenly start rocking the cart. Instead Newman began explaining about the band around his head.

'It's made of a substance called celesdain, or 'moon iron' as it's sometimes known. It's a very rare and very powerful material which, if you care to believe such stories, was woven around the earth by the moon himself.'

Kattis checked the grin which threatened to spread across his face. 'Do you believe it?' he asked instead.

'I…' Baramir began, and then frowned. 'The Makech believe it. Yetzi believed it,' he said, 'and I… I,' Baramir closed his eyes for a moment. 'When I concentrate, I can see flashes of strange and wonderful things. Images. Do you understand, Capell?' His companion noted the seriousness in his voice and nodded slowly. 'Gidus says they are memories from long, long ago –'

'From the moon?'

'No! Not from the beckin' moon, you fool!' exploded Baramir. 'From the crystal!'

It was Capell's turn to frown. 'What crystal Newman?'

'The beckin' crystal in my beckin' head!' snapped Baramir. 'That's what crystal!'

Kattis mouthed a silent 'O' but said nothing. Baramir shook his head and flicked at the reigns again. As Kattis pondered the strange fact that Newman thought he had a crystal in his head his eye was caught by two brightly coloured birds flying

233

tight turns in the air close by. Again and again the birds circled, diving towards one another before disappearing into a bush to a raucous chorus of twittering. Capell watched the aerial display with fascination and sighed: realising it was the first time in memory he had been even close to relaxing. When had the last time been? Obaln? Kattis frowned... No, Rurset. At The Barleyman Inn. Where this whole, sorry nightmare had begun and they had made their escape in a cart not too dissimilar to the one in which they now travelled. Kattis sighed again, remembering the superb food which was always on offer at The Barleyman. The battered fish, roast pork with stuffing, the beef stew with –

'What's the matter with you?!' Baramir snapped. 'You're sighing like the wind through a broken shutter.'

'Sorry, Baramir,' Kattis said sheepishly. 'It's just that I was remembering the menu from The Barleyman.'

Newman arched a brow. 'If only we could swap your brain with your stomach. You'd be the smartest man alive. Now, be quiet. We'll eat when we arrive at our destination.'

As if in protest, Capell's stomach growled audibly, despite Kattis's efforts to muffle the noise with his hands.

'And you can keep that quiet, as well,' said Newman sternly and, with that, they rode on into the wilderness until the grey daylight turned to black.

It took the procession two full days to reach the small village of Urawiir and during that time Kattis learnt more about their reasons for travelling to this tiny backwater. The Philiri, so Commander Tanikalin had gruffly informed him, were rumoured to use the place as a communication point. Because of this, Baramir had added, it was the perfect place to gain information about King Ciro's whereabouts.

Around a roaring campfire, Baramir, Gidus, Tanikalin and the rest had toasted to a quick capture of the 'Fool King'.

Newman, standing as proud and confident as Capell had ever known him to be, had then entertained the group with stories of Ciro's womanising, gambling and fighting around the kingdom of Feirlan. Feeling a little uncomfortable with his friend's tales, Kattis had retired to the back of the cart soon afterwards. It was not because the stories were untrue, but because Baramir attributed them to the wrong Torrman. If he had said 'Bdann' in place of 'Ciro', Kattis would have readily agreed to join in the revelry – he knew some great stories about the wayward prince himself. But to attribute such scandalous behaviour to Ciro made Kattis worry about the fate of the young king once he was captured. He had slept with a heavy heart that night but it was nothing compared to the mind-numbing shock that their stay in Urawiir produced.

They needed, Baramir had said matter-of-factly as they rode across the deserted bridge west of Urawiir by moonlight, to get some information from the townsfolk about the king's whereabouts.

'Who will you ask?' Kattis had said.

'Oh, everybody,' came Baramir's cryptic reply.

Capell was left under the grinning charge of Tanikalin as Baramir joined Gidus. Together the two Soulcatchers brought the bow-legged Wraith cackling and gibbering from its velvet carriage then led it by the hand into Urawiir's village square. The old Soulcatcher had bound the little monster's eyes for some reason and, as Capell followed their progress from the edge of the village, he wondered just who the pair were hoping to question. To Kattis's eyes, the whole place looked deserted.

All the buildings were dark windowed, ramshackle huts topped with unkempt thatch and there was not a sound save the murmur of Tanikalin's men and the occasional rustle from the surrounding trees. There was a half moon glowing brightly through shifting clouds and then on the breeze came the faint smell of burning. Kattis sniffed the air again, turned to see the red-masked Beck Iph guards walking casually amongst the huts which bordered the square: lighting every structure that they passed with a flaming torch. By this fast growing light, Capell could now make out his friend, standing with the old man and the wraith by what appeared to be a solid stone horse trough in the centre of the square. The sight was an incongruous one amongst such flimsy surroundings but its mere presence made Capell smile. Its slab sides and rounded corners were familiar to Kattis and – from this distance at least – it looked identical the one his trinket stall had stood next to in Obaln market.

Gidus began to pace. While the Beck Iph guards spread out to stand watch at the exits to the square, Baramir kept a firm hold on the little Omerk and studied the old Soulcatcher's movements. Gidus stepped one way, then another: gradually circling the square while muttering an ancient chant. Though Baramir did not recognise the incantation, he began to feel its power.

Looking on, Kattis shivered. The wind grew in intensity; fanning the flaming roofs into bright and savage life. Yet, apart from the crack and hiss of burning thatch, the square remained eerily silent.

Then the first scream sounded, and quickly the square began to fill with running, terrified villagers: spilling from their homes by the dozen. Round and round the square the crying locals ran, seemingly blind to the fact that they ran in circles or that Baramir and Gidus stood in their midst. Then, into the swirling human torrent, the pair let loose the blind Omerk and it waddled at speed into the oblivious throng.

Unnerved by the genuine fear of the villagers, Kattis looked on and tried to fathom why – by Fidiann's beard – the poor townsfolk did not run out of the square? There was a Beck Iph guard at each exit, but all were facing outwards, not in. If the crowd decided to bolt, Kattis considered, the single guards would do as well as the Watchman he had once seen trying to keep order in Obaln market when Baramir had shouted 'Plague!'. Whatever the predicament of the poor souls before him, they did nothing but circle round and round while Baramir and Gidus stood stock-still by the horse trough. Beside the screams and the roaring fire, Capell now heard a chant rise up from Tanikalin's men – accompanied by their stamping boots.

'Unzekka! Unzekka!' Stamp! Stamp! Stamp!

'Unzekka! Unzekka!' Stamp! Stamp! Stamp!

The chant continued as Kattis watched and then he caught the eye of Tanikalin. The commander smiled and stepped closer.

'Do you see the power of the Makech?' he said proudly, pointing over his shoulder to where the people still milled. There were old and young alike in the throng and, as Kattis followed Tanikalin's outstretched arm he saw an old woman fall to her knees and writhe like so many rags as the crowd trampled over her. Kattis bit his lip and attempted a smile.

'I cannot begin to tell you how happy I am to be on the right side, Commander,' he said. Kattis hoped the words conveyed the sincerity he intended and not the nervousness he felt.

Tanikalin sneered. 'Just remember why you're not out there running with the rest of the cattle. If anything happens to your friend...' He let the sentence tail off but there was more than enough menace in his words to make Kattis pale.

Capell dropped his gaze to the ground and turned away. He was heading back to the cart when the screams of the crowd grew to a ferocious level and he turned to see a whirlwind of fire erupt in the heart of the square. Dumbstruck, Kattis looked on as Baramir and Gidus stared out from the maelstrom while the now uncovered eyes of the Omerk glowed like cinders. The savage wind, somehow contained within the square was uprooting terrified villagers by the dozen: hurling them into the spark flecked air. Their cries of terror were distorted by the rushing wind and again Kattis caught the chant of Tanikalin's men, loud enough to be heard above the unnatural fury as the poor locals were spun and tossed higher and faster. Now the flames from the surrounding buildings bent acutely; glowing fingers spiralling into the vortex as the screams grew louder. The villagers were burning.

Kattis felt numb. Rooted to the spot he could not wrench his gaze from the hideous obscenity which span up into the darkness before him. He found himself mouthing the words that his mother had always whispered to him at bedtime before kissing him on the forehead and blowing out the candle.

'Never fear the dark, Beck Night,' she would say softly in his ear. 'It may be dark, but does not bite.'

Over and over he repeated the line, wishing that, even for a moment, the words might bring as much comfort to the wretched villagers as it had to him as a child. After what seemed like an eternity of pain the cries had faded into the flames. Another sound arose: at once familiar to Capell's ears and all the more chilling because of it. Kattis turned away feeling more miserable than he ever had before and the sound followed him all the way back to the cart. In the centre of the square, standing upright and proud amongst the dying wind and burning corpses; Baramir was laughing.

Baramir slept badly that night but, unlike Kattis, it was not from any remorse over the events of the evening. On the contrary, Baramir had been exhilarated by the proceedings – especially his own new found skills. If it had not been for the overwhelming and unexpected tiredness brought on by causing so much mayhem to the unsuspecting villagers, he would probably not have retired to bed so soon after their triumphant dispatch of the sad citizens of Urawiir. As it was, he was carried bodily from the square by Tanikalin and some of his men soon after the fires had dissipated and placed in the tent Gidus had had erected on the edge of the village. Newman had been barely conscious when the old Soulcatcher had leant over him and muttered something about 'greed' but, though he had slept for what felt like an eternity, that sleep had been disturbed. Running constantly through Baramir's mind had been harsh, persistent voices, bleak images and, from somewhere, the continuous barking of a dog.

'Will you SHUT UP!?'

Baramir was already sitting up as he shouted the words and noted abstractly that a pale light was illuminating the heavy canvas of the tent. He saw too that some form of ornate stand glinted dully amongst the shadows as he cast his eyes about the tumble of cushions which occupied the floor. His immediate concern however was just who was making that damnable racket. He shut his eyes again when he realised the noise was emanating from within.

How many had it been? How many frightened souls had he plucked from the burning night and locked away in the mansion he was building in his mind? Too many, Gidus had thought and, listening to the cacophony of noise which rang through his thoughts, Baramir was inclined to agree. Like some cerebral hangover the sounds jarred against his consciousness and he listened for a fraction of a second longer before lashing out his will and shaking the cage which held his new souls captive. There was an instant and welcome hush before Yetzi came to the fore: pleased that he now had others to bully. Baramir dismissed his seeming joy with a swift rebuke and attempted to discern just who his new acquisitions were. There were three in all: their presence an avalanche of sometimes bizarre, always disjointed memories and emotions which all but overwhelmed Newman as he attempted to view them. He held firm against the rushing jumble and raged at the new souls, quietening them once again. Yetzi sniggered.

Carefully Baramir peeked at each captive in turn. First bringing his will to bear on them and then demanding specific information – no more. He would peruse their lives at his leisure later but right now he wanted only one thing. Information on the Philiri, and with it (hopefully) the whereabouts of the fool king.

The first was a woman: Insa by name, but apart from her name Baramir could discern nothing of value or interest by her presence. She was the partner of a woodsman named Lybec and collected mushrooms once a day in the forests beyond Urawiir. There was a lifetime more but, even skipping and jumping as quickly as he could, Baramir found nothing to interest him. The most notable event in her life seemed to be his arrival the previous evening.

'I must find out how to purge myself of rubbish,' Baramir said aloud: and noted how his captives quailed.

The next was a girl whose thoughts leaped and shivered with his briefest touch and shrank away from him into the darkest recesses of his mind so quickly that Baramir could not even find out her name. He sent his will chasing after her, annoyed that his captive even contemplated eluding him but, at the same time, admiring the girl's swiftness of thought – so different to sluggish Yetzi. She seemed, Baramir mused as she continued her futile flitting, more 'alive' than the others in some way, but how did not become fully apparent until Newman managed to snare her spirit and demand to know who she was.

Baramir, his eyes closed with concentration, suddenly had the nagging sensation that he was not alone in Gidus' tent. Half expecting to see the old man or Tanikalin standing before him Baramir opened his eyes and was shocked to see the pale outline of a girl crouching nervously a few feet away. Recovering his composure, Newman stared harder at the apparition which, second by second, solidified until almost real.

'Who are you?!' Baramir demanded. The girl, whose gaze had darted continuously around the tent, now settled on the Soulcatcher. Baramir could see the fear in her wide eyes as well as sense it in his mind and so knew her to be the young soul he had just been chasing.

'My name is Elbeth,' said the girl: though Newman could not be sure if her lips produced any sound. Inside his head, Baramir suddenly saw that the previously elusive thoughts were now still and enveloped them with his own, flicking quickly through the brief history of her life while the apparition looked nervously on.

'Mmhm, mmhm,' Baramir muttered to himself as Elbeth's childhood replayed for his benefit. At another time Baramir might have been intrigued by an adolescent girl's antics and her love for her dog. Newman had never understood women but now was not the right time to gain an insight. He wanted information but, like Insa before her, Elbeth's thoughts shed no light on the activities of the Philiri. Baramir was reluctantly beginning to consider seeking Gidus's help to rid himself of these useless entities when a persistent problem the girl had with her father caught his attention.

It was so inconsequential that Baramir had not noticed any

detail during his first perusal but, now that he focused upon that area of Elbeth's life, the intriguing information sprang up like shoots from the bed of her memory.

It seemed that the girl's father, a man named Deran, worked in the compound where the Makech had their garrison. Or rather he had worked there – Baramir now saw Elbeth's memories of the man blazing in the air before her. Deran had sewed and repaired the Legion's uniforms as well as providing woollens for the harsh winters. There did not seem to be any reason other than financial for Deran's job – Baramir could certainly find no love for the Makech in anything the man was remembered as saying – but even so, Elbeth despised him for what she, and all the other children in the village, saw as complicity. With no mother to act as mediator, her contempt for her father was left unchecked and had long since reached the stage where she had been banished from Deran's house and taken in by her mother's sister Lisal and her husband, Mara.

With them she found kindred spirits. Mara left the village frequently and would always return with fresh vegetables and tales of distant days when Rial had been stronger than Makech. Elbeth loved the stories and told Mara that, one day, she would join the Philiri and fight the Bonemen. Mara had laughed at the suggestion.

'How would you find the Philiri?' he had asked.

'Don't you know any of them, Uncle Mara?' she had replied and to this he shook his head.

'They are everywhere and nowhere,' Mara had said. 'But, when you're bigger I shall take you to the hare's house and introduce you to Tenc. He knows where the Philiri are.'

As baffled as Elbeth had originally been with Mara's cryptic statement, Baramir stopped his perusal and snapped at her ghost; still flickering like a candle in the gloom of the tent.

'What, by Fidiann's beard, is 'the hare's house'?!' he demanded.

Elbeth shook her head. 'I don't know... Mara never explained and neither did Tenc when I met him.' The girl looked miserably around the tent. 'Will you let me go now?' she asked.

Baramir smiled. 'Yes. You can go back inside,' he said and slammed the door shut on Elbeth's spirit. The shape before him was instantly snuffed out.

Newman grinned and lay back on the cushions: pleased with himself. If there was a place called the hare's house, Tanikalin would probably know of it. Baramir remembered that he had one final soul to peruse and decided to see if there was any more information to be had. Whoever it was had not uttered a sound since he had silenced the racket which greeted him when he awoke and now he peaked curiously into the space it had been held in. His curiosity was met by a cacophony of noise and jumbled thoughts.

'Oh, no! No!' shouted Baramir, instantly re-closing the space. He jumped to his feet and kicked at the cushions, furious with himself for not paying more attention. 'Beck! Beck!' he thundered and left the tent in search of Gidus and Tanikalin. He would tell them of the information he had gleaned from the capture of Elbeth but not one word would he mention about the fact that he had also captured Elbeth's dog.

The morning was cold with a sharp breeze and the smouldering ruin of the houses around the town square belched grey smoke into an otherwise clear sky. Baramir smiled at the dereliction and wrapped his heavy cloak more firmly around him. There was a tight huddle of soldiers away to his left and Newman headed towards them. There was no sign of Gidus, or indeed Capell.

'Lazy... Fat... Useless...' Newman muttered to himself as he crossed the ground to the soldiers, intending to ask one of the Makech to go and rudely awaken his companion. As he drew closer his approach was noticed and, with much sudden activity the huddle of men parted to reveal Commander Tanikalin and an old soldier whom Baramir had never seen before. Tanikalin smiled and gave a curt bow: the other soldiers following suit as the Soulcatcher approached.

'Good news, your reverence,' Tanikalin said. 'This man is from the Urawiir garrison. He believes he has seen this Rial King.'

Baramir looked levelly at the man. 'I thought you'd instructed the garrison commander to make shields, Tanikalin?' he said curtly, not releasing the grey-bearded soldier from his gaze. To this the soldier bowed his head and Tanikalin struck him soundly on the shoulder.

'Where's your shield, soldier?' Tanikalin said icily. 'I gave strict instructions to that pompous arse Tzimek that all his men should be equipped by morning. Where is it?'

Pronyes hung his head even lower and muttered. 'I'm very sorry sir, your reverence; I left it back at the bridge: thought it would slow me down sir.'

'SINCE WHEN WERE YOU PAID TO THINK!!?' bellowed Tanikalin into Pronyes' ear so loudly that even Baramir winced. 'You don't think, you just do! Do you hear me!? Whenever and whatever we tell you! UNDERSTOOD!?'

Pronyes nodded so furiously that his helmet almost flew off. When he finally lifted his head the helmet had tilted so much that it obscured one eye.

'Now,' continued Tanikalin in a more moderate tone. 'Straighten yourself up and tell his reverence what you just told me.'

Pronyes yanked his helmet level and looked at Baramir's feet, not daring for an instant to look the Soulcatcher in the eye. 'I…If it please your eminence – your reverence – meself and me colleague just saw a Makech patrol cross the bridge.' Pronyes took a deep gulp of air and continued. 'Thing is, they carried no spears,' he said to the mud at Baramir's feet. 'And my colleague, he says: "Look on, Pronyes, one of them ain't got no boots on!" An' so I says: "That ain't right: no boots!?" An' so I came straight over here as fast as I could to tell ya – leavin' me shield – beggin' your pardon, sirs.'

Baramir tilted his head and regarded the old soldier intently while silence hung heavily in the air. 'So what?' he said, flicking his gaze between Pronyes and Tanikalin. 'One of your patrols went out in a hurry,' he said with a shrug. 'So what? How does that make him a king?'

'Tell him the rest, you fool!' Spat Tanikalin. 'Before his reverence decides to make you walk the square.'

'The patrol leader had b-blue eyes, sir,' Pronyes spluttered. 'No mistake, I saw it myself sir. Blue eyes.' Pronyes finally managed to raise his gaze but, instead of the surprise he expected to see, the Soulcatcher simply stared back malevolently.

'No one but the Rial have blue eyes, your reverence,' added Tanikalin – realising Baramir's incomprehension.

'I see,' Baramir replied. 'And this patrol came from where, precisely?'

'Don't know precise, like, begging your pardon, your reverence, but somewhere west,' said Pronyes. 'Wait a minute!' he added suddenly. 'They was all muddy too! They'd been off track!'

'We sent out several patrols to search the area between here and Forht,' Tanikalin explained to Baramir. 'Everywhere from the north coast to the South River. We even sent one to search the Rabbit Warren.'

'Rabbit Warren!?' Baramir repeated, his interest peaked.

'Yes, your Reverence,' continued Tanikalin, 'it's a maze of stone walls that surrounds a deserted village called Olbas Osanti.'

Baramir threw his head back and laughed. 'Tell me, Tanikalin,' he said, barely containing his mirth. 'What does Olbas Osanti mean in Rialan?'

'Rialan, sir? I... I don't understand?

'Humour me.'

'It means 'Hare's House'.'

Baramir grinned. 'Hare's House!' he repeated with glee before pacing around Pronyes and Tanikalin. 'So,' he said, thinking aloud. 'A group of people led by a man with blue eyes came from the wilds between here and Forht – correct?' He stopped and pointed a bony finger at Pronyes.

'Yes, yes,' stammered the old soldier, surprised by the sudden digit in his face.

'And this Hare's House, this Olbas place, it's deserted – correct?'

'For many years, your reverence...' said Pronyes

'But, even so your reverence,' Tanikalin interjected, 'Ciro might have stumbled across it, that's why we sent a patrol there.'

'Quite, but if this hawk-eyed soldier is right about our wayward monarch, that patrol was not enough,' replied Baramir and took some small pleasure from the discomfort that realisation brought to Tanikalin. 'Where did this patrol go after it crossed the bridge?' he asked Pronyes suddenly; flashing his finger back into his face.

'They circled south around the outskirts, your reverence.'

'Wouldn't a Makech patrol have reported to the garrison, Tanikalin?' Baramir asked, Yetzi's knowledge of Makech procedures springing, unbidden to his mind.

Tanikalin nodded. 'Usually, your reverence, yes.'

'Then it's them!' Baramir laughed and clapped his hands before slapping Tanikalin on the arm. 'We have them, commander!'

'Have whom, Baramir?' said a dry, rusty voice from behind them. Newman span round to see the skeletal form of Gidus resting heavily on his staff. The old man and his four huge guards had approached completely unobserved.

'Our quarry, dear Gidus,' replied Baramir with a grin. He took a few steps closer and gripped the sleeve of the old Soulcatcher's robe. 'The Fool King himself. He passed this way less than –' Baramir snapped his fingers at Pronyes. 'How long ago!?' he barked.

'Half hour, no more, your rev'rence,' came the instant reply.

'A half hour...Can you believe it?' said Newman grinning. He turned to Tanikalin. 'Where would they head? Do we have a map?'

'We need to talk, Baramir,' Gidus said to his understudy's back and when Baramir turned there was anger written plainly across his face.

'We need to capture Ciro!' Newman hissed through gritted teeth.

The old Soulcatcher waved a dismissive hand. 'Tanikalin is better able to carry out that task. We need to talk.'

With that Gidus turned away, his guards instantly following. Baramir watched the receding figure for a few moments before flicking his gaze back to Tanikalin.

'Find him!' He spat and stomped off after Gidus.

III

Finding Urawiir burning had been a chilling experience for

Ciro's group yet, perversely, the disturbing sight aided their disguise as a Makech patrol. So ingrained into the Rialan mind was the edict that they were not allowed on horseback that, had it not been for the distraction caused by the smoking village, Ciro would have crossed the river alone.

As it was a chorus of gasps had escaped the group as the two Makech guards were spotted on the far side of the bridge but, now scant feet away from the span, the group had no other choice but to cross. Ciro had tried to settle their nerves.

'Ever seen a Rialan dressed as a Makech?' he asked as he led his horse onto the bridge. There had been silence. 'Well,' Ciro continued, 'neither have they.' He had turned and managed a grin which was nervously mirrored by Nesh. Arper and Tenc seemed too tense to respond. 'Keep your heads down and your wits about you,' continued Ciro. 'We are just another Makech patrol.'

With that Ciro had turned back to face the soldiers by the opposite bank and, instantly ignoring his own advice, stared unblinking at one of the Makech soldiers as if daring him to challenge them. They had plodded on at a steady pace and at length the Makech had dropped his gaze. Suddenly the guards were behind them and they found themselves on the far bank. Ciro was just beginning to relax when the soldier had called out and turned the king's blood to ice.

'Ey!' the Makech shouted and Ciro had slowly wheeled his horse about to face the bridge. The rest of the group, still with their backs to the bridge, watched him wide-eyed.

'Get ready,' Ciro had whispered and stared back at the soldier, noting that the man had placed a hand on the pommel of his sword.

The Makech removed his hand and waved it. 'Lith sestan har Forht?' he shouted.

'He said: "Any news from Forht?"' Tenc whispered.

248

Ciro wanted to smile but kept his face an impassive mask. It was just a simple query – nothing more. He shook his head gravely at the soldier then wheeled his horse about. 'We'll ride slowly around the village,' he muttered, 'until we're out of sight.'

'Then what?' whispered Arper nervously.

'Then we ride like the wind away from here.'

The road from the bridge curved north towards the village and was bordered on both sides by ancient stone walls. Beyond them were tilled fields and hedgerows but, though the barriers could have been easily jumped by their horses, Ciro did not want to draw attention to themselves. He searched the roadside for any break in the walls and tried not to think about what would await them in the village itself. It stood to reason that whoever had inflicted the damage on Urawiir was still close by.

'They're still watchin' us, Ciro!' hissed Arper. 'Can't we speed up?'

'Don't look back at them, Arper,' replied Ciro, frowning. He looked at Tenc. 'Does this road go straight into the village, Tenc?'

Tenc nodded and pointed up the road to a small brake of trees. 'Yeah, but there's a little track which leads down to Low Brook Mill up ahead.'

Ciro tried not to let his relief show. 'Can we get into open country from there? Get past the village?'

'Well, yeah,' Tenc replied. 'But it will make it difficult to get to The Cut – we'll be headin' towards Low Wood.'

Ciro remembered reading about The Cut and considered the route for a moment. 'There's no way off of The Cut for miles if I recall correctly,' he said. 'Wasn't most of it cut through a thick wood?'

'Yeah,' admitted Tenc, 'but it's the quickest route to Kal

Gians.'

'I went huntin' in Low Wood once,' said Arper. 'There's a track.'

Ciro nodded. 'The Cut may be quicker but the wood will be safer. I say we keep as far from the main routes as possible.'

There were nods from everyone and with relief Ciro saw the lane before them suddenly divide. Still moving at a gentle pace they turned right into the southern track and headed away from the smoking wreck of Urawiir.

'Are we gonna ride fast again, Ciro?' Nesh asked as they descended the muddy lane.

'Why, are you planning to fall off again?' replied Ciro with a grin.

Like Arper and Tenc, Nesh had never been on a horse until two days before and her bare foot style, instead of the usual stirrups, had led to one or two muddy tumbles on her first day. But now, after quickly finding her balance, she now rode better than any of the others.

'Nah, it's not that,' Nesh replied. 'It's jus' that if I get any more muddy I ain't gonna be able ta see.' Nesh ran a finger down her cheek and held out the dirt covered digit for Ciro's inspection.

Ciro smiled. 'Think of it as a disguise,' he said. 'If we get covered in enough mud and grass the Makech will think these horses rider-less.'

Nesh smiled back and they continued on down the winding track.

Ciro thought about King Antius's Grand Avenue as they trotted between the high hedgerows which bordered the lane. The Cut (as it became more generally known) had been carved through the middle of a low lying, wood topped range of hills and stretched for fifteen miles until it reached level ground on the eastern side. It had been hailed as one of the wonders of its age when finished and had been undertaken after years of Makech skirmishes around Forht. Its completion had meant troops could move rapidly from Torr Betram to defend the furthest tip of the kingdom and never again had the Bonemen been able to pose the same type of threat. It was one of the things Ciro had looked forward to seeing but he knew now that safety dictated he stay as far away from it as possible.

'Do you know anything about The Cut?' Ciro asked Tenc as the Philiri's horse drew alongside. 'I'd hoped to see it. Did you know King Antius used Makech prisoners to complete it?'

Tenc shrugged. 'There are bound to be documents about it in the Philiri Great Library: though I can't say I ever felt the urge to sit down and read about it.'

As a final gesture, Antius had then had built a massive statue of himself to stand sentinel at the eastern end of the avenue. Ciro inquired if it was still standing.

'No,' Tenc replied with a shake of his head. 'That I do know about. It lies on its side where it fell after the Makech invaded and pulled it down. It's now a canvas for every Makech insult imaginable.'

Ciro nodded, but his attention was taken by the view up ahead as the mill came into view. There was a cart parked before the main building and three Makech soldiers were busy piling grain sacks onto the back of it. At the head their group, Arper was the first to be spotted and the Makech instantly stopped what they were doing to wave. In response Arper gave a cry and bolted his horse for the tree line beside the mill.

'Blood'n sand!' muttered Ciro as Arper's nervousness spurred on the others. He dug his heels into his horse's flanks and darted after them before the confused Makech had time to react.

Beyond the tree line the ground opened out onto rolling meadows, edged on the right by the distant, misty curve of a wide river. Arper was racing on ahead towards a daisy covered rise and Ciro had to push his own horse hard to catch up. Behind them the Makech were now shouting from the trees.

'Slow down Arper!' Ciro shouted as he began to gain on the others. Arper disappeared over the rise and Ciro cursed. Did he even know which way he was going?

Now the king was level with Tenc as they reached the top of the rise and the Philiri glanced sideways towards him. He frowned and pointed past Ciro.

'Look!' he shouted.

There was a nervous edge in Tenc's voice and Ciro turned to see the smoking ruin of Urawiir on the hilltop in the distance. At least a dozen dark figures where racing rapidly down the hillside towards the mill.

They were more than two miles back and quickly hidden as Ciro raced down the far side of the rise but the king was positive he knew their purpose. Their crossing of the bridge had not gone unnoticed and now the Makech were starting to search for them. Ciro looked ahead and saw that the rolling meadows finally faded into a mass of woodland. Arper, with Nesh in close pursuit, was heading straight for it.

'Is that the Low Wood!?' shouted Ciro to Tenc.

'Yeah!' cried the Philiri.

Ciro nodded, dipped low in his saddle, and urged his horse on harder.

Arper and Nesh had already disappeared inside the straggling edge of Low Wood by the time Ciro and Tenc arrived and the pair had to move on into the deeper shade of the forest before they spotted them.

'Sorry, Ciro,' said Arper as he and the Philiri approached. 'I panicked a bit.'

Ciro shook his head, dropped from his saddle and crouched down to look back across the meadows. 'You did the right thing, Arper.' he replied, scanning the green horizon.

'Are those Bonemen followin' us?' asked Nesh.

No,' Tenc replied. 'But there's a bunch of 'em comin' out of Urawiir.' he frowned down at Ciro. 'See anythin'?' he asked.

Ciro nodded and watched as several dark shapes appeared on the daisy covered rise they had previously passed. He had wondered whether they might not have been spotted, but the sudden rush of horses which now sped down the slope towards them dispelled any such illusion. The Makech were giving chase.

'They're coming,' said Ciro with a calmness he did not feel. He leapt back into his saddle and surveyed the dark forest ahead

'We'll head south,' Ciro said. 'We'll ride fast so stay low in the saddle and let your horse be your guide. Come on!' he shouted and spurred his horse into a gallop.

Keeping close they followed Ciro as he cut a thundering path through the thick undergrowth which edged Low Wood. At length the trees began to soar above them and they sped on faster as the dense vegetation faded to a thick carpet of leaves. Ciro led them on a winding course, ever southwards through the heart of the forest and by this circuitous route he hoped that their pursuers would find any trail difficult to follow. At worst, Ciro thought, his efforts would split their pursuers into smaller groups. He knew from personal experience how a wily fox could lead horsemen a merry dance through woodland.

He kept his head low, almost glued to the horse's neck as the tree lines swept around him and occasionally stole a backward glance to reassure himself that no one had fallen from the saddle. Ciro did not want any more loses on his journey. He gritted his teeth, ignored the sharp pain in his side and galloped on towards what he hoped would be safety.

He could not be sure how long they had ridden for, but Ciro's own fatigue and the rasping breaths of his horse told him it was time to finally slow their flight. Rain had been pattering the leaves for miles and now a steady deluge of water was pouring through the forest canopy, making visibility difficult and soaking his Makech armour. Slowly Ciro reigned in his mount and tried to feel his injured side without Nesh noticing. He was sure the sword wound had reopened because, for some time now, it had stabbed and seared with every loping yard. Despite his attempted secrecy, Nesh, with a hawkish look, drew level and inquired whether Ciro's wound was troubling him.

He smiled despite the pain. 'It's nothing a few minutes out of the saddle won't cure,' he lied.

Arper jolted to a halt a few feet behind them: almost flying headlong from his saddle as he wrestled the horse to a standstill. 'Bugger's to stop, ain't they?!' he gasped, pushing his helmet back. 'This one goes like the wind!'

'Do you think we've lost our friends?' Tenc asked. The Philiri sounded as tired as Ciro felt, and slumped in his saddle the moment his horse stopped.

Ciro looked back through the trees for any sign of pursuit but the shadows were grey with rain. And, except for an occasional bird call, there was no sound above the clatter of water on leaves.

'If we're lucky, they will be far away from here – if they haven't already given up,' Ciro said hopefully. 'We've ridden a long way but we should keep moving. The horses need rest but we'll have to push them for perhaps another hour and then find somewhere to camp.'

The others nodded wearily and urged their horses into a reluctant trot. Nesh, riding alongside Ciro, pointed ahead.

'What's beyond the forest?' she asked.

'I've been trying to remember the same thing,' Ciro replied. 'If my memory serves, we should be heading towards Birin and the South Wall – Tenc, any idea if I'm right?'

Tenc was in the process of removing his helmet. He wrenched it free with a sigh, ran a hand over his rain-soaked face and looked absently into the distance for a moment. 'Mm,' he said before nodding, 'I think that's right.'

'Any idea how many Makech we might find there?' Ciro asked.

Tenc shook his head. 'None, that I know of, I don't think Birin's been lived in for a long while: the Makech don't seem to like going by boat.'

Ciro nodded. He knew little about Birin apart from the fact it had been a small trading port for Torr Betram in King Elson's day. But, with the enemy city of Kal Santra down river, passage had often been referred to as 'notorious'. There must have been scope for far greater traffic once Prince Idirnon had wrested control of Kal Santra away from the Makech, Ciro thought, but that had been only a few years before the blight. Ciro made a mental note to ask Tenc more about the Great Library he had mentioned. He wondered just what records they had stored there about the plague.

They journeyed on; finally letting the horses plod at their own pace and attempting to ignore the rain which had now soaked every one of them to the skin. The gloom of the forest deepened as they negotiated a seemingly endless procession of troughs and peaks in the ground and every new rise showed the same vista as the last: another water-logged mire beneath them and another grey tree-line beyond.

'How long 'till we stop?' Nesh asked with a frown. 'Only me feet are gettin' cold.'

Ciro smiled. 'When we get to Peimonac I'll have someone make you a pair of boots like mine. In the meantime…' Ciro fished inside one of the saddlebags and pulled out his Feirlan boots. '…You can wear mine. They may be a little big but they should warm your feet up.'

Nesh took the boots one at a time and, careful to keep her balance, slipped them on then pulled on the laces so that they would not fall off.

'You look very King-like, with them boots on girl,' quipped Arper.

Nesh poked out her tongue. 'An' you look just like a Boneman, Uncle Arper,' she retorted.

Arper frowned. 'Steady, girl,' he said, 'some thin's ain't right ta say, even in jest.'

Ciro was just about to change the subject when Tenc, who had ridden ahead to the next rise, called back to them.

'Come and look,' he shouted and the others urged their horses up the slope to join him.

At the top of the rise the ground dipped away again but this time in a gentle curve which stretched down onto level ground. The wood was brighter here and all could see that the trees in the distance gave way to open countryside.

Ciro smiled. 'Wait here while I see what's out there,' he said and trotted down to the edge of the forest. Dismounting, he tied his horse to a sapling, stepped slowly out of the tree line and peered through the rain.

To his left the trees continued in line with where he stood and beyond that loomed a vague grey mass which Ciro reasoned must be the hills of the South Wall – the hill range which sat just south of the city of Torr Betram. Straight ahead an expanse of tall grass ended with a barely visible break of trees and to his right the line of the forest curved away into the distance. Ciro cast his gaze around, searching for any sign of the Makech, and only when he was sure they were unobserved did he call the others to him.

They trotted down slowly and, with groans and grimaces, dismounted to crouch with him at the forest edge. Ciro, kneeling beside a patch of exposed earth, scratched a map into the dirt and explained where he thought they were.

'I'd say it's fairly obvious we've reached the far edge of Low Wood and, with those hills to our left, I'd say Birin wasn't far from here.' He looked at the tired rain-soaked faces around him and the lowered heads of their steaming horses. 'I know we're all weary, but if we can get to Birin we should find some dry shelter and it's doubtful the Makech will want to search beyond the forest.'

'Night'll be down soon,' said Tenc. He squinted up at the grey sky.

'All the more reason we find somewhere dry to rest up and plan where to head tomorrow.'

It took a supreme effort of will to climb back into saddles which instantly made them sore and uncomfortable but Ciro's logic and the vague promise of a dry place to lay their heads overrode such immediate discomfort. In ragged file they followed the young king through the tall grass and in silent procession they journeyed east beside the grey hills in search of Birin.

An hour later the rain had at last run dry and a warmer southerly breeze broke the late sun free of cloud. Their eastward course was soon halted by a broad river and, though they had no choice but to travel north beside it, Ciro was confident that it would lead them straight to Birin. His only concern (which he kept to himself) was whether they would find a way across once they got there.

The sun was dipping behind the distant, dark expanse of Low Wood as they entered the outskirts of Birin and, rounding a bend in the river, the deserted port could be clearly seen ahead. Broken stone walls had already begun to cut pale lines through the vegetation but now, as they dismounted and surveyed the place, they could see that the centre of the town remained largely intact. Around a harbour flanked by rotting wooden wharfs and the skeletons of jetties, the shells of store houses still stood firm against the carpet of green which had spread through the town.

'Reminds me of home,' said Tenc.

The others agreed. Trees and scrub choked the streets and clung to the buildings just like at Olbas Osanti but the western quay side was clear enough for them to lead their horses on towards the centre of town. At the end of the harbour they found the only bridge which spanned the river.

It was a single stone arch gripped by ivy at its eastern end but time had not sat lightly on its span. Blocks were missing from its side and when the group reached its western end a hole could be seen near its centre.

Arper rubbed his beard. 'I ain't no mason,' he said, 'but that don't look safe ta me.'

Ciro nodded, gave the reigns of his horse to Nesh and stepped closer. 'I'm going to test it,' he said, eying the bridge warily. It was only about fifty feet to the far bank but Ciro was in two minds about how best to cross it. Should he run and risk causing further collapse, or inch his way across in the hope that the structure was strong enough to hold him? He opted for the latter approach and, keeping well away from the hole, strode slowly to the other side. He reached it without incident, gave a sigh of satisfaction then turned straight back and crossed again; this time faster. The looks of relief on the faces of the others when he made it back were plain to see.

'Well, it seems sound enough,' said Ciro. He took his reigns back from Nesh. 'Now let's try it with a horse.'

'D'ya think it wise?' asked Nesh.

'Yeah,' agreed Arper. 'Couldn't we just leave the 'orses 'ere?'

Ciro shook his head. 'We have come such a distance with them it would be a shame to let them go now. As long as we're careful I think it's worth the risk.'

He turned and led his horse slowly across the span without incident then grinned back at the others. 'Who's next?!' he shouted. 'Or do you want me to come and get another horse?'

'I'll go next,' Nesh called back. She frowned at the bridge and followed the path she had seen Ciro take. A minute later she was standing beside him, a broad smile on her face.

Next was Tenc who inched across without incident and finally all were looking back at a nervous Arper. Ciro waved him on.

'It seems to be alright, Arper,' he said. 'Just be careful.'

Arper puffed out his cheeks, looked dubiously at his horse then shuffled his way onto the bridge. He had just passed the hole when a rumble of stone froze everyone.

The colour drained from Arper's face. 'Beck!' he mouthed as the others looked on wide-eyed. Splashes began to sound beneath the bridge

'Run!' shouted Ciro.

Arper did not need to be told twice. With a scream he darted towards the others as fast as he could – his horse trotting behind him. He made it to the bank, clutched his leaping heart and everyone waited for the bridge to fall. The hole in its centre widened by a block then the grinding and splashing ceased. The bridge remained standing.

Arper gripped Ciro by the shoulder. 'If we come back,' he gasped, 'can we go another way?' He pointed at the bridge and shook his head. 'I don't wanna cross that again!'

Ciro smiled. 'Neither do I, Arper,' he replied.

Nesh was scanning the buildings on the eastern side of the port. 'Are we gonna make camp soon, Ciro?' she asked, pointing to her feet. 'Only yer boots are killin' me.'

The others laughed. From the other side of the harbour he had been hoping to spot a structure that could house both them and their horses. He had discounted most of the buildings as seeming either too unstable or too small for the purpose but one building had caught his eye. Now he led them down the wide eastern quay side towards a circular structure which was partially obscured by a thin break of trees.

'There,' said Ciro as they moved closer. 'It looks solid enough to still be safe and there should be more than enough space for both us and the horses.'

They led the horses closer until a high, dark arch in the wall allowed them to see inside. Ciro had assumed it to be just another store house but now he revised his estimation.

'This must have been some kind of stronghold,' he said as the others joined him in the doorway. The walls were several feet thick and pale daylight from numerous arrow slits dotted the interior.

'At least it's mainly dry,' said Tenc. The Philiri's voice echoed strangely as he stepped further into the gloom.

Ciro looked up. There had originally been three stories to the structure but now the darkening sky showed through a raged hole in the floors above. Water from the rainstorm was still dripping down. At the back of the stronghold, what remained of the first floor still gave enough cover to leave the place dry and it was here that they led the horses.

'I could sleep for ever!' announced Arper. He dropped the

reigns of his horse and collapsed. There was a murmur of agreement from the others.

'You can sleep later,' said Ciro.

The king led his own horse into the rear of the stronghold before tethering it to a rusted iron ring he found attached to the wall.

'This looks like this was supposed to be for horses,' he said, pointing out the other rings along the wall. Beneath them was a shallow stone ledge which he guessed would have served as a feeding trough. 'Nesh,' he said as he tied the other horses to the rings. 'If you could start a fire, Arper, Tenc and I will collect grass for the horses.'

'Damn horses!' groaned Arper. 'Why can't they get their own food?' The others laughed as he wearily got to his feet and he followed Tenc and Ciro back into the open.

Dusk was rapidly reducing the town of Birin to a sight which reminded Ciro of a row of broken teeth, set against the sky. As they searched around the back of the stronghold for more open ground, Ciro mused on whether his brother, Bdann, would find Peimonac in a similar state of decay.

'I imagine Peimonac looks much the same as this,' Ciro said, thinking aloud. 'Derelict and overgrown.'

'I've never been close enough to say for sure,' Tenc replied. 'But on a clear day you can see it from the south shore of Bull Lake. It's miles away but in the sunlight it shines on the horizon.'

'Is it big, like Torr Betram?' Arper asked. The three of them had found a large patch of open ground behind the stronghold and together they began hacking at the tall grass with their swords.

'It's bigger,' Ciro replied as he swept his sword at the space before him. 'Where we are now, the South West Wold, was always the furthest outskirt of the Rial Kingdom – no less

261

important though,' he added in case Arper should take offence. 'But the Heart Wold was always where the main life of the kingdom went on.'

'Not much life left there now,' said Arper.

'Have you visited any other cities in Rial, Tenc?' Ciro asked. The question was one which either alarmed or surprised the grey haired Philiri for his eyes widened and he shook his head.

'I'm more adventurous than most,' he replied, 'but even I stayed close to Philire. When I came west – what – four year or so ago, it was a relief to be past the black apples. I knew then that what was behind me would, like as not, stay well behind me.'

Ciro was intrigued. Were all the Philiri as superstitious about the old kingdom as the brave and unfortunate Amec had been? 'Are you referring to the plague?' he asked. Tenc looked blank for a moment before realisation animated his face.

'Arper mentioned that to me a while back,' he said, shaking a clump of grass at Arper. 'You think Rial was destroyed by it, don't you?'

Ciro nodded. 'Well, yes…' he replied. 'We know that's what happened to the kingdom … We have records.' Tenc seemed amused. 'I know that you, well, I know that Amec believed it was some punishment of Milla's on King Elson which destroyed the kingdom but,' persisted Ciro, 'as I say, we have records of the blight which struck Rial. Eye witness accounts of bodies by the dozen being pulled out of the North Horn River.'

To this Tenc nodded slowly. 'I've no doubt that there are such records: they were very bad times back then, very bad indeed. And you're right, some Philiri do believe that it was Elson that started the whole thing. The accounts of Stal and

Gurnius didn't help – it made us feel abandoned – and superstitious tales about what happened to them and the rest of the kingdom have carried down through the generations. We have our Great Library and records of our own, but there are few scholars that I know of who can be bothered to dispel such wild stories. But, when the truth is just as wild as the myth, what difference does it make?'

'What do you mean by that?' asked Ciro.

Tenc sighed. 'It's a long story, so why don't we finish here and I'll tell you all I know by the fire.'

Ciro nodded and hastily slashed at the grass.

Nesh had produced a roaring blaze by the time they returned and Ciro was pleased to note that the glow of the fire could not be discerned from outside the stronghold. They dumped their armfuls of grass in the troughs for the horses and, while Nesh boiled the last of their meat in a pot with vegetables from Olbas Osanti, Tenc began telling Ciro what he knew of the last days of the old kingdom.

'I'm lucky enough to be the son of an Elderman which means, unlike many of my people, I had – or rather my father had – access to the Great Library.'

To this Ciro smiled, thinking of his own fortune in having access to the Ascension Chamber library in Torr Sarvie. Without that access he would never have known about Reilan, let alone Rial and King Elson. Tenc continued:

'When I was a boy my father came to me and said that, now that I was almost a man and was displaying a wanderlust, I should know about the world outside so that I didn't wander into trouble. I already knew all the tales of the Beck Night, the Firehearts and Omerk in the mountains and I'd already seen the bones of the Skaeling, but –'

'– Sorry,' interrupted Ciro. 'You'd seen the bones of the

what?'

'Skaeling,' repeated Tenc with a humourless grin. 'We have its bones on display outside the Great Library, but I'll get back to that in a moment…' Tenc dismissed the point with a wave of his hand. 'Anyway,' he continued, 'my father sat me down and told me that it was all very well knowing the tales but only the facts were worth paying any attention to. He said that it was important to know how and why the Philiri lived like they did from the first-hand accounts of people who had seen what happened to the old kingdom. Now our main information about what you say was a plague is from two sources. The first is the account of a dispatch messenger named Stal; the second is from a man named Gurnius who later went in search of Stal.' Tenc nodded into the fire. 'Now Stal, as I say, was a messenger, and his job was to ride from Philire to Peimonac with dispatches for the city's Elders –'

'Aldermen,' corrected Ciro. He was not sure that Tenc's claim that his information came from documented sources as reliable as Ciro's own where true but, even if they were, he wanted the telling to be as accurate as possible. 'They were known as Aldermen, not Elders,' he explained when Tenc looked confused.

'Oh,' said Tenc, 'Aldermen… Anyway, Stal had documents for them and, as he tells it, he arrived at the Great Bridge – they did have a great bridge outside Peimonac didn't they?' Ciro nodded. 'So, Stal crossed the Great Bridge and rode into the city but there was nobody there –'

'They were all dead?!' Gasped Nesh.

Tenc shook his head. 'No, not dead. They just weren't there.' Tenc adjusted his posture and leaned forward towards the fire. 'Stal rode through the empty streets and found the east of the city deserted but, when he rode west towards the docks, he came across an old man sitting on the quay side watching the water.

"Hail! Old man," Stal said, "What goes on here. I have important messages for the Eld -Aldermen, but Peimonac is deserted."

"You're too late," said the old man and he pointed to the empty docks. "They've long gone, every man, every woman, every ship: even the Queen herself and little Prince Sarvie."

"Gone where? And why!?" asked Stal'

"For a man with a message, you don't know much do you?" The old man replied. "They've gone away, far away because of what happened in the north. Death and doom, so they said, and it's heading this way."

"Death and doom?!" cried Stal. "Whatever do you mean?"

"I mean what I say I mean, young 'un, nothing more. Death has come to our kingdom and not even the King – not even brave Elson himself can stop it."

"Where is the king?" Stal inquired. "Did you see him?"

"He never came," said the old man sadly. "They waited and they waited for news but in the end they got everyone on ship and sailed away. Prince Idirnon himself had to drag Queen Lusiac aboard."

"I can't believe it!" Stal exclaimed. "What in Milla's name could do such a thing?"

'To this the old man laughed. "Milla's got nothing to do with it," he said. "Beck's here, they say, and a wall of night has fallen, blighting the landscape and everything it touches. They waited and waited," the old man said, "but, when they saw the night on the horizon they got everybody they could and sailed away."

"Why didn't you go, old man?" Stal asked and to this the old man shrugged.'

"My boy is Padia: he's a soldier with Meanon's lot – you know – the Wayward Prince?" Stal said he did. "Well, some say Elson won't go 'till he knows that his brother, Meanon, is safe, and I won't go until I know likewise 'bout my son. Meanon may be a rogue but he's always been good to the men and, like as not, if he's safe then my boy is too."

"You can't wait here, old man," pleaded Stal. "You must come back to Philire with me, tell them your tale."

"You tell 'em," the old man said. "I'm staying here 'til my boy comes home." And with that the old man would not move no matter how much Stal pleaded.'

'When, at last, Stal gave up attempting to bring the old man with him and said his goodbyes, the old man said:'

"Before you go son, you'd do well to climb Watch Hill and look to the north. That's where the Eldermen came running down from before the ships started boarding. My legs don't agree with hills the way they used to, but I'm pretty sure they saw enough up there to make 'em want to leave."

'So Stal rode his horse to the top of Watch Hill and, sure enough, he saw that, even though it was broad daylight, night sat heavily on the northern horizon. He rode back as fast as he could to tell the Elders of Philire all about it.'

Tenc sat back and for a moment just the crackle of the fire sounded in the stronghold. Ciro examined his Makech boots, thinking about what Tenc had just said. He was as sceptical of the Beck Night theory as he had been when Amec had told his tale, but the rest of the story was not so far removed from what he already knew. There had been great confusion in the last few days at Peimonac and Elson had ordered his brother Idirnon to escort the Queen and Elson's children away. What this messenger, Stal, had seen from the hill had most probably been a distant storm but, if that was what the Philiri wanted to believe, it did not ultimately matter. The Beck Night was merely a threat to the imagination – nothing more. Ciro looked up to find everyone was looking at him.

'Waddya think, Ciro?' asked Arper. There seemed to be a touch of awe in his voice.

'I'm sure that Tenc's story is as accurate as he remembers it, but I'm still intrigued to know about this 'Scary' thing. What did you call it, Tenc?'

'You mean the Skaeling? Yes, I was just about to tell that tale.'

'And then we eat,' said Nesh, prodding a stick into the bubbling pot.

Tenc leaned forward again and stared into the fire. 'After Stal had returned to Philire and told his tale,' he began, 'the Elders sent him north to Torr Adenair in search of the King. A month later, after Stal had not returned, a friend and fellow messenger named Gurnius volunteered to go in search of both Stal and the King – to settle the fears which had now gripped the city. As fast as his horse could carry him, he headed for Torr Adenair but, once he got there, he found that – just like Peimonac – it too was deserted. He searched high and low for any sign of life but, finding nothing, he began to make his way back to Philire to tell them the terrible news.' Tenc's eyes widened and he stared at the others in turn before continuing. 'Gurnius said that he was near the south of the city when he heard an unearthly roar, and he wheeled his horse about to find a massive beast standing in the road behind him… It was a hideous thing,' growled Tenc, 'and it snarled at him so fiercely that his horse bucked from underneath him and Gurnius fell to the ground. He was at the mercy of the monster…' Tenc raised his hands and slashed them through the air as if they were claws.

Very dramatic, thought Ciro to himself, noting how the others were spellbound by the tale. Tenc continued:

'The beast was almost on him and Gurnius was staring helplessly at the monster's huge teeth when he saw a flash of light in the air. In an instant the monster fell dead at his feet.'

'Blessed lightening, no doubt,' said Ciro dryly, trying to dispel the impact of what sounded like superstitious rubbish.

'No, no, that's the whole point,' replied Tenc, misreading Ciro's sentiment. 'You see, when Gurnius got shakily to his feet and looked at the beast, he saw that there was a strange hammer lying beside the monster – the head of it covered with the monster's blood. He said he didn't know which was stranger, the creature or the hammer, for this thing was bound with leather at the handle but made up of separate pieces –'

'– Don't tell me,' interrupted Ciro. 'They were made up of four separate pieces – each one symbolising the four elemental forces.' Ciro shrugged. 'At least that's what Calian always said their Quorum Hammers signified.'

Tenc frowned. 'You know the story about Calian, then?' he said. Ciro looked confused and frowned. '...One of the brothers who Gurnius met?' Tenc explained.

Ciro smiled and shook his head. 'Sorry, no I don't know this story,' he replied, 'but I do know a man – a Songsmith – named Calian. He was with me on my ship when I was washed overboard. The Songsmith's carry musical instruments known as Quorum Hammers which they play. I've never seen them bound together to make one hammer but it struck me when you were describing the hammer from the story that it might be such a thing.'

'Gurnius said it was metal, wood, stone and crystal,' Tenc explained.

Ciro nodded. 'Yes, that sounds about right, each one produces a different sound.'

'So what 'appened next?' Arper asked Tenc.

'Well, er…' began the Philiri. 'Oh, yes. So Gurnius was looking at this hammer and this beast in wonderment when a shadow fell upon him. He looked up to see two men walking towards him dressed in strange white clothing.'

Songsmith clothing, thought Ciro, but said nothing.

"We mean you no harm," said one of the men. He held out a hand towards the fallen monster and the hammer which lay beside it suddenly flew straight into his palm.'

'Wow!' Exclaimed Arper. 'Can yer friend do that, Ciro?'

Ciro arched a brow, shook his head and said. 'Go on, Tenc. Then what happened?'

'Well, they pulled Gurnius off of the floor, dusted him down and he said: "Who are you? What is that thing on the ground?"

"My name is Calian," said one with a bow, "and this is my brother, Pesarian. That thing is a Skaeling, and its presence here means your kingdom is in danger. Do you know what has happened to your King?"

'To this Gurnius shook his head. "I fear Elson and his armies are no more, for he sent his family far away from here."

"Where?" asked the brothers as one.'

"We do not know," replied Gurnius sadly. "We were told that they all sailed away to the west before the night fell. Now I fear that Philire stands alone."

"Take heart," the brothers said. "The night which has fallen on your kingdom will pass but you must tell your people to keep safe. You must return and tell your Elders to strengthen your defences and guard against the outside. This beast that lies at your feet is a sign of the danger which now lies beyond the protection of your hearths."

'The brothers then found a cart for Gurnius, and hitched his horse to it so that he could take back the Skaeling to show as proof of his tale. As he left he turned to thank them and, because of their strangeness, he asked them if they were gods.'

269

'They shook their heads: "We are the sons of Galisius," the brothers said. "And no more gods than you and yours. Take care on your journey back and remember our words. A dark winter has fallen on your realm and only if you stay safe will your children live to see the spring."

'So Gurnius rode back with his strange prize and there was much disquiet over the tale he had to tell, but one look at the beast he brought with him and, till this day, no one has ever doubted his story.' Tenc sat back and there was silence for a moment.

'Did anyone ever see another of them beasts?' asked Arper.

Tenc sighed. 'For several years after – when the black apples began to grow and the Dark Wood seemed to be full of savage Omerk – many Philiri disappeared. There were rumours and some reports that Skaelings had been sighted and that was when the Elders decided we should move west. So we made a new Philire, safe against such monsters.'

'You moved?' exclaimed Ciro. 'Where?'

'West, as I said, to the hills behind the old city of Monides. And there we have stayed, safe – by and large – from the evils of the South Jaw till this day.'

'We should eat,' Nesh said. 'An' then, Mr King,' she added, pointing her stick at Ciro, 'I wanna look at that wound o' yours.' Ciro opened his mouth to protest but the Nesh simply frowned at him. 'No arguin',' she said.

While Arper quizzed Tenc about Philire and what lay in store for them once they crossed the barrier of black apples, Ciro ate in silence and pondered the stories which Tenc had told. He came from a society – certainly from a family – which had moved away from the superstitious realm of gods and monsters, so the Philiri's tales of magical men and terrifying beasts jarred with his rational disposition. He would have to suspend judgment on precisely what the monster was that Gurnius had returned with from Torr Adenair, but it seemed logical to assume that it was probably a bear of some description. He had not seen one himself (Feirlan was poorly stocked with any large animals) but he had read accounts of various hunts in Rial which had tried to rid the White Wall and the South Jaw of such beasts. Torr Adenair – with its proximity to the mountains – may have been the perfect place for a wandering giant to roam around once the people had all departed. More intriguing to him though, was the evident appearance of two Songsmiths. That one of them was named Calian was of no concern at all. It was the fact that they were there that was perplexing. According to Calian, the Songsmiths had formed their first band years ago in New Kindor: the country south of Feirlan, past the Nelan desert. Ciro had never found records which told of their existence in Reilan so it was a little strange to find two people who could easily have been described as Songsmiths in Tenc's story.

But then a month ago I expected to find the whole of Reilan, and definitely Rial, deserted, thought Ciro to himself. Perhaps Calian was wrong, perhaps the origins of the Songsmiths went back further than even he had been aware of. Ciro smiled. If that had been the same Calian back in Elson's time, he thought, the Songsmith had certainly never mentioned it! The idea of an ancient Calian miraculously reaching five hundred without looking a day over thirty years old made the young king chuckle.

'It's nothing,' he said brightly as the others noted his humour and looked his way.

He decided to leave the problems of black apples, Omerk and other monsters to a more appropriate time and concentrate on more pressing matters. Ciro asked Tenc if he knew the best way of passing Torr Betram: the city renamed Kal Gians by the Makech.

With Ciro's help, Tenc drew a rough map on the muddy cobbled floor which showed their own position beneath the South Wall and where Kal Gians sat on the north of the hill range.

'There's the Kal Santra road running south here,' Tenc said, drawing a line in the mud east of their position, 'but I'd suggest we cross the South Wall before that and come into Kal Gians from the south west.'

'You want to go to Kal Gians?' said Ciro. 'Why?'

'It's our best route east,' Tenc explained. 'We'll have to keep our heads down until we reach the docks but, if we're lucky, Tamarail should be there with his boat and with that we can cross the black apples and get to Philire.'

'I thought the only way past the black apples was through Ebo's Mire?' said Arper. 'Tenc never mentioned no-one called Tamarail.'

Tenc shrugged. 'He wouldn't have done. And for Amec, you're right; Ebo Pamessi was his best route back to Philire. He...er,' the Philiri scratched his head and looked uncomfortable. 'Let's just say that Amec – may the stars guide his soul – and Tamarail did not get on. But, I assure you, boat is not only the best way to cross the black apples, it's also the swiftest.'

'What if this friend 'o yours ain't there?' queried Nesh.

'Then we'll have to borrow a boat,' said Ciro.

'It's best if we use Tamarail's,' cautioned Tenc. 'His is the only boat I know with metal plates on its hull to protect it from the water around the black apples.'

'Meaning what?' asked Ciro.

'The black apples don't just burn the skin; the juice gets into the river. I've heard it said that they can eat right through a wooden hull in minutes.'

Ciro was dubious. He felt it was safer for them to stay away from populated areas. 'If you don't know whether this friend of yours is going to be there,' he asked, 'why risk going into the city?'

'Your arrival appears to have worsened an already bad situation,' Tenc replied: though Ciro detected no animosity in the words. 'There are several Philiri, other than Tamarail, who have been based in Kal Gians since I travelled over here – keeping an eye as best they can on Perlenz, the Makech High Lord. With Mara and Amec dead and Urawiir burnt, it seems obvious the Makech are becoming more aggressive. That could mean the lives of my fellow Philiri may also be in grave danger … I've got to at least warn them.'

'They've still got a slave market in Kal Gians,' muttered Nesh.

Ciro remembered the fears she had expressed about her safety in such places. Looking at her now, with her muddy face and bulky Makech armour on, no stranger was going to suspect that she was anything but a scrawny boy, but Ciro did not want to take the risk of putting any of them in a dangerous environment – unless absolutely necessary. He mulled the problem over for a moment then hunched over Tenc's rough map.

'This is Kal Gians here, yes?' he asked, pointing just above the hills of the South Wall. Tenc nodded. Ciro then drew a line which led east from the city. 'This is the river which runs east from Kal Gians. Do you know it?'

'The Handle river, yes,' agreed Tenc. 'It runs from Kal Gians until it joins the Ice Water.'

'And there's another town along the Handle?' asked Ciro.

'Mm, Formoss,' confirmed Tenc. 'That's where Tamarail does most of his trade.' The Philiri took the stick from Ciro and quickly etched more detail into their map. 'Beyond Formoss the Handle splits into two forks before it joins the

Ice Water and it's around there that the black apples grow. South of that are the swamps of Ebo's Mire an' then the mountains.'

'So if Tamarail is in Kal Gians harbour, he'd be taking us east along the Handle River, yes?' Ciro ran his finger along the line he had drawn. Tenc nodded. 'Alright,' continued Ciro, 'here's what I think we should do. We keep the horses with us and travel past the South Wall until Kal Gians is miles behind us, then ride north until we reach the south bank of the Handle.' Tenc opened his mouth to comment but Ciro held up a hand. 'One moment, Tenc,' he said with a smile. 'When we reach the river we make camp close enough to monitor it and then Tenc and I will travel back to Kal Gians to find Tamarail. How does that sound?'

'Dangerous,' said Nesh.

'Less dangerous than all of us goin' back, girl,' muttered Arper.

'An' wha' do we do while yer gone?' asked Nesh. 'An' what if anythin' 'appens to ya?' She fixed Ciro with a scowl then switched her attention to the Philiri beside him. '…Both,' she added.

'Don't worry, Nesh, we'll just be another couple of locals.' Ciro cast his gaze around the group: saw Nesh's face set firm in the firelight. 'While we're gone you can move the horses a safe distance from the river and let them go… And,' he added, pointing at Nesh's bare feet, 'perhaps some of this Makech leather can be used to make you some boots that fit. Before you know it Tenc and I will be back with a boat.'

Nesh did not look convinced. She sighed then searched amongst their jumbled baggage and pulled out some cloth. 'Let's see that wound o' yours,' she said, changing the subject.

Ciro carefully removed the leather jerkin which was now stuck by blood to his side and Nesh moved forward to clean and dress the wound. She stopped, gazed down at her hands then wrinkled her nose.

'I'd better wash first,' she said and stood up. 'I dunno 'bout the rest of yer but I can't stand this smell no more!' Nesh tugged at the Makech jerkin she was wearing. 'I've gotta dunk meself in the river.'

There was a general murmur of agreement about the rank smell which emanated from their armour. Not only had their previous occupants appeared to live in their clothes, they had very definitely died in them. Everyone had washed the tell-tale blood stains from the uniforms as best they could but, whatever else had permeated the leather, a lot more than a quick scrub with water was needed to dispel its odour. That, and several days riding across country had made everyone muddy, smelly and uncomfortable.

'We should probably all try to clean ourselves a little,' said Ciro, who had noticed his own grimy torso. 'But stay close to the bank, Nesh,' he warned as she made for the door of the stronghold. The water had looked quite placid but there was always the possibility that the current was stronger in the centre. Ciro looked across at Arper. His black beard; now tangled, matted and flecked with grey, was beginning to assume what the young king could only describe as a more 'organic' air. It was a world away from the neatly trimmed affair Ciro had first seen him wearing.

'You look like you could do with a dip yourself, Arper,' said Ciro with a smile.

Arper grinned, sniffed his armour and grimaced. 'Nah, I'm fine,' he replied.

'Well, could you keep a watch on Nesh?' Ciro asked. 'We shouldn't be too confident that no patrols will come here.' To this, Arper shrugged, rose and made to exit the stronghold.

'Don't forget your sword, Arper,' advised Ciro. The

prospect seemed to cause him a vague discomfort, so Ciro smiled and said: 'If you see anything, come straight back and tell me.'

With unrestrained relief Arper left the pale flare of the fire and disappeared into the dark. Ciro sat debating for a moment whether to completely rid himself of the disgusting Makech uniform in favour of Menzir's borrowed clothes or to endure the stench for another day or so. Practicality quickly won over sensitivity and he elected to endure the wretched outfit for a little while longer. As soon as they made camp by the Handle River they could all be rid of them. For the time being Ciro removed his star belt and holster. He laid them beside him and noted that Tenc seemed lost in his own thoughts.

'What's on your mind, Tenc?' Ciro inquired.

'Urawiir,' he replied with a frown, 'and whether poor Mara's wife and his niece escaped the flames. 'He shook his head. 'He was like a father to that girl... Poor Elbeth, I hope she's alright.' Tenc was silent for a few moments and Ciro's thoughts also sped back to the terrible sight they had seen that morning. Of Urawiir burning and the pain and suffering it no doubt signified.

Ciro felt a tremendous sense of guilt over the fate of the village. Whether it was the painful suspicion that the destruction had been carried out in retaliation for his actions in Forht or whether it was the fact that, as Monarch, it was his sworn duty to protect his citizens that caused him the distress, he did not know. In retrospect, both seemed equally valid. The distraction of the Makech pursuit had relieved him of the burden of contemplation on the subject until now and he tried his best to convince himself that his guilt was misplaced. He was in no position to help anybody at the moment.

Despite his best efforts, guilt still coloured Ciro's thoughts.

'When we get to Peimonac,' he said, 'I'll prepare some plans with General Alanti for an offensive: push the Makech back south.'

Was he saying this to show Tenc his commitment, or to publicly placate his own guilt? Tenc nodded but said nothing and Ciro dropped his gaze to the fire for a moment. Calian had always said that a leader must try to be sensitive to others but never so to one's self. Such emotion was an indulgence and one that, right now – so far from his friends and his men – he could not afford to have. He simply had no time to feel guilty. Ciro sighed but Tenc didn't seem to notice.

'I'll also need your help to plan the attack,' Ciro said.

'How?!' Tenc sounded surprised.

Ciro shrugged. 'Information on Makech troop numbers. Garrison positions? Anything like that would make a big difference.'

Tenc frowned. 'Olbas Osanti, as you know, was a little out of the way for such information. It was a safe haven for Philiri to come to but there was never any such talk that I heard. Amec – may his star shine brightly – probably knew of such things, but your best source now would be Tamarail. I'm sure he'll know something of what goes on in Kal Gians, but as for Forht and the rest, you probably have a better idea than either of us.'

Ciro considered this for a moment. Tenc was right: poor Amec had been the one who had claimed to know all sorts of information, yet perhaps Ciro already knew enough about the smaller towns and villages to dismiss them as threats during a full-scale campaign.

It all comes down to the board, he thought. It was a popular term in the Feirlan military and referred to the old board game of Soldiers which so many people, Ciro included, loved to play. For the minor villages and towns such as Forht, you could read opposing 'Footmen' pieces: weak and only a threat in numbers. Kal Gians and Kal Santra however, were 'Castles' in both senses. But if he could turn those pieces to his colours then the game would be almost won: and Ciro had pieces to commit which had never appeared on the board before. How Ciro longed to see just one of his steam ships again. What a difference that would make, he thought, and his mind strayed to the city of Peimonac. How were his friends and his men faring?

Ciro was turning his thoughts to the capture of Kal Gians when there was a scuffle of feet from outside. Flushed, Arper ran into the firelight.

'There's!...There's –' gabbled Arper breathlessly. He flailed his sword towards the harbour but further explanation failed him.

Ciro was already on his feet and drawing Amec's sword before Arper had finally forced out the word 'Bonemen!' He swung his leg back to kick out the fire then stopped an inch from the glowing wood. His mind racing, he looked around the stronghold interior. The flames barely flickered and the light was weak enough, he felt sure, to be almost unnoticeable outside. If they were to flee, they would need to grab their possessions and the horses in a hurry. That would not be possible in the dark.

'Heard 'em when I was up by the bridge,' Arper was explaining rapidly to Tenc. 'Don't think they saw me – I came right back.'

'Where's Nesh, Arper?' Ciro asked.

'Oh, Beck!' he cried. 'She's still in the water!'

Frowning, Ciro ran to the door with Tenc and Arper right behind him. 'How many are there?' he asked, peering out into the darkness. The night was black enough to completely obscure the river, let alone the far side, so Ciro doubted Arper would know but he thought he could hear noises on the opposite bank.

'I dunno,' Arper replied miserably, 'but Nesh was down over there.' He waved his sword towards the bridge.

'I want you to –' Ciro began when the harrowing sound of a scream cut through the night. No one had any doubt that it was Nesh's cry.

In response there were cries from the far bank and, keeping low, Ciro ran towards where he had heard Nesh's scream with Tenc right behind him. Arper hung back by the stronghold door.

Nesh was still screaming and shouting and the thrashing of her naked body was the first thing to emerge from the night as Ciro and Tenc raced nearer. What she was struggling against became clear too as the pale glitter of metal showed the figure of a Makech soldier behind her. With his sword in one hand, the other clamped tightly to her throat, he was attempting to drag her away towards the bridge.

'Hey!' Ciro shouted, running to within a few feet of the pair.

The soldier scowled in response, raised his sword close to Nesh's throat and jabbered something Ciro couldn't understand.

'He said: "Philiri scum. Any closer and she dies," translated Tenc.

The Makech was flicking his gaze between the two of them: backing away as best he could while Nesh still struggled. There was a call from the darkness of the far bank and in response the soldier shouted back.

'He's told them we're here,' Tenc said nervously.

Ciro nodded, but kept his eyes locked firmly on the soldier in front of him. There was hatred in the eyes that stared back, but the constant flicking of his gaze from Tenc to him betrayed something else. Outnumbered and out-armed, this man was scared. On the far bank, Ciro heard the sound of horses and knew that the other Makech would make towards the old bridge. There had been at least a dozen in the party that morning and Ciro had to assume that the rest were on the opposite bank. The bridge was perhaps two hundred yards away so the other Makech could be here in minutes. He had to save Nesh right now: or they would be overrun.

The Makech had moved back another couple of paces and was still holding his sword at Nesh's throat.

'Listen to me, Nesh!' said Ciro quickly, praying the Makech soldier could not understand Rialan. 'When the Boneman loosens his grip, you run to Tenc, not me – Tenc.' Ciro moved two paces to his right. 'Tenc, do as I say: drop your sword on the floor.' Ciro threw his own on the ground before him and, with no time to explain, snapped at the Philiri to do as ordered. Ciro kept his eyes on the Makech and, with the clatter of Tenc's sword hitting the quay side, saw a rapid change in the man's expression. Surprise was quickly replaced with confidence and a grin quickly spread across the soldier's face. Ciro kept his arms slightly aloft, praying that the Makech's diminishing fear would to allow his grip on Nesh to loosen. Then the sound of grinding stonework, splashing masonry and screams caught them all off guard.

The Makech turned instantly as the cries of men and horses ripped through the darkness and with it, Ciro seized his opportunity.

'Now!' he yelled and felt a surge of relief as Nesh broke free and ran the short distance to Tenc.

The Makech swung his sword at her back as Nesh ran but her fear put her out of reach in a split second. The moment she was free, Ciro's hand flashed down to grab his hand lance. After the battle at Olbas Osanti the king knew that he only had two flights left in the chamber but this, he felt sure, was close enough to make the shot a simple one. Or would have been if he had remembered to put back on his star belt when they had all hurried out.

Ciro froze as his hand gripped nothing but air: disbelief and horror striking him in equal measure. He had taken the belt off when he had removed his Makech tunic. Any further reflections on his own stupidity were curtailed by the lunge and roar of the angry Makech.

'Run!' Ciro shouted, diving right as the blade cut the air where his head had been.

The Makech's attack, clumsy and hopeful at best would ordinarily have proved no challenge to Ciro's sword skills. But unarmed, he was going to have to rely on every other ability he had simply to stay alive. As Ciro had shouted out to Tenc and Nesh the soldier, aware that their swords still lay close at hand, had slashed left to push the pair away from the weapons. That done he focused his attention back on the still-rolling Ciro.

The young king came up into a crouch, feinted to dive forwards towards his sword, and then rolled back the way he had come as the Makech launched another thrust at him. The man's momentum, fuelled by his anger and aided by the weight of his body armour caused him to overrun. He swung wildly to his right, span on the spot to counter any potential attack from behind but Ciro, unhindered by the weight of armour, was too quick. The sword slashed at thin air as Ciro dived for his own weapon then rolled back up to a crouch. Amec's sword was now in his hand.

As Ciro had leapt for the sword, a strange cry sounded somewhere in the night. Ciro barely noticing the odd, wailing sound as he grabbed for Amec's blade and rolled away but, by the time he came up into a crouch, the noise was enough to distract both himself and the Makech who was bearing down on him. Out of the darkness a screaming Makech soldier ran into view: his sword gripped in both hands and held high above his head.

'Aaaaaaaaaahhhhhhhhh!'

The painful yell didn't falter or waver in its pitch and, for a vital fraction of a second, both Ciro and his adversary were spellbound by the sight. The screaming man's face seemed distorted with pain and it was only in the instant that the raised sword flashed down to strike the soldier that Ciro recognised the running man as Arper. The Makech, killed in an instant, hit the ground wearing the same puzzled look that had greeted the arrival of what he assumed had been a fellow Makech.

Ciro got to his feet and walked over to Arper: still frozen in the same pose that had finished the soldier. He smiled, patted Arper's shoulder and with that the tension in Arper ebbed away. He looked wearily at Ciro.

'Is 'e dead?'

Ciro looked down at the body just as a pale shape flashed in from his left.

'Bastard!' yelled a still naked Nesh. She kicked the corpse as hard as she could then yelped with pain and fell over, clutching her bare foot.

While Tenc helped her up, Ciro spotted her discarded clothes a few feet away and gave them to Nesh before walking a stunned Arper back to the stronghold. He still seemed shocked and stared at his sword as if it were the strangest thing he had ever seen.

'You saved our lives, Arper.' Ciro said and to this Arper seemed to brighten.

He grinned. 'I did, didn't I?' he said and waggled his sword.

Ciro smiled, patted Arper on the shoulder again before Nesh ran forward to embrace her uncle.

Birin now seemed quiet but the group quickly collected

their possessions and readied the horses. Ciro picked up his discarded star belt and held it in his hands.

Of all King Elson's possessions that had been stored away in the Ascension Chamber of Torr Sarvie, the star belt had always been Ciro's favourite. He could not remember a time since his Ascension Day when he had forgotten to wear it. He put it on and, as he removed his hand lance to confirm that he had only two flights left, vowed never to forget it again.

Ciro checked that his hand lance was fully wound and turned to the others. 'I want to check on our silent friends,' he said. 'And find out what happened to the bridge.'

Arper pulled out his still bloody sword. 'Want me to come with you?'

Ciro smiled and shook his head. 'Help get the horses ready. I'm certain the bridge is down otherwise those horses we heard earlier would be charging around outside, but I'd like to see how many bodies there are – if they're all dead we might not have to move at all tonight.'

Accompanied by Tenc, Ciro moved swiftly along the quay side until they saw a flickering light by the bridge they had traversed so carefully that afternoon. Creeping closer they could see that the whole arch was now just two stumps of fractured brickwork on each bank. Between them the ink-black river swirled around a single peak of masonry sticking out above the water.

There was no sign of Makech bodies – or horses for that matter – but Ciro felt sure that some riders must have perished in the bridge's collapse. The far bank had been quiet since the screams and noise of earlier but the light from the opposite bank proved that not all their pursuers were dead. As Ciro and Tenc drew closer to the eastern edge of the bridge he could clearly see the figure of a Makech standing on the western stump. As well as the vile skull helmet and familiar armoured

283

jerkin, this figure wore a polished metal square on his chest. It glittered in the light as he swayed the burning torch over the dark water.

Tenc shrank back at the sight of the man, tugged at Ciro's sleeve and whispered: 'That man is Beck Iph! We should go, Ciro. Right now!'

It could have been the noise of Tenc's boots on the flagstones as he turned away, or the hiss of his voice carrying across the water. Ciro did not know but, at that moment, the Beck Iph figure glanced up and stared unblinkingly across the river towards them.

Now that the torch was held high and the man was looking up it was easy for Ciro to make out his sharp features and neatly trimmed beard. Ciro stepped onto the eastern stump of the bridge and into the very edge of the torchlight. He stared at the man defiantly and saw a rapid change in the Makech's expression: first surprise, then frowning hostility.

Ciro smiled. 'Lost something?' he asked, pointing down at the debris in the river.

In response, the Makech's face became an impassive mask.

'Well, well,' he replied in passable Rialan. 'Do I have the dubious honour of addressing Ciro Torrman: the Fool King himself?'

Ciro tried to hold the smile, but knew that it had wavered at the mention of the word 'King'. That the Makech knew his name was more than likely due to Menzir or Tersic, the farm hand who had been with the Makech in the wood by Menzir's farm. But Ciro had told no one his true title until they had got beyond Forht and he doubted either Menzir or Tersic could have pulled the truth from thin air. The only other explanation he could think of made his blood run cold. Had Bdann and his men also encountered the Makech? Ciro had no time to consider the frightening questions this man's knowledge seemed to pose, so he put as brave a face on the matter as he could.

'If I am the King of Fools,' he replied. 'Does that make you one of my followers? You are following me, aren't you?'

The Makech let out a short, mirthless laugh. 'Only to inform you of your error in coming here, your highness.' he sneered. 'We have no need of drunken, brawling fools in this country, so why don't you set course back home for Obaln and leave this land in peace.'

Drunken, brawling fool?... Strange, thought Ciro. It was unnerving that the man seemed to have been in contact with at least one of his people – or had Ciro mentioned Obaln to Menzir? He couldn't remember. But, to be described as a drunken brawler was curious. Whoever had imparted the information had no love for his King, or indeed any real knowledge of him.

'Is what you did to the people of Urawiir your idea of peace?' replied Ciro tersely. He held on to the anger which began to well up inside him at the thought of the lives that must have been lost in the burning village. This was the very face of the enemy – for all he knew the very man who had orchestrated of the destruction of Urawiir. 'If I'm a fool!' spat Ciro, 'Then Milla save all fools from the peace of Makech like you who kill without thought and value nothing but your own self-interest!'

The Makech shrugged off the insult. He shook his head fractionally, smiled and said: 'What should the Makech care for the cattle of this world, Rialan? What is that if not a sign of weakness? A badge of shame to mark you down the centuries from the strong of this land. If we had never needed slaves, do you think you would still exist? The lives of all Rialans have for ever depended upon the grace and goodwill of the Makech. Yet you have the audacity to moralise about the petty feelings of livestock!' The Beck Iph stabbed a finger at Ciro. 'You're the worthless monarch of a worthless country full of worthless people who haven't got the sense to realise that God himself and all the Kolben hate you and wish you as dead and forgotten as I do!'

The Makech leered across the water and, as he did so, another Boneman emerged from the night beside him. The bearded man gave a short laugh, passed the torch to his comrade and drew his sword.

'Why don't you do the world a favour,' he said, beckoning to Ciro. 'Cross the river – if you're man enough – and try and kill me. Let me show you the fate that awaits all fools.'

Ciro sighed and, for a second, hesitated as the action which instantly crossed his mind crashed straight into his conscience. The words of Alanti, his friend and the General of his army came to the fore:

'A piece unseen by your enemy,' Alanti had said after routing Ciro's Soldier pieces in an unforeseen attack, 'must come to his notice as painfully as possible.'

Ciro had such a piece in his possession and the staying hand of his conscience was pushed away by bloody recollections of his journey. He saw Urawiir burning, Qisala dead on her own kitchen floor and Amec breathing his last in his arms. All doubts vanished. Ciro raised his hand lance and fired, missed and fired again: this time hitting his target and shooting the torch holder dead.

The torch fell from his grasp as the Makech slumped backwards. It bounced in a shower of sparks, hit the river with a hiss and plunged the bridge into darkness. The Beck Iph had crouched as Ciro fired the second shot but now, in the blackness it was impossible to tell if he had fled or was still there.

'That's the difference between us!' Ciro shouted across the

water. 'I don't have to cross the river to kill you. Remember that the next time you think of following me!'

Ciro re-holstered his now useless hand lance, turned to walk away then paused. 'And by the way!' he shouted into the night. 'If you are fool enough to pursue me, teach your bloo'sandin' men to swim!'

Ciro saw the vague shape of Tenc as his eyes grew accustomed to the darkness and together they started back towards the stronghold. They had gone mere yards when something heavy landed inches away from Ciro's heel. Both he and Tenc ducked as several more spears thumped into the quay side around them.

'Are you dead?!' Came the call from across the river.

The bearded man's voice sounded almost jolly in the darkness. 'I hope not,' he shouted. 'Because I want you to see my face when I add your life to my kill-count and your skull to my helmet. You're as stupid as you are arrogant, Torrman, and when I tell your friends about you they're going to be very pleased to know they didn't miss your capture. We'll meet again, I promise you.'

'You'll meet me at the head of an army,' muttered Ciro as he and Tenc retreated through the darkness.

The King of Nothing

PART FOUR

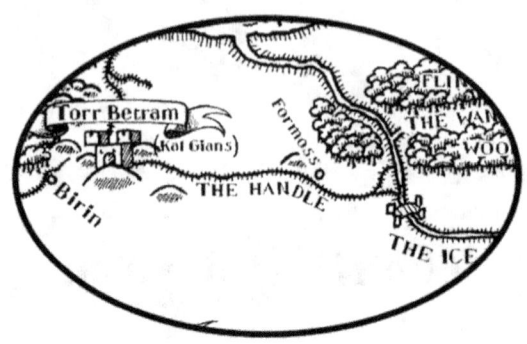

*Having promised my friends a rare sight, Aldermen and aides
alike gathered on deck expectantly as we neared Torr Betram:
watching the horizon for their first glimpse of the Grand
Falls. Neither Alderman Chaime nor Alderman Baulenus
seemed particularly impressed by their initial view but, as our
vessel was hitched to horses at the pullway and dragged
through the increasing current into harbour, I watched their
faces closely and waited for realisation to strike.*

*From a distance the Grand Falls are nothing but mist – its
roar a mere murmur – and it was this which had given my
companions a false impression of the Grand Falls' majesty.
Having suffered the same delusion myself when first visiting
the city, I was fascinated to see just how long it would take
for their eyes to be truly opened. I did not have to wait long.*

*Alderman Baulenus was the first of our party to become
awe-struck. Pointing up stream into the mists of the South
Harbour, he called my attention to a boat which was drifting
past the light house and about to leave the port. Barely had
he raised his hand to point before the vessel turned its bow
towards us and flashed past on its way down stream. Disconcerted by such a rapid passage, the Alderman walked to larboard, gazed down at the speeding water below, then mouthed
words of surprise totally drowned by the ever-increasing roar
of the falls. As the noise and the mists grew and the towering*

waterfall filled our senses, both Chaime and Baulenus held firmly on to the handrail and inquired of anyone within earshot whether it would not be the sensible course to get off of our vessel. Though I assured both that we were perfectly safe – that we would neither drown nor be tossed with the current – neither man was happy until they had stepped onto the firm ground of the North Harbour quay side.

'Never again, Lacey,' Alderman Chaime repeated over and over to me and he eyed the Grand Falls with what I took to be the deepest suspicion.

We were met by a captain of the Torr Betram garrison named Sharce, who was to be our guide during the Spring Stone festivities. The Aldermen of Torr Betram had also sent a delegation to meet us and it took the combined efforts of all those who greeted us to try and convince my fellow travellers to brave the city's second challenge: a ride in the remarkable sky carriages.

These marvels of the Master Maker's art connect the busy harbour to the city which sits on the cliff tops above. Using an ingenious system of water pipes, wheels and pulleys, the carriages act much like the bucket in a well, but do not need the assistance of either men or horses to draw them aloft. Instead the Grand Falls themself act as the power source and so either men or cargo can be raised or lowered at considerable speed. If ever a man wanted to know the thoughts of the birds, a sky carriage is the place to go.

Unfortunately, having just found their feet firmly back on the ground, neither of my colleagues wanted to then experience flight. Both Chaime and Baulenus hired horses from the North Pullway and plodded the long route to the city's north gate.

Alderman Lacey. My travels to the South West Wold.
NC 659

The Cotisann Problem

Gidus eyed his new Soulcatcher in the swinging lamp light and frowned. For the second time in as many minutes, Newman pulled aside the dark velvet curtain a fraction and stole a glance at the passing world outside the carriage.

'Careful, Baramir,' repeated the old man, but his understudy had already closed the curtain.

'I know, Gidus. I know,' Baramir replied, his tone mocking. 'It's bad for the Wraith. I just wondered where we were, that's all.'

Despite himself, Gidus could not resist a smile. It had been such a short time since Baramir's transformation yet already he had ceased to call him 'Master'. How long would it be before he lost control of this remarkable man altogether? Long enough to set things in motion, he felt sure. Who was Gidus to question the prophecies of Thiutheer? His pupil sat impassively for a moment then frowned and placed a hand on his temple.

'How are your charges?' Gidus asked although, judging by Newman's discomfort, the answer was obvious.

Newman winced. 'Noisy,' he replied.

To this Gidus placed a gentle hand on the sleeping Wraith beside Baramir and slowly the grotesque Omerk opened its huge eyes.

'I'll command the Wraith to aid you,' Gidus said and spoke some soft words to the little beast.

It sat up, smiled at Baramir and, before he could protest, the Wraith's eyes seemed to blacken to pitch. The noise from his captives died away to a whisper.

Newman blinked and frowned again, this time in confusion. He had been attempting to silence his 'guests' all morning yet only Yetzi had obeyed his command. The others – especially the bloo'sandin' dog – had been proving increasingly hard to control.

'How did it do that?' Baramir asked.

Gidus grinned and watched the Wraith fall back upon the cushions which littered the carriage: asleep as soon as it had reclined. 'The Omerkfel have an affinity with the spirit realm which even Soulcatchers would be hard pushed to match,' he replied. 'But,' he added with a heavy sigh, 'Wraiths are a rare commodity these days.'

'Rare, eh?' Baramir replied, eying the little monster with only slightly less apprehension than he had the first time he saw it. Even asleep, the bulbous head and bulbous eyes atop its infant frame were still quite disturbing. 'Where can I get one?' he asked.

Gidus laughed so hard it caused a coughing fit. He banged on the floor of the carriage with his cane in exasperation and their motion slowed: the voice of a Beck Iph guard sounded from outside.

'Are you alright, Master?' inquired the concerned guard.

'Quite… Ride on,' instructed Gidus between splutters and finally the coughs subsided. The Soulcatcher shook his head and dabbed a cloth against his lips as the carriage resumed moving. 'Oh, Baramir, Baramir… You really are quite unique,' he said with a smile.

'Thank you,' replied Newman testily; he did not particularly care to be laughed at. 'So,' he said, 'do I take it from your agonised mirth that the acquisition of an Omerk is impossible?'

'No,' said Gidus with a shake of his head. 'Omerk are plentiful – like weeds – but Wraiths are an altogether different commodity. Have you not heard that even now Makech fights a war against the Omerkfel for the possession of such rarities?'

Baramir sifted through the memories of Yetzi and found rumours and stories of a battle at a place called Nish Huiss: deep in the mountainous passes of the South Jaw Mountains.

'Yetzi seems to think that the fight was simply against the Omerk,' observed Newman. 'Nothing to do with Wraiths.'

Gidus waved the words away. 'What would scum like Yetzi know about the nuances of the world? If the Lords and Masters of Makech were ever keen to throw their power away, then the Yetzi's of this world would be raised to positions of great responsibility.'

Baramir smiled. Not because of Gidus's cutting words but because of the reaction they invoked in Yetzi. *I wonder what would happen if I let him loose on the old man?* Baramir mused. He instantly quelled the thought along with Yetzi's fury, and instead wondered aloud: 'I wonder how Tanikalin has fared?'

'He'll return in time,' Gidus replied. 'But don't count on your errant Rialan being with him. If I've learnt one thing in life it's that you can never predict the actions of royalty: they are as strange a breed as Wraiths.'

'I can't say I've had the pleasure to observe them at close quarters,' Baramir responded.

To this Gidus nodded. 'When we get to Kal Gians you'll get your chance. My quarters are there. And I shall introduce you to High Prince Perlenz.'

The name threw up a whole wealth of information from Yetzi: none of it complimentary. It seemed that the High Prince and all the members of the 'Eternal High House of Mala Kech' were notorious targets for the type of wild rumours and outlandish insinuation which made Prince Bdann's antics back in Feirlan seem modest and conscientious by comparison.

'What's this Prince really like?' asked Baramir, doubtful of the validity of some of the stories he had uncovered.

Gidus smiled. 'Worse than anything Yetzi can think of.'

The old Soulcatcher shuffled forward in his seat and leaned across to lay a bony palm on Baramir's knee. 'You must be careful in the company of the High Prince, Baramir. My men will protect you but the House Guard at Kal Gians serves no one but the High Family. Remember that.' Gidus sat back and gave a sigh. 'It is not unknown for a wayward Soulcatcher to fall foul of the Family – and many, some of whom were friends of mine, did not survive the experience.'

'I'll bear that in mind,' Newman replied and wondered at the precise reason for Gidus's warning. It hinted at an unspoken hostility between the Beck Iph and the High House. Baramir was reminded of the 'Eight' back in Feirlan, the Children of Milla, and their running feud with the Feirlan Royal House. He knew that once the Eight had been an integral part of the ruling family but that a rift had formed some two or three generations ago. Since then the pompous 'Saviours' and their followers had been pushed to the outskirts of court life. Baramir had never felt sympathetic towards such superstitious fools before, but now? Now he felt that there may be some truth in the Eight's following of Milla. After all, wasn't he following something which could be perceived as being similarly intangible?

Baramir smiled to himself. No, the Eight were fools. If their blessed Milla had any other power apart from lighting up the day then their decline in Feirlan would never have happened. Being a Soulcatcher was something altogether different. He didn't have to argue that it was a real force; he could prove it at will. He wondered aloud to Gidus if there might be some justification in the beliefs of the Eight.

The Soulcatcher frowned. 'Never heard of them, but then

Rialans were never a particularly powerful voice to the Kolben's ears – even in the old days. But as far as I know they've always prayed to their blessed Milla: the one force that couldn't care less about the drab lives of this world.'

'But there is a force there, isn't there?' Baramir tugged at the black velvet curtain. 'Why else would you shield the Wraith from her gaze?'

To this Gidus nodded. 'Oh, Milla shines all right, but it's a passive force. There's been no way of harnessing that mighty power for many an age…' Gidus sat in silence for a moment and it was obvious to Baramir that the old man was thinking.

'Tell me,' Gidus said presently. 'What is it you see when you look up into the night sky?'

'Well, stars,' Baramir replied with a shrug and wondered why such an obvious question had been asked.

Gidus smiled. 'What do you see if you look at a candle?'

Despite his irritation that Gidus was obviously playing some game with him, Baramir answered.

'A flame,' he said slowly, attempting to stop his annoyance from showing.

Gidus laughed. 'My dear Baramir, you are bristling with indignation! But let me ask you one more question: which will, I'm sure, allow you to 'see the light' so to speak.' The old Soulcatcher chuckled. 'What is around the candle, around the stars?'

Baramir thought for a second before the answer dawned on him. 'Darkness,' he replied.

Gidus grinned. 'That's right, darkness. Stars are no more than celestial candles flickering in the great darkness. Slowing waning as the wick burns down and the glowing ember fades into the shadow it came from. The eternal night, the Dark Square itself which is, was, and ever will be the only true power. It is our duty to return man, especially those unbelievers who look to the sun for guidance, back to the darkness they came from: to snuff out their lives and make ready for the return of Unzekka himself.'

The name caused Baramir's celesdain band to glow and the novice Soulcatcher suddenly experienced a curious sensation. It was as if, just for a fleeting moment, he were one with the forces of nature: standing side-by-side with the mighty Kolben Lords.

'You can feel something?' Gidus asked with a smile. 'You should, the black crystals connect all Soulcatchers to the spirit of the great Unzekka.'

'Who was he?' Baramir asked as the sensation of power faded.

'Some say he was the son of God,' Gidus replied. He tapped his own celesdain band. 'Through the black crystals a part of him lives on inside all Soulcatchers.' The old man settled himself back into his seat. 'You'll learn more when we reach my apartments, Baramir, there's much to –'

'– The power I felt, will you teach me to harness that?' Baramir interrupted.

Gidus looked amused. 'That was Unzekka's power, Baramir – lost when his throne was destroyed. What you have in your head is but a mere sliver – a shattered remnant of that mighty power. What you felt was an 'echo'.'

Newman frowned. 'Where are all the other slivers?'

The question removed Gidus's good humour in a moment to leave the old man looking sad. 'Scattered, Baramir,' he replied with a shake of his head. 'Shattered and scattered like the poor Indecestain.' The old man lapsed into a brooding silence and the still sleeping wraith began to twitch and mutter.

Left to his own thoughts, Newman began to ponder how best he was to proceed with his own advancement. Just how he could get his hands on more black crystals? If he only had a sliver now, what would he be capable of with a dozen?! Baramir searched vainly through his mind for more information (and a location) for the throne which Gidus had mentioned but could find nothing. Instead he wondered idly what they would make of him back in Feirlan. The thought led to an idea so outrageous in its scope and audacity that he could not contain his joy.

'Why the grin, Baramir?' asked Gidus from across the carriage.

Baramir controlled the smile and shook his head. 'I was just marvelling at my good fortune, dear Gidus.' He said and began to plan how, when he was strong enough, he could return to Feirlan. King Newman! He thought to himself and laughed.

II

Ciro and Tenc had spent the night huddled in a bush by the bank of The Handle River and woken to find both the ground and their clothing wet with dew. The blankets they had wrapped around themselves had proved no defence against the invasive moisture so they got up, stretched as much of the cold, wet stiffness from their bodies as they could and blinked at the new day.

It was now the second morning since they had left the others safely hidden (they hoped) far downstream and Ciro wandered to the water's edge to splash his wits awake. The Handle was a beautiful sight in the pale gold of the morning sunshine and the young King smiled to himself as he watched the mist rise from the water. He stepped down the bank to the river, threw a handful of water at his face then cast his gaze to the north bank. From this distance, the trees which lined it seemed no taller than his fingers.

Ciro returned to their makeshift camp to find Tenc crouched beside the bush. The Philiri yawned at the king and held out his hands.

'Ah!' responded Ciro, laughing. 'Breakfast!'

On Tenc's outstretched palms sat a square of stale bread and a misshapen lump of mottled cheese. The Philiri grinned back.

'Breakfast and lunch, I'm afraid,' he said. 'But I reckon we should sight Kal Gians by nightfall.'

'Good,' said Ciro as he took the food. 'I'm looking forward to seeing it...' He frowned. 'Well, from a distance at least.'

'With the Makech High Prince there,' nodded Tenc, 'believe me that's the best way to see it.'

'Tell me about – what was his name again?'

'Perlenz,' Tenc replied as if the word left a nasty taste in his mouth. 'The Wasp, some Rialans call him, on account of the fact that, by comparison to the last High Prince that was here, Perlenz is considered lenient.'

Ciro laughed. He knew the old saying. "Just because it doesn't sting you, a wasp is still a wasp."

'So,' Ciro asked, 'is he lenient?'

Tenc spat. 'No,' he replied. 'I think he was for perhaps the first week, but then he slipped into the same disgusting ways as all the other Bonemen.' Tenc counted off on his fingers: 'Executions, terror, murder, rape – the usual Makech lifestyle.'

'Nesh says they still have slave markets in Torr Betram. Is that true?'

Tenc shook his head. 'You're going to have to get used to calling Torr Betram 'Kal Gians' from now on, I'm afraid. Any talk of Torr Betram will get you arrested.'

Ciro smiled. 'I can't speak Makech, so any talk from me will do the same thing. But,' Ciro added, 'I take your point.'

Tenc nodded. 'As for slave markets. Unfortunately, yes, they still exist. Although one of the reasons that Perlenz was considered softer than his predecessor is because the slave market was slimmed down; less people taken south. But anyone who's wandered this land will soon realise what the real reason for that was.'

'What?' asked Ciro.

Tenc shrugged. 'After generations of slave taking, there are hardly any Rialans left.'

Tenc skimmed his piece of stale bread across the dewy grass to soften it and the pair finished their breakfast in silence. As they watched the river and listened to the song of the birds Milla climbed higher and chased away the mist. By the time they collected their packs to move on, The Handle was shining in the sunlight.

Ciro looked ahead to the eastern horizon and inquired how they would get past the city gates and into the harbour.

'It shouldn't prove too difficult,' Tenc replied as they set off up stream. 'Last time I was there the gates were unguarded.'

'We can't expect the same to be true now,' mused Ciro, remembering the trouble they had in passing through Forht. 'There are bound to be guards there now.'

'Still shouldn't be a problem. We just say we're from the North Pullway.'

Ciro had forgotten about the Pullway towns. Both sides of The Handle had small villages just down stream from the main harbour where horses were stabled to pull boats up the final mile of the river. The Grand Falls which plunged down from the city into the centre of Kal Gians harbour created a rapid stream which made progress impossible without the aid of horse power. The same torrent of water created a perpetual rainstorm in the harbour and was the reason the place was generally referred to as The Cauldron.

'Won't we be heading through the South Pullway,' Ciro asked, realising that they were on the wrong bank of the river to enter from the north.

Tenc shook his head. 'Tamarail's boat is always moored in the north side of the harbour so, unless we want to travel right through Kal Gians itself, we are going to have to find a way to cross the river before we get too close to the city.'

Ciro tried to picture details of the old city map of Torr Betram but could not remember much. All that came to mind was that the city itself was enclosed completely by a vast perimeter of battlements and perched upon the cliffs above the harbour. Even so, he felt sure there was a bridge somewhere near The Cauldron.

'There's two,' Tenc replied when Ciro voiced the question. 'The Fall's Bridge right above the waterfall and High Top Bridge just beyond the Pullway towns. But High Top – or Broken Back as it's called now – collapsed years ago so, as I said, unless we want to climb the cliffs and wander through the city, our best bet is to swim across The Handle.'

Ciro looked over the wide expanse of water beside them to the miniature tree line on the far bank. He did not want to risk wandering the streets of Kal Gians to find Tamarail but, weighed down with their clothes and baggage, just how was Tenc proposing to cross the river?

'Does the river narrow when it gets close to the harbour?' Ciro asked.

'Some, but that's when the current picks up. We can't cross there.'

'You really think we can swim The Handle like this?' Ciro tugged at his cloak for emphasis.

Tenc grinned. 'We'll use a rat raft.'

'A 'rat raft'?' Ciro repeated.

Tenc nodded. 'As soon as I see one I'll show you. Not only

will it get us across the river but our clothes should be bone dry by the time we reach the other side.'

Ciro shook his head and laughed. Images of fiendishly clever rats who could not only build boats but do laundry wandered through his mind. 'I look forward to seeing it,' he said.

They walked on beside the gently curving river. The sun climbed higher to beat upon their backs while a gentle breeze fanned their faces and played amongst the rushes. Ciro revelled in the abundance of wildlife as they walked and smiled at the constant twitter and call of the birds around them. There were ducks paddling almost the whole length of the river and the occasional rustle and splash amongst the reeds made Ciro wonder if those clever rats were hard at work boat building. By degrees his thoughts turned to the old city of Torr Betram up river and the collapse of the High Top Bridge. Ciro wondered if the same fate had befallen the great span at Circia – marvel of the old Rialan Kingdom. Bdann would know by now, he thought, the whole fleet would have passed beneath it on their way to Peimonac.

Milla had overtaken them by the time Tenc called a halt and both the clouds and the landscape had begun to close in. The thick woodland which they had been walking beside had thinned out enough for Ciro to make out the vague shoulder of the South Wall hills to the south and that meant that Kal Gians could not be far away. Tenc's attention however seemed to be occupied by something lying in the grass at the edge of the wood.

'See?' said the Philiri.

Ciro followed the pointed finger but could make out nothing of significance. Just the shattered bole of a tree accompanied by its long dead trunk.

'That's perfect!' Tenc enthused, running over to the spot.

He turned to Ciro and pointed to the bleached and bark-less trunk. 'A perfect rat raft.'

Ciro mouthed an 'O' as Tenc's idea became clear. The tree trunk, easily cleared of its few remaining branches, would make an ideal raft to cross the river with.

'What do we use for paddles?' Ciro asked as he helped pull the surprisingly light trunk down to the water's edge.

Tenc waggled a leg. 'These,' he said with a smile. 'We hang on with our hands and kick like mad until we reach the far bank.'

'And how do our clothes stay dry?' Ciro asked.

Tenc grinned. 'Lay your cloak on the ground and I'll show you.'

Ciro put down his pack and removed his cloak.

'Now take off all your clothes, boots – everything, stuff them into your pack then put your pack in the centre of your cloak.'

Tenc laid out his own cloak to do the same and within a minute they were both standing naked. Tenc held up his belt.

'You'll need your belt to secure everything,' he said.

Ciro pulled his star belt out of his pack then shook his head at his companion. 'You don't mind if I say that this has to be one of the strangest moments in my life, do you?'

Tenc laughed. 'There's only one thing a travelling Philiri hates more than having to swim across a river and that's having to swim across a river and be soaking wet on the other side. With the rat raft our heads and shoulders will be clear of the water and, if we knot up our cloaks and then fasten them to the back of our heads with our belts, our packs and everything in them will stay out of the water and keep perfectly dry. You see?'

Ciro grinned. 'Tenc, you're a genius!'

The Philiri smiled back and grabbed the corners of Ciro's

cloak, pulling them together before making a large, four stranded knot. He picked up the bundle by the knot and passed it to Ciro, instructing him to hold it behind his head while Tenc secured the belt tightly around his temple. That done, the Philiri stepped in front of Ciro to get the young king to help him with his own bundle but Ciro simply frowned.

'Something's wrong,' Ciro said slowly. He held his hand up to his face as if it was the strangest thing he'd ever seen.

The second Tenc had placed the star belt around his head, Ciro's world had changed. Though the clouding day, the river and the countryside still remained in view, Ciro suddenly found himself aware of a strange interplay of shapes and forms which overlaid the scene. He frowned, for a second considering that Tenc had simply put the belt on too tightly but dismissed that possibility when the Philiri moved into view.

Ciro could not work out why Tenc was moving so slowly, or for that matter, why his body appeared to glow like a candle. He could hear his own voice as he said that something was wrong – but it sounded slurred. He had lifted his hand to see that it too was radiating an inner light.

'Are you alright?'

Tenc's words also seemed slow but Ciro managed a nod and looked down to where the glow around Tenc's feet faded into the grass. Beyond the glow, thin filaments of colour splayed out amongst the green shoots of grass and, as Ciro cast his gaze around him, he found that everything was intertwined with the same shimmering patterns. Everything except the shattered log which they had dragged from the forest edge.

'Can you see this, Tenc?' Ciro murmured, pointing to the dark filaments which seemed to hold off their brighter neighbours to dominate the rotten wood.

'See what? Ciro?' Tenc replied. 'What's the matter?'

'See the…' Ciro was about to attempt a description of the endless swirl of colours when something bright caught his eye amongst the trees beside them. What looked to be a more identifiable form composed of the same strange patterns had separated from the trunk of a tree. As he looked on the shape began drifting through the air towards him. Amazed Ciro turned to point the shape out to Tenc then recoiled in shock and fell backwards onto the grass. Tenc was no longer alone. With a familiar grim expression on his face, Amec stood beside him with arms crossed.

'Are you alright?' asked Tenc, a half-smile on his face. 'What happened?'

Ciro tore off the star belt, blinked and accepted his companion's outstretched hand. He ignored Tenc's concern for a moment and there was a pensive expression on his face as he stared at the belt on the ground. Around it, the grass was just green, and when he looked up it was to find that the light around Tenc had vanished. As had Amec.

Ciro took a deep breath and shook his head. 'I'd like to tell you what happened, Tenc, but I'm not sure myself.' He picked up the star belt and examined it closely. 'It was probably just a dizzy spell, but I just saw some very strange things which I couldn't begin to…' Ciro frowned and weighed the belt in his hands. '…One moment,' he said and placed the belt around his temple again.

Instantly the world resumed its strange colour palette and Ciro noted that a bright outline framed Tenc once again. A yard beyond him, Amec stared back grim-faced then kicked out at their tree trunk.

'By the stars!' Tenc exclaimed as the rat raft suddenly rolled over into the water.

Unnerved by Amec's hostility, Ciro snatched the belt off again.

305

'Did you see that?!' Tenc exclaimed. He jumped amongst the reeds to haul the log back. 'It flew into the water!'

Ciro bit his lip, threw the belt on the ground and helped his companion lift one end of the log clear of the river. With their raft secured Ciro returned to his star belt and turned it over in his hands.

'That log didn't have anything to do with your dizzy spell, did it?' Tenc quipped, though there was a nervous edge to his voice.

Ciro managed a half-smile in return. He shrugged. 'I'll tell you on the far bank,' he said then searched through his pack to find some other way of securing his possessions to his head.

It took what seemed like an age of effort to cross The Handle and its swift current threatened to push them all the way back to Arper and Nesh before they reached the far shore. The rat raft, though an indispensable aid to their leg sapping passage, was a cumbersome craft and it span and drifted in the slightest eddy. It was shear luck that one such current pushed them close to their goal and kicking hard, the pair forced their way to the north bank. Exhausted but elated, they also had the further satisfaction of completely dry clothes.

'Ooh!' Tenc groaned, spraying water as he attempting to shake the tiredness from his legs. 'Who'd want to be a duck?'

Ciro smiled wearily but said nothing as he dressed alongside his companion and checked the aching wound on his side. It was still tightly strapped in a now sodden bandage and Ciro glanced across to the south bank as he pulled on his other clothes. Far upstream he could just make out the stump of the tree that had provided their transport and, as he picked up his star belt from his pack, he again reviewed the strange events which had taken place there. As he had for the entire crossing, Ciro went through the questions which kept running through his mind.

Why on earth would a belt – however beautiful – have such...? What? What was it that the belt appeared to have? And whatever it was, how did it come to have it and since when?

Tenc chortled. 'That belt of yours seems to be causing you some rare problems, friend Ciro.'

Ciro sighed. 'You don't know how right you are,' he replied. He bit his lip and regarded the Philiri blankly for a moment then held out the belt. 'Would you do me a great favour, Tenc?' he asked.

The Philiri looked puzzled but took the offered star belt. On Ciro's instruction he placed the leather band tentatively against his forehead.

'Oh... my...' said Tenc vacantly. His eyes flicked around Ciro for a moment before settling on some unseen point behind him. Then Tenc's expression changed to one of distress and he threw the belt onto the ground at Ciro's feet.

'Are you alright?' Ciro asked, concerned as Tenc backed away.

The Philiri shook his head, stopped and pointed an accusing finger at the belt. 'I dunno what that thing is – but it's not right.'

'Did you see the patterns? Ciro inquired, relieved that Tenc had also experienced something. He picked up the belt and strapped it to his waist as he had a thousand times before.

Tenc pointed past Ciro. 'I... I saw Amec.'

Ciro nodded and placed a reassuring hand on his companion's shoulder. 'So did I, Tenc,' he said. 'I'm sorry to startle you but I wasn't sure if I was seeing things or not.' Ciro returned to his bundle and reattached his cloak. 'Well, at least it proves I'm not mad,' he muttered under his breath.

Tenc still seemed disturbed. 'Ciro, there's only one animal I know of that can conjure up ghosts, and that's a Soulcatcher. Where in Milla's name did you get that belt?!... It wasn't off a Boneman, was it?'

Ciro shook his head and tried to calm the worried looking Philiri with a smile. 'It was King Elson's,' he explained. 'One of his personal possessions that was shipped to Feirlan during the exodus.'

The attempted placation only deepened the frown on Tenc's face. 'The old folk tales say Elson tried to usurp the power of the sun. Put the stars themselves in his back pocket.'

Oh, no, Ciro thought to himself, not the bloo'sandin' Philiri folk tales again. 'They're just stories, Tenc,' he replied.

'But, what if the stars on your belt are those same stars? What if that's what the folk tale means?'

It was Ciro's turn to frown. 'You can't seriously think that King Elson – or anybody else for that matter – stole some stars out of the sky and pinned them to this belt? Come on, Tenc: does that make any sense to you?'

'Sense an' magic rarely mix,' Tenc replied with a shake of his head. 'I don't know much about – whatever that thing is –' he continued, pointing to Ciro's belt. 'But I know it's no ordinary belt. An' Elson must have known it was special: why else would it have been sent away to safety?'

Ciro sighed. 'Whatever it is, it is unusual I'll grant you, but all Elson's personal possessions were shipped to Feirlan. There's no record or mention of this belt being 'special', it was simply King Elson's belt. When we get to Peimonac I'll show you all his armour and swords: we brought the entire collection with us.'

'Why?' asked Tenc.

Ciro shrugged. 'To be honest you'd have to ask Calian. He talked me into the idea. "A King needs his regalia" I think

308

were his exact words.'

'Your friend Calian is one of these Songsmiths, isn't he?' Tenc asked. 'Like the ones you think the messenger Gurnius met in the old story?'

Ciro nodded. 'Yes, their description sounded just like that of a Songsmith – but,' he added, 'before you ask, Calian is not five hundred years old and he's never mentioned having a brother.'

'But you think he might know about…that?' Tenc pointed to the star belt.

'He might,' replied Ciro with a smile. He picked up his pack. 'Now let's get moving,' he insisted. 'We can argue about whether I'm carrying stolen stars or not on the way to Kal Gians.'

A dark horizon of rock framed the sunset ahead as the pair finally reached the North Pullway village. A few patchwork structures of wood, plaster, straw and stone clustered around the dirt track which bisected the village and both Ciro and Tenc rested in the cover of a bush to watch the town and wait for darkness.

The bush was at the straggled end of the woodland the pair had walked through since crossing The Handle in preference to the road they had found running parallel to the river. Even though they could have claimed to have come from Formoss if met on their journey, Ciro's inability to speak the obligatory Makech tongue had made travelling unnoticed a paramount concern in the young king's mind. That and the fact that he had neither hand lance nor sword to defend himself. He was reticent enough as it was with their diversion to Kal Gians so he wanted the entire episode to pass as swiftly – and with as little incident – as possible.

Ciro shifted his gaze from the pullway shanties and

followed the line of the river upstream to where the dark, turreted silhouette of Kal Gians – old Torr Betram – sat upon the cliff tops. With the sun now setting fast the towers and battlements where mere dark shapes against the reddening sky but, in its centre, the sweeping outline of the city wall was masked by a ballooning cloud of mist. As he sat there: when the bird song lulled and the breeze lessened the rustling of the leaves, Ciro was sure he could hear the torrent of the Grand Falls crashing into the harbour.

He remembered Alderman Lacey's glowing account of Torr Betram's life: its theatres, annual games and grand avenues. There were the natural wonders too: the Great Fountain, which plumed up before King Betram's old estate to feed the Grand Falls and the whole of The Handle. And then there were the temples. Four, enigmatic and ancient structures whose purpose was as forgotten as their builders, but whose sight – like the Sun Temple in Peimonac – had left Lacey and his fellow travellers awed.

Ciro remembered the Alderman's descriptions well. How many times had he pictured himself in the shadow of those strange towers? Or standing before the Great Fountain? Now he was less than a couple of miles away from the same wonders yet, for all the good his proximity gained him, he might as well have been that same boy dreaming by candlelight in the Ascension Chamber of Torr Sarvie.

'I've been thinking…' Tenc whispered. He moved closer and peered out through the bush for a moment, as if making sure they were not overheard.

'About what?' Ciro asked.

Tenc frowned and was silent for a moment. 'Why do you think we saw Amec?' he said finally.

'I wish I knew,' replied Ciro with a shrug. The same question had crossed his mind more than once since crossing the river. Along with why Amec appeared as annoyed in death as he had been in life.

'Do you think that belt has some sort of power over him? Like the Soulcatchers have?' Tenc said.

Ciro gave a rueful smile. 'I don't know the first thing about Soulcatchers or magic or anything like that. I only know reason and common sense.' Ciro sighed. 'And, though this belt makes no sense to me, I'm sure there's a reason why it does whatever it is that it does, and a reason why Amec's ghost seems to be following us. I just wish I knew what those reasons were.'

Tenc fell silent again. 'Have you thought about putting it on to see if Amec's still here?'

Ciro looked puzzled. 'Why would I want to do that?'

'Well…' began Tenc. 'We can't move until it's fully dark… And, perhaps, he could scout ahead for us…'

The suggestion took Ciro by complete surprise. He was barely comfortable with the fact that the belt around his waist appeared to grant the wearer an insight of the world unknown before; but he had certainly not thought about attempting to use it to communicate with the dead. Ghosts and strange patterns on the landscape were realms far beyond his logical comprehension and, as such, Ciro had no mind to begin dabbling in matters he knew nothing about. If the belt – and the thought made the young king cringe – possessed some form of 'magical' ability, then he was the wrong person to be toying with it. He wanted to get back to Peimonac and show it to Calian. If anyone would know why the belt gave nature such a strange perspective, Ciro was sure it would be his friend the Songsmith.

'I don't think that's a good idea, Tenc,' Ciro advised. 'I'm not sure we should attempt using something we don't understand. Like you said yourself: "Whatever it is, it's not right".

Tenc looked disappointed. 'I'll use it... I don't mind. I mean, it can't do any harm, can it?'

Ciro shrugged. 'You threw the thing off the last time, are you sure you want to?'

'It took me by surprise, that's all,' replied Tenc. 'No... If you don't mind, I'd quite like to try it again: see if Amec is here.'

'Alright,' said Ciro. He removed the star belt then pointed to the pullway village. 'But, if anything surprises you this time, don't cry out.'

Nodding, the Philiri took the belt from Ciro and placed it against his forehead. Open mouthed he slowly shifted his view from the pullway until it settled on the black sprawl of Kal Gians.

Ciro watched Tenc's face intently for any signs of distress, but instead the Philiri's mouth continued to widen in awe as he looked at the shadow of the city.

'You have to see this, Ciro!' Tenc hissed after a few moments as he removed the belt. There was a grin on his face as he handed the star belt back and pointed to Kal Gians. 'Look over there!'

Curious, and despite his better judgment to leave Elson's belt alone, Ciro followed Tenc's direction and raised the belt to his forehead. At once the world resumed its colourful overlay but Ciro's attention was instantly taken by the beacons of light which flared from the centre of the city. It was as if someone had built several incredibly large and powerful oil lamps and had pointed them at the sky. Their glow was such that, not only did they illuminate the clouds directly above them, but the shadow hidden detail of Kal Gians' battlements suddenly seemed bathed in sunshine. Now Ciro could clearly see the Grand Falls cascading from the cliff as well as the bridge which crossed its drop to reach the Falls Gate. Ciro also noted that the light – though its source was hidden by the enclosed city wall – seemed to emanate from directly beyond that point of the city.

'Where the ancient temples are....' whispered Ciro to himself.

Something moved – close by – across Ciro's field of vision and he blinked to see Amec once again standing before him. The king flinched reflexively with the sudden reappearance of the Philiri's ghost but, despite the disconcerting presence, held its gaze as it stepped closer.

'What do you want, Amec?' he said nervously and, beside him, his companion tensed.

Amec opened his mouth and though no sound emanated, the shaking of the spirit's head and the single vowel his silent lips formed were easily understood. Amec was saying 'No.'

Ciro frowned, a mirror of the ghost's expression. "No"?' he repeated. 'No, what, Amec?'

Now Amec's hands moved to either side of his head to make rapid lifting gestures. His lips moved, his eyes locked on Ciro's own, but the young king could not make sense of the rapid words.

"Take"?' echoed Ciro. It looked like that had been the first word. Amec nodded and circled his own head with a finger, repeating the sentence. 'Take the belt off?' Ciro inquired.

To this the spirit nodded furiously but Ciro just shook his head and frowned. 'Why, Amec, what is it? I don't understand.'

In exasperation Amec gave a deep sigh, went to speak then shook his head and went down on one knee on the ground before Ciro.

'What's happening, Ciro?' asked Tenc anxiously.

'Wait,' replied the king. He watched as Amec began

scrawling letters in the dust.

Whatever state Amec now existed in it seemed interaction with the physical world was a difficult thing for him. Ciro watched as the Philiri's finger repeatedly scratched at the soil to leave little impression but slowly a line of letters began to take shape. It seemed a frustrating process for Amec but finally, the word 'D A Y N J U R U S' appeared in the dirt at Ciro's feet.

"Daynjurus," read Ciro blankly. 'Dangerous?' he repeated with a frown to Amec.

The ghostly Philiri nodded, pointed to Ciro's head and again performed his mime of removing the belt.

'I don't understand, but I trust you, Amec,' Ciro said and at once removed the belt. Just as the light patterns disappeared and the world returned to night, Ciro caught one last expression on Amec's face. It appeared to be relief.

'What was all that about?' Tenc asked anxiously. In response, Ciro pointed to the faint words scrawled in the dirt.

'Amec says the belt's dangerous. I don't know why but, from now on, it's going to do nothing more than hold up my trousers.'

'I bet it's a Soulcatcher's,' Tenc said with a nod. 'It would explain a lot.'

'Not to me it doesn't,' replied Ciro, half to himself as he put the belt back around his waist. He was picking up his pack to begin moving off when a thought occurred to him and he placed a finger in the soil by Amec's word. 'ARE YOU STILL THERE?' He wrote.

'What are you doing?' asked Tenc, the Philiri had picked up his own belongings and crouched beside Ciro as he finished writing.

'I just wondered if Amec could still communicate even if we don't use the belt,' Ciro said with a shrug and they both

314

sat on their haunches to see if any new words would appear.

This time the letters formed quickly but their presence only made the pair look quizzically at one other. Frowning at the unusual request, they rechecked what Amec had written to find that the word had now been underlined for emphasis.

RUN

Both Ciro and Tenc sprang into motion as a deafening clap of thunder sounded overhead. Scant yards behind their flying feet the ground exploded as a lightening bolt struck the earth.

Ciro threw himself to the floor as the force from the explosion ripped through the air. He landed heavily, rolled onto his back then looked up to find that what remained of the bush they had been hiding behind was now ablaze. Lying beside him, Tenc grimaced and sat up, rubbing the dust from his hands as he watched the fire consume the remaining branches. He gave a hollow laugh.

"Sakoom blows hard, but Sosh burns brighter," he said with a shake of his head. Tenc managed a grin but he looked nervous.

Ciro frowned as he climbed back to his feet. 'What do you mean by that, Tenc?'

'Oh, it's an old expression,' he explained, 'but what I mean is that Amec was right about the danger. Having both the Kolben Lords of Wind and Fire as your enemy is about as dangerous as things can get...' Tenc gazed up at the dark clouds above. 'I wonder how Amec knew?'

Ciro was about to say he didn't believe in such superstitious rubbish as the Kolben Lords but the sight of the shattered, burning bush held his tongue. The event was beyond coincidence. Despite his better judgment he had the unsettling suspicion that the lightening had – somehow – been directed. A deliberate act by someone or something which, thankfully, Amec had warned them about. No wonder he keeps looking agitated, Ciro thought. He had known the belt was a threat to their safety: their lives.

'You're right, Tenc,' Ciro said quietly. 'How did Amec know?'

The Philiri shrugged, got up to brush the dirt from his leggings and cast his gaze around the Pullway village. Despite the noise and fire there was still no sign of life. 'It's odd, you know,' he said, tugging absently at his beard. 'The Pullway wasn't so quiet the last time I was here.'

Ciro was also patting the dust from his clothes and took in the gloomy structures by the river. It was almost completely dark now, yet there were still no figures around the buildings or a single light from a window. Neither could he recall having seen a single boat on the river during their journey.

'Whatever the reason, we're in no position to find out about it,' said Ciro. The words and their sentiment left a sour taste in his mouth. The King of Nothing, he thought bleakly, come to visit the darkened homes of his people and simply pass them by.

'Do you think we should move from here?' Tenc pointed to the smouldering remains of the bush. 'Just in case?'

Ciro glanced up at the clouds. There had been no further rumbles since the first one but Ciro was not sure that meant they were safe. It made him nervous to think that another bolt might fall at any moment, anywhere. He sought solace in the fact that he had worn the star belt for years without a single incident. Just as long as I don't put it round my head, he thought.

Ciro knocked dirt from his pack and nodded to the Philiri. 'Let's get to the Cauldron,' he said and hitched a thumb at the clouds. 'And pray for a clear sky as well.'

To this Tenc grinned and, skirting the quiet village the pair walked the final mile towards the lights of Kal Gians.

Ciro's concern about what they should do if Makech guards were present at the harbour gateway was answered when Tenc suggested they pretend to be 'Pullers' from the village, looking for money owed to them from a boat in the harbour. Despite the fact that neither had seen any vessels going to or coming from the Cauldron, Ciro had to agree that it was the most plausible excuse they were going to come up with. A little way from the entrance the pair crouched in the darkness to see if there was any activity around the gate.

Points of light here and there gave shape to the battlements which ran the entire edge of the cliff above them while the unmistakable roar of the Grand Falls thundered relentlessly in the darkness straight ahead. It also gave Ciro his first taste of harbour conditions as a fine mist blew on his face.

'See anyone?' he whispered.

'No, looks unguarded to me.'

'Alright,' said Ciro, standing. 'You do the talking while I try and look as simple as possible.'

They approached the formidable front gates of the North Harbour as carelessly as their racing hearts would allow and Ciro tried to prevent his equally rapid thoughts from conjuring up one worse scenario after the next. He puffed his cheeks out, released a sigh as quietly as he could and tried to convince himself that they would find Tamarail in minutes and be casting off before a clock could strike the next hour.

'Lith'eer dec?!' called Tenc into the night. The abrupt cry made Ciro's heart skip. There was no reply to the call and the grey haired Philiri turned to Ciro and winked. 'Just seein' if anyone's about,' he whispered.

They were almost at the open gateway now and Ciro could see that, through the shadow of the arch, a pool of torchlight revealed the foggy curve of the quay side and the dull glitter of water beyond it. Then three dark figures moved into the light and headed straight towards them.

Tenc and Ciro stopped on the threshold of the gateway as the three shadows resolved themselves into Makech guards. The Philiri instantly raised a hand in greeting.

'Anacelestion!' he said cheerily, but the three men simply stood in silence and stared at the newcomers.

Keeping his head bowed, Ciro glanced at the Makech in front of them. The first was a massive, barrel-chested individual – well over six feet tall – with a face almost completely obscured by a beard more akin to a bush. The middle guard was almost identical to the first in appearance, yet on a smaller scale and a necklace of bone poked out from beneath his grey-flecked beard. The third Makech was younger, thinner and darker skinned and sported the sorriest excuse for facial hair that Ciro had ever seen. All three carried badly made – though solid – wooden shields but, unlike his hirsute companions, the youngster had no skull perched on top of his helmet. That omission brought the memory of crossing the bridge at Urawiir to Ciro's mind. It was the only other occasion he had seen a Makech 'unskulled'. The recollection sparked another. The bearded man in the middle had been the one who had shouted out to them after they had crossed the bridge.

'Who in Beck's name are you?' asked Pronyes in Makech.

'We're from the Pullway,' Tenc replied in kind. 'We're owed a fare from one of the boats.'

'Is that right?!' Pronyes sounded incredulous. 'Well, you certainly value money, I'll give you that.'

The other Makech laughed as Tenc shook his head. 'I'm sorry, I don't understand,' he said.

'No, we didn't think you did,' replied Siort with a grin.

Pronyes pushed aside his cloak and drew his sword, his

fellow guards mirroring the move. 'Right, this way!' he barked, waggling his blade towards the harbour. The two other Makech parted to let Tenc and Ciro through.

From Ciro's perspective the entire exchange had been completely unintelligible yet the tone, and now the swords, were enough for him to make an accurate enough guess of the general context of the conversation. He cursed himself bitterly for ignoring his own advice: they should never have come back to an inhabited area.

Tenc cast a glance in the king's direction as the guards fell in behind them but, without being able to speak the forbidden Rialan, there was no way for them to communicate.

'Where are you taking us?' Tenc asked but in reply the Makech merely laughed.

Beyond the shadow of the gateway the vast horseshoe of Kal Gians harbour opened up before them: or would have done if the thunderous cascade of the Grand Falls had not fogged the darkness beyond the torchlight. To their right the black facade of the encompassing cliffs was dotted with fires while, beneath it, a vague crisscross of masts and rigging patterned the mist. Straight ahead, a single point of orange light seemed suspended in the gloom and it took Ciro several seconds to work out that the glow emanated from one of the harbour's light houses. Despite the lack of visibility it should have been a wondrous sight yet Ciro's mind was otherwise occupied.

They were herded right, along the harbour road which ran beneath the outer battlements and would eventually lead them to the base of the cliffs. If Ciro's memory was correct, they would eventually reach the sky carriages – mechanical marvels of the old kingdom – which carried goods and livestock up the cliff face to the north market. Was that the route they would take, he wondered? And what Makech

319

pleasures awaited them when they reached the city: the slave market? Ciro didn't think they would be that fortunate. He wracked his brain for an idea of how they might escape their sword-wielding escort but, with no exit other than the one they had just passed through and no weapon with which to attack the guards, he was at a loss to think of a single way out of their predicament. He could not even ask Tenc if he had thought of anything.

The guards where chattering and laughing heartily as they walked on when suddenly Tenc lifted his downcast face to reveal a bleak and forlorn expression to Ciro.

'They've just said they're going to kill you for the boy's first skull,' he hissed in Rialan.

Before Pronyes, Siort or the giant, Gisker could intervene to silence the pair; Ciro had grabbed Tenc's hand and leapt into the harbour.

'Hey!' Pronyes shouted as their recent captives disappeared into the water. Gisker gave an angry roar and dived in after them.

'No!' Siort yelled, realising too slowly Gisker's intent. Their captives were already swimming into the mist shrouded harbour as Gisker hit the water and – clad as he was in finest Makech armour – sank like a stone.

'Idiot!' cried Pronyes, shaking his head in disbelief at their companion's stupidity. There was a stream of bubbles floating to the surface, but Pronyes had been in service long enough to know that Gisker was as good as dead if he could not remove his armour. So far, not even his wooden shield had floated to the surface.

Siort was shouting into the fog. 'You won't get away!' he screamed. 'There's no way out!'

'C'mon,' said Pronyes. 'Let's get up top and get some help to hunt them down. They won't get far.'

'No, I'll stay here just in case they try for the gateway,' replied Siort. He pointed to the black water below. 'And maybe Gisker will remember how to swim.'

The pair stared at the water for a few moments more but the surface was still. Pronyes shook his head, gave a silent prayer to Shernn: Kolben Lord of water then ran off towards the single working sky carriage.

Ciro and Tenc swam for their lives into the heart of the north harbour until the sight and sounds of the Makech were lost in the mist and the roar from the waterfall. Tenc's initial shock had given way to a broad grin of relief as Ciro pulled him in his wake for the first few strokes and now, hidden by the fog and the rumble of the Grand Falls, the pair eased their furious paddling.

'That was an even better idea than my rat raft!' Tenc exclaimed, grinning and spitting water.

'I'd like to say I'd thought it through,' Ciro replied. 'But it hadn't occurred to me a second before I grabbed your hand.'

'Well, it certainly got us rid of the Bonemen,' answered Tenc cheerfully.

Perhaps, thought Ciro as they paddled on in silence. It was a big harbour but there was no telling how many other Makech were nearby and it was difficult to remain hidden when you did not know where to hide.

The Cauldron was made up of two separate harbours: north and south. Divided by the racing torrent of the Grand Falls, each harbour was protected from the rapid stream by stout stone breakwaters. The lighthouse Ciro had seen sat at the tip of the north harbour breakwater and, with its light still glowing to his left, he was sure that they were heading towards the most inaccessible part of the north harbour. But what they did once they reached the breakwater was a question which weighed heavily on Ciro's mind.

At length, the dark shapes of wooden hulls began to emerge from the murky night, moored beside the long jetties which sat at right angles to the breakwater. The pair made instantly towards the bow of the first ship they saw and Ciro posed the question of how they were going to find Tamarail's vessel.

'Would you know it from down here in the water?' Ciro asked, certain that patrols would await them somewhere on the quay side.

'I can't say I'd ever really considered the question before,' replied Tenc. 'But I'm sure I'll know it when I see it.' The Philiri trod water for a moment and regarded the ship above them. 'It's definitely not this one...' he said, '...too big.'

'Then we'll just have to paddle around until we find it,' said Ciro.

It was an unappealing prospect but the safest course the king could think of. And what would they do if Tamarail's vessel could not be found? Drift back downstream, thought Ciro: to resume a journey they should not have interrupted.

Several bells chimed above the sound of the waterfall as the pair swam on between the moored shapes and then Ciro made out the sound of voices coming from the vessel before them. Swimming closer it quickly became clear that, whoever was talking, he was speaking Rialan.

'That's illegal, isn't it?' hissed Ciro as the voice from the boat was answered by a fainter reply in the same tongue.

'It's the least of our worries, isn't it?'

'No,' persisted Ciro. 'I mean, anyone speaking Rialan can't be a friend to the Makech. And that means they might be able to help us.'

Tenc attempted a shrug but got a mouth full of water for his effort. 'Worth...a try,' he managed to splutter.

Ciro swam more rapidly towards the voice but as he neared the bow the sound stopped. He trod water for a few moments, listening intently before a barge pole suddenly struck the water inches in front of him.

'Hey!' he cried, instantly swimming backwards and a stream of unintelligible Makech issued from the figures on the boat as they thrust the barge pole at him again.

'We're not tryin' ta spy on you!' shouted Tenc, replying to their accusation in Rialan. 'We're simply tryin' to escape from the Bonemen!'

'The 'ole city's tryin' t'do that,' came the dour response. 'S'clear off!'

'Please,' said Ciro. 'We didn't mean to startle you, but we need your help.'

'What're ya doin' swimmin' in the 'arbour anyways?'

'Like my friend said,' replied Ciro. 'It was the only way we could get away from the Bonemen. Will you help us?'

The figures disappeared from view for a moment before the barge pole reappeared. This time however, it was merely placed into the water.

'Climb up quick,' said one of the men. 'But any funny business an' we'll throw you straight back.'

The pair scrambled up the pole, shivering in the sudden cold of the night as they crouched on the deck. Tenc's teeth began to chatter and both men threw down their sodden backpacks as the boatmen looked on in silence. By the pale light of the lantern which sat on deck behind the strangers, Ciro watched for a moment as water poured from his clothing in torrents to pool and soak the already damp deck.

'We're much obliged,' he said with a wan smile.

'Are ya from up top?' one of the men asked. He hitched his thumb in the direction of the fog covered battlements.

Ciro and Tenc shook their heads. 'We're... From Forht,'

Ciro replied. 'We've come looking for a friend of ours, a man named Tamarail. Do you know him?'

'Maybe,' replied the other man cautiously. 'Oo wants ta know?'

Tenc was wringing his soggy sleeves in a vain attempt to dry them. 'My name's Tenc,' he said, 'and this is –'

'– Fidiann,' cut in Ciro quickly. 'My name is Fidiann.' The Beck Iph soldier at Birin Bridge had known his name so perhaps it had now become widely known. There seemed no point in risking its use with strangers; however benign they appeared.

The boatmen took a few steps closer. One was short, thin of build with long, straggled hair circling a bald crown. He sported a drooping moustache which framed his stubbly chin. The other was far taller, totally bald and wore a circlet of shells around his temple. The tall man's face was heavily pock-marked; the scars barely hidden by a mass of grey stubble. In his hands he still carried the barge pole. The shorter man introduced them.

'I'm Dent, this is Borlin,' he said. 'Now, 'bout this friend o' yours?...'

'His name's Tamarail,' Tenc repeated. 'He owns a vessel named the Pesarian and brings goods up from Formoss. If you could point us in the direction of that boat we'd be much obliged.'

Dent nodded. 'Weell...' he drawled, 'that's all well an' good. But these are dang'rous times for us Rialans – which ya'll know y'self after bein' chased by the Bonemen – we've gotta be careful. So, if I did know some such person as this 'Tamarail', what's ta prove that you know 'im? Maybe yer just a couple o' Soulcatcher's Wraiths come ta find 'is whereabouts.'

Ciro frowned. The man seemed earnest in his reticence,

nervous even and it seemed certain to Ciro that news of what had happened at Urawiir had reached Kal Gians: the Makech soldiers from the bridge certainly had.

'If you can get a message to him,' said Tenc. 'Tell him that Tenc has come from the Hare's House with grave news. He'll know what that means.'

Dent and Borlin exchanged a long, deliberating glance before the short man shrugged. He turned to the pair on the deck.

'There's blankets in the 'old,' Dent said. 'Borlin'll show ya where.'

He stared intently at his companion again then, with a swift pat on Borlin's shoulder, moved to the hand rail on the far side of the deck and clambered out of sight.

'He's not going to swim, is he?' Tenc asked Borlin as Dent disappeared.

The big man smiled. 'Nah, we've a boat down there. It's the best way ta get around the docks… The Makech don't like water,' Borlin added then grinned at the soaked pair before him. 'But ya already know that.'

Despite himself, Ciro could not stop shivering. The wetness of his clothes had, by degrees, turned to a freezing clamminess and so it was a great relief when Borlin brought out a pile of dry blankets: even offering them a change of clothing. Ciro eyed with interest the smocks and leggings that Borlin brought up from the hold. Both were simple shapes woven from heavy, grey fibres but Ciro noted instantly how they matched the fishermen's garb worn around the harbours of Obaln and Rurset.

They wasted no time relieving themselves of their dripping attire and quickly dried themselves with the blankets. After Ciro had finally secured his baggy leggings with the star belt and placed his squelching Feirlan boots back on his feet, they thanked Borlin for his hospitality.

Borlin had settled himself on the hand rail near where Dent had disappeared. 'We've got an 'old full of 'em,' he said with a shrug. 'Might as well put 'em ta some use.'

'You've not been able to sell them?' Ciro inquired. The garments were not exactly the height of court fashion, but as sturdy working clothes they were perfect. Ciro knew, he had commissioned his army's 'dun' uniforms from a

business which made almost identical clothing back in Feirlan.

'Did ya not see the boats tied across the harbour mouth?' asked Borlin. 'No one's been down river for days.'

Ciro frowned. 'You mean the entrance has been blocked, why?'

The boatman shrugged. 'Rumour is that the Grand Bastard 'imself: 'igh Prince Perlenz, has been killed. No one knows for sure 'ow it 'appened, but the way the Bonemen've been slaughterin' up there –' Borlin hitched a thumb in the direction of the Grand Falls, '– they certainly don't think it was no accident. An' it looks like they're not lettin' anyone out 'til they get some answers.'

'Then we were lucky to get away from that patrol when we did,' said Tenc.

Ciro nodded. 'Did you notice that two of them were from the bridge at Urawiir?'

Tenc shook his head. 'I was too nervous; I just kept my head down.'

'I thought there was more Bonemen around than usual,' mused Borlin. He scanned the mist behind them for any sign of Dent's return when his body stiffened. 'Wha' was that?' he asked, turning.

Both Ciro and Tenc listened above the perpetual roar of the Grand Falls but heard nothing. Then the flame in the lantern suddenly went out and plunged the deck into darkness.

Knock. Knock. Knock.

'You hear that?!' hissed Borlin with alarm.

'Yes,' Ciro replied. It had sounded like someone rapping on the deck. He could barely see the tall figure of the boatman now but then another light source began to glow in the misty night some way along the quay side. Seconds later the faintest sound of voices could be heard. Shouting in Makech.

'I think we've got company!' hissed Tenc.

'I'll bet it's that patrol looking for us,' replied Ciro. He scrabbled about in the darkness, collecting his wet clothes to shove them quickly into his pack. Tenc did the same beside him.

'Beck it!' hissed Borlin. The boatman crouched down behind the handrail and Ciro and Tenc joined him to watch as the glow of light and the voices drew closer in the mist.

'Do you have any weapons?' whispered Ciro.

The question seemed to surprise Borlin momentarily, then he shook his head and picked up his boat hook. 'Only this,' he replied.

Ciro considered their situation, contemplating jumping back into the harbour. 'What do you think they'll do?' he asked. 'Will they come aboard?'

'Yeah,' drawled Borlin with distaste. 'They always do.'

'Why don't we swim for it?' Tenc suggested. 'It worked before.'

'I'm not swimmin' away from my boat,' said Borlin firmly. 'The bastards can swing on a rope far as I'm concerned.'

'I can't say I disagree,' said Ciro. 'I know swimming is an option, Tenc, but I'd rather stay dry. And I'm not leaving Borlin behind.'

The light from the Makech torches illuminated the dark outline of another vessel along the quay side. It was the only one between them and the patrol and Ciro watched as a swarm of shouting figures stormed aboard.

'What are they saying?' Ciro asked. 'Can you make it out?'

"Check there… Check there," Borlin replied. 'Someone's barkin' orders from the dockside… "Check the 'old," he's just said.'

'Is there anywhere aboard they might not find us?' Ciro asked.

Some of the Makech were starting to clamber back onto the quay side. Borlin shook his head. 'No, there's not much space, other than two cabins an' the 'old – an' that's pretty easy searched.'

Ciro cast his gaze around the vessel but in the darkness there was not much chance of him finding a hiding place which Borlin might have missed. The boat was a single long deck and, apart from the two masts and a central hatch leading down to the hold, almost completely uncluttered. Ciro continued to glance around vainly before, looking up, he spotted a canvas awning three yards overhead which he had not previously noticed. It stretched the entire length of the deck and had been put there, he supposed, to keep out the perpetual drizzle of the Cauldron.

'Did they climb the rat lines?' Ciro asked.

'Not that I saw,' Tenc replied.

'How tall are your masts, Borlin?'

'Tall enough ta 'ave a crow's nest,' the boatman replied with a grin. With the large man leading, the three of them scuttled quickly to the far side of the deck away from the torch light and clambered into the rigging.

It had been a while since Ciro had gone aloft, the last time being a distinctly nerve-wracking experience while the King Elson was crossing the deep ocean. This time the vessel was not rocking wildly in a swell but the unsteady sway of the ratlines as the three men climbed instantly brought back the same sensations which Ciro had experienced the last time he had climbed above deck. He did not, he decided, really care for heights and specifically the unsteady heights of a ship's rigging. As he had done before however, Ciro ignored his fluttering stomach, bit his lip and kept climbing.

From their new vantage the world was now a swirl of mist with just the glow from the Makech torches to show them where the enemy – and the ground – were. And the torches were heading towards Borlin's boat.

On the boatman's suggestion, the trio ignored the crow's nest, level with the mainsail yardarms, and continued higher until they reached the precarious peak of the main topsail. There was barely space for the three of them to cling around the masthead, so Borlin deftly side-stepped along a foot-rope until he was a good ten feet from the others.

'One of you come 'ere with me,' he hissed above the noise of the Grand Falls. 'We'll straddle the sail. Shouldn't be seen then, even if they bother climbin' up a way's.'

Ciro motioned Tenc to join Borlin before inching himself along the opposite foot-rope with both hands clutching tightly at the furled canvas of the sail. The king felt his legs begin to shake and, looking down to check his footing on the slender rope, he noticed the torch lights now illuminated the canvas which covered the deck. Holding his breath as well as his nerve, Ciro heaved himself on top of the sail and wrapped his arms about it with all his strength.

'Oash! Nilidroi!' Came the gruff call from below and Ciro could make out shadows as a dozen Makech soldiers clambered onto the deck and moved beneath the canvas. He craned his neck to look along the yardarm but even from this short distance the shapes of both Tenc and Borlin were barely discernible from the bulky sail.

With much stomping and shouting the patrol explored the bowels of Borlin's boat but not once did they seem to give a second thought to what might lie above their heads. The minutes seemed to drag as the search went on but soon the Makech were clambering back onto the quay side to continue their hunt elsewhere. Relieved, Ciro watched as the torchlight became fainter in the fog then stuck out a leg to find the foot-rope. Carefully he inched his way back to the mast.

'They've gone!' he hissed and the pale faces of Tenc and Borlin appeared from the shadow of the sail.

'They'll be back,' Borlin replied. 'There's three more boats moored at the far end, near the light'ouse. But once they've done, they'll 'ave ta come back this way. We'd best stay put.'

Ciro was about to inch back to his hiding place when a noise from below, barely audible against the background of the waterfall, caught his attention. He looked down. There was nothing to see apart from swirling mist but the sound came again. A voice? A bird call? Ciro thought. He looked at the others, still clinging to the sails and saw that they too were listening.

'That's Dent!' said Borlin, swinging his large frame onto the foot-rope. 'Climb down ta the deck.'

Ciro nodded, gripped the rat-line beside him and began to descend.

'What were ya doin' aloft?' asked Dent as first Ciro, then Tenc and Borlin jumped from the rigging on both sides of the boat.

'Makech patrol,' explained Ciro.

'But they'll be back,' Borlin said. 'So we should go.'

To this Dent nodded and led them to the bow. 'Climb in,' he said, pointing over the side.

Ciro looked down. There was a small rowing boat moored alongside with a rope ladder leading down. Borlin was already descending and, as Ciro motioned Tenc to go before him he noticed a tell-tale glow in the fog.

'They're coming back!' he whispered and Dent followed his gaze to see the torches of the Makech patrol coming closer.

The boatman smiled. 'They're too late,' he said and nudged Ciro. 'Climb down, I'll follow.'

Ciro vaulted the hand rail and descended, stepping into the little boat as gently as he could to sit beside Tenc. Dent instantly joined them, untied the boat from its mooring and nodded to Borlin who gripped the oars.

'Alright, Borlin,' he whispered. 'Let's go!'

Silently, the little boat pulled away into the harbour and both Tenc and Ciro heaved a sigh as the glow of the Makech torches became lost in the mist.

'Where are we going?' Ciro asked as the fog closed in around them.

'To see a friend o' yours,' Dent replied. 'It's not far.'

The noise and mist from the Grand Falls increased as they moved further into the harbour until nothing could be seen but the few feet of water which surrounded the boat. After a time of travelling through this blankness, Ciro was about to enquire whether Borlin could navigate in such conditions when the lopsided hulk of a vessel suddenly emerged from the gloom directly before them.

From the acute angle of the ship and the algae covered woodwork it was not hard to deduce that it had been a wreck for some time and, as Borlin deftly navigated around its sorry form to expose the leaning deck, Ciro noted that the fore and main masts had been removed. There was still a web of slime-covered rigging clinging to the hulk and even a sail which bowed out from the stump of the mizzen mast to hang into the water. Here was a vessel, thought Ciro, that was now only capable of travelling in one direction: down.

'What happened to it?' he asked as they passed alongside.

'Oh, we scuppered 'er a year or so back,' Borlin replied and pulled in the oars to let the boat drift into the black shadow of the sail.

Dent stood up and gripped a hanging rope to guide them further into the darkness. 'Safest place in the 'ole city,' he said. 'Looks like a wreck by day an' can't even be seen at night. The Makech've never caught on.'

Tenc laughed. 'Was this Tamarail's idea?'

'Sort of,' Borlin said as their boat bumped the slanted deck of the derelict. He stood up beside Dent and made a scratching noise on the woodwork of the wreck. A few seconds later a square of pale light appeared just above them as a hatch opened.

By the weak glow which spilled out, Ciro could just see that the overhanging sail formed a hidden harbour and that at least half a dozen rowing boats were already moored in its lee.

'Up ya go, Fidiann,' said Dent and Ciro gripped the edge of the hatch to pull himself inside.

The cramped cabin they found themselves in was so askew that one of the walls now served as the floor. Illuminated by a single candle firmly held by a dour young man in the far corner, first Ciro then Tenc slithered in to stand uncomfortably on the incline. They waited while the boatmen followed them through the hole. The man in the corner, dressed in what looked to be the same thick garments worn by Ciro and Tenc, watched silently until Dent had shut the hatch behind them. Then, casting a frowning glance at the newcomers, he pushed aside another hatch in what had once been the floor.

'In 'ere,' he said and disappeared into a brighter room

beyond.

The chamber which they now found themselves in had once been the cargo hold but, though the walls and deck still leaned, a straight floor of planking had been put in to provide a level space. There were oil lamps hanging from the curving hull of the ship and a candle-lit table occupied the far end of the space. What drew Ciro and Tenc's attention though were the forty or so people – men, women and children – who lined each side of the chamber. They looked on sullenly as the young man with the candle led them to the group seated around the table.

The faces of the group were similarly impassive with one exception: a broad-shouldered man with blonde hair platted to his shoulders and a pale, wide face grinned at Tenc. He rose to embrace the Philiri, patted him on the shoulder, then seemed to remember himself. The welcoming smile faded.

'I'm happy to see you again, Tenc, but I hear you bring bad news.'

Tenc nodded. 'It's good to see you too, Tamarail,' he replied then gave a heavy sigh. 'The Makech finally discovered Olbas Osanti. Urawiir has been burned to the ground... Amec was murdered – Mara too.'

Tamarail frowned and leaned back onto the table's edge. Lost in thought for a moment he stared at the floor.

'That is terrible news. Poor Mara...' he said distantly. '... And Amec: it's a shame.' Tamarail shrugged the emotion off in an instant and looked up at Tenc. 'The Makech are raging like Sakoom everywhere: there's been nothing but slaughter in the city since that bastard Perlenz was brought back dead a few days ago.'

'Yes,' said Tenc. 'Borlin mentioned that he'd been murdered.'

Tamarail shook his head and took in a sharp breath. 'Oh, he

wasn't just murdered –' The Philiri turned to the table and motioned a slim, dark haired woman to come forward. 'Dowen worked as a servant up at Perlenz's Mansion 'till this afternoon. Tell 'em what you overheard, Dowen.'

The woman held a clay mug in her hand which she sipped from before setting it down and joining Tamarail.

'The guards up top're scared,' she said and grinned a brief smile of brown-stained teeth. 'They ain't supposed ta talk but can't stop chatterin' 'bout what 'appened... Seems 'is Lordship's 'untin' party got 'unted by somethin' nastier than 'e was. Shot to ribbun's – all of 'em – by arrows big as swords.'

Ciro frowned. 'Did you see these arrows?' he asked.

Dowen stared back blankly. 'No, I didn't see 'em – I just 'eard about 'em. Like I says, the guards keep talkin' 'bout it.'

'There were two Rialan cooks with Perlenz's party who survived and came back with the tale and a few of the bodies,' explained Tamarail. 'We don't know much of what these cooks said but, after they were tortured and killed, an entire Makech caravan left the city and raced south towards Kal Santra.' Tamarail gave a humourless smile. 'Now more troops have come from the west and, ridiculous as it sounds, rumours are rife of a Rial King – come to free his people.'

There was a murmur amongst the crowd huddled on the floor of the chamber and Ciro noticed Tenc give him an uncomfortable, sideways glance.

Tamarail also spotted Tenc's discomfort. 'Do you two know something about this?... Tenc?'

'I...' Tenc began and looked back at Ciro.

'I can't be definite;' said Ciro, 'but Perlenz's injuries sound like they may have been caused by a fire-lance.' Tamarail and the others around the table stared intently at him. 'It fires,' he continued, 'what could be described as "arrows big as swords."

The chamber suddenly became very quiet.

'How do you know about these – arrow things?' asked Tamarail with a frown.

What should I say? Thought Ciro. Do I lie and tell them I'm simply a member of the expedition? Or do I tell the truth and risk raising hopes which I cannot satisfy?… No, he thought, whatever happens I must be truthful. He saw the expectation in the faces around him. 'My name is Ciro Torrman–' he began.

'– That was it!' Dowen suddenly exclaimed, her face alive, her hand pointed towards him. 'I couldn't fer the life of me remember that beckin' name! Ciro! 'E's the one I 'eard mentioned up at the palace – 'e's the beckin' King!'

Now there was consternation in the chamber and Tamarail waved his arms and hissed for silence. 'Quiet! By Ebo's Mire, do you want the Bonemen to hear?!' The incredulity was subdued and Tamarail turned to Tenc. 'Is this true, Tenc?'

Tenc nodded. 'I believe he is the King. And I know the Makech certainly believe it. It's a long story, but Ciro's the one to explain it.'

Now all eyes were on Ciro and Tamarail shook his head in wonder. 'How under Milla's Gaze did a youngster like you become a King?' he asked.

Ciro sighed, straightened his shoulders and, as briefly as he could, told them exactly how.

Once the shock had sunk in, and Ciro had answered the many questions put to him as best he could, there was disappointment when the crowd realised there was no avenging army camped outside the city gates.

'As soon as I get to Peimonac,' Ciro explained. 'I can bring thousands of my soldiers here. But first I must get to

Peimonac.'

Tamarail seemed as disappointed as the others and turned to the group around the table. 'Then we go on with our original plan,' he said. There were nods in response and the blonde Philiri turned to Dent and Borlin. 'You two had best be busy.'

'What about the patrols?' Borlin asked.

Tamarail shrugged. 'I never said it would be easy,' he replied and with that the two boatmen left the ship.

Tamarail spent some minutes conversing with the group at the table then, after offering both Ciro and Tenc a mug of what turned out to be apple juice, the Philiri walked amongst the recumbent lines of people before finally returning to the pair.

Ciro had listened to Tamarail's earlier exchange with Dent and Borlin with interest and, as the Philiri boatman joined them, he asked what plan it was he had spoken of.

'You were lucky to get here when you did,' Tamarail replied. He swept his gaze around the chamber 'Since the death of Perlenz the city has turned into a slaughter house. The people you see here are those who we've managed to convince to come back with us.'

'You're returning to Philire?' Tenc asked.

Tamarail nodded. 'The last few days have been bad for all of us – Philiri and otherwise – many have been killed. So, when they blockaded the harbour I knew it would simply be a matter of time before the killing spread down here. I spoke to a few of the sailors I could trust that I planned to break the blockade and set sail past the black apples. It's a hazardous trip, but these are the people that have agreed to take the risk.'

'It's not that dangerous with your ship,' said Tenc. 'The Pesarian was built to travel through the dead lands.'

To this Tamarail looked sad. 'The Makech took her almost a year ago, Tenc. I was lucky they didn't get me too. I haven't seen her since.'

'She had metal plates on her hull, did she not?' asked Ciro. 'To protect her from the black apples?'

'Yes,' replied Tamarail with a sigh. 'She was a fine craft, the only ship ever built by Philiri hands.'

'But isn't it impossible to get past the black apples without it?' continued Ciro. 'Won't an ordinary boat sink?'

'It's a risk, but we have no real future here: we have to pray that Milla shines, that Miri blows fair and that Gallia speeds our course,' replied Tamarail. 'We also plan to wrap sails around the hulls of the ships when we pass Formoss – that should protect us for a time.'

'How many vessels are you taking?' inquired Ciro.

'Just two. Getting more out of the harbour would prove too risky, but we're positive that two can get loose without any trouble from the Bonemen. Besides...' Tamarail indicated the people still lining the chamber. 'We sadly have no need of further vessels.'

'Borlin said there was a line of boats tied across the harbour mouth,' said Tenc. 'Have they gone to cut them free?'

'Not quite yet, but soon,' said Tamarail. There was a murmur in the crowd and all eyes turned to watch as the entrance hatch opened and the young man with the candle led in a stocky figure with a dark black beard.

'Orlis, is it done?' asked Tamarail as the man drew closer. The man named Orlis nodded and with that the people on the right hand side of the room collected the sacks and bags at their feet and stood up.

Led by Orlis they slowly filed out through the hatch, followed by the group seated around the table. They said brief goodbye's to Tamarail as they departed and many a curious glance was cast in Ciro's direction before they had all left.

'The first boat's ready,' explained the Philiri once the

chamber had half emptied. 'Dent and Borlin told Orlis to cast off and drop anchor in the centre of the north harbour. Now my crew will do the same with my boat while Dent and Borlin cut a hole in the blockade.'

'Won't the Makech notice?' asked Ciro.

'You saw the mist out there – this time o'night you can't see a thing.'

'What about the lighthouse near the harbour's mouth?'

Tamarail shrugged. 'That's a risk we'll have to take but, by now, the Makech should have noticed the little distraction we've created for them. It should keep the patrol occupied.' He smiled and then explained: 'Orlis's crew cut the water lines to the only working sky carriage, which means there'll be no more Makech coming down from the city for a while.' The smile widened to a grin. 'And they do hate to be stuck down here at night.'

The candle man appeared back through the hatch.

'We're ready, Tamarail,' he announced and the remaining people got up from the deck.

'We'll get into the launches outside,' Tamarail explained. 'Once Borlin and Dent have broken the blockade, we'll meet with them aboard the Gallean and head out.' He slapped Tenc's shoulder. 'Within a week we should be home in Philire.'

Back in the cold, damp air of the harbour, Ciro climbed into the rowing boat moored beneath the hatch to find the lee behind the sail empty of other craft. He crouched down and placed a hand in the dark water – icy to the touch – and wondered if the temperature had dropped dramatically. He could not remember it being cold at all when he and Tenc had swum in it.

Tamarail was the last to climb down from the wreck. He

gently closed the hatch behind them then, as he sat in the prow and gave the order to cast off, Ciro was sure he caught an expression of sadness on the Philiri's face as the lop-sided hull disappeared into the fog.

They rowed for several minutes through the blank night until the dim shape of another crowded rowing boat emerged from the mist. It sat stationary in the water as, unseen, they drew closer then a call from Tamarail alerted them to his presence. The lead boat returned the call, dug its oars into the water and together the boats moved on, deeper into the centre of the North Harbour.

Soon another rowing boat was visible ahead, this time with the stern of a much larger vessel rising from the mist beyond it. As Ciro watched the lead boat slipped around the stern of the ship and within seconds silent figures could just be made out as they clambered up its side.

They drew level with the larger vessel to find several rope ladders hanging from its starboard side and leading to the deck. Like the boats before them, Tamarail's moved swiftly alongside to off load his passengers and, in almost complete silence, the final refugees boarded the ship. Tamarail stayed below until lines were securely fastened and, still aboard the rowing boat, he was winched clear of the water and up onto the deck.

Ciro and Tenc declined the offer to go below with the other passengers and looked around at the familiar sight of the Gallean. It was, they quickly realised, the same vessel which they had been on earlier and, as they moved to the bow of the craft to get out of the way of the tense crew, Tenc found the extinguished oil lamp which had gone out earlier.

Tenc was still holding the lamp as Ciro reached the prow to stare fixedly into the gloom beyond the boat.

'Did you find it strange that the lamp blew itself out?' Tenc asked.

Ciro had been watching the shape of a similar vessel to their own merge then re-emerge from the mist in front of them but turned to regard his friend.

'I found the three knocks even stranger,' he observed. 'But fortuitous, none the less. Don't you think?'

Tenc put down the lamp. 'You think?...' He let the question tail off but Ciro nodded.

'Yes,' Ciro said with a slight smile. 'I think we have Amec to thank for –'

'– There you are.'

The roar of the falls had covered Tamarail's approach and now he lent alongside Ciro to look out into the harbour.

'Any sign of Borlin or Dent?' he asked.

Ciro shook his head then returned his attention to something which had just caught his eye on the vessel in front. Was it his imagination, or were they loosing their sails?

'They're moving off,' said Tamarail. He too had caught the vague square of canvas suddenly appearing in the night and moved quickly to alert his crew to make sail.

'Look out for Dent's boat,' he said over his shoulder as he left. 'They're sure to be alongside shortly.'

Ciro moved to the starboard bow to scan the water below. The first boat was disappearing rapidly into the mists when the shape of a rowing boat suddenly sped into view. Though there was no sense of motion in the blank confines of the fog, a curve of white at the Gallean's water line confirmed Ciro's suspicions that they too were underway.

'Tenc! Rope!' hissed Ciro, scanning the deck at his feet as the rowing boat rapidly drew close. He waved back as Dent stood up and signalled in their direction.

'Here!' said Tenc a second later and offered Ciro a coil of rope.

Instantly the king tossed the coil down towards the rowing boat then wound his end around his waist. Tenc moved in front to grip the rope firmly and together they took the strain as first Dent, then Borlin scrambled up the line. There was a loud blast from a horn somewhere on the quay side to their right and, as Ciro quickly recoiled the rope, both Dent and Borlin grinned.

'That'll be the lighthouse,' said Dent. He prodded his tall companion in the chest. 'Best tell Tamarail ta veer ta starboard by the time you've counted thirty.'

'Aye,' replied Borlin.

He ran up the deck muttering the numbers and Ciro looked to see an orange glow appear in the mist. He placed the coiled rope on the deck.

'You did it?' Tenc asked Dent. 'You broke their blockade?'

'Yup, cut clean away. No stoppin us now.' Dent followed Ciro's gaze to where the firelight was slowly becoming brighter and a small tower to their right could be discerned as they drew nearer. 'Right about... Now,' muttered Dent. On cue the Gallean began a slow turn then straightened her course.

Ciro glimpsed the end of the final jetty pass close to starboard as they turned and soon the breakwater quay side could be seen as the fog began to thin. There were voices in that direction, bellowing in Makech and Ciro made out the figures of several guards running towards the lighthouse. They waved angrily. Smiling, Ciro, Tenc and Dent waved back.

'I'd best tell the cap'n ta turn again,' said Dent then thumped Ciro firmly on the shoulder. 'Thanks for the line,' he said and then rushed off to find Tamarail – counting as he went.

Ciro watched the Makech soldiers as they reached the

lighthouse, still only a vague outline but becoming more defined by the moment as their course brought them nearer to the mouth of the harbour.

'Do you think they'll try anything?' pondered Tenc.

As if in response three guards reappeared carrying spears but, when they loosed them through the air, it was not in the direction of the Gallean.

'They're trying to hit the other boat,' said Ciro. He automatically reached for his hand lance before remembering that it was both flightless and also with Arper. 'That reminds me,' he said. 'We have to tell Tamarail to stop.'

'Why?'

'We have to pick the others up – remember?'

Tenc mouthed a silent 'O' and the pair crouched down as the guards by the lighthouse launched a fresh volley of spears – this time at them.

Two fell short. The third, obviously thrown by a far more experienced hand, hit the deck with a thump behind them. Ciro instantly scurried over to retrieve it and watched as the guards went back into the tower.

'How's your aim, Tenc?' Ciro asked.

'Rubbish,' Tenc replied.

Ciro shifted his grip on the shaft of the spear then hurled it as hard as he could when the first Makech re-emerged. It hit the quay side short but skipped to strike the wall beside the soldier's feet. He jumped with surprise to avoid it.

'Bloo'sand'it!' cursed Ciro and ducked down as the Makech returned the attack with interest.

This time the spears were closer to their mark and three loud thuds sounded as they struck the hull beside them. Tenc went to peer over but Ciro grabbed his arm: pulled him back down as the spear which Ciro had thrown once again flew over their heads.

'Grab that spear!' ordered Ciro. He jumped up to see the Makech disappearing inside the lighthouse again and also noticed that the Gallean was moving beyond it. He reached down and managed to pull free the single spear which had stuck fast into the boat's side then crouched again as the trio came back out to launch another volley.

'Look out on deck!' he bellowed.

The fog was thinning rapidly now as they passed the lighthouse and Ciro saw many of the crew dive for cover as the spears struck somewhere near the stern. Then a cheer went up from the darkness before them and Ciro chanced a look ahead to see the first boat, its dark shape framed by moonlit water, swing to larboard and gather speed. He also saw a bobbing string of rowing boats, tethered to the quay side at one end, but drifting freely as the strong current of The Handle tugged at them. Within moments the mist became a cloud framed by a curving cliff face and the Gallean turned downstream to catch the rapid flow of the river.

'Sails!' came a cry from along the deck and the half-loosed canvas instantly dropped and filled.

With a speed Ciro considered even his own, steam assisted vessels would envy, the Gallean hurtled from the harbour mouth. Soon the city, the thunder of the Grand Falls and its cursing Makech, were lost in the night behind them.

'We're free!' exclaimed Tenc. He gripped Ciro's shoulder and grinned.

Ciro nodded. There were cheers resounding around the deck and Ciro stood up to watch the brightest lights of Kal Gians finally merge with the stars above the city walls. There was not a cloud in the sky now and a bright moon illuminated the night sky to a deep blue. He should have felt the same elation as Tenc, yet his overwhelming mood was one of sadness. They were free, but how many Rialans were suffering and dying inside the city walls still? He sighed and tried to concentrate on matters more immediate.

'We must talk to Tamarail about picking up the others,' he said, breaking his silence. 'At this rate who knows how quickly we'll get back to where we made camp.'

Tenc frowned. 'Do you think we'll be able to spot it in the dark?'

'We'd better,' Ciro replied and went to find the captain.

The request was a shock to Tamarail: souring his jovial spirits after their success at breaking from the harbour. Both Dent and Borlin, removing the embedded spears from the near the tiller where Tamarail sat, shook their heads in unison as the blonde Philiri flatly refused to stop until they had passed the town of Formoss – almost a day's sail away.

'I can't allow the Makech a single chance to catch us,' he said. 'We'll need all the time we can get just to rig the sails around the hull. I can't afford to stop twice.'

There was no malice in the man's words and Ciro fully understood his concerns – yet he was not about to abandon Arper and Nesh to the wilderness.

'Captain,' said Ciro, 'I understand you want to keep the people you have rescued safe. By the stars, I applaud your actions… But, these people who are waiting down stream will surely die at the hands of the Makech if we do not pick them up.'

'Tell that to the passengers in the hold, King Ciro,' Tamarail replied. 'They have all lost people dear to them, and we are by no means safe yet. Do you think I can balance the lives of two against the lives of my passengers – and of my crew?'

No, thought Ciro. But there had to be some way. 'I promised them,' he said. It was all he could think to say.

Tamarail gave a humourless laugh. 'A King's Promise…

That was worth something once. But the promise you made was your own: not mine; I'm not bound by it.'

'What if you don't stop?' Ciro asked. 'Can you at least trim to half-sails? That would give me a chance to row ashore and pick them up.'

'I'm sorry. I really am,' Tamarail replied. 'But we sail at full speed for Formoss…' The Philiri smiled. 'Perhaps, if what you say about this army of yours is true, you can sail back yerself in about a week or so and pick them up.'

Ciro frowned at the jest. 'I have every intention of returning this way, Tamarail, but my friends will not survive that long. They're not trained to live off of the land like the Philiri can – they do not have the skills Amec had: they're just ordinary folk.'

'I've never heard the words 'skill' and 'Amec' used in the same sentence before!' Tamarail said. He grinned at Borlin who grinned back.

'That's uncalled for, Tamarail!' Tenc said angrily. 'You may have had your differences with Amec, but there's no need to dishonour his memory. He died trying to save Mara from a Makech patrol.'

'Only a fool like Amec would attack a Makech patrol!' Tamarail barked in response. His eyes blazed for a moment at his fellow Philiri then he shrugged and stared levelly at Ciro for a moment. 'My decision still stands,' he said. 'If you want to rejoin your friends, the only thing I can suggest is that you jump overboard when we pass them. We're not stopping.'

Ciro nodded. 'Thank you, captain. That's precisely what I intend to do.' He turned to walk away and then stopped. 'One thing though, Tamarail,' he said, turning back to face the Philiri. 'I would advise you not to say anything more discourteous about Amec.'

'Oh, really?' Tamarail replied. 'Why's that?'

'He won't like it,' said Ciro with a humourless smile and walked back towards the bow.

Tenc joined him a little later and found the young king silently scrutinising the dark southern bank of The Handle. The Philiri sat down on the deck, listened for a moment to the creak of the rigging and looked up to see that the canvas awning had been removed from above the deck. Now he could clearly see the cream mainsail billowing in the moonlight. Tenc was no sailor, but it seemed to him that their speed had dropped slightly.

'Perhaps the breeze will lessen enough for us to get the others aboard after all,' he said hopefully, then held out the piece of bread he had brought from the hold. 'I thought you might be hungry,' Tenc said and with this the king turned.

Ciro took the bread but did not eat. 'You would be best off to stay here when I jump, Tenc,' he said earnestly.

The statement took the Philiri by surprise.

'I'm not staying aboard while you jump!' he replied, getting back to his feet. 'I'm coming with you!... Anyway, I'm sure Tamarail will see sense once the others are seen on the shore. Frankly, I can't believe he won't stop – it's not like him.'

Ciro shook his head. 'Tamarail's doing what he thinks is right; you can't blame him for wanting to protect his people.'

'Well, even so...' muttered Tenc. He gripped the bow rail and stared at the dark water.

'Right now, the Makech may well be heading downstream after us,' said Ciro with a sigh. 'I'm sure that's what Tamarail fears.' He bit his bottom lip and stared again at the moonlit river bank. 'And I think they will come after us.'

'Why?' Tenc asked. 'It's just a couple o' boats, no real threat.'

Ciro shrugged. 'You know the Bonemen better than I do, but I think they will definitely come hunting for us. Their supremacy here has been defied. They already know I'm on the loose, and by now they've probably figured out that it was strangers like me that killed their High Prince. They may even consider this break-out to be my work as well...' Ciro looked glum. 'They'll come,' he said quietly. 'If they know who I am and why I'm here they won't want me to escape.' Ciro lapsed back into silence for a moment, and then gave Tenc a weary smile. 'I only hope Arper hasn't let the horses go,' he said. 'We're going to need them.'

Lost in their own thoughts the pair sat down, leaning their backs against the bow rail. Tenc considered attempting to argue with Tamarail again. He had tried after Ciro had left but, no matter how much he had pleaded the answer had always remained the same. Ciro appeared to have already accepted the fact that their diversion to Kal Gians had been a waste of time; and for that Tenc was bitterly sorry. As Arper and Nesh had trusted Ciro, so the king in turn had trusted Tenc: and he had let them down. He knew Ciro would not blame him for their fruitless trip but, Tenc wondered, how far would they have travelled by now without having turned back? To the edge of Ebo's Mire, he imagined. Now they would have to return to that dangerous course – but days later than they should have done. And how would they fare with no knowledge of those treacherous swamps and marshes? Could Amec's spirit help them?

Pondering the difficulty of their situation, Tenc's exhaustion crept up on him. He dropped his chin onto his chest for a moment and the next thing he knew, it was morning.

Despite his own tiredness, Ciro had refused to sleep and kept his attention firmly locked on the south bank of The Handle. Whenever the soothing creaks of the boat and the murmur of the river threatened to lull him into unconsciousness he simply reminded his dulling wits that two people would die if he did not stay awake. So with red-rimmed eyes and a head that felt numb, the young King of Rial saw another dawn rise over Reilan. With the growing light he also saw the first of the markers he and the others had placed by the water's edge.

Ciro jumped to his feet, all tiredness forgotten as the willow tree, clearly festooned with white rags, suddenly appeared in the distance. There were three such marker points: one further along, closer to the camp and a final one of silver Makech armour which would signify the camp had been passed.

Ciro checked the sails. Though the wind had lessened during the night the canvas was now taut and the first marker approached rapidly. Ciro shook Tenc and put on his pack – still damp from their swim of the previous evening – then focused on the shore. Was that a figure waving?

'Uhh?' Tenc rose groggily. 'Are we?…'

'We're here,' answered Ciro. 'If you're coming, get your pack and get ready.'

'CIROooo!?'

Faintly, Arper's voice carried across the water and the young king cursed himself for the disappointment he would bring when he jumped overboard and swam back with nothing. He had just glanced back to see Tenc fumbling with his pack when the Gallean suddenly lurched to starboard and threw him off of his feet.

'What the –!?' cried Tenc, falling on his backside as Ciro sprawled beside him.

Ciro quickly scrambled to his feet, grabbed the bow rail for support and took in the frantic scene at the stern of the vessel. Gallean crewmen, Tamarail and Dent among them, were spilling from the hold in confusion as Borlin, both hands on the tiller, appeared to have spun the craft towards the southern bank. Ciro frowned up at the sails – still fully set – and wondered what Borlin was doing. Ciro considered himself a novice sailor, but even he knew you did not throw a vessel into a tight turn with all sails set unless it was some form of emergency. What was the man thinking?

Now Tamarail and Dent had joined Borlin in grasping the tiller and it quickly became apparent to Ciro that Borlin was in trouble. All three sailors were shouting and shaking their heads but, no matter how many hands came to help, still the tiller continued to point to larboard.

'Furl sails! Furl the sails!' Tamarail yelled and, as the Gallean crew sped for the rigging, Ciro looked forward to see that the Gallean itself was now speeding straight for the south bank.

'Are we going to crash?!' cried Tenc as he joined Ciro on the bow rail.

Ciro said nothing. He looked back to the stern where four people were fighting to control the now straightened tiller then glanced aloft to see a swarm of sailors struggling with the sails. Ciro could see they were not going to furl them in time which meant they only had one option to prevent the Gallean from striking the bank... Tamarail voiced Ciro's next thought.

'Cut the mainsail! Cut the mainsail!' the captain screamed. He ran from the struggle around the tiller to bellow the command again into the rigging.

The main topsail – the highest from the deck – and the triangular fore and aft spanker sails, had been half-furled already, but the large mainsail was still untouched. Its full spread alone continued to power the Gallean towards the river bank. Now the frantic actions of the crew aloft were switched to concentrate on cutting the mainsail free and in moments the spread of canvas billowed its last to flap wildly in the breeze.

'Secure that!!' Tamarail shouted. He cast a worried glance at the bank, now less than two boat lengths from them, then span round to see that Borlin and the others had finally got control of the tiller. Slowing with each second, the Gallean gently turned until it drifted in the current: parallel to the two people who were waving on the bank. Tenc waved back. Ciro ran aft.

'I'm sorry to disturb you, Tamarail,' he said. 'But I'd quite like to bring those two people aboard.'

Tamarail frowned as he found Ciro standing before him and his face flushed with anger. He was about to demand an answer to how Ciro had affected the Gallean's tiller when the ridiculousness of the question struck him. How in Milla's name could he have affected the vessel like that?! Not only was he nowhere near the tiller, but –

'Take that launch,' muttered Tamarail through gritted teeth.

He stabbed a finger at the rowing boat beside him, shook his head and went to organise re-splicing the mainsail lines. Ciro and Tenc quickly set about lowering the launch into the water.

Nesh was jumping up and down on the spot while Arper, his beard neater than Ciro remembered it, waved happily as they approached.

'Are you both ready to go?' asked Ciro as they touched the bank. He waded the few steps to dry land then nearly fell backwards as Nesh launched herself forward to hug him.

'Ciro! Ciro! Ciro!' was all she could say and the young king hugged her back before exchanging equally frantic greetings with Arper.

'We thought ya weren't gonna stop!' exclaimed Arper with a grin so broad it looked almost painful.

'We'll tell you all about our trip when we're safely aboard,' said Ciro. 'But you have to hurry, the boat can't wait.'

Quickly they grabbed their packs, swords and saddlebags from the bank and passed them to Tenc. Then a large number of blood-stained, rush mat parcels were brought out and piled beside their belongings in the bottom of the boat. Finally Arper, Nesh and Ciro clambered in.

'What are those things?' Tenc asked Nesh. He nodded towards the strange, blood tinged parcels while Ciro pushed them away from the bank.

''Orse meat,' replied Nesh as if the answer was obvious. She frowned at Ciro's shocked expression. 'Well, wha' did ya expect us ta do with no food an' a 'orse that was lame?'

'That was a fine idea, Nesh,' said Ciro as brightly as he could.

'Yeah, an' good eatin'!' added Arper.

'We best get back before the boat drifts too far,' Tenc said and, with an oar each, Ciro and Tenc quickly covered the distance to the Gallean.

There was a crowd of people lining the side of the deck and, with their assistance, the boat and its occupants were quickly winched onto the deck. One of the Kal Gians women offered the newcomers bread and, in return Nesh handed over the horse meat to be shared out equally.

After some brief hellos from the Kal Gians refugees and some sour looks from the busy Gallean crew, Ciro led the others to the bow of the vessel. All sat down while the king and Tenc quickly explained what had happened at Kal Gians harbour.

'So,' said Arper, scratching his trim beard, 'if this Tamarail's so sure on not stoppin', how come ya stopped?'

Ciro glanced at Tenc and realised the Philiri had reached the same conclusion about their sudden halt as he had.

'This is not to go beyond this group,' whispered Ciro. 'But, as odd as it may sound, we think Amec did it.'

351

Nesh made the sign of the Eight, Arper just looked confused.

'Amec?' he said slowly.

'We've both seen him,' said Tenc, nodding earnestly. 'He even saved us from a bolt of lightning –'

'– We'll go into that a little later,' cut in Ciro quickly. He had just spotted Tamarail moving purposefully along the deck and drew their confidential conversation to a close. 'We're guests on this vessel, so we must try to pitch in and help these people but, whatever you do, don't mention Amec to Tamarail: the captain has enough problems on his hands at the moment.'

Arper nodded. 'I never met the man but I know Amec never liked 'im.'

The group stood to greet the captain as he approached but he ignored the thanks and salutations and stared at Ciro.

'Well, I hope your guests are comfortable,' he said dryly. 'We've managed to repair most of the damage and – if you don't mind - we'll set sail and continue.

'Well… Yes, of course, Tamarail,' Ciro replied. 'Thank you.'

'I only ask, because the crew and meself don't want anythin' more to happen to this vessel. An' if we do have any more 'accidents', we'll throw the lot of you into Shernn's arms as quick as possible.'

'Tamarail!' exclaimed Tenc. 'These people are your friends, not your enemies! You don't know what you're saying!'

'I know magic when I see it, Tenc: and I'll have no more of it on this boat. I don't care if he's a King or Beck himself; I'll not suffer for a Torrman like our forefather's did.'

'I see what you mean about not mentioning Amec,' whispered Nesh once Tamarail had returned to order the sails set. 'If what ya say is true about 'im turning us, the last thing we'd want to tell 'im is oo did it.'

Ciro nodded but did not speak. He felt sympathy for Tamarail, felt the same nervousness himself when considering the whole bizarre question of Amec's spirit and his 'magical' belt. They were sentiments he could understand. But to hear once again the same jaundiced grudge against his own family made him bristle; as did the threat of being thrown overboard. He sighed quietly to himself and the weariness of his vigil crept up on him. He sat down, leant his back against the bow rail and managed a smile. At least the others were safely aboard. Listening absently to their chatter, Ciro fell sound asleep.

III

Kattis Capell had never seen a city quite like Kal Gians. The vast line of its towered battlements could be seen from many miles away and, as he rode alone on the ox-drawn cart, Capell found himself awed by its increasing presence on the landscape. The sight left him feeling a grudging respect for his new 'friends' but how, he wondered, could a group as brutal as the Makech produce something which looked so graceful? As the column proceeded steadily towards the grand battlements, Kattis found he was eager to discover what marvels lay within.

They were still some miles distant when a Makech horseman thundered down the road to meet the column. With some haste, he delivered a message to the Soulcatcher's coach at its head and with that a note of urgency rippled through the entire column. With cries and calls Kattis found incomprehensible the entire procession sped up and soon he had to drive his oxen hard just to keep the rest of the group in sight.

Closer to the city a rich patchwork of fields crisscrossed the landscape punctuated, like Urawiir, with the smouldering remnants of farm buildings. Shaking his head at the senseless destruction, but with no time to consider its implications, Capell spurred his oxen on faster and at length reached the massive double arch of the Grand North Gate.

He was the last one through and was instantly greeted with a scene of greater carnage than the farmlands outside. A large, disfigured statue mounted on a dais stood directly in front of the gates but its impressive scale was marred by the piles of rotting bodies strewn around its base. Capell attempted to ignore the bloody destruction, held his breath and dutifully followed the rapidly diminishing convoy.

Despite the carnage, the city of Kal Gians was still as impressive as the mighty battlements had suggested to Capell and, as he steered around the statue and into a grand avenue, the city opened up like some long discarded jewellery box. There were traces here and there of bright paint work on the buildings and an elegant vista of grand facades and towers stretched on to reveal the glint of golden spires, marble walls and the distant water plume of a massive fountain. In all it was a glorious sight but also, Kattis thought, an empty one. The wide, fanning avenues of the city were deserted of all bar the ever-present Makech and, though smoke rose from several points above the rooftops, Kattis did not believe they were the result of roaring hearths.

The rest of the column was still a distant sight and, all alone, Capell began to draw glances from the patrols which were roaming the city. Avoiding their curious gaze, he spurred his oxen into rapid motion once again and switched his attention to the right hand side of the avenue.

Beyond the tall elms which lined the road a vast, rolling park land occupied the entire western half of the city. Its natural beauty, bounded by the distant battlements seemed a perfect counterpoint to the elegance of the city and again Capell wondered how a race like the Makech could devise something so pleasing to the eye. Then the realisation struck him. The vandalised statues, the decay and disrepair were because this was not a Makech city but an ancient Rialan one, misused, like the people, because of brutal Makech contempt. This was the reason King Ciro had come: to reacquaint himself with the marvels of his past – their past! The thought sent a shiver of joy down Capell's spine but, as his eyes focused on the trees beside him, his happiness evaporated. Every single tree along the avenue was occupied with an upturned, headless corpse; nailed by its bloody feet to the trunk. Capell gave a sigh, locked his gaze firmly on the oxen and followed the distant convoy towards a golden-spired palace set in the middle of the park.

In the stable yard which sat to the north of the palace, Baramir waited impatiently for Capell to arrive. Most of the Makech had already dismounted and disappeared through the trees towards the grand buildings a short distance away but, still awaiting Capell, Baramir spent a few idle moments taking in the massive fountain. It sprang ferociously from a large lake directly before the palace and the air was alive with the roar of its descent. It was an impressive sight but, though he kept his attention on it as he paced the stable yard, Newman's mind was elsewhere. He had the strangest sensation that somebody, just out of his own sight, was watching him.

'You'd have been quicker walking!' he shouted as Kattis finally appeared. 'Well, come on! Come on!'

'Sorry, Baramir!' Capell called back apologetically. He clambered quickly from the cart even before it had stopped. 'Why is everyone rushing?'

'The Makech Prince – a fat man named Perlenz – has

apparently been murdered,' Baramir explained with an arched brow and a smile. 'Now, hurry up, I want to find out what happened.'

Kattis was just fetching their meagre baggage from the rear of the cart when the clatter of rapid hooves announced the return of Tanikalin's party from their pursuit of Ciro. The commander did not look happy.

'Where's the beckin' King!?' bellowed Baramir angrily when he saw that, dead or otherwise, Ciro was not amongst the group. He pointed an accusing finger at Tanikalin who quailed under the Soulcatcher's glare. 'Where are the rest of your men!?' Newman roared and the celesdain band around his head glowed momentarily.

Tanikalin dropped from his saddle and then to his knees, the rest of his patrol instantly following his lead.

'I am very sorry to report, your reverence,' Tanikalin said with his head bowed. 'That the Fool King evaded us. We also lost some men attempting to cross a bridge... It's my mistake.'

'Of course it's your mistake!' yelled Baramir so loudly it made Kattis's ears ring. 'How can you loose men crossing a bridge?! What did it do, collapse?!'

Tanikalin looked up curiously. 'Yes, your reverence, we had–'

The commander's explanation was cut short by the arrival of a Beck Iph guard. He dipped his head to Baramir and said:

'His Reverence, Gidus, demands your immediate attention.'

Baramir nodded and shot Tanikalin a withering glance. 'Get up, commander,' he said impatiently. 'You can grovel later.'

The castle at Forht seemed now like some pauper's hovel as Baramir and Kattis were led through the opulent, cavernous rooms inside Perlenz's Palace. Baramir's bad mood lifted as he took in the glorious wealth brazenly displayed around him and, by the time they were led into the vast, silver throne room, his spirits were high.

At the far end of a marble floor, bisected by a single garish line of carpet, Gidus and his Beck Iph guards stood at the base of a large silver dais surmounted by a single throne. Around the chamber intricate silver panels glittered in the lamp light but the mass of dark velvet which hung from each wall gave the space a sombre air. Newman, his spirits undiminished by the funereal mood, was half inclined to quip who had died but, already knowing the answer, he instead focused his attention on the outlandish looking individuals who stood beside Gidus.

Dressed in black robes adorned with more silver and jewels than Baramir had ever seen on a single individual, the most stunning feature of these strangers was their heads. Instead of being round they had been squeezed out of all proportion to assume the rough shape of a melon and, though their faces seemed normal, their foreheads rose almost a foot before reaching the crown of their heads. Fascinated, Newman searched through Yetzi's memories to find that these were waisslenii – royal aids – and that the black stains which stretched from each man's mouth to his chin was the result of drinking the juice of the black apples since childhood.

'I must say,' said Baramir jovially as he strode up the carpet. 'This is a fine place, Gidus.'

The old Soulcatcher nodded but said nothing: he looked serious.

'Is that them?!'

The voice was high, the tone one of unreserved contempt and Baramir saw a thin, sallow-faced man push through the group of royal aids to stand beside Gidus. He wore the uniform of the Makech but, instead of iron, every strip of

metal on his polished leather uniform was gold. His name –
so Yetzi now informed Baramir – was Commander Dinevre:
50. He was second in command to Lord Chinek back in Forht
but a distant royal connection meant that he spent most of his
time in Kal Gians. He was thought of as a manipulative
schemer with a dubious kill-count by some, a cowardly
bastard by many and Tanikalin believed he was poisoning
Chinek to get his command. Even before Yetzi's opinions
filled his thoughts, Newman had already decided he did not
like the man.

'Commander Dinevre!' exclaimed Baramir with a bow.
'What an honour! Your presence is still missed back in Forht.'

The statement took Dinevre by surprise and he cast a glance
towards Gidus. The old Soulcatcher smiled.

'Allow me to introduce his reverence, Baramir Newman,'
said Gidus.

'He's one of these new Rialans?' replied Dinevre with a
frown.

'If by that you mean: "Will he be able to shed light on the
fate of our High Prince?" Then the answer is probably yes,'
said Gidus. 'Where he comes from is far less important than
who is now is. Remember that, Dinevre.'

Dinevre scowled. Even harder when he saw that a mud-
spattered Tanikalin was now standing behind Baramir.

'Well, well,' he sneered. 'Patrol Leader Tanikalin. Been
playing in the dirt again? Where's that ape, Yetzi: 12?'

Tanikalin ignored the jibe and tapped the brass plate on his
chest. 'That's Commander Tanikalin, Dinevre.'

Dinevre smiled and tapped his own golden armour. 'That's
Acting Lord Dinevre, Tanikalin.'

That's enough,' said Gidus with a weary voice. 'We all
know each other's ranks and none of us likes Dinevre. But,'
added the old Soulcatcher as Dinevre's face reddened with

anger at the insult, 'until this situation is rectified, Dinevre is the acting lord here. So let's skip the petty differences and concentrate our efforts on more important matters.' Gidus turned his attention to the waisslenii. 'Tain,' he said, 'will you bring in the objects please?'

The most ornately decorated of the royal aids looked briefly at a scowling Dinevre for conformation. After a fractional pause he dipped his long head at Gidus and led the other aids from the room. He returned a few moments later followed by ten of the palace staff. Between them they carried a large table covered with a red velvet cloth which they set down at the base of the dais before backing away.

'We need some maps as well,' Gidus announced and Tain and his staff retreated again.

'Now,' said Gidus, gripping the edge of the cloth. 'We all know that our High Prince, Perlenz has been murdered –' Tanikalin gasped. '– Quite, commander,' nodded Gidus in response. 'A terrible thing but, as you've no doubt seen in the city, we are taking our revenge. Now, according to the waisslenii, and Dinevre, Perlenz's hunting party were north – where's that map!?'

Tain returned at a brisk pace carrying a large piece of animal hide which he unrolled and handed to Gidus. With a nod of thanks, the Soulcatcher laid the map on top of the covered table and pointed to a spot where the name Torr Betram had been crossed out and the words Kal Gians written underneath it. Both Baramir and Kattis looked on with interest: it was the first time they had seen what Reilan looked like.

'Now,' said Gidus, 'Perlenz's party went north from Kal Gians then along the High Water River towards the coast. The party consisted of –.' The old man held up his left hand to count off on his fingers. '– Perlenz himself, Lord Doiya, Commander Gers, Soulcatcher Kompek plus his Beck Iph

Guard, twenty Makech from the Kal Gians garrison, a handful of royal aids and five peasant cooks. According to the survivors, Perlenz had become frustrated by a lack of decent hunting around the marshes so led them even closer to the north coast and the mouth of the High Water.' Gidus pointed to where the thin blue line of the High Water met a vast area of open sea. The Soulcatcher sighed. 'Most of the bodies that hadn't been taken by the tide were found on the beach, including his Highness, Perlenz. There was no indication as to who committed this terrible act but –,' Gidus passed the map to a Beck Iph guard and lifted the cloth from the table. '– These items were found in the bodies and in the woods at the edge of the beach.'

Sitting on the table were two dun coloured, pill-box caps with the Rial sun emblem emblazoned above their peaks. In a pile beside them, sat a number of slender wooden rods roughly four inches in length. They were iron-tipped and triangles of leather jutted from their base. There were at least two dozen of the things and Gidus held one up.

'These look remarkably like the flights that you have in that watch of yours, Baramir,' he said.

Baramir nodded. 'They are flights from a fire lance,' he explained. 'It's a device which works similarly to my clockwork repeater, only the fire lance can launch these things across a great distance. It's little wonder Perlenz was killed.'

Tanikalin had also seen something similar. A flight half the size of the ones now before him had been pulled from the forehead of the man Ciro had shot at Birin Bridge. The commander however, was not about to mention his failure in front of Dinevre. Instead he asked the question which had been on his mind since encountering Ciro's weapon. 'Was the High Prince wearing armour?' he asked.

'Of course he was wearing armour, fool!' Dinevre spat. 'It

went straight through it!' The Acting Lord picked a flight from the pile and thrust it under Tanikalin's nose. The iron tip was twisted and splayed and still showed traces of blood. 'We pulled half a dozen of these from Perlenz alone!'

'Where are the survivors?' Baramir asked. 'Perhaps we should search their minds?'

'They told us all they knew – which was nothing,' Dinevre said dismissively. 'I don't think a Soulcatcher could have extracted any further information.'

'The only people to survive the assault were the peasant cooks,' Gidus explained. 'They were at the camp Perlenz had made that morning about a mile or so from the beach and were found by the search party wandering back to Kal Gians. After the palace staff had tortured them for information, Dinevre killed them personally.'

'So where does that leave us?' Tanikalin asked. It came as no surprise to him that Dinevre would add a couple of half-dead, chained prisoners to his kill count but he had little faith in Dinevre's ability to coax answers from anybody.

'I thought that, perhaps, Baramir might know something we don't.' Gidus shrugged. 'Is there something I might have missed, Baramir? Some clue to Ciro's intended destination, or a plan which you might have overheard?'

Baramir shook his head. 'Captain Talwood had little to do with us once we were hidden aboard Ciro's ship. Even if I had heard a destination mentioned, it wouldn't have meant a thing to me.'

'What about him?' asked Dinevre. He pointed at Kattis.

Baramir smiled at the fearful expression which instantly sprang onto Capell's face. 'No,' he said, still speaking Makech so Kattis would not understand. 'He knows even less than I do.'

'Well, then we have a problem.' Gidus sounded glum. 'Why

would these Rialan soldiers appear here –' he pointed to the mouth of the High Water river '– and then disappear. Are we about to be overrun by these sunmen and, if so, from where?'

'I believe that wherever they are, they could be fortifying their position,' Dinevre said. He took the map from the Beck Iph and put it back on the table. 'We found that some of the trees around the mouth of the High Water had been felled, but there was no sign of where the logs had been dragged to.' He pointed at the map and tapped a hill range north of Kal Gians. 'I've since ordered lookouts to the old High Water Harbour and sent out continual patrols along the river. There's been no reports of either vessels or a camp yet.'

'I wonder if Perlenz's death was an accident,' pondered Baramir, half to himself.

'An accident!?' exploded Dinevre.

Baramir frowned and was just about to let Yetzi loose on the man when he felt a strange restraint on his thoughts. He flicked his gaze angrily to Gidus and in response the old Soulcatcher shook his head.

'You would do well to remember who you are speaking to, Dinevre!' snapped Gidus sternly. He gave Baramir a smile and his tone changed to one of affection. 'My understudy nearly threw you across the room. Next time, I'll let him.'

Dinevre's face reddened as his initial anger was hastily brought under control. He gave a short bow to Baramir but refrained from making eye contact. 'My apologies, your reverence,' he muttered.

'Thank you,' replied Baramir graciously. 'Now, as I was saying. I think Perlenz's death was accidental because I'm certain that no one from Feirlan knew about the Makech.' He flicked a finger at himself and Capell. 'We certainly didn't. And these logs that were felled but can't be found… Well, the Rialans could simply have been chopping them down to use as fuel.'

'For a beacon fire?' Tanikalin asked.

'No, for their ship,' Baramir replied. 'Ciro's ships were travelling along the coast so it's possible that one, or several of them, stopped at this beach to get fuel for their engines. Unfortunately Perlenz stumbled across them doing it.'

Dinevre looked puzzled. 'What in Beck's name are 'engines'?'

'We'll explain later,' said Gidus, noting the Acting Lord's bemusement. 'But it's enough to know that these vessels are like nothing you have ever seen before.'

'So, perhaps these ships had a long way still to go,' mused Tanikalin.

Baramir hadn't thought of that, but it was a valid point. Why would a vessel close to its destination feel the need to refuel? He smiled and nodded. 'Exactly, Tanikalin!' he said.

'So we can discount Monet as a destination,' Gidus said, pointing to the map. 'It's too close.'

'Circia?' mused Tanikalin. 'Would they dare go past the black apples?'

'If they do then they're no longer a threat to us,' replied Dinevre.

Baramir thought better of asking what Dinevre meant by that and instead quickly questioned Yetzi. He found that the Makech believed the land beyond the strange, deadly barrier to be cursed. So much so that not even the bravest Makech would think to journey beyond it.

'I think we must assume,' said Baramir. 'That they have travelled beyond these black apples.'

Dinevre shrugged. 'Good. Then they are already dead.'

'I would not be so sure,' cautioned Gidus. 'Don't forget the Philiri come from beyond the barrier.'

'With respect, Gidus,' Dinevre replied, 'I've never believed in the Philiri rebel myth. They call themselves Philiri, and we naturally think that means they're from Philire, but I think they're simply Rialan cattle who have a hidden base somewhere on this side of the barrier. No one ever comes back from beyond the barrier.'

The old Soulcatcher shook his head. 'That sort of blindness only hampers our options, Dinevre. The Philiri have survived all this time precisely because of that sort of belief. And now this new threat has, as far as you're concerned, travelled beyond our grasp. If we are to defeat them, then perhaps we will have to follow them into the cursed lands.'

'I've already sent a convoy back to get reinforcements from Kal Santra,' Dinevre said. 'It will then travel south across the desert to Kal Iet with the news of Perlenz's death.' He sighed. 'I've asked for as many men as possible but I can't see any Makech, no matter how fearless, wanting to walk a river of blood which leads past the black apples.'

'We'll face that problem when the time comes,' said Gidus. 'Our chief concern must now be: are we safe until the reinforcements come?'

'The locals are becoming more hostile,' Dinevre replied. 'We had been systematically questioning the cattle in the city for information concerning the High Prince's murder and, though we could find no evidence that they had anything to do with it, they are certainly aware of it. We've killed over a hundred suspects, trouble-makers and protesters so far and most areas of the city are now secure. We've also barricaded the harbour to prevent news of Perlenz's death spreading.'

'A wise precaution,' responded Gidus with a nod. He looked briefly at the map before his gaze rose to meet Tanikalin's. 'I take it your attempt to capture the Fool King met with no success?'

Looking distinctly uncomfortable, the commander bowed

his head. 'We managed to sight him several nights ago in a deserted town... Here,' Tanikalin pointed to Birin on the far side of the South Wall. 'But the only bridge across the river collapsed when my men attempted to cross and capture him. He escaped.'

'Remind me not to pray to the same Kolben you do, Commander,' Dinevre sneered. 'You are obviously out of favour.'

Tanikalin bristled but remained silent while Gidus studied the map. 'Baramir,' he said. 'If you were a young and foolish king, had a lot of ships and were heading to a land you were only vaguely familiar with: which of these cities here would seem the best suited for you to use as a base?'

Baramir studied the map of Rial and ran his finger along the thick blue line of The Channel to the large expanse of Bull Lake. 'Well,' he said, 'we must assume from the course of the ships that they were heading up this way. But once here... I really couldn't say – this one, Peimonac? Or perhaps Piilour? Perhaps further on to this one, Torr Adenair.' Baramir shrugged. 'Frankly, Gidus, he could have been heading anywhere.'

'Peimonac would be the best defensively,' observed Tanikalin.

'Why, commander?' Gidus asked.

'Well, I believe that it's an island for one which makes defence practical – especially with these ships of his. And from there his ships can go anywhere.'

Dinevre shook his head. 'I could give you a dozen equally plausible reasons why Circia or Monides would make just as good a base as Peimonac, Tanikalin, but the fact still remains that, no matter where they have gone, they are probably dead by now.'

'Because nobody survives beyond the black apples?' asked Baramir.

'Precisely, your reverence,' replied Dinevre with a sickly grin

'Speaking as someone who has travelled through the barrier and returned,' said Gidus. 'I'm afraid I must ask you to stop repeating that nonsense, Dinevre. It's dangerous beyond the black apples, I'll grant you, but it's not an instant death sentence.' The Acting Lord fell silent and Gidus continued to peruse the map.

'You saw Ciro here, Tanikalin?' he muttered a few moments later.

'Yes, your reverence.'

'Hhm…' Gidus tapped the name of Birin on the map. 'If he is heading east to meet up with his fleet then where will he be heading to now? Does he stay south of The Handle and attempt to cross the swamps of Ebo Pamessi? Or does he cross the river and head north towards The Channel?'

'Why not take a boat?' asked Baramir.

'He'd be a fool to come here,' Dinevre replied. 'Our harbour is completely sealed.'

'Maybe, but he doesn't know that,' countered Tanikalin. 'He may still try to get in.'

'How many guards do you have down in the harbour, Dinevre?' asked Gidus.

'A few men, but enough, your reverence.'

Gidus frowned. 'Tanikalin, get some of the men we brought from Urawiir down there – especially the one from the bridge – tell them to arrest anyone coming into the harbour, no matter who they are.'

Tanikalin nodded, gave a low bow and went in search of the guards.

'What does the whereabouts of one man matter anyway?'

Dinevre asked as Tanikalin left the throne room. 'It's this army of his that we should be concerned about.'

'He's the head of that army, Dinevre,' Gidus explained patiently. 'He knows more about its strengths and weaknesses than anybody else. He also knows of its whereabouts. Catch him and we not only have a valuable source of information but an invaluable hostage.'

'Are there boats at Formoss?' inquired Baramir, still studying the map. 'Perhaps he'll head there rather than come here.'

'Dinevre, dispatch a rider to Formoss,' said Gidus. 'Inform the garrison commander there to watch the harbour.' The Acting Lord motioned to Tain who instantly turned on his heals. 'Also…' continued the old Soulcatcher, 'send a patrol to the edge of Ebo Pamessi. He may just be stupid enough to try and cross the swamp.'

'And what do we do in the meantime?' asked Baramir.

'We'll go to my quarters and eat,' replied Gidus.

It was dark by the time Baramir and Kattis where led up into Gidus's chambers and, in a well-practiced routine; the Beck Iph guards quickly illuminated the candles which sat in clumps around the room.

'It's not as grand as the throne room,' Gidus said. 'But it's home.'

Baramir nodded and tried to hide his disappointment. The opulence of the palace appeared to end where Gidus's quarters started and, though there were several doors leading from the main chamber: the low-beamed ceiling, threadbare carpet and general air of decay did not make Baramir suppose that the other rooms hid any sights more glorious.

'It's very… You,' he said, attempting to mask his disappointment.

The old Soulcatcher laughed. 'A man rich in spirit does not need material wealth,' he said and tapped his flaking forehead. 'That wealth comes from within.'

Baramir and Kattis made their way to a pair of wooden chairs which sat before a row of large, leaded windows.

'I'll try to remember that,' Baramir replied half-heartedly and turned his attention to the roar from the darkness outside.

'It's the Great Fountain,' Gidus said, noticing Newman's face pressed against the window. 'A magnificent spectacle.'

Baramir turned away, frowning. 'I don't know whether it's these damn spirits of mine,' he said. 'But I keep getting the distinct impression that someone is watching me.'

Gidus chuckled. 'I'd be surprised if you didn't,' he said. 'There are four Kolben Temples just beyond the fountain. They've been in ruins for many an age but there's still a great power in them.'

'Is that why I feel uncomfortable?'

The old Soulcatcher shook his head. 'No, you feel uncomfortable because they were not built by our kind, but by an old, old enemy.'

'The old Rialans?' mused Newman. 'I had no idea.'

'No, not the Rialans,' corrected Gidus. 'Those things out there are far older than either the Rial or the Makech. The Brihma made them... Or was it the Pomarri? I forget which... It doesn't really matter now though, those tribes are long gone.'

'So why do you leave the temples standing?' asked Baramir. 'Why not knock them down?'

Gidus smiled. 'You'll learn in time that there are some things that even a Soulcatcher has more sense than to meddle with. Those things out there are very powerful tributes to the Kolben and, as such, untouchable.' The old man nodded to himself. 'I have a library here that will help you to understand

368

more about what you are, and what you can become. I must start teaching you words of power – like the few I taught you at Urawiir – you'll certainly understand the temples better after that.'

To this Baramir looked blank.

'They are covered in them, Baramir,' explained Gidus. 'Hundreds and hundreds of words of power all aimed at harnessing the strength of the Kolben are written upon the walls of the temples.'

'Can we use the temples?' Newman asked.

Gidus shook his head. 'The soldiers here hold an annual competition of bravery to see who can get the closest to the temples. No matter how many times they try they can't get closer than about thirty feet.'

'The power from these temples forces them back?'

'Oh no,' Gidus replied. 'It just kills them.'

The old Soulcatcher, still grinning from Baramir's open-mouthed surprise, disappeared through one of the doors and the creak of the hinges was followed by a large rumble from Capell's stomach.

'Are we going to eat?' Kattis asked sheepishly.

After a meagre meal of bread, cheese and some poor, acidic wine, Baramir was led by Gidus out of the room and down a narrow hallway which ended in a discoloured silver door. Newman had found no real appetite himself, so to escape from the perpetual chomping of Kattis was a welcome relief. It also seemed that Gidus was about to show him the expensive part of his chambers.

Embossed into the silver door was the insignia of the Beck Iph and Baramir noted that the panels surrounding it were painted with a dark and flaking paint which, on closer inspection, appeared to be blood.

'You'll sleep in here tonight,' said Gidus. The old Soulcatcher fished out an ornate key from inside his robes and unlocked the door to reveal a dark chamber beyond.

While Gidus disappeared inside, Newman hung back on the threshold and attempted to ignore the smell which now emanated from the room to fill his nostrils. It was a strange, rancid odour: both repulsive yet compelling in equal measure and, by the time Gidus had illuminated the room and returned, Baramir felt quite light headed.

'What is that smell!?' Newman asked, wrinkling his nose as Gidus led him inside.

'The scent of black apples,' replied the old man.

Baramir was escorted to a padded chair which sat in the centre of the room. Like the door, the floor was also silver, marked with the sign of the Beck Iph and discoloured with the same poor paint which Newman had also noted on the door. Around the chair, four tall torches threw the silver-red sheen of the floor onto the bookcases which flanked the room and glinted on the cage housing Gidus's wraith in the far corner.

Newman sat in the padded chair and watched with mild interest while his old companion pottered around in the gloom. Muttering to himself, Gidus moved to a cluttered corner opposite the cage and rummaged around in the desk which sat there.

'Far be it from me to question my host's hospitality,' said Baramir. 'But I thought you said I was supposed to sleep in here?' Newman's voice echoed strangely from the metal at his feet and he craned his neck to recheck the other corners of the room. No, he thought, there is definitely no bed.

'That chair will be your bed,' Gidus replied absently.

'I see…' responded Baramir quietly.

The old Soulcatcher returned grinning and in his bony hand

he held a small, round bottle which he handed to Baramir. Newman frowned while Gidus returned to the far end of the room and slowly pulled black velvet curtains into place which completely hid the cage and desk.

'What's this?' asked Baramir, holding up the bottle.

'That, my dear Baramir is the fermented juice of the black apple,' Gidus replied. 'Drink it.'

Newman pulled the silver stopper from the neck of the bottle and recoiled at the overpowering stench which wafted out. 'Drink this!?' He gasped. 'Why?'

Gidus sighed. 'That juice will expand your thoughts. Focus your mind. Make you stronger.'

Newman did not look convinced. 'You drink it,' he said.

'Do you want to get more powerful or not!?' snapped Gidus. 'We walk the square, Baramir,' he continued firmly. 'If you want the riches and power I know you crave then you will drink it – all of it. Before you lies greatness, behind only mediocrity... So drink it.'

Still frowning, Baramir placed the small bottle to his lips. 'It can't be any worse than your wine,' he said and emptied the bottle in one gulp.

The searing pain which burnt his throat was instantly accompanied by a numbness that flashed out from his head to reach every extremity of his body in a heartbeat. Newman looked curiously at the bottle in his hand which he could no longer feel then looked around to find Gidus. The process of turning his head seemed to take an age and, by the time he had focused on the spot he felt sure the old man should be occupying, he found that there was no one there. Instead, the torches appeared to be going out and Baramir smiled, trying to catch sight of the dying flames as the chamber slowly fell into total darkness.

'Gidus?'

Newman was sure he had said that but his voice simply echoed into the night. He felt dizzy and the black, impenetrable dark expanded around him until a gentle voice began reciting:

'Tala sanmilla dec ilbek dir jal,

Urnia ui abatin beckia…'

The words continued. A chanting rhythm which seemed to pulse in Newman's head and focus his attention on a single point of greater darkness. He felt a familiar sensation – yet could not recall from where – and slowly his mind seemed to tumble over: spin and turn until the deep black point had swallowed him whole and the words began to take a tangible shape before him…

By the window, Kattis sat alone and stared sleepily out into the night. The continual splashing of the fountain outside had been gently lulling him to sleep and his anxiety, a state which had dogged him worse than any hunger he could remember, was slowly ebbing away to leave him feeling more at ease. Then one of the chamber doors threw itself open and the savage gust of wind which accompanied it blew in to knock a group of candles onto the floor.

Wide awake, and terrified by the sudden commotion, Capell watched wide-eyed as each group of candles was upturned and extinguished until only a single candle on the table beside him remained lit.

'B-Baramir!?' stuttered Kattis as the darkness closed in around him. He jumped up to crouch on his chair as scampering footsteps sounded somewhere in the room.

'Hahahahaha!'

The voice was light, childlike and Kattis was debating whether to shut his eyes and stick his fingers in his ears when the slight figure of a girl suddenly broke into the weak circle of light around him.

'H-h Hello?' Capell managed to say.

The girl stared intently at him for a second then produced a grin that seemed out of place on such a sweet-looking countenance. 'Hello, fatso,' she said, then disappeared back into the gloom laughing.

Terrified, Kattis managed to call Baramir's name once again but the only response was the return of the girl's footsteps. She reappeared before him once again and prodded him in the chest.

'Whaddayawant?'

'N-nothing, nothing,' Kattis whispered. He shook his head frantically but the girl's attention seemed to suddenly go elsewhere. There was a clatter in the darkness across the room and suddenly one of the candle clumps was back upright and re-lit.

'On,' said the girl firmly.

The candles snuffed themselves out.

'Off,' she said and gave Kattis a sly wink.

Capell attempted to smile as the girl now proceeded to return the groups of candles around the room to their former positions and wondered nervously why nobody had come in to see what all the noise was about. His relief was overwhelming when a curt knock at the door heralded the arrival of Tanikalin but, the moment the door began to swing wide, the girl simply disappeared.

'By Sakoom!' snapped the commander from the doorway. 'What are you doing?!'

'There was a girl here,' Capell attempted to explain nervously as he jumped from the chair. He scanned the room but there was only himself and Tanikalin present.

The commander frowned hard and stomped into the chamber. 'Where's Baramir?'

'He - he went through there with Gidus a little while ago,' Kattis said. 'Would you, er…like some food, Commander?'

Still frowning, Tanikalin seated himself beside the table and chewed on a hunk of bread: his eyes still firmly locked on Kattis.

'I'll see if I can find Baramir,' Capell said quietly after gazing at the carpet for a few seconds. He walked to the door, opened it but found his way barred by a red-masked Beck Iph guard.

'Igena esc!' barked the guard the second the door was opened and Kattis quailed. He did not understand the words but made no mistake about the sentiment.

'He says sit down,' Tanikalin said gruffly from behind him.

Capell closed the door and walked towards the chair he had recently occupied.

'Not here!' barked the commander. He pointed the wine bottle he held at the opposite wall. 'Sit over there, on the floor.'

Sheepishly, Kattis crossed to the other side of the room and sat on the floor. He drew his knees up, bowed his head, shut his eyes tightly and hoped that the dawn would bring something to make him smile.

Kattis woke to the sound of raised voices and opened his eyes to find the room full of people. Gidus's Beck Iph guards were all there and stood with Tanikalin around a Makech soldier who was talking quickly and pointing to the grey light through the windows. Capell didn't understand a word of what was said but looked on at Tanikalin's frowning face until Baramir and Gidus entered the room.

'What are you doing down there?!' shouted Baramir as he saw Kattis sitting on the floor. 'Get up you lazy fool!'

Capell quickly got to his feet. He tried not to stare but the livid, red burn marks either side of the celesdain band around Baramir's head drew his attention. He wanted to inquire whether Baramir was quite alright but his friend was already involved with the conversation taking place near the door. Kattis sighed as the incomprehensible dialogue continued and looked through the grimy windows to see dawn brightening the city outside.

An hour later a column of Makech soldiers were lined and waiting in a shingle courtyard beside the palace. Baramir grudgingly enlightened Kattis with their plan of action as they tramped across the gravel to their cart.

It had been reported, he said, that two armed strangers had stormed into the city harbour during the night, fought and drowned a Makech patrolman, rallied their fellow Rialans into rebellion and then broken through the blockade in two large vessels. Baramir suspected – as did Gidus and Tanikalin – that Ciro had been the main protagonist of these despicable events.

There was no other destination along the river apart from Formoss, yet still the boats had decided to risk their lives and run. That made it almost certain that the boats where going to move on past Formoss into the barrier of black apples and attempt to reach the cursed lands which lay beyond.

'We intend to follow Ciro right through the barrier,' explained Baramir as they passed the line of immobile Makech. A soldier on the far end of the line frowned as the Soulcatcher walked past speaking Rialan but Baramir simply grinned back at him in response. The man very quickly dropped his gaze.

Baramir laughed. 'That weasel Dinevre believes that not even the bravest Makech dare go beyond these black apples… ' He drew close to Kattis and placed an arm around his shoulder. 'But Tanikalin and I,' he whispered, 'have devised a plan to get around that particular problem.'

'What's that?' Capell asked.

'We're simply not going to tell them!' Baramir cried jovially and led them on to their ox cart.

Their ox cart had undergone something of a transformation. It was still weather worn and humble but now it was drawn by a fine pair of horses. Beside it, Commander Tanikalin sat waiting on his own mount.

'Good morning, your reverence,' he said, bowing as far as he could in the saddle as Baramir and Kattis drew near.

Behind them the soldiers filed off to form into two lines then marched forwards the short distance to where Gidus's black coach waited.

'Do we have a boat?' asked Newman as he climbed onto the cart and took the reigns.

Tanikalin nodded. 'As well as a crew,' he said. 'They needed a little persuasion... But we have members of their families now, so they'll co-operate.'

A frown creased Baramir's cheerful countenance. 'Will we be able to catch Ciro before he reaches the barrier?' he inquired. There was an order barked from Gidus's Beck Iph guard up ahead and slowly the procession began to move off.

'The rider we sent to Formoss last evening should beat the boats there,' Tanikalin replied. 'It should give the garrison time enough to prepare for their arrival.'

Baramir had just flicked his horses into motion when another call from the Beck Iph up ahead halted the procession.

'What the–!' exclaimed Baramir.

He pulled the horses to a standstill then leaned to his right to see that a group of dignitaries – Dinevre amongst them – had suddenly appeared through the tree line beside the gravel track. They made straight for Gidus's black coach.

'That's Lady Perlenz,' said Tanikalin quietly.

Baramir looked on as a stick-thin woman dressed, like the

rest of her waisslenii group in bejewelled black, stepped past the flanking Makech escort to rap loudly on the carriage door.

'Is that a…?' Baramir let the question tail off but pointed instead to the celesdain band around his head.

The commander nodded gravely. 'Lady Perlenz is also a Soulcatcher.' He lent in his saddle to get closer to Baramir. 'Rumour is she did it herself,' he whispered.

Baramir looked blank. 'Did what herself?'

Tanikalin tapped his own forehead by way of reply. 'No woman has ever been allowed to walk the square, but she found a holy crystal from somewhere and did it herself.'

Baramir frowned. 'I'm not sure I like that sort of presumption in a woman.'

'Is there a problem, Baramir?' Kattis asked. He too was craning over to see the continuing commotion ahead.

'Be quiet,' replied Newman curtly. 'I'll explain later.'

Up ahead the black carriage door now opened with a bang. A very annoyed Gidus stepped down onto the track.

'By Sakoom!' he cried, waving his bony arms. 'Must you thunder so?!'

'I would speak with you, Gidus.' Lady Perlenz gave a polite bow but Gidus was still fuming.

'Yes!? Well?! Out with it, woman!' he spat.

'Acting Lord Dinevre informs me you intend to chase these Rialans past the barrier.'

'If necessary, yes.'

There was a murmur amongst the Makech troops: cut short as Tanikalin yelled for silence. Both Gidus and Lady Perlenz gazed in his direction and the woman's eyes fell on Baramir. For a moment Newman felt as if another mind was connecting with his but the sensation passed as Lady Perlenz returned her attention to Gidus.

'You would be unwise to visit the cursed lands,' she said.

Gidus smiled and arched a brow. 'Is that so, my Lady? Why?'

'You risk the lives of your men and go against the will of Unzekka.'

Gidus smiled even more broadly. He tapped his celesdain band and said: 'I am the will of Unzekka, Lady. I was chosen to walk the square in his name, not serve my own dubious self interest.' With that rebuke the old man clambered back into the carriage and called for the convoy to continue.

'You will find nothing but your own death there, old man!' Lady Perlenz shouted as the coach and its escort moved on.

Baramir spurred his horses and jolted the cart forwards. Within seconds he was level with Lady Perlenz's group. He gave a curt nod to the pale woman as he passed by but in response he felt the same curious feeling of another person's thoughts attempting to enter his.

'I am the voice of Ishenzia,' said a faint voice in Baramir's ear. 'And she can see you, Baramir Newman.'

Disturbed, Newman turned to see if Lady Perlenz had spoken but her group was already walking back towards the palace. Frowning, he followed Gidus's carriage out of the grounds while ruthlessly scrutinising his own spirits to see which one of them was playing games with him.

As the procession travelled slowly through the city of Kal Gians, Tanikalin pointed out various sights of interest to Baramir while Capell attempted to fathom the city for himself. Looking back to the palace grounds the lake and the Grand Fountain which sprang from it was an impressive sight in the morning sunshine, as were the four towering structures which sat in a wide strip of park land beside the ensuing river.

'Those are the old Kolben temples,' Tanikalin said and pointed through the double tree line which they were travelling beside.

'More bodies,' observed Capell sadly as the trees alongside displayed more examples of Dinevre's revenge.

'Shut up,' came Baramir's reply. He frowned at the strange towers poking through the tree line and looked away: uncomfortable with the feeling that many eyes were watching him from their heights. The structures also seemed to give off a continuous sound: higher pitched than the dull roar of the Grand Fountain behind them but just as persistent. Like a wasp trapped inside my head, he thought and tried to focus his attention on the buildings to the left of the road.

The majority of the structures were weathered, run down or simply derelict but, as their procession moved along the avenue, Baramir caught the glint of a single golden turret and some larger, yet equally dilapidated, buildings beyond their road.

Capell had also noticed the grand relics beyond the avenue. 'This must have been very beautiful once,' he said: more to himself than anyone else. 'It reminds me a little of…' His self-consciousness got the better of his reverie and he turned to see Baramir scowling.

'I hope it all falls down,' spat Tanikalin. 'Then the memory of Rial will be put finally where it belongs: in Ebo's belly.'

They travelled on in silence while the roar of the fountain faded and was quickly replaced by a greater noise.

'It's the waterfall,' explained Tanikalin. He pointed to another hanging corpse on one of the trees. 'I'm surprised Dinevre didn't throw them from the Fool's Bridge. The red falls are a rare treat these days.'

The commander looked wistful for a moment while Baramir, searching Yetzi's memories, found reference to Tanikalin's statement. He laughed.

'Do you know what the Makech do for recreation around

here, Kattis?' he asked.

Kattis shrugged. 'Is it that Judgment Ring thing?'

Baramir smiled and shook his head. 'No. They take a group of Rialans to that bridge down there –' Newman pointed through the trees to where a single brick span crossed the fast flowing river. 'Then they paint numbers on their backs and then bet on the numbers.'

'How do they bet on the numbers?'

'Well,' grinned Baramir, 'they throw the Rialans off of the bridge together and watch them swim for their lives. There are referees in the harbour below and the last Rialan body to float out from the base of the waterfall is the winner.'

Capell attempted to share his friend's joviality but his mouth simply refused to form a smile. He put his head down and stared at the road.

'Your problem is that you get no enjoyment out of life,' observed Baramir when Kattis failed to respond adequately to his anecdote. 'I've a good mind to let Yetzi loose on you again.'

To this Capell mouthed an apology but kept his head down. Perhaps tomorrow will be better, he thought.

IV

After another fitful sleep full of strange unsettling images, Ciro did his best to occupy his mind by sorting through his meagre belongings. In doing so, Ciro reached the conclusion that he would change back into his Rialan uniform. There seemed to be no particular, practical reason for this but, the second he had removed it from his bag, Ciro felt an irresistible urge to put it back on. He was tired of running and hiding from the enemy and, with the Gallean making steady progress downstream, he felt confident that his journey was nearing its end. There was another, nagging motivation which crossed the king's mind but he decided that, even if it was his real reason for changing he would still do it. If Tamarail was going to throw him overboard, Ciro wanted the man to see just who he was doing it to.

The rest of the group were in an optimistic mood. Tenc was busy telling Arper all about the hidden realm of Philire while Nesh was arranging her sea shell dowry on the deck. As quietly as he could, Ciro moved a few feet away and, still unnoticed, quickly changed back into his white leggings and blue jacket. He retied Tenlern's scarf around his neck and was just pinning his gold Rialan sun broach back onto his breast when Arper caught sight of him.

'Now there's a fella I ain't seen in a while,' he said with a grin. Ciro gave a bow.

'You look…' began Nesh. She gazed into his eyes for several seconds, blushed and returned to her shells. 'Ya look very nice,' she muttered.

Tenc leant back and regarded Ciro's attire for a moment. 'You would've had no trouble convincing me you were a King if you'd worn that outfit earlier,' he said.

'Unfortunately, neither would the Makech,' replied Ciro with a grin.

The young king sat down and pushed his discarded clothes back into his bag. It was then that he noticed the roll of parchment which he had carried, but not read, since Calian had given it to him in the forecastle storeroom of the King Elson. With time now on his hands, Ciro pulled out the roll and began tentatively peeling away the sheets which the sea had endeavoured to stick together.

The ink had run for the most part but the faint impressions still left made the majority of the pages still legible. As he separated the papers he noted scripted addresses and dates and the name at the bottom of the pages made his heart skip a beat. As it had always done when he had searched through the Ascension Chamber's library as a child, the name of King Elson always grabbed his attention.

The pages, as the covering letter remarked, were copies of some ancient correspondence between King Elson and his brothers, Meanon and Idirnon. But, wondered Ciro, if they were of genuine origin, why had he never come across them in the Ascension Chamber? With a frown the king began to read what Calian had believed to be evidence of a plot and, as he lost himself in the ancient correspondence, the Gallean carried them ever onwards to Formoss.

Be it known to all you brave souls that our prayers travel with you on this desperate journey into the night. The letters enclosed should give enough information as to where to begin your search and convince you, beyond all doubt, that you must not be swayed by the infantile dreams of the Fool King. The originals of these letters have been safely stored since the time of Prince Tenlern, the last fool to make this journey, and it is our firm belief that nobody in the royal court since the wise King Erin has ever seen them. If they had then I do not doubt that Ciro would never have decided on his present course of action, but then it is not our place to worry of the unbeliever's fate and we must give some thanks to his sacrifice for providing us with this 'golden' opportunity. Read these messages well, memorise every word so that you know you do God's work in retrieving her image from the darkness and, when you have it, return safely home. As for Ciro and his mindless followers, let their folly be the final one of our people. A pyre to light our way finally out of the darkness.

May Milla shine!

From King Elson Torrman, Torr Adenair
To Prince Meanon Torrman, Romunesse.
19th/Third of Spring. New Calendar: 723

My dear brother,

I have this very moment finished hearing our little Idirnon's communication from the lips of one of his generals and just had to share my joy with you. Kal Santra has fallen! The Rial flag flies from the ruins! Who would have thought little Pipsqueak could be so bold? The details which General Solford has just given me are astounding, and of a nature so unorthodox and audacious that I thought for one moment he was referring to you! The full report will be posted in dispatches to you as usual, and I know that Idirnon will want to give us moment by moment recollections – but I cannot restrain myself from giving you the outlines of his dazzling scheme.

Idirnon massed five divisions of the Western Army at Torr Betram, and sent a further four from Forht down the South River in grain barges towards Kal Santra. Half way down, the troops disembarked and filled the barges with wood and kindling from a nearby forest and then covered the whole with lamp oil. At this stage Idirnon had set off from Torr Betram and night marched his troops to strike camp in the plains to the east of Kal Santra. The four divisions under General Solford did likewise on the western side of the South River and waited for the grain barges to arrive on the appointed night.

Skeleton crews piloted the barges into Kal Santra harbour at dusk on the tenth of the month and, raising sails, they lit all six vessels and made off in row boats as the barges drove at full speed into the jetties. General Solford says that the flames were magnificent and lit the sky for miles around, signalling the advance for Idirnon's forces. As Idirnon had cleverly surmised (and he does appear, may I say, to be getting very clever) the fire took hold wonderfully and soon the garrison beneath the castle was ablaze and all available men were sent to try and contain it, including most of the force stationed in the castle! As planned Idirnon then used archers to decimate the fire fighters, while the remaining mass of troops swarmed from east and west to take the castle. Our brother says that the Makech were so surprised, and not to say terrified by the sudden onslaught that most just dropped their swords and ran! Idirnon reports that, as the Rial flag was raised, he looked from the ramparts and by the fire light could see what remained of the Makech warriors fleeing towards the desert! I am sure you will agree that Idirnon deserves full honours for such a victory and what is now Torr Idirnon will be a fine monument to his endeavours. He will be returning at month's end to Peimonac for his celebration and I am sure you will be there with me to greet him.

Now, about this other intriguing matter which you wrote to me about. That you should ask my permission for such a venture is heart-warming but completely unnecessary, dear Meanon. Just because I am King, and tied by the affairs of our Kingdom, do not for one moment think that I have forgotten what it is to want to roam and explore, or that I would prevent my dear brother from doing so. I may be so constricted but that does not mean I have forgotten what wanderlust is, especially yours, you vagabond! I think an expedition into Taisin an excellent idea for, like you, I believe there must surely be more there than just a wasteland. Who knows, you may discover another Kingdom beyond those mountains!

I have been pondering this idea since I received your letter, and the more I have thought on it, the more I think it quite possible. If you remember your history (and of course I know you do) you'll remember that, when King Adenair led our ancestors out of slavery in Makech and into Rial, it is written that they found the land littered with ruins but, apart from the disgusting Omerk, completely deserted. You have only to see the remains of the sun temple at Peimonac to know how wonderful that kingdom must have been, and even the foundations below me as I write are from that lost people! Such things were not created by the thuggish Makech, or by those Unmen – the sun fearing Omerk – so perhaps the people responsible still survive beyond the mountains? A fanciful thought perhaps, but never-the-less they must have gone somewhere!

We can talk at length when we meet in Peimonac for Idirnon's festival, but in the meantime make whatever preparations you feel are necessary.

May Milla shine on you

Elson

From Prince Meanon Torrman, Taisin
To King Elson Torrman, Torr Adenair.
25th/2nd Autumn/723

My dearest brother,

my apologies to you and Queen Lusiac for filling your grand hall with relics, but I know that these things will interest you as much as I: and mark my words, what I have returned to you is the merest fraction of the 'antiquities' (as the learned Frisia would have us call them) that we have collected from this strange domain. They will give you an idea of the wonders which we continually stumble across here in Taisin – this land of broken cities – but I wish you could see for yourself the sheer scale of the ruins which we encounter daily. You were right when you thought that there may be another kingdom beyond the mountains but, sadly, it would seem to be a realm of the dead. We have encountered nobody in our travels here, but the disgusting Omerk appear to be everywhere. And they are bolder here too! Just last evening I had to personally kill five of the creatures when they swarmed our camp – attracted no doubt by the fire and smell of food – but, as the saying goes, these Unmen continue to be as stupid as they are vicious.

Today we travelled further south and east and you will be fascinated to know that we have sighted another mountain range to the east! Superior, it would seem from this distance, to our own White Wall! Our mapmaker has diligently charted our every step and I hope to send you details of this place with my next dispatch. We also found and explored the deserted remains of a great citadel carved into the rock face of a hillside and a forest of oaks the size of which I have never seen before: they are huge! Even taller than our highest clock spire!

I cannot help but be saddened in the knowledge that whoever built these monuments has long departed and you will note from the tablets I have sent you that, whatever language they used, it is all but indecipherable. The learned Frisia (what a good idea of yours it was to bring him) has attempted to unravel the lettering, but he does not seem confident of success. Instead we must content ourselves with marvelling at the wondrous sights we constantly encounter, that and the breathtaking scenery – for it is very beautiful here.

We have camped on the bank of our second river and tomorrow will continue south into the unknown. There seems to be the remains of a road or, to be more precise, there is a straight depression of grass under which Frisia assures me there is a road, which heads off towards the south horizon. Ah! Another mystery to chase!

Give my love and blessings to everyone and tell Pipsqueak to stay out of trouble. I wish you could be here with me.

May Milla Shine

Meanon

From Prince Meanon Torrman, Taisin
To King Elson Torrman, Torr Adenair
10th/3rd Summer/724

My dearest brother,

thank you from the bottom of my heart for your concern. Who else would send five divisions of the Northern to dig me out of the snow? I hope that the general who delivers this message has impressed upon you the importance of reading this letter before opening those huge crates I have sent back to you, because I must tell you the details of our discovery before you feast your eyes on the wonder which lies within!

By my reckoning it has been almost a year since I last wrote to you, and for that I apologise. The winter set in fast and bitter below the further mountains soon after I last communicated, and so fatigued were my men with the exertions of travel in such conditions that we eventually sought refuge in yet another ruined citadel to sit out the worst of it. If that was not enough, we then had to contend with the increasing presence of the vile Omerk who, if I did not know better, appeared to be trying to lay siege to us! Needless to say, such plans – if they had any – came to naught but such hindrances have prevented me from dispatching riders safely back to you for some time.

How glad we were when we heard the horns of the Northern Army, and saw the Rial flag flashing through the snow! I did not realise how homesick I had become until I saw that majestic sight! And how pleased I was that I had given you directions enough to find me. After their arrival, and the final turn in the weather, we were been able to continue south along the grass road until we crossed the river we had been following since my last letter. If it had not been for your concern and rapid response I do believe we would have turned back and, in so doing, missed what has to be the most amazing structure I have ever had the good fortune to witness. You will be amazed as were all present here in Taisin at what we found – the most staggering part of which sits snugly in the crates before you. But enough of my teasing, let me attempt to describe the scene that we encountered so that you may fully comprehend the stunning monument that we have unearthed.

After several weeks of travelling beyond what I shall call the Taisin River, we came across a wide plain of discoloured grassland, in the centre of which was what appeared to be a massive grave site marked by large, irregular tombstones. This in itself was enough to make most jaws drop as the stones stretched on further than the eye could see and appeared to fan out in perfect, concentric circles. We made camp on the outskirts of this strange site and Frisia pointed out what an ideal opportunity this was to find evidence of the builders of all the cities and monuments that we had previously encountered. I agreed wholeheartedly with his suggestion and so we planned to dig at the base of a few of the tombstones the following morning.

During that night I was summoned by loud and disbelieving cries from my tent to see my entire party crowded and staring at the graveyard. Drawing nearer I too witnessed the cause of the commotion. The stones, all of them, were glowing! As if lit by some pale inner light! You cannot believe, my dear brother, the consternation that this caused, and though I do not claim to be a religious man, I too found myself making the sign of the seasons. It was Frisia, dear learned Frisia, who broke this spell of fearful awe. It was he alone who had the temerity to approach one of the stones and deduce that it was not stone at all, but a metal the like of which no-one has ever seen before!

By dawn we had cleaned several of the 'stones' of the lichen and dirt which had caused us to mistake them for rock and our efforts soon brought forth the real nature of the metal. It is, as I have said, the most amazing substance I have ever seen and its appearance spurred on our efforts as we excavated deeper to find the graves. But instead of graves, after ten feet of hard labour, we found a floor of patterned stone in which the columns – for that is what they appear to be – are set. Suffice to say that we were all a little disappointed and not a little confused that our initial theory had been wrong, but such was our wonder at this mystery emerging from the earth that I endeavoured to unearth as much of it as possible, and that was, if you can believe it possible, when our real amazement began!

Seeing that this was a grand structure of magnificent proportions I decided to make a concerted effort at uncovering its central circle and to that end I set our entire party to work. It is a large area and the work took us several days to complete but, when it was done, we had to slap ourselves to prove we were not in some dream. The centre circle of the structure is surrounded by twelve pillars of the same miraculous metal and in each of them is a recess containing a bronze container. The stone floor, which seems to sit at the base of all the many thousands of pillars, ends at the edge of this central circle and is replaced again by the same metal of which the pillars are made. But inset into this central circle of metal, we found another, greater substance, and that is what I have dispatched to you with all haste.

Brother, brace yourself, for what I am about to tell you will take your breath away. Inset into the floor of this structure was the image of Milla, identical to that which graces our flag and exact (Frisia assures me) in every way to the stone recess in the sun temple at Peimonac. It is made from a metal which has the appearance of gold, yet is not gold, for it shines like Milla's gaze and is warm to touch. We do not know if this is the object that would have originally occupied the floor of the sun temple, for even though it is the same in all respects we can, none of us, think of a reason why it would have been moved to this isolated spot. We can only assume that the original from the sun temple was looted by some ancient rogues. You will see for yourself when you gaze upon the metal how likely that explanation will seem for it is without doubt the rarest and most wondrous thing I have ever seen.

Though I long to return to the civilisation of our kingdom, I feel compelled to first uncover this monument in all its splendour, for I have a strange suspicion that all its secrets are not yet unearthed. I will of course keep you informed of any developments as they occur. Give my love to Lusiac, your children, and of course Idirnon and his family and I promise to return as soon as possible.

With all my love, may Milla shine

Meanon

From King Elson Torrman, Torr Adenair
To Prince Idirnon Torrman, Peimonac
17th/2nd Spring/725

My dear Idirnon,

it has now been eight months and still there is still no word from either Meanon or the divisions of the Northern I sent to aid him. Though I know he is sure to be safe and well and that the winter months can drag on in Taisin, this strange development in the town of Cotisann worries me, even more so because it is near to where Meanon should be making his return through the lower mountain passes. There was no sign of battle, no damage to the village itself, so how can an entire town's population simply vanish overnight!? General Gossil has informed me that he is sending several brigades from Romunesse to scour the surrounding area for possible witnesses or survivors and I am sure that there will prove to be some logical explanation for this odd occurrence. In the meantime, I suggest you alert the Western Army to be ready – for what I do not know – but if it proves to be some sly Makech trick I want to be ready to bloody their noses.

Because of this I will not be coming to the Spring Stone as I had planned this next week and though I am sure they will understand my reasons, please convey my sincerest apologies to the Aldermen when they arrive. My love to Talia and your children.

May Milla shine
Elson

From King Elson Torrman, Torr Adenair
To Prince Idirnon Torrman, Peimonac
4th/3rd Spring/725

Brother,

if you have not already been alerted by dispatches I now give you the order. Call all able men to arms. This Cotisann problem appears to have worsened and we here are still at a loss to fathom its cause. I have not heard from General Gossil since his last communication over a month ago, nor has the party I sent to Romunesse returned. And now, Lady Orias, one of my Chief Ministers has disappeared after travelling to Solriar to meet with Gossil. I have sent a division of Royal Guard to Solriar to investigate and have put the Heart Wold on full alert. I advise you do the same but do not make any rash moves north until you receive my signal. If you hear of anything from either Romunesse or Solriar let me know, but let us pray to merciful Milla that this is nothing but a terrible breakdown in dispatches. As father used to say: beware, be wise. My love to you and yours.

May Milla shine

Elson

From Prince Idirnon Torrman, Peimonac
To King Elson Torrman, Torr Adenair.
23rd/3rd Spring/725

Brother,

I beg you, please do not send any more troops to Solriar! Just as I received your communication I got disturbing reports from our coastal town of Formisse that bodies have been sighted in the river floating down from Romunesse. Then, this very morning, riders from Erlar came to me with news that they had fished out the bodies of several Royal Guards from the White River which flows from Solriar. What is going on!? In spite of your order I have dispatched troops to Formisse to quell the panic which appears to be spreading there, and ordered divisions from Circia, Monet and Lamann to move up and strengthen our position here. I know you will approve of this action and I will not make a further move until I hear from you. I pray that this letter finds you well.

May Milla shine
Your obedient brother
Idirnon

From King Elson Torrman, Torr Point
To Prince Idirnon Torrman, Peimonac.
14th/1st Summer/725

Idirnon,

I have assembled 5,000 men at our stronghold at Torr Point and by the time you receive this letter my family should be with you at Peimonac. I will also have, by then, advanced to Solriar to engage the enemy.

Two of my Royal Guards made it back from Solriar, and from the state of them it would seem that the bodies you found in the river is the very least of our problems. One of them is burnt and disfigured terribly and can say nothing other than to gibber about the 'Beck Night' descending. The other, a Captain Darrit who I knew well, is now a wide-eyed wreck who cannot stop shaking. We have been able to press him enough for him to give us some information, but what use it will be I do not know. He says the Royal Guard arrived at Solriar to find it deserted like Cotisann, and heeding my orders they made no move to travel any further, but instead made camp and prepared to dispatch a rider to inform me. That rider was Captain Darrit. He says that, as he got into the saddle, a storm bank rushed across the sky and within minutes it was as if night had abruptly descended – so dark did it suddenly become – and that the whole division was thrown into dismay. The captain does not know, or will not say what happened next other than he made his escape out of the darkness to the Solriar bridge and it was there he rescued the sorry form of the battered corporal. I do not know what such things portend but I do know this: if the devil himself is abroad I will make him regret it.

I have sent scouts forward to the north bank of the White River, but there is no sign of an enemy. Never the less I am about to move forward to attempt to flush them out. My troops are of the stoutest heart, fearless and ready for battle and I know they will serve me proud. I have kept a further correspondence back with the garrison here at Torr Point and, in the event of anything happening to me, it will be dispatched to you. By Milla's grace I pray it will not be necessary. Take care my dearest brother, of yourself, Lusiac and my children whom I now entrust to you. Do nothing until you receive that final communication, or my next one. Be safe.

May Milla always shine

Elson

From King Elson Torrman, Torr Point
To Prince Meanon Torrman, Peimonac.
15th/1st Summer/725

My dearest brother,

this is the last communication I shall ever send for I know that as sure as Milla shines the night is about to fall upon me. Those that are not dead have fled in panic but still my closest regiments stand with me; yet even as I write these words I can see from my window that my kingdom is being devoured by a wall of darkness. For the sun's sake do not send reinforcements! They will do no good. Though they be as brave as tigers, they will surely fall like the thousands I have seen slain this day.

All my troops, the flower of our army, have been destroyed, and the words from that deranged corporal who I took to be mad now ring like wisdom in my ears. The Beck Night has indeed come upon us and all my efforts to prevent the devil from walking here have come to naught. Heed my words brother, for I have not much time to impress upon you their importance, or my insistence that you follow my orders.

You are not, I repeat NOT to send reinforcements. It would be a fool's errand and serve no purpose. The fate of our people now lies in your hands and you must not make rash or senseless decisions other than to protect their lives and that of our families. To that end I wish you to ready every ship and transport necessary to convey our people away and you must impress upon them – CONVINCE THEM – for their own safety to follow your orders just as I hope you will follow mine. Seek out a seafaring explorer in my wife's group named Feira who knows of a place far away from here where you can go and be safe. Pay the closest attention to what he has to say. Do not balk at this demand brother, for it is my final one and, though your heart will surely pound for the battle, understand this: it is already lost.

My general is calling me, I do not have much time. Please tell my darling Lusiac that I love her more than any words can convey and tell my children not to mourn my loss. They must be brave and resolute and one day their time will surely come. I have failed my kingdom and my family. YOU MUST NOT. I wish, oh how I pray that Meanon is safe and free from harm. Be wise Idirnon, beware. But above all else be safe.

May Milla shine
Elson

V

'Are you alright, Ciro?' Tenc asked. They had all noticed him reading the papers but so complete was his concentration that none of them had wanted to disturb him.

Ciro shook his head and said nothing. He gathered up the papers and walked to the handrail, his gaze set on the distant riverbank but his attention elsewhere.

They had to be forgeries. It was the only explanation that made sense, yet still Ciro found himself disconcerted by what he had read. Without the reference of the Ascension Chamber library it was difficult for Ciro to be certain, but he was fairly confident that the correspondence dates tallied perfectly with other letters he had read and re-read back in Feirlan. There were Idirnon's official dispatches about his assault on Kal Santra, eyewitness accounts of bodies floating past Formisse and many reports of the panic which had gripped the kingdom. All these things were well documented. But the personal correspondence he had read from the time of the plague had all come from Peimonac: carried to safety with the populous when the blight had swept the land. And wasn't that how Elson's son, 'Wise King Sarvie' had later described it: a blight?

Ciro recalled that, about twelve years after the exodus, a bitter correspondence had been written between King Elson's widow and her eldest son and heir, Prince Sarvie. Prince Idirnon had left two years earlier to return to Reilan and search for his brothers and Sarvie, now twenty one years old, had been pressured by his mother to follow his uncle back to Reilan and claim his rightful throne. Considering his first duty as monarch was to protect what was left of his people, he had flatly refused, set up the Feirlan throne beside the Rialan one and written to his mother:

"The blight which claimed the flower of our nation, my

father and now both my uncles will not claim me. I will be King of Feirlan only."

It went something like that, Ciro was sure, and was an understandable response to the catastrophe which had claimed so many. But nowhere, in all the reports that Ciro had read from before the exodus had there been talk of a wall of darkness, or of the missing villagers of Cotisann. Of a 'Beck Night' descending and 'darkness on the horizon', well yes, those phrases had often been used; but surely they had simply been colourful metaphors for the plague which had ravaged the land. Hadn't they?

Ciro was uncomfortable with the fact that the writer of the covering letter believed that Ciro himself would not have attempted the expedition if he had known of the existence of the letters. If they were forgeries, concocted to encourage Captain Fars in his task of reclaiming this Rial sun emblem – the symbol of the Children of Milla – then their content was irrelevant. But if they were forgeries, what was the point of sending a man into the unknown with no chance of completing his task? It simply did not make sense! Ciro had to assume that the writer of the covering letter believed the content of the correspondence, and even he had to admit that the letters were compelling. There was a thread of truth woven throughout the correspondence which added substance: but how much of it was true?

Ciro considered the stories Tenc had told about events he claimed were documented after the fleet had sailed: of the messenger who had seen darkness on the horizon from Peimonac and the other who had encountered Songsmiths and strange creatures in Torr Adenair. Neither those nor Amec's wild tales that the Beck Night had been sent to punish both King Elson and the kingdom made mention of a plague. In fact, and Ciro recalled Amec's vociferous contempt well, the

Philiri had been adamant that there had been no plague.

Ciro still found the possibility of some god-like punishment inflicted on the Rial Kingdom a far-fetched idea, but then how was he to rationalise a myth which had sprung up on two unconnected continents? It just didn't make sense. How could a wall of night descend? How could people simply disappear? It wasn't logical. Ciro looked down and found that he had hitched his thumb underneath his star belt. He sighed. Was the belt logical? He could not explain it but he had no doubts about its strange abilities.

He gazed at the river beneath him and the foam shearing a white line from the bow of the ship. Clouds were beginning to dull the sky with grey and he felt a shiver run through him. What if I'm wrong? He thought. What if the letters, rather than fakes, were the truth; and the warning given with them equally genuine and sincere? If that were the case then he really was the 'Fool King', the king of nothing but his trusting men's doom. Ciro looked north, past the tree line which bordered the river, wishing with all his heart that he could somehow spy Peimonac and assure himself that his men and all his friends were safe. If he was wrong then, like Prince Tenlern who had disappeared on the same journey two hundred years before him, he had led his followers into terrible danger.

Ciro felt like screaming at the horizon in frustration, but instead bowed his head and gripped the bow rail. 'Please let me find them well,' he muttered.

'Wha'sup, Ciro?' asked Arper. The king looked up to see Arper standing beside him while both Tenc and Nesh looked on with concern.

Arper pointed to the papers. 'Bad news?' he asked.

Ciro managed a weak smile. 'Possibly,' he said. He rolled up the letters and walked over to Tenc. 'This library of yours in Philire?' Ciro asked. 'Is there much material from the time of the exodus?'

'I think so,' Tenc replied. 'My father would know more about it than me, but I'm sure they'll let you read as much as you like.'

Ciro nodded. He felt a nagging sense of disorientation from reading the letters and stuffed them back into his bag: as if their disappearance would nullify the effect. He could do nothing now, he reasoned, but wait and see if the Philire library could verify either story. Then he would travel swiftly on to Peimonac and get to the truth about the correspondence – even if it meant breaking Captain Fars in two to get it. He did not like to be played for a fool.

Tamarail sauntered up the deck and called Tenc over. The Philiri returned sheepishly a few moments later and whispered to Ciro.

'Tamarail says we're about to pass Formoss and he'd… Well he says that he'd appreciate it if you kept out of sight.' Tenc pointed at Ciro's golden badge and, while the others decried the captain's cheek, Ciro smiled, pulled his cloak from his pack and attached it to his jacket.

'Shall we take a look at Formoss?' Ciro said. He wrapped the cloak around himself and moved to the edge of the deck.

The others followed and together they watched for a sign of the town on the northern shore.

'I'm surprised Tamarail wants to pass in daylight,' Ciro said, half to himself as a line of white stonework appeared through the trees in the distance.

Tenc shrugged. 'It's probably for the best, I suppose.' He did not sound too convinced.

Slowly, the town of Formoss slipped into view. It was bigger than Ciro had expected and he pointed to several large wooden structures set back from the river. 'They look new,' he said, then corrected himself. 'Well, less ramshackle than usual.'

The buildings were a contrast to the rest of Formoss which was, like every other settlement he had seen, in a bad state of disrepair. These structures, set slightly apart from the main town seemed well cared for and were surrounded by a protective wall.

'Any idea what they are?' Ciro inquired. The others looked blank.

Gradually the buildings slipped past and the walled harbour of the main town drew level with the Gallean. There was activity all along the harbour wall and the dull glint of metal gave Ciro no doubt that the Makech were somehow alerted to their presence. He switched his gaze to look down river and spotted the other boat which had left Kal Gians harbour before them. They were distant, but Ciro was sure he could see the sail of another, smaller craft close by it on the water.

'Ciro look!'

Nesh was pointing to the harbour mouth where two small sailing boats were being rowed through the harbour entrance. Once clear of the breakwater, they raised sails and veered swiftly towards the Gallean.

So much for the Makech having no skill with boats, Ciro thought. They were some distance away but Ciro was certain of one thing: there was no Formoss welcoming party aboard either boat.

'Will they catch us, do you think?' asked Tenc.

Ciro looked along the deck and saw that Tamarail had ordered his men to drop extra canvas. There were sailors hurrying to scale the rat lines while some of the Kal Gians refugees were beginning to come up from the hold to line the larboard rail.

'Looks like the captain knows what he's doing,' Ciro said.

'With full sail I can't see them catching us.'

The breeze was slight, but enough to show a noticeable difference when the sails were fully unfurled. The Gallean began to increase its distance from the town and the pursuing craft. Ciro looked to see that, further downstream, the other boat was making similar headway on its pursuer. Then the smaller boat came swiftly about and began a zigzag course upstream.

'Tenc,' Ciro said, stepping away from the handrail. 'I want you to take Nesh down to the hold and tell Tamarail to arm his men with whatever they can find.'

Nesh protested but Ciro shook his head and, as gently as he could, insisted she listen to reason.

'Tell the captain to get those refugees out of harm's way too!' he shouted as the Philiri led Nesh to the safety of the hold. Then Ciro sifted through their pile of belongings and pulled Amec's sword from its sheath.

Arper too removed his own sword as Ciro returned to checking the position of the Makech boats. Nesh's Uncle looked downstream and eyed the rapidly approaching craft nervously.

'Can we get past 'em?' Arper asked.

Ciro checked that the trailing Makech craft were still falling behind before concentrating on the boat before them. It was swinging wide to their larboard side now, avoiding the danger of being run down by the rapid approach of the larger vessel. All they had to do, thought Ciro, was hold a stationary position until the Gallean was within range, then tack to starboard to come alongside. Over a short distance, Ciro was sure the Makech boat would be fast enough to complete the task and the shallow deck of the Gallean would make boarding a fairly simple affair.

Tenc returned and with him came the diminutive figure of

Dent and the towering Borlin. They said nothing, but stood watching the Makech boat getting closer.

Dent frowned. 'Borlin,' he said, 'tell Tamarail ta turn about when I give the word.'

'You're planning to turn?!' Exclaimed Ciro. 'No! Borlin, tell Tamarail to hold his course. If we turn about we'll have three boats to contend with, not one!'

Borlin paused and looked questioningly at Dent, who shook his head and pointed down the deck.

'Wait!' cried Ciro as Borlin went to convey Dent's message. 'If we turn now, that boat will still catch us. What you're proposing is suicide!'

'If we don't turn round we're gonna be trapped,' replied Dent firmly. 'We need time ta put the sails round the vessels if we're ta get through the black apples, an' with those boats trailing us we'll 'ave no chance. If we turn round now we might 'ave a chance to reason with 'em.' he sneered at Ciro and pointed to his sword. 'We ain't warriors.'

'I am,' said Ciro with feeling. 'And I'll kill any Boneman who attempts to board this ship.' He looked levelly at Dent. 'You took a risk in breaking free from Kal Gians and the Makech know what you've done. They aren't going to listen to reason, they are simply going to slaughter us: a task you'll make easier if you turn this boat around.'

'I don't like ta say it, Dent,' Borlin said. 'But I think 'e's right. We've come this far.'

Dent shook his head and was about to give the order himself when the Gallean began to veer away from the centre of the river. Without Dent's advice, Tamarail appeared to have chosen to turn anyway and slowly the Gallean began to come about. Alarmed, Ciro, Tenc and Arper watched helplessly as the Makech vessel seized its chance to move in and it skipped across the water as the larger vessel fought both the current and the breeze.

'Turn her you fool!' shouted Ciro as loudly as he could in the captain's direction. He ran along the deck in close pursuit of Dent and Borlin and looked back just as the Makech boat disappeared beneath the hull and thumped alongside.

There were harsh, guttural shouts from the vessel as several grappling hooks were thrown to bite into the hand rail and a volley of accompanying spears shot into the rigging to claim two screaming sailors.

Ciro stopped. He was close enough now for Tamarail to hear him. 'They'll kill us all if you don't turn down stream!' he shouted then ran with Arper and Tenc to meet the Makech threat.

The height from the deck of the Makech boat to their own was an easy climb now that the two vessels were firmly tied together. Ciro could see that there were seven Makech soldiers crammed onto the smaller vessel but their lack of deck space hampered their ability to swarm aboard in sufficient numbers. While two Makech secured the grappling lines, another pair were rearming themselves from a spear rack at the base of their mast. That left three who now leapt in unison to grip the Gallean handrail and pull themselves up.

'Stay low, cut their lines!' Ciro shouted to Arper and Tenc. Two spears whistled over their heads and the king ran to attack the first Makech head he saw rise above the handrail.

Screaming, Ciro charged at the figure who, with one leg now over the handrail was in no position to defend himself. The Makech stared back wide-eyed but, before Ciro could bring his sword to bear, the man threw himself backwards from the boat.

There was a yell of pain as the falling Makech hit the edge of his own craft before striking the water and Ciro almost received a spear in the face as he glanced over the handrail.

He span and ducked as the shaft flew past his nose then recovered quickly enough to strike out at the second Makech head which appeared.

As the Makech, fatally wounded, lost his grip and fell, Arper appeared beside him. Ciro pulled his friend down as another two spears flew overhead.

'I cut it!' Arper said, grinning and the pair watched as Tenc, a few feet away, slashed through the other grappling line to cut the smaller boat loose.

Keeping low, the Philiri ran to meet them. 'I got one!' he said and showed his bloody sword. Ciro nodded and risked a look over the rail.

The Makech boat was still moving alongside the Gallean: the helmsman bouncing the smaller vessel into their hull as they began to fall behind. Ciro noted with relief that the Gallean now appeared to be heading back downstream. Spears were still being hurled up onto the deck but the Makech appeared to have abandoned any thought of boarding again.

'Come on,' said Ciro and ran down towards the stern where most of the crew had taken cover. On his way he plucked a spear from the deck and threw it at as hard as he could at the enemy boat. His aim failed him and the spear fell short to strike the water.

Dent was screaming and thrashing around on the deck when they arrived: his bloody side pierced by a spear. While Tamarail, casting nervous glances overboard, crouched down and gripped the tiller, Borlin and several other crewmen were fighting to keep their stricken colleague still. Ciro saw the Makech boat finally clear their stern and the soldiers, now spear-less, could do nothing but hurl abuse in their direction.

'Bastard!' spat Dent in agony from the deck. 'This is your fault!'

Ciro frowned, but made no comment to Dent's accusation and crouched down beside the injured man. He held his waist as Borlin pulled the spear free and Dent's body convulsed with the pain and he fainted.

'Arper, go below and see if Nesh has any more of that moss left,' Ciro said. 'And get some cloth to bind Dent's wound.'

While Arper went in search of Nesh, Ciro stood and, ignoring the hostile faces around him, looked back along the sunset river. The two other Makech boats were now close to the third and their sails cast long shadows on the glinting water. Watching them fall behind, Ciro's attention was drawn to a fourth and larger sail. The vessel it belonged to was much further up stream but it was definitely heading their way.

'Were any other boats supposed to escape from Kal Gians?' Ciro asked Tamarail.

The Philiri, with undisguised hostility, ignored Ciro's question. He got to his feet and pointed to the tiller.

'I told you that if anythin' else happened I'd throw you overboard!' he yelled.

Ciro shrugged. 'I'm not responsible for either your dangerous about-turn or the actions of the Makech. You should have known they would attempt to kill us.'

'I don't mean the beckin' Boneman!' Tamarail spat. 'I mean the beckin' tiller, look!' The captain gripped the wooden handle with both hands and pulled on it. It moved easily towards him and he cursed.

'I don't understand,' replied Ciro with a shrug.

'The tiller turned on its own again! Back downstream!' shouted the captain. 'Like last time when you're friends came aboard!'

Ciro resisted the smile which threatened to split his impassive countenance and ignored the glance which Tenc gave him.

'The gods would appear to be helping us despite your actions, Tamarail,' he replied. 'Or do you still think we should turn around and attempt to reason with the sharp end of a Makech spear?'

Tamarail pointed over his shoulder. 'If they continue to follow us: prevent us from protecting the Gallean's hull, then we will be in a far worse situation. I know what's waiting just a few miles downstream an' if this boat sinks you'll wish I 'ad turned back.'

'You knew the risks, Tamarail,' Tenc said dismissively. 'Even with a piece of canvass wrapped around the hull our journey'll still be hazardous. Stop blaming our situation on a man who has done nothing but risk his own life to protect you, your crew and your passengers. If it hadn't been for Ciro, you'd be knee deep in dead people by now.' Tenc shook his head. 'I don't know you anymore, Tamarail,' he said and walked away.

Nesh arrived and while she knelt down to staunch and bind Dent's wound Ciro asked: 'How far are we from the black apples?'

Tamarail ignored the question and stared back upstream where the larger sail could still just be seen on the river. Borlin stood up from beside the groaning Dent.

'Hour, maybe more,' he said. 'But, like the captain says, I can't see us gettin' a chance ta put the sails round the 'ull.'

'I don't know precisely what to expect,' Ciro replied. 'But is there nothing we can do while we're on the move?'

Borlin, with a glance at Tamarail's back, motioned Ciro aside and the pair, followed by Arper, walked along the deck.

'I've been through the barrier a couple o' times,' said the boatman. He leaned back against the handrail and pointed to the heavy pock marks on his face. 'I was lucky just ta get this,' he said. 'The man next to me 'ad his 'ole face –' Borlin stopped when he realised Nesh was now standing behind Ciro.

Ciro, realising the same thing, turned to Nesh. 'How's Dent?' he asked.

''e'll live,' she replied with a shrug.

'Then I have another man who needs your assistance,' said Ciro. He pointed to the bow where Tenc stood alone. 'Can you go and cheer Tenc up?' he asked.

Nesh narrowed her gaze. 'You just don't want me ta 'ear Borlin's gruesome story, do yer?' she said.

Ciro smiled in response, but said nothing.

'Uncle Arper's told me worse,' replied Nesh with a grin then moved off to join Tenc.

'Thing with the black apples is they float on the water,' continued Borlin once Nesh had gone. 'One touch an' POOF! They explode an' eat right through anythin' they touch.'

'Are there many off them?' asked Ciro.

Borlin grinned. ''undreds, thousands – on the shore anyways – in the water, I dunno… But enough ta sink us if we're not lucky an' hit enough of 'em.'

'Have you ever struck one in the water?' Ciro inquired. 'I mean, have you tried to prevent them touching the hull?'

'Yep, that's 'ow I got these scars,' said Borlin. 'Beckin' thing came right beside us when we was in a row boat. Oarsman panics an' 'its it with the oar, next thing I know the bloke in the back of the boat is dead an' me face is on fire.' Borlin shook his head. 'Most painful thing I can ever remember.'

'I've 'eard similar tales,' said Arper. 'All of 'em bad. Strikes me a sail won't do much good.'

Borlin shrugged. 'It was the best we could think of without Tamarail's old boat, the Pesarian, to hand.'

'You planned to take the sail right under the hull?' Ciro

asked. Borlin nodded and Ciro stared out into the dusk for a moment, thinking hard.

'Just you wait now, sailor-boy,' said Arper with a wink to Borlin. 'King's thinkin'.' He grinned. 'Last time 'e did that I 'ad to dress as a Boneman an' ride an 'orse. The uniform stank like Ebo's Mire, but it saved me life.'

Ciro studied the Gallean's prow for a moment: returned Nesh's wave and then returned his attention to Borlin. He passed Arper Amec's sword and, with both hands free, held them before the sailor.

'This is the Gallean,' he said, holding one hand straight with its palm down. He cupped his other hand and held it beneath the first. 'And from the starboard side right the way under to the larboard side is how you planned to fix the sail, right?' Borlin nodded. 'With us travelling at speed,' continued Ciro, 'it seems the greatest danger from these floating apples would be to our bow, so why don't we simply fix the sail to the bow and let it drape into the water. The speed of the boat will stop it from slipping away and perhaps we can fix it wide enough to give us a bigger lee: it's not perfect, but it might help.'

Borlin frowned for a moment with concentration and then his face split with a grin. He slapped Arper on the shoulder. 'Better'n dressin' up as a Boneman!' he said.

'You think it will work?' asked Ciro.

'Aye, that'll work,' Borlin replied. 'I'll get the lads to bring the mainsail up an' we can start fixin' it now.' The tall sailor moved off to tell the rest of the crew then paused. He turned and smiled.

'Thanks, mate,' he said to Ciro then hurried on to get the sail.

It took a little co-ordination to tie the spare mainsail to the spar once both were brought up from the hold but, with the crew, Ciro's group and some of the Kal Gians refugees lending a hand the work was completed by the time darkness had descended and The Handle split into two separate rivers.

'We'll be takin' the North Fork, I expect,' Borlin told Ciro as he stood back and watched the crew manoeuvre the completed sail into position over the bow. The pair looked on while the sail was then weighted and the spar, with its furled sail attached, was secured across the width of the boat.

'Then where?' Ciro asked.

Borlin smiled. 'If we get through the black apples in one piece, then we'll 'ead down the Ice Water a few miles then up The Wanderer to Monides.'

'Have you been there before?'

Borlin nodded. 'But never off the boat. It's safer.'

Ciro looked puzzled. 'Safer than what, getting off?'

'Yep – Fix that line there!' Borlin snapped at one of the crew and then shook his head. 'Tenc must've told you about the dangers past the barrier, didn't he?'

'You mean the Omerk?' Ciro replied. 'Yes, he said they were still around.'

'Omerk!' Borlin whistled, and then drew Ciro out of earshot of the refugees still on deck. 'Omerk are the least of it,' he whispered. The tall boatman pointed downstream. 'We came down here, what? Two year ago? That was when Tamarail still 'ad the Pesarian an' this trip was easy. Anyway, we dropped anchor just below the old city of Monides. Tamarail an' Dent went off to visit the Philiri an' that left me in charge.' Borlin looked earnest. 'Now, I'd 'eard all the stories, all the tales an', well… Like any man would be, I was a bit – y'know – didn't really believe 'em. So, anyways, I stayed aboard while we're anchored an' darkness comes down – I mean right down like that!' The sailor clapped his hands together. 'Comes down in the middle of the beckin' afternoon! BANG!

It's night-time.'

Ciro was curious but couldn't help trying to rationalise the phenomenon. 'Was it cloudy? A storm perhaps?' he asked

'Naa,' Borlin replied with a shake of his head. 'It was a bit patchy up there,' he said, pointing to the sky, 'but this was like snuffin' out a candle. But that's not the worse of it. See, after me an' the crew got our nerve back an' starts lookin' around on shore, one o' the men sees a light on the 'ill by Monides and we think: "Oh, it's Tamarail come back." So, ta 'elp the captain find us in the dark, we light lanterns in the rigging an', sure enough, Tamarail's light gets closer an' starts comin' along the riverbank.' Borlin shook his head. 'I don't know what it was, but it weren't Tamarail.' The sailor looked cautiously around the deck and dropped his voice down even lower. 'We starts hearin' this weird 'owlin' noise as the light comes closer,' he continued. 'An' a sort o' – I dunno – clunkin' sound like, like Makech armour: y'know?'

Ciro nodded.

'So luckily, we're sittin' in mid-stream an' this thing can't get to us but it sees us, we're sure of it, cause it jus' stomps an' stomps about on the bank, 'owlin' an ragin' like Sakoom.'

'You've no idea what it was?' asked Ciro, still searching for the plausible explanation.

Borlin shook his head. 'We couldn't see too good in the dark: just the torch it were carryin'. Heard it plain enough, but couldn't see much.' He sighed. 'Even the bravest of us stayed below that long night. Come mornin', thank the stars, it was gone.' Borlin paused for a moment. 'Tamarail an' Dent came back later that day an', when we told 'em what we'd seen, the captain shakes 'is 'ead an' says: "Boys, you're the luckiest men alive. You saw a Fireheart an' lived to tell about it."

Ciro recalled Tenc mentioning the word but it had never

struck him as anything he felt the need to enquire of further: just another piece of superstitious nonsense. With everything that had happened now though, Ciro didn't hesitate to believe at least the sincerity of Borlin's story. Logic still nagged at his own credulity, but Ciro was starting to doubt that the logic of Feirlan applied in this land of strangeness.

'Sail's ready!' shouted a crewman, and Borlin moved to the prow to oversee the final unfurling of the sail.

'It might be best to unfurl it half way, rather than completely,' said Ciro, moving to stand beside Borlin.

Borlin had raised his arm and was about to drop it as a signal to the crew, but now he paused and looked questioningly at the king. 'Why's that?' he asked.

'If these black apples only sit on the surface, then we only need the sail to sit just below it,' Ciro replied. 'I was thinking that, if the sail then gets burnt through we can drop more sail into the water to replace it. You see?'

Borlin looked blank for a moment, then smiled. 'Alright, boys!' he said. 'You 'eard the King! Unfurl it 'a quarter an' we'll see 'ow she sits.'

Ciro looked on as the crewmen gripped the sail and gradually lowered it into the water, measuring out the canvas until the sail just dipped below the water line. Borlin checked the starboard and larboard sides and then returned grinning to the king.

'Perfect!' he beamed. 'That should give us a better chance!' He patted Ciro on the shoulder. 'Thanks, Mr King, I'll go tell the captain.'

Ciro smiled and watched the man walk aft. Night was falling fast now and he joined the others sitting near the bow.

Tenc waved a pale root at Ciro as he sat down. 'You should eat,' he said. 'When was the last time you ate?'

The king shrugged and took the food from him. Arper was

411

already eating noisily while Nesh was leaning over the handrail and looking at the water.

'What can you see, Nesh?' Ciro asked.

Nesh looked back. 'Not much,' she said. 'It's gettin' misty and the water's just black.' She returned to scan the water then leaned over the bow rail. 'What's that?' she muttered.

The three men crowded around Nesh as she pointed at the dark river: all could just make out a pale white shape bobbing on the water.

'Look's like a fish,' Arper said.

'A dead fish,' added Tenc. 'We should stay back from the water,' he said. 'I think we're at the barrier.'

Borlin had returned and pointed to the lamp which they had been eating by. 'Mind if we turn that off?' he asked.

Curious, Ciro looked back along the boat and noticed that, where there had been several lamps glowing before, now there were none but theirs.

'Isn't that a bit dangerous, Borlin?' asked Tenc. 'I think we're at the barrier. How will you spot the black apples in the dark?'

Borlin shrugged. 'Captain wants as little light as possible.' He pointed back along the deck and Ciro suddenly saw the reason for Tamarail's decision.

The evening was getting darker by the moment, leaving the countryside a grey expanse, yet upstream a single light glowed steadily in the distance.

'Blow that thing out, Tenc,' Ciro said. 'It looks like we've got company.'

Borlin nodded as the deck was plunged into gloom. 'Tamarail knows we'll need light ta keep a watch on the water, an' maybe later we can use some. But 'e's not sure if the other boat's reached the fork yet an', though we 'ope they'll turn about anyway, he doesn't wanna let 'em know which fork we've taken.'

The sky was patchy with cloud yet, once their eyes adjusted, there was still just enough dim light to make out the deck and the dark water around them. Borlin, the shell band around his temple now a grey line, sniffed the air and grimaced.

'Smell that?' he said, moving to the edge of the deck.

The others also noticed the pungent smell which was suddenly in the breeze.

'Smells like shit,' said Nesh.

'Hm,' Borlin replied. 'You was right, Tenc. We're at the barrier... Listen– '

Ciro and the others lent on the rail and looked out. The shoreline was obscured by both the encroaching night and a gentle fog which rose from the river, but a faint noise, not unlike the creaking of the boat, carried across the water.

'What is it?' Ciro asked, straining to catch the sounds. 'It sounds like logs crackling in a fire.'

'That's pretty much what it is,' replied Tenc. 'It's the black apples spitting off their branches.'

'We'll be in the thick of it soon enough,' Borlin said. 'I warn ya, the smell'll get worse an' the noise louder, so ya might wanna go below.'

The others looked at Ciro.

'Sounds like a good idea,' he replied. 'But I'd rather stay on deck. I'd like to help if I can.'

'Nothin' to be done at the moment,' replied Borlin. 'Just pray ta that god o' yours ta steer us clear o' trouble.'

Ciro smiled and turned to the others. 'Perhaps you should get out of this bad air and get some rest,' he said.

'So should you,' replied Nesh. 'It's been another long day.'

'I'll rest up here,' Ciro said. 'You go below.'

'Nah, it's too cramped down there,' Nesh said with a shake of her head. 'An' it smells just as bad as up 'ere. I'm stayin' put.'

There was a chorus of agreement from the others and Ciro shrugged. 'Thanks for the offer, Borlin,' he said, 'but it looks like we'll camp here again tonight.'

The boatman smiled. 'Jus' don't light any camp fires,' he said and made his way aft.

Though all were tired, the sense of unease which the noise and smell of the barrier produced drove all thoughts of sleep from their minds. They clustered around the bow to one side of the protective sail and watched the water nervously.

'You've travelled this way before, Tenc,' said Ciro. 'Any idea what we can expect?'

Tenc grimaced. 'Nothin' good, I'm afraid,' he replied and returned to scanning the water.

The pursuing vessel it seemed, was not about to give up the chase. Once it had been determined that the distant lamp light was still following their course, Borlin returned to the prow with some crew members armed with boat hooks and several lamps. After listening to the strange noises in the mist for long enough, Ciro seized the opportunity to do something practical. While Nesh responded to Borlin's request to check on Dent, he and the others joined the sailors in checking the protective sail.

'There, look!' exclaimed Borlin. He swung a lamp over the side to illuminate several large holes in the canvas then craned his neck to check the hull. 'Nuthin' yet,' he said with evident relief.

Ciro squinted at the holes in the canvas and spotted something dark and round bob through the gap. 'There!' he shouted. He grabbed a boat hook from the sailor beside him and stabbed at the black apple before it could touch the boat.

There was a hiss as Ciro struck and burst the thing and it

414

disappeared beneath the surface. Ciro pulled the boat hook free from the smoke the black apple had left on the water's surface and, to his amazement, found that most of the metal tip was now missing.

'Blood and sand!' he said, scarcely believing his eyes.

'Keep that pole straight,' advised Borlin. 'There might still be some juice on it an' ya don't wan' it on yer 'ands.'

Nodding Ciro exchanged a wide eyed glance with Arper and Tenc and, while Borlin instructed his men to lower another yard of canvas into the water, the three of them took positions either side of the sail to check the water.

While Tenc stood watch with some crewman on the larboard rail, Ciro and Arper moved to starboard. They were joined moments later by Borlin carrying another boat hook.

'When ya see one,' the boatman said. 'Don't whack it, jus' prod it. These things burst at the slightest touch.'

'I've never seen anything like it,' Ciro replied. 'Where on earth did they come from?'

'Milla knows,' said Borlin with a shrug. 'But ya wait 'till dawn: it's the Beckist sight you'll ever see.'

'There's one,' announced Arper, pointing and Ciro instantly jabbed out to strike it: losing another inch from his boat hook in the process.

Its arrival heralded another, then two, then six, then more. There were cries coming from the larboard rail as a similar number appeared to be swirling in their direction and Borlin handed Arper the remains of his boat hook to call more crewmen and adjust the steadily disintegrating sail. Ciro, between prods, looked out across the water and, at the very edge of the lamplight, he saw that the entire river was awash with dark, glinting apples.

'By the stars,' he said, awestruck by the sight. He called for Arper to move further aft and cover the centre of the vessel.

As the hours passed, every member of the crew but Tamarail – who seemed glued to the tiller – was lending a hand on deck to combat the endless, bobbing menace. The boat hooks, now nothing more than stumps were finally thrown at their targets and, in a last ditch attempt to protect the Gallean's hull, Borlin brought up the entire store of shirts from the hold. Hastily he began nailing them to the boat's hull at its waterline.

By now the acrid fumes from the continually bursting black apples were beginning to sting both eyes and lungs and Ciro tied his old scarf over his mouth in an attempt to keep out the worst of the burning mist. Then Arper, his eyes streaming and his sleeve held over his mouth suddenly staggered out of the fog and made a grab for Ciro's shoulder. The man's legs gave way as he stumbled into Ciro but the king gripped him firmly around the waist and managed to keep him upright. Arper's eyes fluttered as Ciro dragged him to the middle of the deck.

Ciro propped his friend against the mainmast and checked to find that he was now unconscious. He was debating whether to drag Arper to the relative safety of the hold when the boat lurched to larboard. Ciro's heart skipped a beat at the thought that they had been holed.

'It's the beckin' rapids!' someone shouted from the prow and Ciro hung on to the mast as the boat performed a number of bucking swerves before settling in calmer water.

Coughing, and wet from the spray which had splashed the deck, Ciro began dragging the limp form of Arper aft. He heard Tenc's voice call his name and shouted back through the fog.

Tenc appeared, wet and naked from the waist up to join the king in dragging Arper.

'He's not…?' the Philiri began.

Ciro shook his head before Arper, as if to dispel any doubts about his health, suddenly came to life in their arms.

416

'Wha' the beckin'!?–' he cried: struggling to his feet. He looked unsteady for a moment, grabbed hold of the hand rail beside him and coughed loudly. 'Wha' 'appened?' he asked with a bleary-eyed frown.

'It's the fumes from the apples,' explained Ciro. 'Damn things release some sort of gas.'

'I'll tell ya wha' sort o' gas it is,' replied Arper with a grimace. 'The beckin' bad sort, that's what!'

Ciro patted his friend's arm and sniffed the air. 'Tenc, have you noticed? The smell's gone.'

The Philiri nodded and hitched a thumb towards the bow. 'Borlin said the black apples don't make it through the rapids: we should be safer for a while, but we're not through yet.'

Arper gazed curiously at Tenc. 'What 'appened to yer jacket?' he asked.

Tenc pointed to a small red sore on his chest. 'Beckin' apple came right over the side in the spray. Burnt right through the cloth. Lucky for me I got it off in time.'

The trio were moving back towards the bow when through the fog came yells that the boat was taking on water. The three exchanged worried glances.

'We should get below,' said Ciro. 'See if we can lend a hand.'

They turned about and were swiftly joined by Borlin and several of the crew also making their way aft. The tall boatman stopped them.

'If we're 'oled, we'll 'andle it,' said Borlin pointing to his men. 'But it'd help if ya'd watch the sail for'ard.'

Ciro nodded and the three made their way back to the prow where Tenc pointed out the unrecognisable remnants of his discarded smock. Ciro checked that the protective sail was intact and the water seemingly clear, then used the stump of a boat hook to prod at the black apple remnants amongst the material on the deck.

'What're you doing?' asked Tenc as Ciro pushed the black apple skin clear of the jacket.

'I'm just curious, that's all,' Ciro replied.

'Careful with it,' warned Arper when Ciro's prodding produced a sudden curl of gas from the remains.

The king got a lamp which he placed beside the dark skin then crouched down beside it. Tenc and Arper, despite their apprehensions, moved in closer too.

'It looks like a plum skin, don't you think?' Ciro mused. 'It's the size of an apple, but –' he pushed at the remains with the boat hook and the deck around it began to smoke.

'Careful with it,' repeated Arper.

After a moment, the smoke died away to leave a dark burn mark on the deck. Tenc shook his head.

'It's always puzzled me how these things grow,' Tenc said. 'It eats through anything it touches.'

'Not everything,' corrected Ciro. 'The skin of the apple hasn't been affected at all –'

'– What've ya found?'

It was Nesh's voice and they rose from their crouch to find her looking over them.

'We were taking a close look at the enemy,' said Ciro and indicated the black apple skin.

'Is that wha' they look like?' Nesh sounded disappointed. 'Thought they'd be bigger.'

'They're bad enough that size, girl. Believe me,' Arper replied.

Nesh peered out into the darkness beyond the boat. 'Are we past 'em now?' she asked. 'Everyone below's gettin' really nervous.'

Tenc shook his head. 'We've still a way to go but, when it's light, it should be easier to spot them on the water.'

Ciro held up the stump of the boat hook before throwing it into the river. 'We had better start looking for some more poles,' he said and went off to speak to Borlin.

Ciro, more from Nesh's insistence than any desire on his own part, attempted to sleep along with the others just before dawn. Ragged nerves coupled with the continual activity around the prow however, made such relaxation impossible for him. Instead he watched the water and pondered the problem of the black apples.

With the dawn the river remained relatively clear of the things and the sun, rising slowly on their starboard side, thinned the mist on the water to a patchy veil. Together with Borlin and many of the crew, Ciro helped check the waterline on the outside of the hull and witnessed the devastation that the black apples had wrought on the ship in the darkness. Much of the clothing which had been hastily attached had either come loose in the rapids or been eaten away and, where the hull was exposed to the water, tell-tale burn marks made plain the damage which had been done to the wood.

'This is the worse one,' Borlin said, pointing to a foot wide scar near the mid-starboard side. 'We've patched it up from inside but there's still some water leakin' through.'

Ciro leaned over the hand rail to stare at the hole. The woodwork looked as if it had simply dissolved and the king shook his head at the sight. 'How many others are there?' he asked.

'Enough ta make me an' the crew worry,' Borlin replied. 'But few enough for us ta keep afloat for the time bein'.'

'How's Tamarail?' Ciro asked.

Borlin shrugged then drew Ciro's attention towards the stern. The king looked to see Tamarail leaning on the stern hand rail beside the tiller, his attention set firmly upstream.

''e's worried 'bout that other boat,' explained Borlin. 'It's

419

madness, I know, but 'e thinks they're still followin' us.'

'Why would that be madness?' asked Ciro, perplexed by Borlin's dismissal of the problem.

Borlin gave a rueful grin and shook his head. 'Ya don't know the Makech like we do. We don't cross the barrier 'cause we know it's dangerous. They don't cross it because it's dangerous an' what lies beyond it scares 'em witless.'

'The Firehearts?'

Borlin shrugged. 'Dunno, but it's kept the Philiri safe for generations.'

'The Makech aren't supposed to like the water either,' Ciro observed. 'Yet they managed to sail several ships after us.'

The boatman considered the fact for a moment then shook his head. 'They'd never come through the barrier – it's un'eard of.'

"Unheard of," echoed Ciro quietly to himself. How many times have I used that statement myself, he wondered. Tamarail was right to be worried if the pursuing Makech were who Ciro suspected them to be. Most likely the same group he had encountered in Birin.

'How close to Philire will we get in the boat?' Ciro asked.

Borlin shrugged. 'About a day from the old city of Monides I think, but 'ow close that is ta Philire I dunno. Like I told yer, I've never been off the boat meself.'

Ciro nodded and looked absently into the mist for a moment. How long, he wondered, would it take two boat loads of people carrying their belongings, to walk the distance from their final destination on the river to Philire? A day? Probably more. But how long would it take a small force of Makech soldiers to follow the path left by fifty people? Ciro didn't need to have his General, Alanti's calculator mind to work out the equation, or to see that the sum was an uncomfortable one. If the Makech boat stayed on course and got through the barrier, then their trailing distance on the river might soon be closed over land. There was no guarantee that the Makech would make it past the black apples, but the fact that they might even attempt such a thing was enough to make Ciro and, he supposed, Tamarail, worry about what they would do if they got through. The hideous black apples were the best defence the Philiri had against the Makech, but only as long as the Makech stayed west of them.

Borlin was looking into the water too. 'Still clear,' he said, breaking Ciro's train of thought. 'An' in the light those apples are a lot easier to fend off.' He looked around the deck. 'I best see how the boys are doin' with our new boat hooks,' he said and left Ciro leaning on the rail.

Ciro looked south towards the grey riverbank. The sun was climbing steadily above the horizon now and the fog was thinning enough to afford the occasional clear view of the landscape beyond the river. It was an eerie sight. Flat and desolate with only one feature: hissing, crackling fields of gently swaying black apple bushes, an uninterrupted vista as far as he could see.

The next few days were anxious and exhausting for all aboard the Gallean. It seemed at times to Ciro that there was a race on between the black apples and the crew: to see who could dismantle the vessel first. After the boat hooks, spare planking and spars were used to fend off the black, bobbing menace as well as repair new holes. Then divisional timber from the fore chamber of the hold was ripped out to aid their efforts and finally alternate strips of decking were taken up simply to keep them afloat. By the time they had navigated the short stretch of the Ice Water river and fought their way across stream into the safe and gentler current of The Wanderer, the Gallean looked not only like a vessel with little time left to her, but also like a boat not quite completed yet.

Despite all their efforts, the journey through the barrier had terminally stricken the Gallean and the holes around the hull accumulated to such an extent that sinking was inevitable. Travelling with sails fully set meant they took on water steadily and, even with the constant manning of the pumps, it was only a question of time before they sank. Soon the Gallean would become nothing more than a water-filled hulk: just like the one they had left behind in Kal Gians harbour. A slower speed might have helped the flooding to a degree but, with the sighting of a distant sail still following their course, no one questioned the wisdom of steering the Gallean to its ultimate destruction.

The main question on Ciro's mind was whether the pursuing Makech vessel had horses aboard.

The King of Nothing

PART FIVE

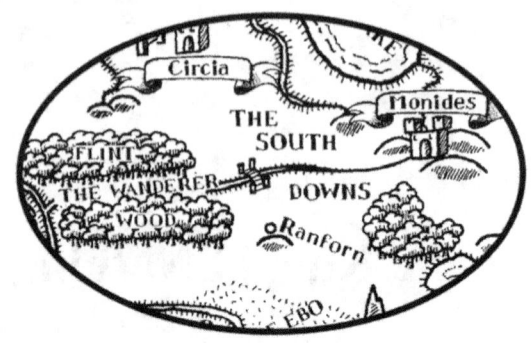

Like the wide division of The Channel separates the north from the south, so The South Downs act as a barrier between the South West Wold and the rest of Rial. Though there is civilization – grand Circia to the north, Ranforn in the centre – the great rolling plains between can make many a traveller feel themselves lost in a green yet unforgiving wilderness. Even the Great West Road, the main avenue of commerce between south and south-west can seem a bleak journey to set oneself upon: especially when your companions are more used to grand living than the rigours of nature. More particularly when said nature comes with the fearful threat of Omerk.

Though far from the foothills of the South Jaw Mountains, many are the tales of these fearsome Unmen stalking the Great West Road at night. With this threat clearly in our thoughts, my learned colleagues and I purchased passage with a merchant convoy, bound for the distant town of Formoss. Some thirty carriages in number, this particular caravan was carrying herbs and spices for the healers of Ranforn and weapons for the traders in Formoss. It was, so the Master Merchant informed us, the safest group that had ever crossed The South Downs and that, what with the armed guards and such, would prove more than adequate if any 'threat' should arise.

With gladder hearts my companions and I set off on this next leg of our travels in spirits which even the grey weather that dogged our first day's travel could not dampen. Only when the day turned to night and our large caravan made camp did the first fingers of fear begin to grip our hearts. It was a fear, I later realized, which came not from our situation, but from the tongue of the Master Merchant himself.

Sitting beside one of the many campfires which had been lit for both ourselves and the merchants, we had feasted well on spit-roasted pig and bitter Monides ale. Content (even Alderman Chaime seemed satisfied) we had greeted the arrival of the Master Merchant with no little praise and I, as I so often do, had then asked if he knew any tales from his own travels through this great kingdom of ours.

The merchant had gazed out beyond the caravan guards to the dark downs beyond and sipped at his ale in silent contemplation.

'I'll tell yer a tale,' he said at length. 'True one at that. Ten year ago I was travellin' to Monides with a merchant friend o' mine along this very same stretch o' the road. Now me friend, Cristan, lost 'is wife to the Makech a year before an' was never the same again. 'e'd talk about 'er often, said 'e dreamt of 'er just as much an' many was the night I'd sit with 'im while 'e talked. In them days there was only a couple 'o wagons in our convoy so we only ever stopped on the downs durin' the day. So this night we're 'eadin' east at a steady pace when Cristan jumps from 'is cart an', cause 'e's in front, I 'ave to stop an' all.

"What's wrong?" I says.'

"Can't ya 'ear 'er?" says 'e. "It's me beloved wife callin'!"

'Now its pitch dark with only stars to light our way an' I can't see or 'ear nuthin', just Cristan pacin' up an' down at the edge of the road. Before I can climb down from me own cart an' join 'im, 'e bolts off onto the downs.'

The Master Merchant, now with our slack-jawed attention, took a sip of ale before continuing. 'So I go to the edge of the road an' stare out into the darkness, listening for the sound of me friend... But I 'ear nuthin'. I call for 'im over an' over an' then finally decide to go back to me cart an' light a lamp. On me way back I 'ear a woman's voice callin' me in the darkness an' with a shakin' 'and I light me lamp an' shine it at the roadside.'

The Master Merchant shook his head and looked grave. 'There, just beyond the road,' he said, pointing into the night, 'was me friend Cristan's 'eadless corpse an' just beyond that was a row of wide Omerk eyes glintin' in the lamp light. Without another thought I jump onta me cart an' spurred me 'orses inta a gallop. I left Cristan's cart to its fate an' threw the oil lamp as 'ard as I could at them murderous devils. I didn't stop 'till the gates of Monides was in me sights.'

The Master Merchant gave a sigh and stood up. 'A terrible business,' he said. 'An' it still 'aunts me ta this day.' He nodded to himself, turned to rejoin the other merchants then left us with a warning. 'If ya wake from yer sleep in the night,' he said, 'an' 'ear someone callin' for Cristan, whatever you do, don't wander off the road.'

Suffice to say, sleep was not something my colleagues and I were troubled with for the next few nights.

Alderman Lacey. My travels to the South West Wold.
NC 659

Beyond the Barrier

I

It was the evening of the fifth day out of Kal Gians when the Gallean, now almost half way up the winding course of The Wanderer, came within sight once again of its companion vessel. Listing and lodged against the south bank, the Waterman had suffered too much damage to continue any further but now the joyous Rialans lining the river bank cheered and waved as the Gallean sailed into view. The smiles quickly faded however when they noted the sails remained fully set on the Gallean and it soon became apparent that the vessel had no intention of stopping. Along with others on the bank who took up the cry, the captain of the Waterman called to Tamarail as the boat drew closer, but Tamarail had already made his decision. He would not risk the lives of his people to save those of the stricken vessel.

Ciro had been discussing precisely how to save the lives of all the Kal Gians refugees with Borlin, Tenc and the others before the Waterman had been sighted. Now, as he gazed from the bow at the anxious, stranded crowd and realized Tamarail's intentions, he grabbed his pack and sword and ran aft to confront the captain.

'Tamarail! You've got to stop and pick up the others!' he exclaimed as he reached the tiller.

Tamarail, with a scowling Dent beside him, simply frowned at the demand. In exasperation, Ciro turned to Borlin.

'The plan, Borlin!' he implored. 'The one we've just been discussing about distracting the Makech!'

Borlin nodded but seemed distracted himself. The cries from the bank were still continuing and the tall boatman looked distinctly uncomfortable. 'What about it?' he asked.

'We do it now!' said Ciro firmly. 'Stop the boat, let the

others on and let me off.'

'What's 'e talkin' 'bout, Borlin?' sneered Dent. 'What plan?'

'Drop the sails and let me off!' insisted Ciro to the captain.

Tenc, Arper and Nesh had now joined the group with their own belongings while Ciro continued his attempts to sway Tamarail.

'I know you're worried about who's following us,' he said with earnest, 'and that they may catch us once we start travelling overland.' Tamarail gave a cautious nod and narrowed his gaze. 'Let me off here and I'll draw them away,' said Ciro.

'How?' Tamarail asked.

Ciro looked overboard. They had now passed the wreck of the Waterman and the stranded refugees were running to keep up with the speeding Gallean. 'I don't have time to explain – ' he locked his gaze on Tamarail's. '– Listen, the people on the bank have no idea what's coming upstream behind us. They'll be slaughtered if we don't get them away from here. I know you're trying to make the best of a bad situation but I know you don't want to leave those people to the mercy of the Makech… I can help, Tamarail.'

'His plan might work, cap'n,' added Borlin.

Tamarail's frown deepened and he lowered his head. He was silent for a moment, then sighed and nodded to Borlin.

'DROP SAILS!' Borlin bellowed. 'All hands ta the lines!' He moved quickly to the starboard rail and shouted to the people on the bank. 'Ready yer launches! Prepare ta come aboard!'

The cheering had resumed from the riverbank and Ciro turned to the others. 'Tenc, if you're willing,' he asked, 'I'd like you to come with me.'

'We're all comin' with ya!' Nesh said with feeling. She

428

flicked her gaze to her Uncle. 'Ain't we?' she asked.

Ciro smiled and placed a hand on Nesh's shoulder. 'Arper isn't coming either, Nesh. It's safer if just two of us go. We'll travel faster that way.'

Nesh sounded crestfallen. 'But, wha' if somethin' 'appens ta ya? What'll we do then?'

Ciro lifted Nesh's chin and smiled. 'I have no intention of being caught, Nesh: I'm just going to lead the enemy away.'

'We'll loose 'em easily on The Downs,' explained Tenc. 'Then we'll meet you back at Philire in a couple o' days.'

'Ciro's right, girl,' agreed Arper. He put his hands upon Nesh's shoulders. 'It's best we stay with this lot,' he hitched a thumb at Tamarail, ''til Ciro an' Tenc get back.'

'And then we move on to Peimonac,' said Ciro. 'Alright?'

Nesh nodded reluctantly then turned away to stand by the larboard rail. Ciro watched her back for a moment, saw her shoulders slump. He sighed and drew Arper to one side.

'I don't intend to get caught by the Bonemen,' said the king quietly. 'But I want you to look after this until I return.' Ciro took off his star belt and handed it to Arper who, though surprised, instantly stuffed it into his bag.

'Now, if I'm not back in four days,' Ciro continued, 'I need you to go to Peimonac and give that belt to my friend, Calian. Tell him all I've told you about it. Understood?'

Arper nodded and the pair embraced. 'See ya in a couple o' days,' said Arper with a smile.

The rowing boats from the Waterman were now pulling alongside the anchored Gallean and, as they unloaded their grateful cargo, Tamarail, Dent and Borlin approached Ciro.

'Looks like two more trips'll do it,' said the captain as the boats skipped back towards shore. 'Are ya ready?'

Ciro adjusted Amec's sword on his back and checked that the hilt sat above his left shoulder: Tenc was doing the same.

'We need an oil lamp and a tinderbox but, apart from that, we're ready,' he said.

'Why are you doing this?' Tamarail asked with a frown. 'If they've got horses you'll stand no chance on The Downs.'

Ciro smiled. 'Though it may seem strange to you, I am responsible for these people.' The king pointed to the refugees along the deck and then at the captain. 'Even you, Tamarail, whether you agree with it or not, whether you like it or not, are my responsibility and therefore come under my protection.'

Tamarail laughed. 'You may win over those poor fools,' he said, indicating the refugees, 'but you'll get no thanks from me. The Philiri have lived without a king's protection for generations.'

Ciro shrugged. 'I'm not doing this for your thanks, Tamarail. I'm simply attempting to protect Rialan lives as best I can. As king it's my duty.'

'Well, yer 'ighness,' sneered Dent. ''ere's yer lamp an' tinderbox.' He handed them both to Ciro who thanked him and placed them in his bag.

The final passengers where brought on board and Ciro and Tenc made their way along deck to where the rowing boats had been secured against the side. Tamarail had already ordered his crew to unfurl the sails and, as the Gallean raised anchor and slowly turned to face upstream, the pair made their final goodbye's.

'We'll come lookin' for ya if ya don't turn up,' Arper said but to this Ciro shook his head.

'We'll be there, don't worry,' Tenc replied with a wave.

'Good... Luck,' Nesh managed to say tearfully. In response Ciro gave her a reassuring hug.

Borlin had also joined them and frowned at Ciro's uniform. 'Do ya think it wise ta wear that?' he asked. 'You'll stick out like a sore thumb on the downs.'

Ciro smiled. 'I'm counting on it,' he replied.

'May Milla shine on ya both,' Borlin said and with that the pair clambered over the side and down into the rowing boat.

There were waves and sad goodbye's from the Gallean as Tenc turned the oars and allowed the current to separate the boats. Ciro smiled and waved back as they gradually slipped away into the evening gloom. He couldn't explain it, but he felt happy as he saw the Gallean disappear into the twilight. He smiled at Tenc.

'Thank you, Tenc,' he said.

The Philiri frowned as he pulled on the oars and moved them swiftly towards the south bank. 'Thank me? Why?'

Ciro shrugged. 'You didn't have to do this…I appreciate it.'

Tenc gave a lop-sided grin. 'You wouldn't last long on the downs without me,' he replied. 'An', like you, I wanna do what I can to help those people.'

They continued on in silence, striking the bank close to the hulk of the Waterman then moved off swiftly towards a wooded hill set back a half mile from the river. The light was fading fast by the time they reached its shallow summit and the pair quickly built the fire which Ciro hoped would prove irresistible to the pursuing Makech.

It was the same plan that Ciro had been considering for their final destination. Light fires to draw the Makech south into The Downs while the main party moved east as rapidly as they could. Though the fate of the Waterman had pre-empted the plan by at least two days, Ciro felt more confident that the added attraction of the wreck would make the Makech stop miles short of their real quarry. He was also greatly relieved that Arper and Nesh were safe and that as few people as possible were involved in what could potentially be a very dangerous exercise. Despite Tenc's assurances, he still felt guilty for having to involve him, but Ciro tempered that unease with the fact that, without him, he would be as lost on the downs as the Makech he hoped to lure. His detailed knowledge of King Elson's old Rialan map made him confident he could find the old city of Monides, but only a Philiri could help him find the hidden city of Philire.

Once the fire was piled high and blazing, the pair moved away to the boundary of its light and waited. Resting against the bole of a tree they listened through the gentle swish of the leaves in the wind for the slightest noise from the river. The night had descended clear and bright and Ciro watched through the swaying canopy of the trees as the sky grew black. Stars began to shine brilliantly overhead.

'It's a wonderful sight,' he said, leaning back and gazing up.

'Mm,' muttered Tenc.

The Philiri seemed uncomfortable and Ciro asked whether he was nervous about the arrival of the Makech.

'It's not that,' Tenc replied with a shake of his head. He looked pointedly into the darkness beyond the firelight. 'It's just that this fire may well bring others. Not just the Bonemen.'

'Firehearts?' asked Ciro.

'Omerk,' Tenc replied. 'I've been away for so long I'd almost forgotten: you don't light fires out here unless you're looking for trouble.'

Ciro had read about the white skinned, wide-eyed Omerk but, in Elson's day, they had seldom been spotted below the foothills of the South Jaw Mountains. Only in the tales of Master Merchants did the Omerk seem to travel The South Downs. He remembered the letter he had read on the Gallean which Prince Meanon had (apparently) written from Taisin. The prince had mentioned hordes of the beasts.

'I thought they didn't like fires?' Ciro asked.

Tenc shrugged. 'They don't. That's the problem. If they see one they'll come to investigate.'

'Perhaps that might work to our advantage,' Ciro said with a smile. 'Maybe the Omerk will fight the Makech for us.'

Tenc returned a grin and was about to speak when a 'snap' sounded close to the fire. Slowly the pair rose. They drew their swords as quietly as they could and crept deeper into the shadows: attempting to see beyond the blazing fire.

'Ciro?'

The voice was instantly familiar and, as the king and Tenc drew nearer to the fire, they were shocked to see the shivering form of Nesh standing beside it. Her hair was dripping and plastered to her face and her nettle green dress was soaking wet. In her hands she clutched her precious box of shells.

'Nesh! What happened?' Ciro asked as he moved towards her. 'Are you alright? Where's Arper?'

Nesh looked sheepishly back towards the river for a moment and then, when she turned and held his gaze, Ciro saw an expression in her eyes which shocked him even more than her sudden appearance.

Since the age of eleven, Ciro had spent most of his life studying about Reilan: dreaming and planning how to follow in Prince Tenlern's footsteps and mount an expedition to the kingdom which so fired his imagination. As such, he had never been particularly aware of, or indeed interested in what his brother Bdann often referred to as 'affairs of the heart'. It was something Ciro considered (on the rare occasions he had considered it) the exclusive preserve of people with nothing better to do with their time. And that applied specifically to Bdann.

There had however been one person who had drawn his attention during his last years at Torr Sarvie and it had

433

concerned him so much that he had brought the matter to his younger sister, Princess Penyatt. Why, Ciro had inquired, was Penyatt's best friend, the young Lady Cassily, acting so strangely around him? The answer, it had transpired, was that she was in love with him and now, when he gazed into Nesh's tear-filled eyes, he saw the same indefinable yet unmistakable expression which Lady Cassily had favoured him with so often.

Shocked, Ciro managed a smile and returned his sword to its scabbard. 'You jumped overboard, didn't you,' he said, attempting to make the comment seem matter-of-fact. 'Nesh, you could have drowned.'

Nesh nodded. 'I... I was worried... Worried about...' she began before tears choked her voice.

Ciro bit his lip and moved forward, wrapping his arms around her while she sobbed and clung onto him tightly. 'It's all right, Nesh,' he said softly. 'It's good to see you.'

After a short time, Ciro dried Nesh's eyes with his scarf and sat her beside the fire to dry out. 'Arper will be worried to death about you,' he said, crouching down beside her.

Nesh sniffed acknowledgement then smiled up at him. 'I told 'im what I was doin' jus' before I jumped,' she said. 'Arper knows I'll be safe. You'll protect me.'

Ciro smiled back. 'Yes,' he replied, the smile broadening to grin. 'I suppose I'll do that much.'

Tenc had kept a discreet distance during this time with his gaze set on the vague reflection of the stars in the river. Now he was hissing Ciro's name with some urgency.

Ciro turned to see Tenc back slowly towards the fire, his eyes locked on something beyond the illumination of the blaze. Ciro, drawing his sword, moved beside him then frowned as another young girl walked up the slope and into the light.

She was a little younger than Nesh, but similarly bare footed and clothed in the same type of simple dress. She smiled broadly as she breasted the rise and Ciro wondered if some of the Waterman's passengers had wandered away from the river and been left behind.

Tenc frowned at the girl. 'I know you,' he said.

The girl stopped and looked around the fire-lit clearing, nodding to herself before her gaze settled on Ciro. Her smile became a sneer.

'Ever the King of Fool's, eh, Ciro?' she said.

'Who –' Ciro began but Tenc was already answering his question.

'Elbeth?' said the Philiri. 'You're Elbeth, aren't you? Mara's niece: from Urawiir.'

The girl frowned back, looking at Tenc as if for the first time until familiarity seemed to show on her face. 'Tenc...' she whispered. A look of fear swept momentarily across her features but instantly the sneer returned. 'Are you a Philiri, Tenc?' she asked. 'I always wanted to meet a Philiri.'

Tenc had moved a pace forward but now Ciro gripped his arm and pulled him back. 'Blood 'n' sand!' he whispered breathlessly. 'Tenc, look at her feet!'

Elbeth, still smiling, continued to walk towards them. As they backed rapidly away, Tenc managed a glance at the girl's feet. They were bare and they were dirty but they made no contact with the ground whatsoever.

'Nesh!' Ciro hissed over his shoulder. 'Get up, we're leaving.'

'Oh, don't leave on my account, Ciro,' Elbeth said as the king and the Philiri retreated. 'You've got such a nice fire going and we've got so much catching up to do. So many stories to exchange – so much pain I want to inflict on you before you die.'

Unnerved by the strangeness of – whatever it was – advancing on them, Ciro turned on his heel to see the fire suddenly flare to twice its height. He dived at Nesh as burning wood and cinders exploded into the air and Tenc gave a cry as a flaming log struck his shoulder. The Philiri rolled on the grass beside Ciro, damping the flames as the king and Nesh scrambled to their feet.

'Nesh, run!' shouted Ciro.

Wide-eyed and propelled by a shove from the king, Nesh grabbed for her shell box and skipped around the burning embers now spread around the clearing. Ciro helped Tenc to his feet then turned to face the girl.

She was no longer there, but a cry from behind him span him round in time to see Nesh thrown to the floor. The grinning girl was now at the back of the clearing.

Disconcerted by the girl's speed, Ciro instantly charged towards her sword first. He was inches away from striking the immobile figure when she let out a very adult laugh and simply disappeared.

'You'll have to do better than that, Torrman!'

Tenc had run to help Nesh to her feet and now Ciro turned to see that the girl was back beside the fire.

'Let's go!' the Philiri shouted. He picked up Ciro's pack and ran past the king with Nesh on one arm.

Ciro could not tear his eyes from the grinning girl, her pale face lit by the dying remnants of their blaze, her eyes bright and staring back with obvious amusement. He felt nervous: uncertain how to deal with the situation. Tenc was urging him to come away but Ciro did not move.

'What are you?' he whispered to the apparition.

'Oh, you'll find out soon enough,' the girl grinned in reply.

Tenc pulled on Ciro's arm – rousing him into motion and

together the three of them fled down the back of the hill. There were horns blaring through the night from the direction of the river now and a man's voice followed their flying feet.

'Don't go too far!' shouted Elbeth after them.

With sword still in hand: his mind a whirl of disjointed thoughts, Ciro ran on with the others as fast as he could into the night.

They sped and tumbled across a wide plain of uneven grassland, cursing their falls and cajoling one another until they encountered a steady rise and had made it to the top. Ciro stopped for a moment, desperate to collect his breath and wits. He looked back to see a tiny patch of light still visible on the hill behind them.

'What in Milla's name was that?!' Ciro panted, uncomfortable with his own sense of nervousness. 'That girl, that 'thing' – her feet didn't touch the ground!'

'It was a spirit,' Tenc replied. 'I'm sure of it.'

'You mean a ghost?' asked Ciro. 'Like with Amec?'

Tenc nodded gravely. 'Like Amec. Do you remember the man we saw on the bridge at Birin? The Beck Iph soldier? Those people serve the Soulcatchers and the Soulcatchers, so the stories go, control the spirits of the dead.' The Philiri shook his head. 'Never thought I'd ever encounter one, but from the stories I've heard…' Tenc's voice trailed off: the king did not seem to be listening.

Though Ciro nodded absently his mind was elsewhere. The talk of Amec had made him feel for his star belt and now he was inwardly cursing himself. Perhaps leaving the belt with Arper had been a bad idea.

'How do we fight this thing, Tenc?' Ciro asked, watching the distant firelight. 'I can fight people; no matter what they call themselves, but how do you fight a ghost?'

'I wish I knew,' Tenc replied. 'All I know is: we run and keep running – try to escape. People don't cross the Soulcatchers and live to tell about it.'

'Aunt Halla didn't,' said Nesh sadly. 'She got caught by a Soulcatcher an' never came back. Uncle Arper never forgive 'imself for it.'

Ciro put a reassuring arm around Nesh's shoulder. 'That's not going to happen to us, Nesh. We'll do what Tenc says: keep running.'

A thought occurred to the king which made him feel a little more hopeful and, as they took one final look at the hill camp they had left behind and continued their flight, Ciro shared his thoughts with the others.

'Maybe that ghost can't go very far from whoever controls it,' Ciro said as they trotted down the far side of the hill. 'Otherwise it would simply have followed us here, wouldn't it?'

'I wish I knew, Ciro,' Tenc replied as he jogged beside him. 'I hope you're right.'

They ran on into the darkness; the land an endless sea of rolling, star lit grass which spread in gentle waves of grey and black before them. Even though there was no evidence of pursuit, they kept to the sporadic tree lines and darker troughs of the downs when possible and headed east as best they could. Tenc assured them they were making steady progress and it would only be a matter of days before they sighted the great hill range at the edge of the downs. There, the ruined city of Monides and safety awaited them.

On and on, mile after rolling mile they ran, until the fear which fuelled their flight gave way to exhaustion and their bodies felt like burning lead. They found welcome shelter in a damp hollow beneath a large outcrop of rock and, while Nesh and Tenc instantly dozed off, Ciro found his fear still strong enough to hold off sleep. He kept watch and tried to make sense of their predicament.

He had expected to draw the attention of the Makech but now the situation seemed out of his control. But above all other concerns he wanted to know how the girl had known him. Like the Beck Iph soldier on the bridge she had recognised him and called him by name. He knew that she could not have known him in life but, as Tenc said, she was controlled by a Soulcatcher and therefore, Ciro theorised, was perhaps an extension of the person in control. So just who was it that was pursuing him and how did he know him by name? By sight?! He tried not to dwell on what such information might mean for what awaited him at Peimonac.

The gloomy thoughts, like the patches of cloud passing slowly overhead, came on in an endless grey procession until tiredness finally claimed his full attention. Wishing Amec was here to help, Ciro fell asleep.

The next day continued as the previous one had ended and the group ran on under a drab and drizzling sky. Ciro was surprised to find that his body ached, his injured side nagging with each stride as the dull morning turned to midday. He called a welcome halt on the lower slopes of a steep and wood lined hill but, conscious of the vantage point the hill would provide, they slowly zigzagged to its summit until they found a clearing. Here Ciro could see the countryside they had traversed since the previous evening and the three of them rested while taking in the rolling plains of grass. They had heard nothing of the Makech since the horns had sounded the previous evening nor had any spirits bothered them since leaving the fire. Now Ciro scanned the gloomy landscape for any signs of pursuit.

'I'm going to check the south side,' Tenc said after watching the downs with Ciro for a while. 'If I can see the Great West

Road we should be that much closer to reaching Monides.'

Ciro smiled and pointed to Nesh. She was crouched at the base of a tree, grimacing while she massaged her feet. 'Tell Nesh that,' he said. 'It looks like she could do with cheering up.'

Tenc smiled, gave Nesh some encouraging words as he passed then left the clearing. Nesh smiled back with some difficulty then got to her feet and hobbled over to Ciro.

'Ya won't be angry with me, will yer?' she asked sheepishly. The king shook his head and Nesh pointed to one of her feet. 'It's cut,' she explained. 'Don't know 'ow I did it or where but it's been 'urtin' for a while now. Sorry,' she added.

Ciro, with obvious concern, got Nesh to sit down while he examined the sole of her right foot. There was a large, irregular gash by the toes and Nesh winced as he made sure the cut was as clean as he could make it.

'I must've run over a stone,' said Nesh glumly.

'You'll live,' replied Ciro with a smile.

He stood up and searched in his pack, tore the arms off of his only spare shirt and proceeded to bind both of Nesh's feet with the cloth.

'The sooner we get you a pair of shoes made, the better,' Ciro said with a grin. 'Until then, these will have to do.'

Nesh smiled back, stood up and took a few tentative steps. 'It still 'urts a bit,' she admitted. 'But it's a lot better. Thanks,' she said and kissed Ciro on the cheek.

Tenc came running back into the clearing. 'I've found something!' he said anxiously and hitched his thumb over his shoulder. 'Come and look!'

The Philiri's agitation made Ciro instantly draw his sword. 'What is it?' he asked.

Tenc shrugged. 'I dunno, but...' He walked closer to Ciro

and pointed to his neck. '...It's got the same markings on it as your scarf has,' he said.

Intrigued, Ciro took a last look at the grey downs behind them then went to follow the Philiri through the trees. He stopped and turned to Nesh.

'Could you keep watch for a few minutes, Nesh?' he asked. 'If you see anything, run and tell us.'

Nesh agreed and Ciro walked with Tenc through the wood until they came to the southern slope of the hill. There was a wide hollow in the ground flanked by trees and deeply lined with dead leaves.

'It scared the life out of me when I first saw it,' Tenc explained as they crossed the hollow. 'But it's definitely dead.' He stopped for a moment and looked around, then pointed to a hawthorn bush at the southern-most edge of the hollow. 'There,' he said.

Ciro stopped for a moment and attempted to fathom what on earth he was looking at. He moved a few steps closer then crouched down, studying the thing which sat, half submerged beneath the earth under the thorn bush.

In overall shape it seemed like some crude parody of a man – yet lumpen, clumsy and much, much larger. It also appeared to be made entirely from metal. The head was a cylinder, its eyes glass-filled holes and its mouth a fearsome snarl of jagged, twisted iron. The arms, one of which disappeared, like the unseen legs, beneath the soil, were rusting bars set in bulky joints while the hand displayed a set of tarnished knives instead of fingers. For all its intended ferocity however – for Ciro could see no other function for the strange object – there was something sad about the forlorn posture and its empty eyes. Intrigued, Ciro moved nearer to get a better look.

'See there?' Tenc said, pointing to the metal head. 'There's that symbol.'

Ciro frowned and brushed at the dirt which covered the lettering the Philiri indicated: quickly revealing two intertwined 't's'. The King removed his scarf and held it up beside the symbol.

'Tenlern Torrman,' he said with a sigh. 'You were right, Tenc. That's Prince Tenlern's insignia.'

'Who was he?' asked the Philiri.

There were other, smaller letters around the symbol and Ciro rubbed at the accumulated grime. 'An explorer,' he said over his shoulder. 'A pioneer who was lost to our people more than two hundred years ago.'

'He came here?'

Ciro nodded. 'But what this… statue is, or what it means about his fate I just don't know.'

The letters Ciro had now revealed where the old, undeciphered script he had seen sketches of from the Ascension Chamber library. They were the same type which the scholars of King Elson's time had reported finding in the Sun Chamber at Peimonac and on countless other ancient relics dotted around the old kingdom. How they had come to sit side-by-side with Prince Tenlern's insignia was a mystery.

Frowning, Ciro began pulling away the leaves and moss piled over the chest in the vain hope more clues would be forthcoming. But his efforts simply revealed the rusty grill of what he took to be a type of fire grate.

'Oh, Beck!' exclaimed Tenc, suddenly back-pedalling away from the thing. 'Ciro, move away from it!' he hissed.

Perplexed, Ciro looked back at the wide-eyed Philiri. 'What's the matter?' he asked.

'I think I know what it is,' Tenc replied. He backed away still further. 'That grate on its chest… I think it's a Fireheart.'

While Tenc made the sign of the Eight, Ciro returned his attention to the metal figure. Its shape and composition seemed to match the description Borlin had given him, but how a man could possibly fit inside such armour was beyond Ciro's comprehension. He looked back at Tenc.

'If it is a Fireheart,' Ciro said with a grin, 'its fire certainly seems to have gone out.'

Tenc did not seem reassured. 'I don't like it,' he said, shaking his head nervously. 'It's not right. I've heard terrible stories about those things.'

'But have you ever heard of anyone getting this close to them before?' Ciro asked.

'Only the dead ones,' Tenc replied grimly. 'That hand looks like it could inflict the sort o' wounds the Elders speak of. But there've been lots of sightings at a distance – their fiery chests and eyes burnin' in the night. The sounds of them walking around and moaning in the darkness.'

Ciro studied the armour. There was no way a person could ever walk with such armour on but there was certainly enough space behind the grate to light a fire. And, he reasoned, examining the 'face', the glass eyes would probably shine like lanterns in the darkness. He was reminded of the steam engines which powered his ships and that train of thought led him back to the insignia on the thing's forehead. Ciro's vessels were based on the old designs which Prince Tenlern had commissioned several centuries ago. Was this 'Fireheart' proof that Tenlern and his people had survived? Was this some form of metal scarecrow: devised to deter the superstitious and fainthearted from this part of the kingdom? Ciro's thoughts were brought back to the present by Nesh's voice, shouting his name through the forest.

They left the Fireheart and ran quickly back to the clearing on the north side of the hill. Nesh was waiting anxiously for them.

'I think they're comin'!' she yelled breathlessly, jabbing an arm at the rolling downs below. Both Ciro and Tenc scanned the landscape but could see nothing. 'I def'nitely saw somethin'!' Nesh persisted.

Ciro nodded. 'I don't doubt it for a moment, Nesh. It was time we were moving on anyway.'

They were collecting their packs when Ciro remembered the reason that Tenc had gone to the south side of the hill.

'Did you manage to spot the Great West Road?' he asked.

The Philiri nodded. 'I think so. We're still a few miles away, but it'll point us straight at Monides. With luck we could be there by this time tomorrow.'

'Good, then let's get moving.' Ciro picked up his pack and smiled at Nesh: pointing to her cloth-wrapped feet. 'Ready for some running?' he asked.

Nesh ran on the spot for a moment and grinned. 'Yep,' she said.

They moved out of the clearing and, avoiding the Fireheart hollow, quickly descended the southern slopes of the hill and continued their flight across The Downs. Instead of the frantic pace they had previously assumed, Ciro tried to keep moving at a steady jog: hoping that, at this rate, their stamina might get them close to the Monides plateau by nightfall. He was also concerned that Nesh's injured foot might not last a more vigorous pace.

For an hour they kept up the same, steady trot and continued to hug the dips for cover. Then a familiar, dull rumble sounded faintly in the air behind them. Alarmed, Ciro had no option but to pick up their pace. The Makech had brought horses.

The group was halfway across a gently dipping plain of grassland when they again heard the sound of hooves. From their position it was impossible to see beyond the rising edges of the depression but Ciro looked back nervously to make sure they had not been spotted. The rise behind them was clear, but the sound was still present. They ran on as hard as they could towards a thicket of bushes and saplings on the far edge of the plain while the sound grew louder. It was only when they had made it to the relative safety of the trees that Ciro paused to take another look behind them.

Back across the plain, three horses appeared on the brow of the previous rise. At this distance it was impossible to make out the riders distinctly, yet Ciro had little doubt that they were Makech. The riders spurred their horses on and began moving rapidly in their direction.

'Beck,' cursed Ciro and ran on into the trees.

Weaving past the border saplings into deeper cover, the three moved as quickly as their legs could carry them. Spurred on by the nearing thunder of hooves on the plain, all sense of fatigue was now replaced by fear. As he ran, Ciro admonished himself for allowing their pursuers to find them so easily. What had he done wrong? He had a half thought that perhaps they should only have travelled at night but dismissed the idea instantly for more immediate considerations. They were not about to outrun three horses.

The ground began to rise slowly as they sped through the trees and now the sound of thrashing plant life could be heard as the riders attempted to drive their mounts into the tangled undergrowth of the wood. Ciro was almost tempted to turn and fight amongst the confines of the trees as they reached the brow of the rise, but a glint of blue through the tree line ahead gave him hope. He shouted to the others as they cleared the trees and grinned at the sight of the broad river which bisected the grassland a short distance ahead of them.

'We'll swim across!' he yelled. 'Even if those bastards can do the same they'll be vulnerable! Keep going!'

They ran on to cover the few hundred yards which separated the wood from the river and broke from the confines of the trees. The river's current looked swift but it was the least of their worries and the sounds of slashing vegetation and the cries of the Makech behind continued to spur on their efforts. It would be a close run thing, thought Ciro, but he felt certain the river would provide a tactical advantage. Even with their horses, the armoured Makech would have the same problems with water as the guard in Kal Gians harbour had. Ciro would make sure of it.

They were less than one hundred yards from the water when Nesh's stride became ragged. She was still moving at some speed, but now her injured foot was causing her to limp heavily. Terrified she might stumble; Ciro grabbed Nesh by the arm to support her. It kept her upright, but his sudden grip loosened the box of shells which she had been cradling tightly at her midriff. They toppled from her grasp as she bounded on and fell into the grass behind her. With a cry, Nesh lunged out to grab them: stumbled and sprawled headlong onto the grass.

Cursing, Ciro tried to pull Nesh back to her feet while she lashed out to retrieve her shell box. The ground was now shaking: the sound of hooves, clink of armour and unintelligible shouts far louder than before. Ciro looked back to see that three horsemen were now a matter of yards behind them. He yanked Nesh to her feet, shoved her with all his might towards the river, then drew his sword and ran at the central horseman.

In the second it took Ciro to lunge at the horse, slash its foreleg and fell it, he was able to take in the disturbing appearance of the rider. Instead of the familiar Makech armour, this figure was dressed in a coat of shining, linked scale mail. He wore an intimidating mask of red whose frozen grimace leered down at the king as he moved across the horse's path, but the spear which the rider levelled just before Ciro slashed and rolled out of danger appeared to have no tip.

Ciro got quickly to his feet and turned to witness Nesh's limping flight being ended by another of the horsemen. He had moved instantly in her direction the second he saw the threat, but was only able to watch helplessly as her galloping pursuer drove his spear into her back. Nesh's frail frame was slammed to the floor.

Screaming, Ciro raced past the thrashing horse he had brought down, and its rider who was unsteadily attempting to rise. The man was well armoured but, without breaking stride, Ciro simply hacked at the pale line of neck which was exposed between his chain mail and his mask. A second later he himself was thrown to the floor by a stunning blow to his shoulder.

Fighting the pain in his left arm, Ciro staggered back to his feet, grabbed his sword and ran on. The third rider, having knocked him to the ground with the butt of his spear, was now dismounting a little way to his right but the king had no other thought than of reaching Nesh. Now the unmasked rider who had felled Nesh leapt from his saddle to face him.

'Well, well,' said the Makech in Rialan as Ciro approached. 'Fancy meeting you here?' He threw his spear to one side, grinned and drew his sword as Ciro lunged at him.

Ciro's initial thrusts met with no success, his opponent easily parrying the blows, but it did allow the king an opportunity to force the Makech back. He grabbed a glance at the prostrate figure of Nesh and heaved a visible sigh. There was no wound on her back. She was unconscious but she was still alive!

The other masked rider, spear in hand, was running to join the fight but Ciro's adversary shouted two words of Makech which made the man hang back. It was then that Ciro recognised the face of the man before him.

'You fight very well,' said Tanikalin conversationally as Ciro continued to drive him backwards.

Ciro said nothing, but the man's obvious skill with a blade and his patronising comment stung him into adjusting his attack. The Makech was reading his thrusts and deflecting them but at no time had he attempted to strike back. This purely defensive approach, coupled with evident ability, gave Ciro no chance to off-balance his opponent so, instead of continually stabbing, jabbing and probing, Ciro suddenly stopped his intended thrust, side-stepped and swung his sword as hard as he could at the Makech's head.

Tanikalin read the move a fraction too late but managed to escape the blow by leaping quickly to one side. Now off-balance, he deflected the second strike when Ciro pressed home his advantage but could not stop the king's glancing third stroke. The tip of Ciro's blade sliced a searing line into the left side of his neck. Alarmed with the realisation that this king was not such a fool with his sword, Tanikalin backed away as rapidly as he could – lost his footing on the uneven ground – and fell backwards.

Instantly the masked Beck Iph guard was charging forwards, pointing the butt of his spear at Ciro's face as the king attempted to finish off the prostrate Tanikalin. Ciro twisted left as the shaft flashed inches from his face and swept his sword in an arc to strike the running man's midriff.

The blow did little except dent the chain mail of his opponent but its ferocity winded the Makech. With his mind racing, Ciro seized the opportunity, twisted and span round to strike at the back of his opponent's neck.

'CIRO!'

In a blur Ciro saw Nesh rise from the ground. The blade hit

the masked man's armoured shoulder. Nesh was running towards him. There came a sharp blow to Ciro's legs, followed a fraction of a second later by a ringing thump to the back of his head. Then he was down: the two Makech raining savage punches and kicks until consciousness deserted him.

Ciro woke to the nagging sensation that something was not quite right. His left eye felt like it had acquired its own heartbeat and there were dull, numb patches of his body which suddenly flared with pain when he tried to shift his position. He also appeared to be kneeling, his arms taut and strapped to his sides.

It took a few moments for his mind to reacquaint him with what had happened but slowly, as he returned to consciousness, he became aware that there was something more painful occurring elsewhere.

Nesh was screaming.

Ciro opened his eyes to find that only his right one would obey but it was enough for him to see that they were back at the edge of the tree line. He could not remember what had happened to Tenc but Nesh, suspended by her arms from a branch, was bleeding in several places and pleading for her life.

'LEAVE HER ALONE!!' Ciro bellowed. He tried to rise but his ankles were bound to his wrists and the action merely toppled him over.

'Oh! You're awake!' said Tanikalin merrily. He left the Beck Iph guard with Nesh and ran over to where Ciro was attempting to crawl towards her. He grinned down at the king then kicked him as hard as he could in the stomach.

'We're to bring you back alive, you see,' Tanikalin said conversationally as Ciro writhed in pain and gasped for breath. 'I don't think his reverence will mind if you're a little dented though.'

'Leave… The girl… Alone,' Ciro managed to say between gasps.

Tanikalin laughed. "Panison ui olla lerir," oir emeira!' he cried to the other Makech. The masked Beck Iph laughed back and shook his head.

'No, I don't think we'll do that, King Ciro,' continued Tanikalin. He grabbed Ciro's shoulders, pulled him upright then waved at the Beck Iph guard.

Nesh, her dress and legs stained red with blood thrashed weakly as the Beck Iph drew his sword. Ciro, his eyes filled with tears, was screaming and attempting to rise but both his bonds and Tanikalin held him firm. He watched, unable to tear his eyes away as the red-masked man thrust his sword into Nesh's chest. With her final breath she screamed Ciro's name then her head dropped and she was still.

'There!' announced Tanikalin above Ciro's wail of despair. 'That didn't hurt did it?' he grinned as he watched the girl's body swing lifelessly from the branch then glanced down at the sobbing king. He frowned.

'Oh, be quiet,' Tanikalin muttered and rendered Ciro unconscious with a swift kick to his head.

Kattis Capell had never seen his friend Baramir leap up and down before but, when Commander Tanikalin returned with their King tied to the saddle of a horse, he did just that. To Kattis it was just another addition to a whole collection of strange, disconcerting and frankly miserable episodes which had culminated in them being here: on an isolated hilltop in the middle of nowhere.

Now grinning broadly, Baramir skipped to Tanikalin as he dismounted. He clapped his hands with glee as the commander hauled the unconscious Ciro from his horse and dropped him onto the grass.

Baramir peered at the king and, in an instant his joy was lost. 'He's not dead, is he?' he asked suspiciously.

Tanikalin shook his head and smiled as he dismounted. 'No, your reverence, just a little battered.'

Newman's grin returned to his face. 'You've done very well, commander!' he announced. Then the shadow of a frown crept back.

He looked for the third Beck Iph guard: found him slumped dead behind the saddle of the second then narrowed his eyes as he took in the bloody bandage on Tanikalin's neck. Baramir nodded to himself and the smile returned.

'You've done very well, commander,' he repeated and patted Tanikalin on the shoulder.

They dragged Ciro to a tree, lashed him upright to its trunk then Baramir ordered the remaining Beck Iph guard to ride back and get the main party which was camped a few hours away on The Downs.

'Would it not be better, your reverence,' suggested the Beck Iph as he climbed into the saddle. 'If we all returned to the safety of Gidus's camp?'

'No it Beckin' wouldn't!' snapped Baramir. 'Unlike you cowardly bunch, this place beyond the barrier holds no terrors for me.' Newman wagged a finger at the masked guard. 'You tell Gidus that if he wants to see the king before he dies, he can drag his bony arse here!'

With a nod the rider left the clearing and Baramir returned to gloat over his prize. Kattis had hung back this whole time but now Newman called him over.

'Come and look, Capell!' he cried. 'Can you believe it?! King Ciro Torrman no less!'

While Capell moved reluctantly closer, Newman snapped

his fingers at Tanikalin. 'Well, don't just stand there, Commander. Wake him up!'

Tanikalin gave Ciro a hard slap across the face and, just as violently, the king came back to life.

Ciro strained frantically against his bonds for a moment and looked wildly around the clearing. Was he dreaming? Hadn't he left this place hours ago? The harsh memories flooded back a second later and he ceased to struggle, focusing his good eye on the thin, leering figure standing a few feet before him.

'Remember me?!' said Baramir with glee.

Ciro looked closely at the man. He did not know him, yet there was something undeniably familiar about both his voice and his rictus expression. He glanced past Baramir's shoulder to catch the eye of a portly, sallow-faced man who instantly dropped his gaze. Then the recollection of the King Elson during the storm returned to him.

'You were stealing supplies on deck,' said Ciro dully. He nodded his head to Newman and then indicated Capell. 'You, and that man there.'

'Ha!' cried Baramir. 'He remembers us!' Newman bobbed his head. 'Allow me to introduce myself. My name is Baramir Newman – but you can call me 'Your Reverence' – and this is Commander Tanikalin of the Beck Iph.'

'Then that gentleman there must be Kattis Capell,' added Ciro.

Baramir frowned. 'How would you know that?'

The king closed his good eye. There was a sharp pain every time he took a breath and the taste of blood was in his mouth. He collected his thoughts.

'If I remember the report correctly,' he said. "Capell and Newman – first names Kattis and Baramir – wanted for the murders of a Watchman and a coachman in Rurset and various charges of robbery and theft. Armed and dangerous, their whereabouts are instantly to be reported." Ciro managed a lumpen-faced smile. 'Yes, I know all about you two,' he nodded to Tanikalin. 'No wonder these Makech scum found you so useful.'

'That's enough!' bellowed Baramir. He clenched his fist and shook its bony mass in the king's face. 'I'm not that petty criminal who sailed out of Obaln harbour hiding in the hold. Now I'm a bloo'sandin' Soulcatcher!' Baramir jutted his head forward and tapped the celesdain band on his forehead. 'A bloosandin' god! D'ya hear me?!'

Ciro looked at the metal strap around Baramir's forehead and noted its faint glow: brightening in unison with the criminal's anger. The band seemed to have burnt the skin badly. Two stripes of livid red and broken veins edged its path around his head.

'Soulcatcher,' Ciro said quietly. 'I've heard of them too… My, Baramir,' he muttered, 'what a long way you've come. From a carrion bird preying on the misfortunes of others to one which feeds on their corpses. The same bird, just a deeper shade of black.' The King managed a pained laugh. 'Baramir Newman: God of the crows!'

Baramir sneered and stepped back. 'Tanikalin, shut him up.'

Instantly the commander slammed his fist into Ciro's midriff and broke another rib. Newman looked on for a moment then, after watching a few more blows strike the writhing king, he caught Tanikalin's wrist in mid-flight. He shook his head.

'No,' Baramir said with a deep sigh. 'We'll wait for Gidus. Then we'll kill him.' He stepped closer to Ciro, grabbed him by the hair and forced his head back. 'Did you hear that, your Majesty?!' he shouted. 'I'm going to kill you, tear your mind and soul from your body and then destroy every Rialan on the face of the earth!'

Baramir released his grip and Ciro's head fell forwards onto his chest. He stepped away, brushed his hands on his robe and then looked to the sky where the first rain drops were beginning to fall. It was dusk now and Newman frowned at the dark northern horizon.

'We'd best find some shelter and light a fire,' Tanikalin suggested as the rain began a steady patter all around them.

Baramir nodded and together they ran into the cover of the trees to the east of the clearing. Unnoticed, Kattis remained standing by the king.

Capell wasn't sure why, but the sight of the king bound and beaten before him made him feel more miserable than ever. This was the prize which Baramir had longed for but, only now, was Kattis sure that it was not what he wanted. I'm as bound and as bullied as our king, thought Kattis, to a man who I no longer know or trust – just fear. He felt a rising urge to release the king from his bonds, seek salvation from Baramir and the Makech with the only act of mercy he could remember ever contemplating. He sighed. He doubted the king would be any more of a match for Baramir and Tanikalin unbound than he had been before. The man looked barely alive, so attempting to escape with him would simply get them both killed.

By Ciro's feet lay his golden sun broach and Kattis moved forwards and picked it up. The king looked up slowly as Capell pinned the brooch back onto his jacket but Kattis dropped his gaze and turned away.

'I'm very sorry, your majesty,' he muttered and left Ciro to the worsening storm.

The rain, for all its relentless pouring, gave Ciro some small measure of comfort. It was enough that it had driven his captors away but the cool, tapping drops also seemed to wash away a little of the pain he felt. The left side of his face was as numb as his bound hands, his jaw ached when he moved it and his ribs complained sharply when he attempted to take anything more than a shallow breath. Despite this he concentrated on the greater pain: of Nesh, poor Nesh who he was supposed to protect, hanging lifeless and bleeding from a tree. What, he considered bitterly, could he have done to keep her safe?

Ciro tried to consider the situation abstractly – like an end-game on the Soldiers board. One side had comprised two foot soldiers and a king, the other, a full army relentlessly driving the weaker force into the corner of the board. And now here he was, the last piece, the king: cornered. Ciro blinked as a raindrop struck him squarely in the eye and managed a pained sigh. No, he thought, not cornered, captured. A captured king: end of the game. Only it was not a game; the board could not be reset. Nesh's life could not be miraculously returned.

He bit his lip to stifle a cry as his ribs flared again and tried to keep his breathing light. He had no doubt that the murderous Baramir would kill him before the night was out but was his threat to capture his soul true? There seemed so little logic in this land that Ciro had to assume it was, but what would it mean to his brother, Bdann and his friends in Peimonac? Would his thoughts, his memories betray them? Would his spirit walk for Baramir's benefit like the ghost of the girl they had encountered by the river? As Ciro gravely pondered these questions the rain grew steadily heavier. The sky was now a black and starless pall, growling and rumbling with thunder as the wind rose and the storm closed in around the hilltop.

It took a little while but, after much bleak contemplation, Ciro reached a resolution which to him seemed his only

455

logical course of action. He would escape: or at least die trying. Die or get away so that Baramir would not gain the prize he seemed to value so highly.

Ciro was well aware that, in his current physical state, escaping back onto the downs would only result in his recapture but, he considered, if he could get free of his bonds at least he would have the chance to die fighting. Ciro tested the ropes and realised that even such a terminal prospect was a distant hope. Even fit and uninjured he doubted he could force his way free. The image of Nesh screaming for him in her final moments flashed like a blade through his thoughts. He gritted his teeth, ignored the ocean of pain which welled up within him and thrashed and struggled against his confinement for all he was worth. The exertion on his battered frame proved too much and Ciro promptly passed out.

Before him stood a slender mountain peak, one of four which spired up into a misty blue sky. Ciro shivered and turned on the spot: trying to get his bearings and remember why he was here. He caught sight of his wet sleeves and with a frown held them out before him. The thin clouds above were patchy yet he was soaking wet! Perhaps the cloud bank which sat between him and the land beneath him was the reason? Still attempting to recall how he had come to be half way up a mountain, Ciro turned his attention to his hands. They were bleeding: cut and bruised all the way to his sopping wrists. Confused, Ciro turned back to face the rock spire ahead and realised slowly that music was spilling from a dark opening a little way further up. He smiled – though the action hurt his jaw – he recognised the music. It was a Songsmith tune!

Ciro tried to call for Calian, but his jaw hurt even more. He shook his head, his thoughts woollen; took a step then gripped his side and sucked in his breath. His ribs did not seem to like him moving quite so quickly. Ciro paused, waited for the pain to subside, and then shuffled his way up a rough path until he reached the cave.

Louder now, the music seemed to wind like tendrils from its depths and Ciro felt the stirring harmony pass right through him. Why would the Songsmiths chose such an unusual place for their performance? He mused. Using the cave wall for balance Ciro crept forwards, stepping carefully through the darkness until a curve in the tunnel revealed a brilliant light beyond.

The illumination came not from any fire source but from the thousands of words which had been written upon every surface of the cave. Ciro watched, dumbfounded as particular lines of text glowed brighter then faded and slowly he realised that the words were flaring in perfect time with the music. Moving closer, Ciro saw that the unfamiliar words continued on deeper into the mountain, but their light was such that the extent of the cave was obscured by the glare. Then a shadow moved amongst the brightness and a figure stepped out of the light.

If the pain had allowed it, Ciro would have dropped his jaw but, as it was he had to content himself with being mentally open-mouthed. The man, though dressed in very different clothes, was the spitting image of himself.

'Did Areil send you?' the man asked, seemingly unsurprised by Ciro's presence.

Ciro said nothing for a moment, his attention switching to the man's right hand as he stepped closer. Jutting from it were the killing words which Ciro had seen before, the strange line of characters which he had seen fell an entire army. Only now he could see that the letters ran the length of a sword blade and that the characters read 'Setin al keb'.

Ciro looked at the man with his one good eye. 'I'm not

really sure why I'm here,' he mumbled. 'I'm not really sure where here is.'

The man smiled and cast his gaze around the cave. 'We're beyond the realm of Our Lady: beyond Areilan.' He frowned at Ciro. 'You're injured,' he said, moving forward to examine Ciro's battered countenance. 'Have you not sung of healing?'

"Sung of healing?" Thought Ciro. He shook his head. 'I don't know what that means,' he replied

The man lent the sword against the wall of the cave and raised the palm of his hand. There came a rapid succession of words from the man's mouth and Ciro struggled to remain upright as the music of the cave seemed to beat in waves against him.

Pushing against the sound, Ciro felt strength in his legs that had not been there before. He blinked and found his left eye no longer closed and the sharp pain of his chest was just a memory. Ciro patted his ribs then, as he put a hand to his left eye, his fingers touched something on his forehead which should not have been there. He was wearing Elson's star belt.

'Tell Areil I will return the crystals when I have finished here,' the man said. 'Not before.'

Ciro was trying to remember why he should not be wearing the star belt and only half listened to what the man said.

'You should go,' the man was saying. 'But be more careful on the plains this time.'

Ciro nodded dumbly, images of rolling downs filled his head and a girl who collected sea shells.

'Do you know the song of Sakoom?' the man continued. 'It should help you fend off those monsters.'

Ciro shook his head absently. He had given the star belt to Arper. That was it! Arper and Tenc and...? His companion did not seem to notice his divided attention and began to recite lines of verse. Suddenly the king was focused on the song, the belt around his head resonating with the tune.

'Do you know it?' the man asked when he had finished, mistaking Ciro's awe for recognition.

Ciro nodded. He had never heard the words before but he knew the tune off by heart. Calian and the other Songsmiths had made it rain on the arid salt flats outside Obaln with the same tune. Thoughts of rain and storm clouds brought back a vivid memory to the King: of a rain-drenched hilltop at night, with himself bound to a tree. This is wrong, he thought. I shouldn't be here.

'I have to go,' Ciro announced to the man. He pulled the star belt from his forehead and flinched as rain struck him hard in the face.

Ciro toppled forwards into the rainy night, the thunder barely covering his cry as he hit the sodden grass and his ribs flared with pain. He writhed in agony, spat mud and blood from his mouth in equal measure then lay still: breathing as deeply as he dared while willing the pain to subside. The rain played a staccato tune through his thoughts and slowly Ciro opened his one good eye to squint along his outstretched arm. His right hand, lacerated and bloody, gripped the star belt.

With great effort, the king managed to turn himself. He cast his gaze around the rain-swept clearing and frowned when he realised he had not struggled free of his confinement. From the wide loops of rope which now lay discarded beside the tree it was clear that someone had untied his bonds for him.

'Tenc?' Ciro whispered. 'Arper?' He could see no one and heard no reply so he held his breath and forced himself into a crouch, his midriff searing like fire with every movement.

The king shuffled a few steps then lent against the tree which had held him as he caught his breath. The storm had intensified. The rain was now a hard, angled force backed by the steady rumble of thunder and it covered Ciro's painful progress as he inched towards the western edge of the clearing. His mind felt too numb to formulate any coherent plan so he decided to hide in the shadow of the trees while he collected his leaden thoughts.

He forced himself on until the trees formed a thin screen between him and the clearing then propped his back against the trunk of an elm. With trembling hands, Ciro plucked at the grass which had rounded his mouth and slid to the wet ground before his equally trembling legs could give way beneath him. He sighed, exhausted and closed his eyes for a moment. Ignoring as best he could the pain which screamed for his sole attention, Ciro tried to take stock of what had happened.

He remembered the cave and the man with the sword but the pain he felt throughout his body proved that it had been nothing more than a dream. He shook his head in an attempt to clear the woolliness of his thoughts then turned his attention to the dark shape of the star belt in his hand. He had definitely given it to Arper, so how did it come to be here? Ciro toyed with the belt for a moment, thinking hard. He knew of one man who might be able to supply an answer and so, ignoring Amec's previous warnings of danger, Ciro strapped the belt around his forehead.

The trees and the clearing beyond remained in his vision yet now the sight was overlaid with shimmering lines and fleeting shapes. Ciro looked up through the tree canopy to where the clouds rolled and grumbled above. Through the driving rain he could see that the colourful patterns continued: red, blue and white lines twisting and colliding through the grey mass of the clouds while here and there, patches of fire flared and faded in time with the thunder.

With the belt around his temple, the night seemed no barrier to his vision now and Ciro looked towards the tree he had been bound to. He could see the reason for his escape now, and the king managed a smile as he saw Amec walk towards him.

'I suppose I have you to thank for this?' Ciro said as Amec stopped before him and crouched down.

Amec nodded. 'I was told ta bring it ta ya,' he said. 'An' not a moment too soon by the looks of ya.'

Ciro attempted a grin but a sharp, painful stab in his jaw curtailed the action. 'I thought you couldn't talk?' he mumbled.

Amec frowned. 'You can hear me?'

Ciro nodded.

Amec's frown deepened. He glanced around the clearing and shook his head. 'Wish I knew what was goin' on. That belt's o' your's been throwin' me all over the place.'

Two faint black spots, far darker than the night, appeared in Ciro's vision to the north of the hill. The King ignored them as mere symptoms of his addled wits.

'Who told you to bring me the belt?' he asked.

The Philiri shrugged. 'A voice, I think… It's difficult to say. Though I was glad to come really. Bein' back in Philire's difficult to take – bein' dead an' all.'

Nodding, Ciro attempted to climb to his feet. His legs gave way and he winced as he collapsed to his knees.

'I've gotta get you out of 'ere,' said Amec with concern.

Ciro smiled weakly and took several ragged breaths. 'The others made it safely to Philire then?' he asked. Amec nodded. 'Good, that's good…' he whispered.

Ciro sighed and, while he fought an overwhelming urge to sleep he thought of Nesh: wondering whether the presence of the star belt might have aided her like it had Amec. He just wished he knew more about it: why it showed such strange

461

patterns on the world, why it had caused lightning to strike down at him.

Ciro inched his arms up the tree trunk and used it for support until he was back on his feet. He looked up at the storm clouds.

'Amec,' he asked, 'why haven't I been struck by lightning this time?'

Amec also looked up. He cocked his head to one side. 'They're waitin',' he answered.

'Who's waiting?'

Amec pointed up. 'The voices. Can't ya hear 'em?'

Ciro listened. Thunder. Rain striking the leaves and thudding the ground was all he could hear: a riot of noise. But he could not discern any voices. He shook his head and was about to ask Amec another question when he noticed that the black spots dotting his vision had grown larger.

'I think we should be leavin',' Amec said but Ciro was watching the figure of an old man on a horse who suddenly bolted into the clearing and reigned in his mount.

Ciro shook his head and moved as quickly as he could back to the edge of the clearing. He was not going anywhere. He had never seen the man before, yet he knew one thing. The black spot which sat on his forehead and the hideous child he held in his arms marked him out as an enemy of all mankind. An evil which had to be stopped. Stamped out. Eliminated in any way possible.

'Soulcatcher,' hissed Ciro as the old man jumped from his saddle and stared back at him through the darkness. Ciro saw that the old man's eyes where just holes, mere slits into an abyss of nothing which occupied the space where his soul should have been. It was not a man, but a flimsy, hollow vessel: an animated skin which carried oblivion as its gift.

Ciro felt his anger rise at the vile sight and a shiver ran

down his spine as he realised the rain had suddenly stopped: the thunder had ceased. The very world around him appeared to have paused. Waiting. Ciro raised an arm and pointed to the Soulcatcher, and the song the man in the cave had recited to him came unbidden to his lips. With it an immense power descended upon the hilltop.

Soulcatcher Gidus was not a happy man. Not only did he resent being beyond the barrier for such a long time, but he was distinctly put out by Baramir's juvenile attitude towards their situation. He had braved the world beyond the black apples once before – travelled all the way to the Siren's mountain lair – but he knew that to bring such a large force of Makech this close to the mountains of the South Jaw would inevitably attract attention. And, as he rode through the rain beside his plodding, bedraggled troops, he felt a sense of foreboding the like of which he could not remember feeling before.

The night and the storm came on in unison as the party tramped the downs and Gidus cast a glance down to where his Wraith, wrapped in a heavy cloak, slept fitfully in his lap. Did it dream of its youth, scrabbling through the darkness in the tunnels under the mountains? He thought. Gidus wondered if it could remember that far back and smiled to himself as it twitched and muttered in its sleep.

'Should we light torches, your reverence? The column's beginning to loose its shape.'

The question was posed by one of his own guards but the Soulcatcher shook his head. It would be difficult to set anything alight in this driving rain and harder still to keep it ablaze. His greater concern however was that its light might announce their presence to the Omerkfel, or worse still, the Firehearts. Night was, after all, their day.

'Tell them to march closer together,' Gidus responded. 'The only thing the men need to do is to keep from tripping over. I know where we're heading.'

The old Soulcatcher looked out into the darkness, a blank expanse of night overlaid with driving rain. Squinting, he saw that there, perhaps a mile off, was a tiny spot of darker night, the tell-tale sign of Baramir's black crystal. He sighed. Gidus knew that his understudy had all the makings of a fearsome Soulcatcher but those very attributes also made him a liability. Once the king's soul had been safely plucked and stored, thought Gidus, they would return to Kal Gians and continue with Baramir's training. He would also have that fool Capell quietly disposed of: he was a weakness which would always hamper his understudy's progress.

The old man rode on, ever wary of the night until they reached the base of the hill and began a slanting ascent up its northern side. The storm had continued to worsen as they had approached and Gidus found himself watching the sky more closely as his horse negotiated the slope. He could not put his finger on it but there was something, some pattern to the way the clouds were deepening that he felt sure he should recognise. Like some long-forgotten memory the shapes assumed tantalisingly familiar forms, yet their exact nature simply perplexed the Soulcatcher.

A few yards on and the nervousness he had felt earlier returned to Gidus. He brought his horse to a stop, allowing the troops to trudge their way past while he peered into the darkness at the top of the rise and tried to find meaning in the fear he was beginning to feel. He stroked the Wraith, now awake and wide-eyed but it struggled and attempted to jump to the ground.

'Sakoom! Sakoom! Sakoom!' it gibbered, its arms flailing as Gidus tried to calm it.

The Soulcatcher frowned at the sky. Yes, he thought, Sakoom would be up there somewhere. He mouthed a prayer to the Kolben Lord of the air then gritted his teeth and spurred his horse up the slope at a gallop. There was something wrong up there and he wanted to know just what it was.

'Sakoomsakoomsakoomsakoom!' the Wraith continued to squeal and Gidus, reaching the clearing his guard had told him of, reigned in his mount and leapt from the saddle. As his boots struck the wet grass the weather suddenly changed.

The rain stopped. The thunder ceased. The clouds overhead seemed to freeze in the sky. Then Gidus saw it: the thing which the black crystal in his head – the little shard of Unzekka himself – had been desperately trying to remember. Across the clearing, wreathed in the light of the sun, a man stood wearing the Eyes of Areil. And his attention was firmly fixed on the Soulcatcher. Gidus, caught in the full gaze of the Eyes, found himself exposed: plucked from the safety of the Great Darkness. Then an intense energy charged the air as the sunlit man sang and Gidus knew to his horror that he would walk the square no more. Sakoom himself had been summoned to the hilltop.

II

There had been great jubilation in Philire after the return of so many wanderers and the tales of their escape from the clutches of the evil Makech were still enthralling everyone in the city. Then Tenc, son of Hothan the Elder, had wandered exhausted into the wood and the tale had been soured. He told of bravery and guile and of the man who had tricked the Makech onto the downs but lost his life attempting to protect a young girl named Nesh. The people had lamented then, for the loss of souls so brave and it was all that Tenc could do to stop Arper's grief from overwhelming him.

Watchman Poori, keeping guard in the east watch tower, was mulling over these events when he heard the sound of trotting hooves in the forest below. He frowned, listened through the canopy of rustling leaves to make sure of what he heard then heaved himself out of the hollowed great oak to get a better look.

Far below, a horse with a rider dressed in blue passed through a gap in the foliage. Poori's heart skipped a beat as he considered the unthinkable: that the Makech had finally found Philire. The horse moved out of view but Poori nimbly stepped along a branch until he reached the platform which overlooked the entrance tree. He watched with his heart in his mouth as the horse slowed to a stop.

Poori squinted at the rider and shook his head. The figure's clothing did not fit with the description of the armoured Makech and the way he slumped forwards in the saddle made the Watchman wonder whether he was in fact asleep. He waited to see if the man would climb from the saddle and search out the bell line then stared in wide-eyed disbelief as the cradle descended from the entrance tree. The horse – apparently of its own accord, for the rider did not move – now stepped into the cradle and was carried aloft.

Poori ran back to the watch tower and rang the alarm signal on his own bell line. As he suspected, there was no reply. No one was outside Philire at the moment so nobody would be watching the entrance. Or manning the cradle controls.

Poori raced down the inside of the tree and descended the entrance hole until he reached the tunnel which connected the east watch tower with the main entrance cavern. Speeding through the semi-darkness and into the brighter light of the cavern, he paused to regard the unmanned cradle controls for a second then rushed to pull on the alarm bells for the other three towers. Finally, he pulled a spear from a rack on the wall and stood nervously listening to the clunk and grind of machinery which appeared to be operating itself.

Vanse was the second Watchman to arrive in the cavern and he called to Poori the moment he saw him standing armed by the entrance steps.

'Grab a spear!' came Poori's nervous reply. 'Can't you hear it?'

Vanse listened to the noise of the cradle descending then hurried to arm himself.

'No one's supposed to be outside!' Vanse hissed, moving to stand beside Poori. 'Who is it?'

Poori shook his head. 'Someone on a horse. Not one of us. Look…' Poori nodded towards the spinning control wheel on the far side of the cavern.

'Ebo save us,' whispered Vanse then ran to get more men.

Alone, Poori tensed himself as the cradle thumped to a stop and the doors drew slowly back.

'Halt!' he shouted nervously as the horse and rider appeared. He moved a few feet to the right, fearing the man might suddenly spur the horse forwards, but the beast simply descended the low steps and stopped. Poori was about to shout another challenge when he saw that the rider would give no response. He was battered and bruised and completely unconscious.

News of Ciro's arrival in Philire spread through the underground city like wildfire, but the exact circumstances of how he had gained entrance was kept to a select few. The Elders felt that the events were strange enough without tales of how the cradle had worked itself alarming the populous. Ciro was swiftly removed from public gaze to recuperate in Elderman Hothan's care but his return to consciousness merely brought him more pain. He had to tell Arper about Nesh's death.

'I know,' Arper had replied, his voice cracked with emotion. 'I knew before Tenc told me. When I found yer belt missin' I got really worried. I didn't tell no one but I knew it was a bad omen.'

Nesh's Uncle leaned heavily on Ciro's sickbed. His head was bowed, his eyes red-rimmed, while his words came choked and whispered. He gripped the king's bandaged hand as lightly as he could and talked on while Ciro nodded dumbly and tried to hold back his own tears.

When Tenc had finally reached the city, Arper explained, he had brought back the tragic news that both Ciro and Nesh were dead. Tenc had reached the far bank of the river just in time to witness Nesh being struck down and, while Ciro had fought for his life against unbeatable odds, Tenc had panicked and fled.

'It were some comfort that she died quick,' Arper continued, nodding to himself. 'But...' his voice faded away. 'I blame me'self. I should've stopped 'er jumpin' off the boat.'

Ciro shook his head. 'You can't blame yourself, Arper,' he replied with feeling. 'None of this is your fault.'

Arper gave a fractional nod in response and stood up. 'Yeah... Well, I'd best let yer rest...' he muttered absently.

After Arper had left, Ciro sat staring at the rock wall on the far side of his room, trying to come to terms with his own grief. Had it been worth it? The realisation of his Reilan dream? An entire farmstead was dead because of him: the girl who had found him on the beach, the farmer who had taken him in, his wife. Even Amec, the man who had come to guide him to Peimonac – all had lost their lives in Ciro's misguided pursuit of ancient glories. Of them all, Nesh's agonising, senseless death hurt him the most and his mind wound back through the days: counting the mistakes which had brought about her loss. The king's only small comfort was that Arper did not know how Nesh had really died.

By degrees, Ciro's health returned. He was tended daily by a Philiri healer and as the days passed his physical wounds healed – the sight in his left eye improved. His ribs still pained him with any sudden movements but then Ciro rarely moved – barely spoke. Tenc visited every day, as did Arper, but the king always seemed distracted: lost in his own bitter thoughts. As the days dragged on Ciro continued to stare at the blank wall opposite and continued to catalogue the deadly mistakes he had made.

Ciro had no idea how long he sat staring intently at the wall but, when his thoughts had wound back to his eleventh birthday, his discovery of Tenlern's scarf and of the Ascension Chamber, he threw himself from his sickbed and began pacing rapidly.

'You're a fool, Ciro Torrman,' he muttered to himself, 'for only a fool would wallow in such a morass of self-pity and self-recrimination.'

If he was to be an effective king, Ciro considered, and then he had to turn such losses to his advantage. He had to learn from the bitter lessons of his journey and use that experience so that others would not suffer the same fate. More than four thousand men depended on it. Sitting back and bemoaning the past the way he had once revered it would get him nowhere: both outlooks were inaccurate. It was the present that was important and the future he could shape with his actions. There was more, far more to this strange land than the faded ink that had fuelled his thoughts before, but he had to accept that and use the knowledge accordingly. He could not repair the damage that had been done but he had to accept

469

that his part in it had been just one of many different and conflicting parts. If he had not been washed overboard then Nesh, Qisala, Amec would probably not have lost their lives but, as a small part in a greater whole his influence had been limited. What would his part have been if he had landed his army on that shore? If he had known that people still existed in Rial?

Ciro stopped his pacing and gave a rueful smile. He was beginning to wallow again. He shook his head then addressed the wall which had been the canvas of his thoughts for so many days.

'I pledge that I will avenge the deaths of my friends and of those poor innocent's whose only crime is to have been born Rialan. I vow to rid this land of the vile Makech.' Ciro turned away and was about to beginning dressing when another thought struck him. 'I also promise,' he said to the wall. 'That if those bastards, Baramir and Tanikalin still live, I will hunt them down like the animals they are.'

Tenc almost fell from his chair when Ciro strode briskly from his room and for a moment the Philiri found himself at a loss for words. The straggling beard which had covered Ciro's face was gone now and, apart from the faded bruise around his left eye, the king looked as fit and well as Tenc had ever seen him. In his pressed blue jacket, white trousers and polished boots he looked, Tenc was surprised to admit, a much younger man. But, never-the-less, the change was miraculous.

'How are you, Tenc?' Ciro inquired.

The Philiri nodded. 'I was about to ask you the same thing.'

Ciro took a deep breath: then winced as his ribs reminded him not to take his injuries too lightly. 'I've been better,' he replied. 'But I'll live.'

Tenc stood up. 'You should meet my father, Elderman

470

Hothan,' he said. 'I think the Elders wish to speak with you.'

Ciro nodded and glanced around the room. It was, like the room he had been convalescing in, carved from solid rock, but this chamber was far more spacious. There were polished panels of wood lining the walls while daylight seemed to spill through an intricately patterned ceiling above. The room was impressively furnished and Ciro wondered for a moment whether any of the objects dated back to King Elson's time. His thoughts returned to more pressing concerns.

'Where's Arper?' he asked.

Tenc smiled. 'He's been staying with Borlin for the past couple of nights, visiting the taverns to tell their tales and sing songs. It seems to have helped him, I think.'

Ciro returned the smile. 'Good,' he said. 'And how about you, Tenc? How do you feel?'

The Philiri shrugged. 'Lucky to be alive, I suppose.' He moved a step closer. 'I feel ashamed that I left you,' he said sheepishly. 'I should have swum back. Tried to help.'

'You did the right thing,' Ciro answered. He put an arm on Tenc's shoulder. 'There was nothing that you could have done. It wasn't your fault, you must know that.'

Tenc gave grudging acknowledgement and changed the subject. 'I must warn you, Ciro, that your arrival has started an awful lot of gossip. My father tells me that the whole city is still buzzing with rumours. Not only of how you managed to steal a horse and escape, but how on earth you found Philire.'

Ciro looked puzzled. 'I had a horse?'

'You don't remember?'

'I remember a storm,' Ciro replied with a sigh. 'I remember Amec. How I gained a horse and how I got here I can only guess at.'

'I could hazard a guess,' Tenc said, looking at the star belt

471

around Ciro's waist.

The king also looked down and patted it. 'Dead or alive, Amec's a good man to have on your side.'

Tenc nodded and placed a hand on Ciro's shoulder. 'I'm glad you're better,' he said. 'Now, if you'll excuse me for a moment, I'll go and find my father.'

While they stood waiting before the Chamber of Elders, Tenc explained to Ciro more about the city of Philire.

'We're about three miles to the north east of the old city of Monides and some of our more ancient parts actually use the Monides water and sewage system.'

Ciro had been surprised to find that the entire city was underground but it explained a great deal about how they had survived undiscovered for so long. The pair were seated at the base of a large ornamental fountain which, with its surrounding flower beds, was the centrepiece of the biggest chamber Ciro had ever seen. The bare rock, smoothed and shaped into decorative columns and floral patterns rose into a domed semi-darkness and all around the square of the chamber were cut the grand facades of magnificent buildings. Tenc pointed straight ahead to where blue marble blocks marked one particular building apart from the others.

'That's the Chamber of the Elders,' Tenc explained. 'It was one of the first grand buildings to be built in Philire.'

Ciro cast his gaze around the vast space. 'It must have taken years, generations to build all this,' he said.

Tenc nodded. 'It still continues to this day, but much of the digging now is only on the lower levels, the hillside we sit beneath is almost completely hollowed out.'

'How many people live here?' Ciro inquired.

Tenc shrugged. 'Thousands and thousands, my father would know for sure.'

A figure came out from the Chamber of the Elders and began the long walk to the fountain where the pair sat. Ciro stood up, straightened his jacket and, with Tenc beside him, went to greet the Elder.

The man stopped and bowed as they drew near. He was pale, thin to the point of illness and what hair he had was white and carefully plastered upon his forehead. His dress was the same style of flowing robes which the Adlermen of Feirlan wore but, instead of Feirlan green the clothing was a washed-out blue. Around his neck was a chain of silver and from it hung a large medallion which showed a sun sitting between two mountain peaks.

'I am Urin,' the man said with a voice firm enough to belie his stature. 'The Elders await you.'

Ciro dipped his head in response and the pair trailed Urin back towards the grand blue facade.

Inside a large circular chamber – wood panelled and lit with torches – the Elders of Philire sat on tiered cushioned seats and watched Ciro's arrival in silence. Before taking his place amongst his colleagues, Urin pointed Ciro to a circle of blue marble set in the centre of the white marble floor and the king, with Tenc beside him, stood for a moment and ran his gaze across the assembled Elders.

'Welcome, Ciro, to the Chamber of Elders,' said a bearded man, standing and stepping down onto the floor of the chamber. 'I am Nera.'

He was dressed in the same blue robes as the others but a chain of gold around his neck appeared to distinguish him as perhaps the leader of the group. Ciro bowed but said nothing.

'We have heard much of your exploits,' Nera continued. He glanced at the other Elders and Ciro noted a slight smile play for a moment on the man's lips. 'Perhaps you would enlighten us as to who you are, what brings you here… And what your curious costume denotes.'

'My name is Ciro Torrman—' Ciro began but his voice was instantly curtailed by a loud guffaw from one of the Elders. Nera frowned and the murmur which had started to ripple through the crowd was quickly silenced.

'My name is Ciro Torrman,' began Ciro again. 'Son of King Fidiann Torrman of Feirlan. I am the true and rightful heir to the throne of the Kingdom of Rial.'

'By who's authority?!' shouted one of the Elders.

'By the authority of the crown,' Ciro replied with a shrug. 'By direct descent from King Elson, the last King of Rial.'

To this, the murmurs began again and many of the Elders shook their heads.

'This realm has had no king for more than five hundred years,' said Nera firmly. 'You will excuse us, your Majesty, if we state that we recognise no such place as Feirlan or that any such royal position exists here.'

'Dully noted,' replied Ciro. 'The people of Feirlan are of a very similar mind. Reilan and Rial are but dim memories to them.'

Nera smiled. 'Then what, may I ask, brings you here?'

Ciro smiled back. 'I am the King of Rial; it is my duty to be here.'

'Philire does not need a King!' shouted one of the Elders vehemently.

Ciro's smile did not waver. 'Elders of Philire…' he began and stepped from the circle. 'Please do not misunderstand either my position or my intentions. I know of your struggle here, of the great darkness, of Firehearts, of the Makech and the Omerk. I can also see how you have prospered under such adversity – the wonders you have built. I want to assure you that I have not come here seeking to usurp such glories: I do not deserve to. I do not want to claim dominion over Philire, over its leaders or its people, I –'

'Then what do you want?!' barked an Elder from the highest tier of the steps.

Ciro spread his hands and shrugged. 'Nothing,' he replied, 'except your friendship.'

Nera looked thoughtful. 'We understand that you have an army based at Peimonac. Would this 'friendship' you speak of involve their presence here?'

Ciro mouthed an 'O' and looked up towards the shadow of the ceiling. Philire was, like Feirlan before her, isolated and suspicious of strangers Ciro reasoned. The only army they had experience of was of the skull wearing variety, so they were naturally cautious of letting another force – however well-meaning its intentions seemed – get too close.

'The army that sits in Peimonac is a Rialan army,' explained Ciro, hoping the meaning would be clearly understood. 'We may be separated by centuries of history but our origins are still the same. Technically I am a Feirlaner,' continued Ciro with a shrug, 'you are Philiri. But, wherever our place of birth, we are all Rialan at heart.' There were approving murmurs from the assembly. Nera smiled but shook his head.

'A noble sentiment,' he said. 'And, in some respects, true… ' Nera put a finger to his mouth and furrowed his brow. '… However,' he continued, wagging the finger at the young king. 'What is also true is that, like this hidden Feirlan realm you come from, Philire has survived because it has remained hidden. I see no reason, despite such fine and inspiring rhetoric, to change the course of our people.' Nera's tone became firm once again. 'I sense in your presence a veritable gale of change: of conflict. History tells us that there is one use and one use alone for an army: and that is to fight. You have already battled your way this far, it would seem logical to surmise that you intend to rejoin the fray once you have rejoined your army. Would that be true?'

'Yes, but–' Ciro began but Nera was already continuing.

'– We want no part of that here!' Nera thundered, sweeping his arm to indicate the assembled Elders. 'No army. No conflict. No war.' He shook his head and gazed at Ciro steadily. 'Now is not our time. There are things in this kingdom which cannot be raged against with force of arms and, if you are aware of the Great Darkness, I need not emphasise what things they are. We, the Elders of Philire, hold this city and its people in safe isolation for the day when the Brothers will lead us back to our rightful home. Until that day we will not fight for the King of Rial or anybody else for that matter. I hope that is understood.'

Ciro bowed. 'Perfectly. But I would just like to clarify one thing. You are right that historically there is just one use for an army but my men are not simply soldiers with nothing but blood on their minds and a weapon in their hands. First and foremost they are farmers, carpenters, blacksmiths, master makers, potters – amongst many other trades – who were trained to defend themselves against the unknown. Since my arrival here I have met and travelled with several of your fellow Philiri of whom much the same could be said. But they learned, like my men learned, new skills to protect themselves against unforeseen circumstance.' Ciro studied the tiers of faces and spread his arms wide. 'We did not come here to wage a war but, if that is what it will take to free this land from the fear which hangs over it, I will lead my men to war. But of Philire I ask for nothing that Philire will not give freely. Only your friendship if you will give it.'

'And if we don't?' asked Mera with a smile.

Ciro shrugged. 'Then someday – how far in the future I do not know – but someday, you will walk out into the sunshine above to find a new Rial has sprung from the soil in which you sit.'

Ciro returned with Tenc to the fountain while the Elders debated. But what they were debating, Ciro was unsure of. He had asked for nothing but their friendship and had promised to leave them out of any conflict but, as he stood with Tenc, his companion's nervousness became more apparent.

'Is there something I'm missing, Tenc?' Ciro asked. 'You seem very ill at ease.'

The Philiri cast a frowning glance at the blue marble facade behind them and shook his head. 'I think it's nothing,' he began then looked around the vast chamber, making sure there was no one in sight. 'I think I have to warn you that the Elders might try to keep you here.'

'What!?' exploded Ciro.

Tenc gritted his teeth and frantically motioned the king to keep his voice down. 'I don't know for certain, but I overheard my father debating with Nera yesterday about how you managed to gain access to Philire without the presence of one of us. There are a number of Elders who see not only your arrival, but how you managed it at all, as a very bad omen.'

Ciro frowned. 'All I know is that Amec must have got me here – nothing more.'

'I know,' Tenc replied, 'and I've spoken to my father about it. But such strange occurrences may only cloud the issue further.' He shook his head. 'My people are very cautious when it comes to dealings with the outside world, and your arrival has started many people asking if it's a sign for us to finally…' Tenc hitched a thumb at the ceiling. '…Leave here.'

'Well, that's understandable, I suppose,' said Ciro. 'But I thought I had made it plain that I would not force them into anything they did not feel ready for.'

'That's the problem, I think.' Tenc answered. He paused for a moment then pointed to an archway which sat to the left of the Chamber of Elders. 'That's the Great Library through there,' he said. 'Come and see it and I'll try to explain the problem.'

'Do we have time to look through the library?' Ciro asked.

Tenc nodded. 'I need to show you something.' He replied and led the way towards the arch.

'Do you remember the story I told you about the brothers, Calian and Pesarian?' Tenc asked as they walked briskly towards the arch.

Ciro nodded.

'Well, that story has become a cornerstone of Philiri philosophy, and even to this day debate still rages as to whether it still holds any significance to us: whether such an old tale has any relevance any more.'

'You'll excuse me, Tenc,' said Ciro. 'But just what does that have to do with your Elders wanting to keep me here?'

'Fear,' replied Tenc. 'Fear that the time we have been told will come is now upon us.'

Ciro shrugged. 'Fear of change is understandable,' he mused. 'But your Elders surely know that my presence is nothing to do with that old story.'

Tenc nodded. 'I think they do,' he said. 'But, from what I can gather, they are worried that your arrival might convince the populous otherwise.'

The pair had reached the arch and Tenc peered down the flight of steps which led down into darkness.

'Usually the library is bustling with Elders,' Tenc said, taking a lamp from its bracket on the wall. 'But I suppose with them all in the chamber there's nobody around.' He swung the lamp before them and led Ciro slowly down the steps.

'You see,' Tenc continued as they descended, 'the fear that the Elders have is that what befell the old kingdom will befall us if we leave our hideaway before the appointed time.'

'And, after five hundred years or more, people are starting to ask if there's any point waiting – is that about right?' asked Ciro.

They had reached the bottom of the steps and the king's voice echoed in the low-ceilinged space. Tenc nodded, studied the wall to his left, then retrieved and lit another lamp. Now Ciro could see the patterned marble floor and the hint of glass and polished wood some dozen or so yards before them. It looked like an entrance of sorts.

'This is why the Elders fear getting the appointed time wrong,' he said and led Ciro towards the wall of wood and glass.

There were two arched doors: highly polished and inset with leaded glass panels. Tenc directed Ciro's attention to a large, glass fronted case which occupied the space between the doors. Inside it stood the seven foot skeleton of a beast so hideous in countenance and oppressive in stature that Ciro took an involuntary step backwards at the sight.

'This is what the Elders fear might still be waiting for us on the surface,' explained Tenc.

Ciro nodded dumbly and stepped closer, his breath clouding the glass as he examined the serrated jaw line, the barrel chest and the lethal looking talons the beast had in place of fingers. He cast his mind back to when Tenc had recounted the tale of the beast's death and his instant dismissal of its threat. But this was no bear. On the crown of the massive, dog-like skull was a cracked hole: made, Ciro assumed, by one of the quorum hammers the brothers in the story had carried. It was long dead – a thing of ancient history – but the thought of it made flesh and moving sent a shiver down the king's spine. What if the Elders were right? What if these monsters still roamed the kingdom?

'Tenc,' said Ciro without taking his eyes from the beast. 'I don't know how and frankly I don't care, but I need you to find me a way out of this place so that I can get back to my people in Peimonac... Right now.' Ciro turned to see Tenc grimace.

'But, what about my father? The Elders?' he responded.

Ciro pointed to the towering thing in the case. 'What about my men, Tenc?' he replied, his tone rising. 'What about my men?!'

Tenc could not mistake the passion and anguish in his friend's voice and sighed. 'You're right of course,' he said. He cast his gaze back up the library entrance steps before turning to Ciro. 'I've no idea how long the Elders will debate, but, with something this important it could be quite a while. If we're going to head for Peimonac from here then the best way will be by boat. Philire does have a small harbour for our fishermen, though it's years since I ever went there. If we leave now, perhaps we can get there without being missed.'

Ciro nodded. 'We'll head back to your chambers, collect our belongings and,' Ciro tugged at his jacket. 'I suppose I had better get back into something less conspicuous.'

'Hm,' nodded Tenc. 'What about Arper?'

Ciro was already heading up the stairs. 'We'll change first and then find him. I'll not leave him behind if he wants to come.'

At the top of the steps, Ciro and Tenc peeked around the archway to view the Hall of Elders. Though no one but Philiri sentries could be seen around its entrance, there were now several people criss-crossing around the central fountain. Ciro and Tenc hung back in the library entrance and watched as the distant figures walked towards other grand facades cut into the cavern's walls. Once again the cavern was empty.

Ciro removed his jacket and folded it under his arm. 'It looks quiet enough,' he said. 'Perhaps if we cross the chamber on the far side we can get out unnoticed.'

Tenc agreed and the pair walked as casually as they could towards the lower end of the great cavern. More Philiri exited from the other buildings as they made a wide loop around the lower end of the chamber and Ciro and Tenc tried not to seem too wary. There were several looks and even a 'Good day' from the Philiri who were also crossing the space but nobody stopped their progress. With relief they made it to the main entrance of the chamber and continued on through a long connecting tunnel until they were in sight of Tenc's father's chamber.

Though the cavern they had just left was the most opulent space Ciro had seen in Philire, the rest of the underground city seemed no less impressive. The cavern where Tenc's father lived - along with many other elders' families - was gently lit by large oil lamps while the rock walls had been intricately carved with the shapes of curving trees. The overall effect of this was to make the cavern appear like a space deep in the forest, rather than one deep underground. In the centre of the chamber was a wide hole, pillared on its four sides and from here it was possible to look down to the next, larger level of the city. Two sets of wide stone steps led below to the lower caverns and the pair passed them as they made their way towards Tenc's home. With all the elders currently in their Great Hall the space was all but deserted.

Once inside the main door Ciro and Tenc made straight to their respective rooms to get ready as quickly as possible. Ciro threw his jacket onto the bed and removed his travelling clothes which were stuffed into his pack. The clothes were still stained and travel-worn but, Ciro thought, that would hopefully mean he drew even less attention. He pulled out his cloak and attached it around his neck, crammed his blue Rialan jacket into the pack and was about to pick up Amec's sword from the floor when the blade shot out of its scabbard.

Ciro quickly recovered from the shock and gave a half smile. 'Hello, Amec,' he said.

In response the blade lifted from the ground and tapped the stone floor twice. Ciro looked on and the blade repeated the motion, this time more quickly. The king removed his star belt and tentatively placed it around his temple. He only had the vaguest recollection of what had happened on the downs but he well knew the belt was dangerous. Once again the room became overlaid in the same swirling colours but this time, Ciro noted, the colours seemed to be duller in tone. Before him, Amec dropped his sword to the floor and stood up.

'I see you've recovered from the hilltop,' he said with a nod.

Ciro smiled, glad that Amec could still be heard. 'I don't remember that much about it,' he replied. 'But I know I couldn't have done so without your help. Thank you, Amec.'

'You don't have much time,' explained the Philiri. 'You've got to ¬-' There came a loud knock on the entrance door. '- Too late,' continued Amec with a frown.

Ciro turned at the sound. The door to his room was open and he looked through to see Tenc exit his own room. Tenc looked first towards the main door, then back to Ciro's room. Seeing the king with the star belt around his head, he hurried over.

'It's the Watchmen,' Amec explained. 'The Elders have decided to place you under arrest.' There came a louder knock on the door.

'How many are there, Amec?' Ciro asked.

'What is it?' Tenc asked. 'Who's out there?'

'Amec says it's the Watchmen,' Ciro replied.

'There are two of them,' continued Amec. 'But they aren't like the Makech, so they aren't expecting a hostile reception. Philire is a peaceful place.'

'I understand,' replied Ciro with a nod. 'But I can't stay here. I have to get back to my men.'

'Get your things together and get Tenc to let them in,' advised Amec. 'I'll do the rest.'

Ciro agreed and quickly re-attached the star belt around his waist. He shoved Amec's sword back into its scabbard and grabbed up his pack. There came a third, booming knock on the door.

'Alright, Tenc,' Ciro said. 'Amec says to let them in.'

With a hesitant nod, Tenc slowly walked towards the door. 'What's he planning?' he asked.

Ciro followed on behind and shrugged. 'I've no idea, but I think he wants to avoid bloodshed.'

Hearing this Tenc seemed relieved. He glanced back as Ciro put down his pack and sword on a table then unbolted the door. Beyond were two watchmen dressed in loose and hooded dove grey uniforms. At each man's waist was a short sword and in each of their right hands they carried a quarter-staff. With a curt nod to Tenc, the two men entered the room.

'Our apologies,' said the first watchman with another nod. 'But we come on order of the Elders of the Great Hall.' He looked at Ciro and pointed his quarter staff. 'Ciro Torrman,' he announced. 'You are, by order of the Elders of Philire, to be placed under arrest.'

Tenc, who was still holding the door open, felt it wrenched suddenly from his grip. With a loud thump the main door shut and both watchmen turned with alarm at the noise. Now the first watchman's quarter staff span from his unwary grasp towards Ciro, who picked it up the second it clattered by his feet. Both Watchmen wore looks of consternation at the sudden, bizarre events but now Ciro, with quarter staff in hand was racing at the two men.

The first watchman drew his sword as Ciro moved in swiftly, while the second, with a wary glance at the unarmed Tenc, moved round his partner to aid him. With a sudden groan he slumped to his knees and hit the floor, rendered unconscious by the small stone statue which had flown out of the corner of the room to strike the back of his head. The remaining watchman thrust his sword half-heartedly at Ciro as he moved to within striking distance but the king, reading the man's movement, simply tapped the blade towards the floor with the left end of his quarter staff and swung the right in rapidly to catch the watchman a stunning blow behind his right ear. As his adversary's legs buckled, Ciro flashed in the left end of the quarter staff to land another blow on the left side of his head. The second watchman joined his colleague unconscious on the floor and both Ciro and Tenc looked on as the statue flew back to the corner of the room.

Putting down the quarter staff, Ciro removed his star belt and once again placed it around his head. 'Thank you, Amec,' he said, seeing the Philiri put the statue back on its pedestal.

Amec nodded and walked to stand over the two fallen men. 'You should head for the harbour right now. It won't take long before these two wake up.'

Ciro nodded agreement then frowned. 'We have to get Arper,' he said.

Amec stared intently into space for a moment then gave a half smile. 'Don't worry about Arper,' he said. 'I'll get 'im. I know where he is. Now get goin'.' Ciro was about to take off the star belt when Amec added: 'Don't use the belt again, Mr

King. Like I said before, it is dangerous, 'specially beyond the black apples. And one more thing…' Once again Amec seemed to be seeing something beyond Ciro's vision. 'You know a man named 'Calian' don't you?' Ciro nodded. 'Take the belt to him as soon as you get to Peimonac, he might have some answers.' Amec grinned, as if there was some unspoken joke then turn and walked through the wall of the chamber.

Ciro removed the belt from his temple and motioned to Tenc. 'Get your pack,' he said. 'We have to make for the harbour.'

Tenc cast a glance at the watchmen at his feet and rubbed his beard. 'I should write a note to my father,' he said, then hurried over to an ornate writing desk set against the wall.

'Make it quick,' advised Ciro.

Tenc nodded, grabbed a quill and wrote: Dear Father, Very sorry but duty to our kingdom calls me on a piece of paper. It was not going to explain that much, he thought, but then he was not sure how his father would ever understand. He left the note on the desk, grabbed his belongings and hurried out of the door with Ciro.

Philire was a bustling place beyond the tranquil upper realm of the Elders and deep below Ciro and Tenc's departing feet lay the beating heart of the city. In the 'Spirit of Philire', several levels down, Arper had just finished another hour long stretch of folk songs from the West Wold and, to deafening cheers from the crowded inn; he slumped into his chair beside Borlin and Tamarail.

'Your star shines bright as a polished button, Arper!' said Borlin with a grin as Arper sat down. In response Arper waved back at the standing crowd behind him then gratefully took the mug of ale which Tamarail thrust towards him.

'Wonderful stuff, Arper!' said Tamarail with a smile.

Arper nodded in response, lifted the mug to his lips then felt it tugged from his grasp. It bounced upon the table, spilling half its contents, before tumbling to the flagstone floor.

'Beck it!' exclaimed Arper. He ducked instantly down to retrieve the now empty mug and shook his head as he sat back up. 'I don't usually start droppin' stuff 'til I've 'ad at least 'arf a dozon o' these!' he quipped. There was no reply and Arper frowned at the shocked faces of his companions. Both were staring, open mouthed at the table. 'Wha – ?' began Arper. He followed their stunned gaze and then quickly mirrored their expressions. Beside the pool of ale which spread across the table, some invisible hand was using the liquid to write a message.

ARPER. GET YOR THINGS. The message began then, underneath, appeared a second line. MEET CIRO AT HARBER – NOW!

Arper stared in disbelief for a moment before Ciro's tale of a ghostly message from Amec flashed into his head. 'Amec?!...' he whispered, flicking his gaze around the table.

'Amec!?' hissed Tamarail. 'Arper, what – '

YES! Continued the writing. GO. NOW! HARBER!

Arper turned to Borlin and stood up. 'Dead or alive, he always was a good friend 'o mine, Amec was. An' if he says 'go' I'm goin'. Borlin, where's this harbour?'

Borlin shook off his incredulity and also stood. 'I'll show you,' he replied. The pair turned to regard Tamarail, still shocked, at the far end of the table. 'Comin'?' Asked Borlin.

Tamarail shook his head slowly and his eyes did not leave the scrawled message. 'I want nothing more to do with that king,' he muttered.

Arper nodded. 'Goodbye, Tamarail – an' thankyou,' he said. With that both he and Borlin turned to leave then stopped when an exclamation sounded behind them. Tamarail's ale mug had suddenly tipped its contents into his lap. Tamarail said nothing but glowered at the pair.

'Amec never did like Tamarail much,' mused Arper as they left.

The pair moved quickly through the busy streets towards their lodgings and Borlin noted an increased presence of Watchmen in the city. They approached a group of Philiri on a corner who seemed concerned by the very same thing and, as they passed the gathering, both overheard a man say that: 'the stranger in blue was about to be arrested'. Borlin and Arper exchanged concerned glances and hurried on.

On his bed, Arper found his things were already packed. Shaking his head he picked up his belongings and exited his room to find that Borlin too was carrying a pack.

'I'm coming too,' said the sailor. 'I think Ciro needs all the help he can get.'

Arper smiled in response and the pair swiftly made their way towards the harbour.

Though there did seem to be more Watchmen patrolling the city, they did not hinder the pair's progress and soon they were travelling down the long, wide tunnel which connected the city to its exterior harbour. The tunnel was well lit and the granite flagstones of the floor showed two parallel grooves worn into the stone from generations of transit between the city and the harbour. In the distance was a semi-circle of daylight and the pair picked up their pace to run towards the harbour entrance. It was only as they drew closer that they found their exit blocked. Three grey clad Watchmen stood around the open exit to the harbour.

The Watchmen were armed but their swords remained in their scabbards. Instead the middle Watchman raised his quarter staff and shook his head.

'I'm sorry, gentlemen,' he said. 'The harbour is... Out of bounds for the moment.'

'Why?' Asked Borlin.

'By order of the Elders,' came the reply.

'Because o' the 'stranger in blue'?' enquired Arper. 'Where is 'e?'

To this the guards exchanged frowns.

'I'm a friend o' his,' continued Arper firmly. 'Where is 'e?'

The middle Watchman sighed. 'He's in the harbour. And we're waiting for an Elder. We've been told to arrest him but – .' The guard shrugged. 'We're not sure how to.'

Arper and Borlin grinned. 'Yep,' said Arper. 'That sounds like our King.'

'He really is the King!?' exclaimed the Watchmen.

'The King of Rial,' confirmed Borlin with a nod.

'Yeah,' added Arper. 'Ciro Torrman, direct descendant of King Elson Torrman. Rightful King of Rial.' Arper pointed to himself and Borlin. 'And we're 'is mates.'

'Please,' said Borlin. 'Let us through. I don't know why your Elders might want to arrest him but, it's a mistake. He's a good man.'

'He's a Beckin' hero!' spat Arper, his anger rising. 'You should be singin' his beckin' praises, not clappin' 'im in irons! Why would you do that?!'

'Let us through, please,' insisted Borlin. 'We may be able to help.'

'Look, we've heard tales of this Ciro,' admitted the middle Watchman. 'We've talked of little else,' added another of the guards. To this all three nodded.

'Very well,' agreed the middle Watchman with a sigh after the group had stood in silence for a few moments. 'I'm not sure what good it will do, but... Come with us.' He stepped to one side and allowed Arper and Borlin through the harbour gate.

Philire's harbour was small compared to the grandeur of The Cauldron yet, like the harbour beneath The Grand Falls of Torr Betram, it too was hemmed in by massive cliffs of rock. A stone quayside curved around the eastern edge beneath the overhanging cliffs and from here fanned several wooden jetties which moored a large collection of fishing boats. The area was quiet apart from the occasional cry of a gull and completely deserted. That was, apart from a small, single-masted boat which lay at anchor: isolated far from the docks in the centre of the water. On its deck stood Ciro and Tenc, long boat hooks in their hands.

Arper and Borlin grinned at the sight as the Watchmen accompanied them along the quayside, instantly realising why the patrol had not attempted an arrest. They were peace keepers – not brutal thugs like the Makech and, if they had heard of the exploits of the young king, then they knew all too well what he was capable of.

Both Ciro and Tenc smiled at the sight of their friends and the King moved to the bow of the small boat to be closer to the quay.

'Are my friends also under arrest?' he called across the water.

'No sir,' came the reply. 'We have only been asked to arrest you.'

Ciro nodded. 'Then will you let my friends join me? I would like to speak to them in private.'

To this the Watchmen conferred. As did Borlin and Arper. Before the patrol had reached a decision there were two loud splashes as Arper and Borlin leapt into the water of the harbour.

The sudden departure of the two men caused consternation amongst the Watchmen. One of them drew his short sword and moved to the edge of the quay but, Ciro noted with a rye smile, he thought better than leaping into the water in pursuit.

'It's quite alright,' placated Ciro as his friends quickly swam towards the boat. He shrugged. 'Beyond the safety of Philire is only danger – is that not correct? So, where would we go?'

The statement seemed to calm the onlooking patrol and the drawn sword was returned to its scabbard.

'I merely wish to address your Elder,' said Ciro. He pointed his boat hook towards the quayside entrance. The patrol turned at the sign to see a larger group of Watchmen enter the harbour. At their head was a figure wearing the unmistakable light blue robe of an Elder.

Tenc helped Arper out of the water while Borlin all but sprang onto the deck. 'No time to stand on ceremony, I'm afraid,' said Ciro. The king was already raising the anchor. 'To oars please, gentlemen. We need to leave quickly.' Scanning the new arrivals, Ciro noted with concern that this new group of watchmen appeared to include several archers.

'Aye!' replied Borlin. He and Tenc took the rowing positions on either side of the deck and quickly the small vessel was turning to surge towards the outer entrance of the harbour. Ciro moved to stand beneath the main mast and gazed back as the larger group of Philiri hurried to the very edge of the quay.

'They've got beckin' bows!' exclaimed Arper, pausing from a vain attempt to wring water from his sleeve.

'I know,' answered Ciro.

To this Borlin and Tenc increased their stroke and Ciro saw with relief that the Watchmen did not raise their bows to fire. Now the boat was entering the narrow mouth of Philire's harbour.

'I'm sorry that I cannot submit to your captivity,' Ciro called across the water. 'But, if you need me, I will be in

Peimonac.'

Arper stood up and held on to the main mast. 'Yeah,' he yelled just before the enclosing rocks hid them from view. 'Jus' go ta Peimonac an' ask for the King!'

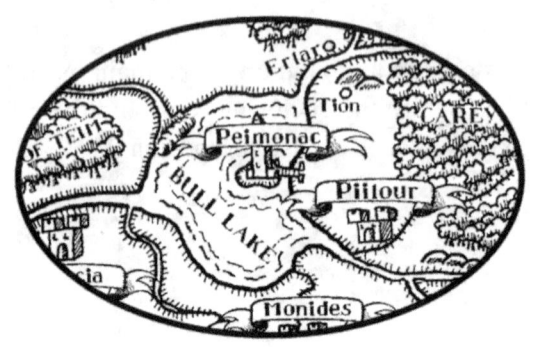

Epilogue: Peimonac

In the shadow of the Queen Irsa's towering starboard paddle wheel, Captain Benus shifted his gaze from the imposing skyline of Peimonac to watch impatiently as a squad of duns ran briskly down the quay side towards him. He shook his head at the sight, removed his pocket watch from his blue jacket and tapped the glass face impatiently.

'Run! You bone idle layabout's!' he yelled as the panting soldiers approached. He tapped the glass face of his timepiece again loudly. 'I wan'ed them stores on this quay 'alf an hour ago!'

Quickly, the ten man squad drew up into an ordered line and saluted, standing to attention while the captain scowled at their flushed faces.

'Right,' said Captain Benus with a nod. 'In pairs, I want you up that gangplank and inta the hold. Quartermaster Trei–'

'– Beggin' yar pardon sir!' said one of the men, stepping out of line and saluting again.

'What!?' barked the captain with a scowl.

'Sail, sir,' replied the soldier and pointed out across Bull

Lake.

Benus turned sharply on the spot and scanned the horizon, narrowing his gaze when he saw the triangle of canvas on the blue water. It seemed to be coming rapidly towards them.

'Sail...?' said the captain to himself. He watched as the small craft continued to approach then turned back to his men. 'Right!' he barked. 'Ya know the drill! You two, up on board an' get the Quartermaster to make steam – I want them lances good an' hot. You, get back and tell General Alanti we've got company. The rest of you, wind up and stand ready!'

While the men unshouldered and wound their fire lances, Captain Benus drew his own hand lance from its holster and took a few steps towards the edge of the quay. He shaded his eyes and tried to get a better look at just who was approaching.

Rapidly the little boat skipped across the water, drawing ever nearer to the Peimonac docks. Twenty yards from the quay side it tacked in a sharp curve to reduce its speed and at the same time dropped its sail. Now parallel with the stone jetty, the boat gently bobbed and bumped to a halt.

'Alright, steady boys,' said the captain to his men. With a stern face and a stiff back, he strode towards the little vessel, first scrutinising the bald-headed man with a circlet of shells who jumped out to secure the boat, then the man who leapt out after him. Benus stopped and frowned.

The uniform was unmistakable, but shabby and weathered, and the man who wore it gaunt and unshaven. The man cocked his head to one side, returned the captain's stare then grinned.

'It's Captain Benus, isn't it?' he said.

Now Benus was rushing forward, his stern countenance lost as sheer joy threatened to overwhelm him completely.

'I...! I...!' It was all Benus could manage. Flustered, he

stopped a few feet before the figure and gazed in wonder at his king: the man they thought was dead and gone.

'Blood and sand!' cried one of the soldiers, the same realisation striking him. 'It's the King! It's Ciro!'

As the king shook Captain Benus's eager hand, the others crowded round. They threw their weapons to the floor as they jumped and cried and hugged one another with joy.

'Yar majesty,' said the captain weakly. 'I, we thought...'

Ciro nodded. 'I'll tell you all about it later, captain, it's a long story.' The King looked along the quay to where Peimonac rose in tiers up the hillside beyond. He smiled. 'I'll need quarters for my friends and a messenger to inform my brother of my arrival.'

'Yes, yar majesty,' replied the captain with a snapped salute.

'And get one of your men to tell Calian I'm here as well, will you?'

Benus's expression changed. 'I'm afraid I can't do that, sir. Mr. Calian's gone.'

'Gone?' echoed Ciro. 'What do you mean, "Gone"?'

The captain looked uneasy. 'A man turned up, sir – out o' nowhere – Calian and them other Songsmiths wen' off with 'im.'

'What man?'

'I know it sounds odd,' explained Benus, 'but 'e said 'e was 'is brother, sir. 'e called 'imself Pesarian.'

Ciro turned on the spot to face an astounded Tenc. 'Calian has gone because his brother, Pesarian turned up,' the young king repeated woodenly. A coldness spread up Ciro's spine and he shifted his gaze from the open-mouthed Philiri to stare vacantly across the water; his thoughts racing. He had to speak to Bdann, to Alanti. There was much to discuss. Ciro shook his head slowly and regarded the gentle ripples on Bull Lake with a deep frown.

'By the stars, Calian,' he whispered to himself. 'Who are you?'

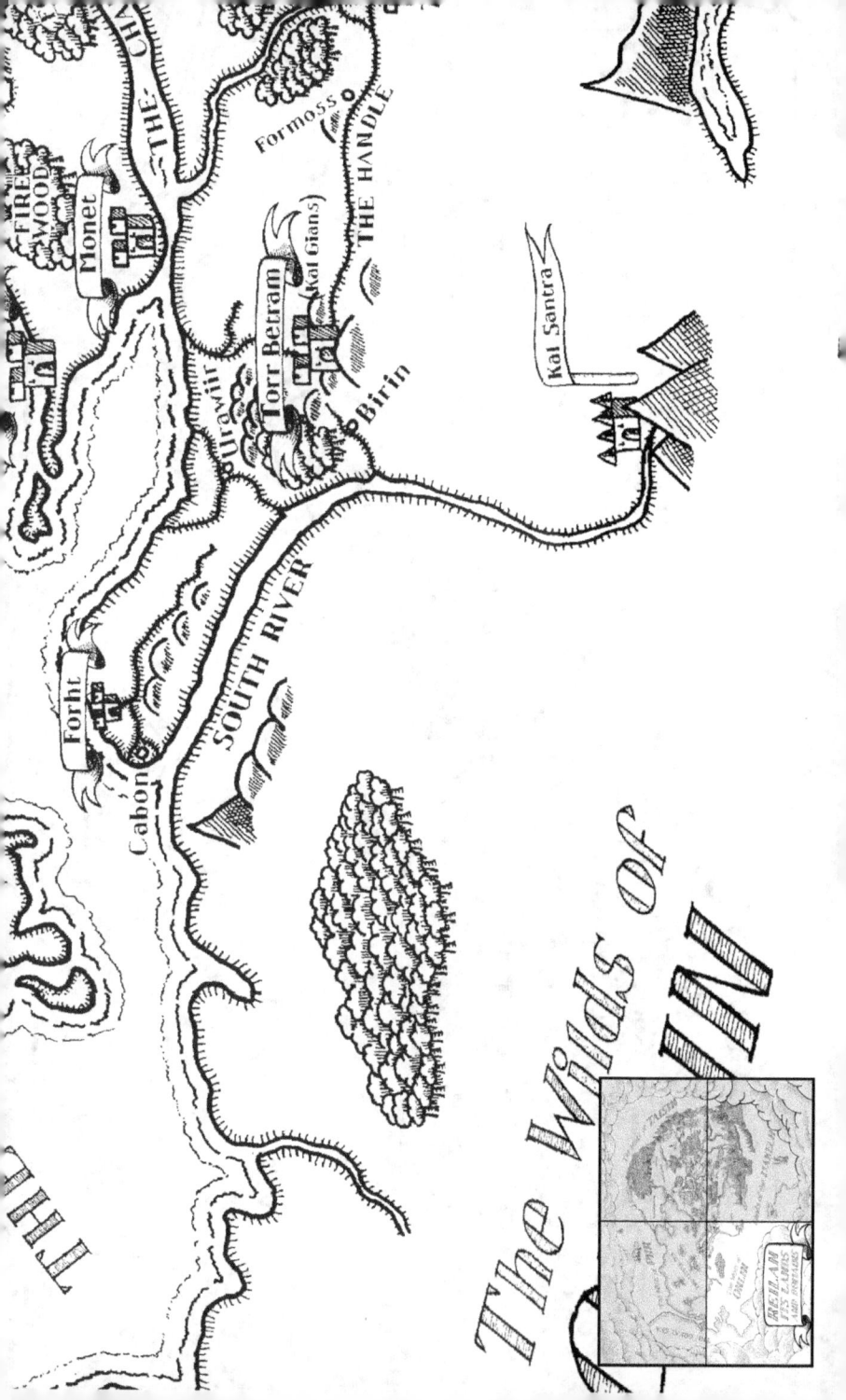

The Wilds of NIN

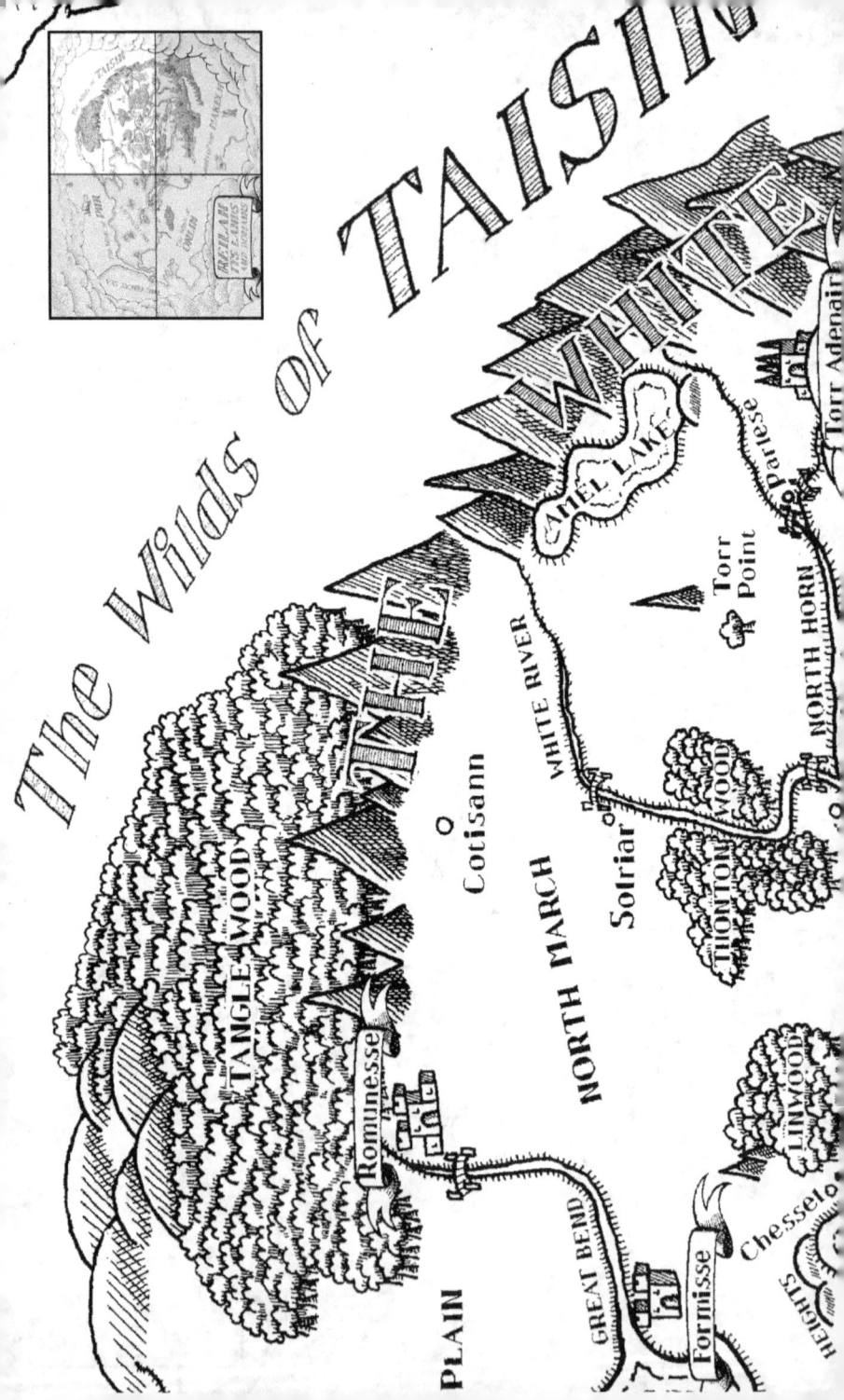

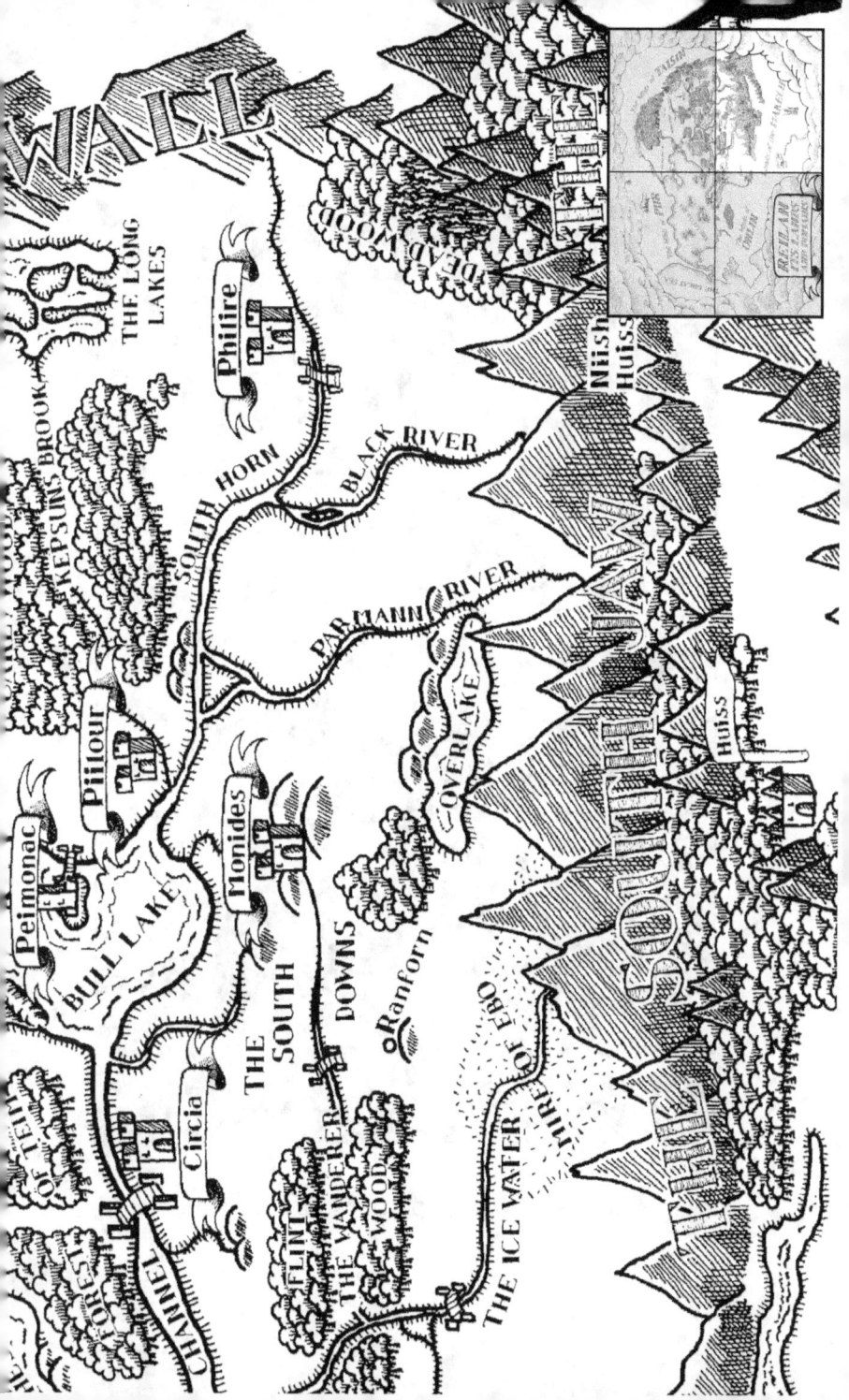

You may also like...

Available now in paperback and for Kindle.